T0368992

The Quest for the Stones:

Part Two

of

The New Earth Odyssey

Robert Blumetti

iUniverse, Inc.
New York Bloomington

iUniverse books may be ordered through booksellers or by contacting:

iUniverse
1663 Liberty Drive
Bloomington, IN 47403
www.iuniverse.com
1-800-Authors (1-800-288-4677)

Because of the dynamic nature of the Internet, any Web addresses or links contained in this book may have changed since publication and may no longer be valid. The views expressed in this work are solely those of the author and do not necessarily reflect the views of the publisher, and the publisher hereby disclaims any responsibility for them.

ISBN: 978-1-4401-5883-4 (sc)
ISBN: 978-1-4401-5884-1 (ebook)

Printed in the United States of America

iUniverse rev. date: 08/06/2009

Table of Contents

Book Three: Out of the Witch's Cauldron and Into the Dragon's Fire   **1**

Chapter One: The Parting of the Ways   9

Chapter Two: A Race Towards Doom   23

Chapter Three: Kidnaped   35

Chapter Four: To the Top of the World   55

Chapter Five: The Witch's Cauldron   73

Chapter Six: Escape!   99

Chapter Seven: The Stygian Hole   117

Chapter Eight: Fire and Darkness   137

Chapter Nine: Out of the Wolf's Jaws   151

Book Four: Fire and Ice   **165**

Chapter One: Faerie Hill and Tales   171

Chapter Two: Dullin's Gate   187

Chapter Three: Dark Clouds Over Northern Lands   201

Chapter Four: In The Hall of Heroes   223

Chapter Five: Ironbone   247

Chapter Six: Rolling Stones Go to War   269

Chapter Seven: A Final Stand - A Family United   285

Chapter Eight: The Siege of Ortangraal   303

Chapter Nine: The King and the Demon   325

Chapter Ten: The Battle of Six Nations   341

Chapter Eleven: The Winds Blow South   351

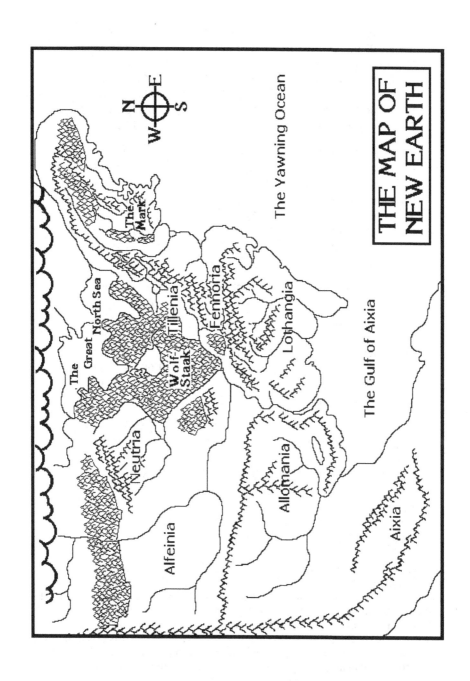

THE DRUID CALENDER

	Sunpass	Frostfost	Melttime
Mon.	01 08 15 22 29	06 13 20 27	04 11 18 25
Tues.	02 09 16 23 30	07 14 21 28	05 12 19 26
Wed.	03 10 17 24	01 08 15 22 29	06 13 20 27
Thurs.	04 11 18 25	02 09 16 23 30	07 14 21 28
Fri.	05 12 19 26	03 10 17 24	01 08 15 22 29
Sat.	06 13 20 27	04 11 18 25	02 09 16 23 30
Sun.	07 14 21 28	05 12 19 26	03 10 17 24 R

	Rebirth	Joyfest	Eremid
Mon.	01 08 15 22 29	06 13 20 27	04 11 18 25
Tues.	02 09 16 23 30	07 14 21 28	05 12 19 26
Wed.	03 10 17 24	01 08 15 22 29	06 13 20 27
Thurs.	04 11 18 25	02 09 16 23 30	07 14 21 28
Fri.	05 12 19 26	03 10 17 24	01 08 15 22 29
Sat.	06 13 20 27	04 11 18 25	02 09 16 23 30
Sun.	07 14 21 28	05 12 19 26	03 10 17 24 M

	Midpass	Highot	Harvestime
Mon.	01 08 15 22 29	06 13 20 27	04 11 18 25
Tues.	02 09 16 23 30	07 14 21 28	05 12 19 26
Wed.	03 10 17 24	01 08 15 22 29	06 13 20 27
Thurs.	04 11 18 25	02 09 16 23 30	07 14 21 28
Fri.	05 12 19 26	03 10 17 24	01 08 15 22 29
Sat.	06 13 20 27	04 11 18 25	02 09 16 23 30
Sun.	07 14 21 28	05 12 19 26	03 10 17 24 P

	Turning	Hollowtime	Eresun
Mon.	01 08 15 22 29	06 13 20 27	04 11 18 25
Tues.	02 09 16 23 30	07 14 21 28	05 12 19 26
Wed.	03 10 17 24	01 08 15 22 29	06 13 20 27
Thurs.	04 11 18 25	02 09 16 23 30	07 14 21 28
Fri.	05 12 19 26	03 10 17 24	01 08 15 22 29
Sat.	06 13 20 27	04 11 18 25	02 09 16 23 30
Sun.	07 14 21 28	05 12 19 26	03 10 17 24 S
			B

The standardized calender used by all Truemans on New Earth was formulated by the druids of Wissenval. The years are always the same, beginning on a Monday. There are twelve months and four extra days that falls between the months. They correspond to the first days of winter, spring, summer and fall and are named; Renewal, Midsummer Day, Passing and Sunmass. After Sunmass and before the first day of the year is one additional day call, Bridgeday. This day celebrates the turning of the year. Every four years there is a leap year day called the Druid's Day and appears after Midsummer Day and before the first day of Midpass.

Book Three:

Out of the Witch's Cauldron and Into the Dragon's Fire

Rullin Ashburn   Palifair Chestnut   Tom Applekean

Huck Lock   Rowena Chestnut   Anna Vineyard

Blondor   Arlindor   Hollin Hillroller

Magin Strongbone   Gordon Rivervin   Milland Pineleaf

Tor Applekean   Kellium Greengold   Olaf Westmorgrove

Vesten   Brim the Bold   Hagrim

Princess Valenda   Pettin   Olaf

Gottron   Thardor   Shandor

King Amthrim

Prince Sagtrim

General Bolthur

Ironbone

Brimknonor

Gorbag

The Mount of Fennoria

Wargana

The real Wargana

Gormath

Kella-Kazok

Gugtuk

Benlich Bramblewood Kemmel Barralbar Sheriff Tod Oaktrunk

Harl Pennypaper Old Grampa Crossway Sam Hammertoo

Tuddy Sweetwater Fred Plumegrove Bob Bogmorton

Caratium Hunthundon Kharz-Zish

Map of Fennoria

Blondor battles the dragon in the Stygian Hole.

Chapter One:
The Parting of the Ways

The druids had just arrived from searching the surrounding hills. "We were exploring the hills after last night's premonitions, and came upon a set of tracks that were clearly made by trogs," Arlindor explained. "We followed the tracks north, between the hills until they finally split and went in three different directions. We followed each set of tracks and discovered that they led to three different hills, but it was not until we climbed to the top of the third hill, that we became aware of the commotion back here in the campsite, and we rushed to return."

"It seemed that someone had laid the tracks to draw you both away from the campsite while the trogs attacked," Vesten said.

"But what about Palifair and Tom?" Rullin asked. "Where are they? We've got to find them!"

"Did anyone see them during the battle?" Vesten asked.

"We searched the bodies, but there was no trace of either of them," Hagrim said.

"I don't remember seeing either of them during the battle," Hollin said "I think they must have slipped out of the courtyard just before the trogs attacked, but I can't be sure."

"We've got to find my brother and Tom," Rowena pleaded. Her blue eyes were filled with tears as she looked helplessly at Blondor.

Arlindor closed his eyes, as if he was searching his mind, and then spoke. "I see many moving bodies to the south of the Yarmil River," he said. "I think they are trogs, but I can't be sure. They are now under the darkness of the forest that hides them from my sight. Wait! There are others. Truemans, but I can't determine clearly how many. It must be Tom and Palifair, for the White Stone calls out. Yes. They are alive and well, but shaken up."

"Thank the Lords of the Light that they are unharmed," Rowena said, relieved for the moment.

Blondor placed his hand on her shoulder to comfort her.

"Wait! There is more," Arlindor continued. "I sense another— not a trog. He is shrouded in mist and I cannot see into his mind. The image is familiar to me, somehow, but I can't place it." Arlindor opened his eyes and stepped forward, using his staff for support. "I cannot see any more. The Darkness is too strong and it blocks my sight."

"Is it the Lord of Darkness?" asked Milland.

"No. It is of a lesser power," Arlindor said. "I think it originates out of Fennoria."

"Wargana," Blondor said. "So she has a hand in this mischief."

"We've got to go after Pal and Tom, "Huck said. He and Rullin were already putting on their backpacks, but they were stopped by Vesten.

"What we don't need right now is hot heads," Vesten said.

"But the boys are right," Magin said. "We've got to go after Palifair and Tom. This is a black day. Both the stone bearer and the White Stone have fallen into the hands of the enemy. Without them, all is lost."

"They have not fallen into the clutches of the witch of Fennoria, yet," Blondor said. "And I'll wager that her henchmen weren't informed of the reason for their abduction. The White Stone is too precious and powerful a talisman for her to confide in her slaves. She must have told them to capture any children that they could find, and return them alive to her."

"If we are able to intercept them before they reach Fennoria, we might have a chance to save the boys before either of them are harmed," Vesten said.

"I don't think they'll be harmed before they reach Fennoria," Blondor said. "Wargana probably wants them brought to her alive. If they were killed or harmed, then her slaves would have to bring the stone to her, and I don't think any of the trogs would be able to handle the stone, and I doubt if she would trust any Trueman servants with it."

"Then I'll go south and follow the stone bearer and his friend, wherever it might lead me," Vesten declared as he raised his sword overhead. "This I swear by my sword, Gordonthal, that was handed down to me by my ancestors."

"But if we turn south, the aid that is needed by my homeland will not be forthcoming," Princess Valenda said, "And the Shadow of Allomania will have triumphed over the whole of the northwest."

"We're talking about the lives of my brother and his friend," Rowena said as she looked at Blondor. "I will not desert him, Blondor. You can't make me."

"I would never suggest such a thing," Blondor reassured Rowena. "And yet, we cannot desert Neutria either."

The princess walked over to Rowena. "Nor will I desert your brother," she said to Rowena. "For I have a brother, and I love him dearly. I say this; I pledge by the royal blood that flows through my veins, to go with Vesten and rescue your brother and his friend, or die in the attempt, if others will go on to Neutria and aid my countrymen."

Rowena was overwhelmed and hugged the princess.

"It's plain that we cannot desert Palifair and Tom for comradeship's sake, if for no other reason," Blondor said. "I have already sworn never to desert Palifair. He accepted the responsibility of carrying the White Stone to Lothar, and I accepted the responsibility to defend him. But even if oaths and comradeship were not part of the equation, I would be forced to follow, if for no other reason than to retrieve the stone. If it falls into the hands of the enemy, all is loss, and the Lord of Darkness will win."

"It wasn't for nothing that two druids were sent on this quest," Magin said. "I'm beginning to think Wissenval knew there would be need of the two."

"You're very perspective, Strongbone," Blondor said. "It was to me that the charge of protecting the stone bearer was given, and I will go with Vesten south to Fennoria. And with us will go a part of the company. The rest of the company will go with my brother druid, Arlindor, to fulfill the second part of our quest. They'll go to Neutria and help to restore the resolve of the Neutrians to resist Allomania, and join the Alliance of the Light."

"Then we will go with you to save Pal and Tom," Rullin and Huck insisted.

"No, Rullin. It would not be wise for you and Huck to go with me," Blondor said. "Trogs out of Fennoria probably have orders to capture all Trueman children. I'm sure Wargana suspects the stone to be in the possession of a youth, but she is not sure which one of you is carrying it. It would be best if the two of you were to go with Arlindor to Neutria.

"No! I won't hear of it!" Huck insisted. "We made a pact of friendship to our dying days. We won't leave Palifair's side."

Everyone expected Blondor to become angry at the youth's outburst, but instead, he just smiled and laughed. He was greatly moved by the boys' loyalty to their friends.

"I don't think you have any choice," Blondor said. "It would seem that Fate has taken Palifair from your charge. Besides, it was not for nothing that the four of you were present when the stone was found, and now it's clear what the role that both Palifair and Tom must play. But your roles in this game are still unclear. No. You both will go with Arlindor to Neutria. I think there is much that needs to be done there. There is nothing that you can do for your friends now. But don't worry. We'll get them back."

Everyone left the house to search the surrounding area for signs of what happened to the boys.

"Here! Come here!" Milland shouted. His sharp eyes spotted the footprints belonging to Tom and Palifair.

"What is it?" Vesten asked, as everyone rushed to see what Milland had found.

"Footprints," Milland said as he examined the prints with his exceptional vision. "I see two pair of prints leading off from the back of the campsite toward the canal. Here. This pair is Palifair's.

He left first, and afterward came Tom. This smaller pair of prints belongs to him. It looks as if Palifair snuck out of the camp by himself, and was followed by Tom. Look how his prints covers Palifair's."

"If we follow them, maybe we can figure out what happened to them?" Vesten suggested.

Following the prints, they soon arrived at the old wine cellar that the boys had discovered. After descending the stairs, they walked down the long passageway until they came to the room where Palifair and Tom discovered the remains of the campsite, and then they retraced the footprints back to the cellar's entrance.

Once outside, Vesten stooped down close to the ground. "Yes. Here. You can see Tom's smaller prints running off in that direction. He was followed by Palifair, who ran after him," Vesten said as he stood up.

They once again followed the prints and turned the corner of a building. Soon they came to the spot where the boys were abducted and looked into the window.

"Wait. There are signs of a struggle in here," Vesten said.

"Yes. There are trog prints in here," Milland said. "I can make out five sets of prints, I think, if my eyes are correct? But wait. What is this? These are not the prints of a trog, and yet, they don't belong to a Trueman."

"What then?" asked Magin.

"Half-trog," Blondor said, ominously.

"Half-trog?" Huck repeated Blondor's word.

"Yes. You remember Blondor telling us about the evil experiments in Fennoria?" Rullin reminded his friend. "How the witch-queen has mixed the blood of Truemans with trogs."

"Very good, Rullin," Blondor said. "This could only mean that Arlindor were right. It was Wargana's trogs that captured the boys."

"And Palifair and Tom are being taken to Fennoria, where Wargana will . . ." Rowena could not continue her thought.

"But first they will have to get them to Fennoria, and that they haven't done yet," Blondor said. "And they won't, if we have anything to say about it."

"Then our choice is clear," Hollin said. "We have to follow the trogs to Fennoria, and try and over take them and rescue the boys, before they get to their destination."

"No. Not follow," Blondor said. "They will be sure to go through the forest, knowing that way will give them the best cover, and hinder us in our pursuit of them. There is no way we can travel as quickly through the woods, even if there was no evil that blocked our way."

"Then how are we going to rescue the boys?" asked Hollin.

"Since we can no longer travel under the protection of the road, and the forest is too dangerous to travel through, we will have to seek another road," Blondor said.

"What other road?" asked Rowena.

"We will ride the Yarmil River," Blondor said. "I flows out of Lost Lake, into the Donnor River farther south. The evil that inhabits this forest does not like running water. We will be just as safe on the river, as we were on the road. If we ride the river to where it joins up with the Donnor River, we might be able to cut off the trogs before they reach the Axis Mountains and disappear into Fennoria."

"Then let's hurry," Vesten said. "We're wasting precious moments, and the trogs are probably miles away by now."

It was decided that Blondor would take part of the company, and follow the trogs to Fennoria. With him went Rowena, Anna and Hollin. Princess Valenda, who had sworn an oath of honor to go after the boys, also agreed to go south. Brim and Hagrim would not be separated from their commander, Vesten, and so they decided to go south.

Arlindor agreed to lead the rest of the company, which included Magin, Gordon, Milland, Huck, Rullin and the two Tillenian woodsmen, Olaf and Pettin, to Neutria. They would continue along the Highway that followed the northern shore of the Lost Lake, until it passed through the Gates of Dullin, and then continue on to Neutria.

Everyone quickly packed their gear and were ready to depart.

There was a heavy silence that hung over the campsite. They were sad to separate after all they had been through together, in the last few months.

"We 'll leave, now," Arlindor announced. "I want to reach the coast of Lost Lake before nightfall. To do that, we have to pass through the Hills of Keel Atumon, and through the outer wall."

"Let's say our farewells now," Blondor said. "May the Light go with you, and watch over every step you take? May you be successful in your quest in Neutria?"

"And may you be as successful in your quest to rescue the stone bearer?" Arlindor. "May the Light be with you?"

Everyone said goodbye to each other. Their hearts were filled with sadness over their departure and tears flowed freely. Huck and Rullin were extremely depressed to have to go on to Neutria. They wanted to go after Palifair and Tom, and felt that they were breaking their oaths of friendship by deserting their friends. Both Rowena and Anna tried to reassure them that it was for the best.

"You both have got to be strong, and go with Arlindor to Neutria," Anna said.

"We know," Huck said, "but we can't help feel that we're letting Pal and Tom down."

"You mustn't feel like that," insisted Rowena. "Blondor and Arlindor are only thinking about what's best for all of us. I'm sure that both Tom and Palifair would agree and understand."

"Just make sure that you get them back safely," Rullin said. "I could never forgive myself if any harm came to them. We should have been more alert and followed Palifair, as Tom did." Rullin fought to hold back the tears that rolled down his cheeks.

Rowena hugged both of them as she was overcome with emotions. "Don't worry. We'll get them back, and then we'll all be reunited once more, after this terrible affair is over, and someday laugh about it all back in Middleboro. But for now, we must all be strong and do what we must for the good of all."

Rowena gave each of them a kiss and hung them once more, and then hurried away so that they could not see her tears.

Arlindor led his group through the remains of Keel Atumon, on the road that ran along the northern shore of the lake and through the hills. They could make out the towers standing tall on top of the lonely hills, and then passed out of the northern gate and into the dark forest once more.

Blondor and his group doubled back along the road they had taken up the cliffs of Tule Amon. He hoped to find a path down the cliffs, next to the falls that would allow them to escape, moving through the forest from the Highway to the river bank of the Yarmil. The distance was only a half of a mile, but it was extremely dangerous walking through the forest. The dangers that lurked within the woods were too great to chance, but they had to try. They came to a halt after walking all morning and part of the afternoon, and finally turned off the road when they came to the edge of the wall that lined the edge of the cliffs. As they passed through the small growth of trees and brush that grew along the river's edge, they made their way through maple and ash trees, mixed with large and ancient oaks that grew there, until they heard the rushing of the river. They could tell that the river was plummeting over the cliffs, as the waters filled the woods with a thunderous roar.

The air was filled with the spray of the falls at the river's edge. Blondor ordered everyone to remain within the tree line while he went ahead and checked on the cliffs.

Rowena was too nervous to rest as she stood under a large shade tree. She would glaze out over the cliffs, and could see the hazy, green forest stretching out below, broken by a long, blue river that shined from the rays of the afternoon sun. She kept telling herself that her brother and Tom would be alright. Blondor seemed sure that they would rescue the boys in time, and she had to keep convincing herself that he was right. But as hard as she tried, she couldn't help but fear that they would not reach the boys in time to prevent them from falling into the clutches of Wargana. She kept asking herself what would happen if they did not reach them in time? How could they defeat the trogs that had captured the boys? There were only eight of them, even though the Guardians were the best fighters in all of northern New Earth, and the power of Blondor could probably defeat hundreds of trogs, but would they be able to prevent them from harming the boys once they reached them?

Suddenly she felt a presence. She looked over at the group and saw Vesten's blue eyes staring at her. She felt that he knew what she was thinking, but instead of saying anything, she looked away, as Blondor came walking back up the path toward them.

"What did you find?" Vesten asked the druid as he walked out of the trees to greet him.

"The cliffs are steep and the wall reaches to its edge," Blondor said. "But there is a small ledge at the edge of the wall that leads to the far side. It shouldn't be difficult to scale down its side. There are many ledges to support the foot and several outgrowing trees to grab onto as we climb down."

The druid led them to the wall and carefully, they slipped around its edge until they were looking over the forest's roof that raced off endlessly into the distance.

"See there," Blondor pointed out to the others. "At the bottom of the cliff there is a clearing on the banks of the river. We can rest and build a raft that will carry us down the river, free from the evil that lurks within the Wolf-Staak."

The cliffs were steep, but the jotting rocks and the few trees that grew along the length of the cliffs provided a natural ladder for them to descend. Everyone tied their ropes together, making two long ropes, one for them to climb down and another to secure them incase they slipped. Blondor was the first to descend. The second rope was secured around Blondor's waist and held by Vesten and Brim, and would prevent him from falling as he slide down the first rope that was secured to a tree. He swung from ledge to ledge, using the boulders for support. A couple of times he lost his footing on the slippery rocks, which were wet from the spray of the falls, but he finally made it to the bottom safely.

Once at the bottom, Blondor checked the area and then shouted for the next person to come down.

Rowena was next. The others lined up for their turn behind her. Rowena refused to look down for fear of getting dizzy, but she made it down with little trouble. The thundering roar of the falls drown out the sound of Blondor at the bottom, trying to tell her to be careful and watch out for slippery rocks.

After she reached the bottom, the others followed her. Anna was next and then Hollin, Valenda and Hagrim in that order. Finally, Vesten and Brim took the second rope and placed it around the trunk of a large tree that grew out from under a stone wall, at the edge of the cliff. They tied the two pieces of rope together to form one long single rope. One end of the rope was tided around Brim's waist, while the other end was let down the side of the cliff, where Hagrim, Hollin and Valenda held it and slowly let it out, as Brim began climbing down. Vesten remained at the top of the cliff, holding the rope from the top. After Brim had reached the bottom and untied himself, the rope was pulled up and Vesten did the same as Brim, climbing down in the same fashion. After he had reached the bottom, they easily pulled the rope down so they could use it to build the raft they would need to ride down the river.

After checking on the quality of trees, Blondor began directing the others on which trees to cut down. The Guardians were very skilled in surviving in the wilderness, and knew how to build a hardy raft that could carry them down the river to the Donnor, with little effort. They stopped only to eat a quick dinner that Anna and Rowena had cooked, and then everyone returned to their work.

It was the first meal they had eaten all day. Everyone avoided the woods and only cut down those trees that laid at the outer rime of the forest.

"We won't be needing the extra clothing that we took with us to protect us from the approaching winter, now that we're heading south," Blondor said. "You'll find that the weather will get progressively warmer with each mile that we travel. Therefore, everyone is to empty their backpacks of their winter clothing and give them to Anna and Rowena, to make into a small sail that will speed us down the river."

After they finished their meal, they continued to work on the raft for the next few hours. The evening air was still cold and the moon rose early in the darkening sky, as the first stars began to appear. By the time they had finished building the raft, it was dark. Though Vesten wanted to wait until morning before getting under way, for fear of maneuvering in the dark, Blondor insisted on getting under way immediately.

"I don't like this, Vesten said. "It will be dangerous to sail down the river at night on an untested raft. We could easily hit rocks and crash in the dark. It would be better to remain here tonight and get under way with the first rays of the sun."

"I disagree," Blondor said. "It's not safe to remain here a minute longer than necessary. We don't have the protection of the enchanted road to keep us safe from the evil that fills these woods, and I do not want to chance spending a single night here." Blondor then looked around, as if he expected something to jump out of the woods at them at any minute. "I can sense evil gathering around us."

"Blondor is right," Rowena interrupted impatiently. "We haven't got a minute to spare if we're going to save my brother and Tom. If we waste time here, we'll never reach the Donnor River in time to prevent the trogs from carrying the boys off, into Fennoria."

Vesten said nothing more. He only looked at Blondor and realized that deep inside, the druid was concern for more than the welfare of the company. Vesten knew the druid for a long time and though he had always been shroud in mystery, he had come to understand something about the way Blondor thought. Blondor was not only moved by Rowena's concern for her brother, but he felt a responsibility for everyone under his leadership that went far beyond that of a good comrade. Everyone was, in a way, his children, and he felt that he had let Palifair and Tom down.

He felt he made a mistake and should not have left their side and gone off to scout the area. Because he did, Palifair and Tom were now in the gravest danger. Finally, Vesten agreed to chance the river at night. Everyone began loading their supplies on the raft.

The raft was about six feet wide and ten feet long, and made from two layers of logs laid across each other. It was sturdy, with a torch at each of its four corners, for light. A shaft was placed in the center of the craft with a small sail that the girls had constructed from their winter clothing. Along each side of the raft was a long log to prevent anyone or anything from sliding overboard.

As they sailed down the river, the forest appeared dark and forbidding on both banks. The black -filled forest rolled pass them on either side, as the raft quickly sailed down the river. The current was swift and they were making very good time. There were no signs of life in the forest, except for an occasional howling of a wolf at the moon, but the cries always appeared far off and distant. The river was not covered by the forest because of its width. They sailed along under a black canopy, decorated by a million stars. All night long the golden face of the full moon slowly sailed across the night darkness that lent a faint light that seemed to gently dance on the currents of the river, until the moon finally sank into the southwest. One by one, everyone slowly fell asleep, all except for Rowena, who was to anxious to sleep, Blondor, who was in deep meditation, and Brim, who was steering the raft.

Everyone else was huddled together on the raft and now lost in a deep and restful sleep. The night silently slipped into the morning, and the air grew progressively warmer as the day wore on. The night had been uneventful and they were all glad that daylight had arrived. The river carried them swiftly and gently southward, as a autumn breeze filled their sail. Brim, Hagrim, Valenda, Hollin and Vesten took turns steering the raft, keeping it at all times in the center of the river, avoiding the river banks and the forest that grew right up to the water. They soon spotted life in the forest, mostly birds and squirrels, though they could hear growls and howls from deep within the woods. Occasionally all the forest noises would cease and the air was filled with an eerie silence. But these periods of silence did not last long, but they were unnerving. Late in the day clouds began to roll in from the west, and a mild shower fell on them. Fortunately it did not last long. Some on the raft thought they should pulled alongside to the river bank during the rain, but Blondor did not want to halt their progress for any reason, not even for a minute. Blondor had to remind them that it was safer to chance the rain in the deep of the river than pull up to the river banks. They continued on their way, taking their meals cold and on the raft.

As night fell on their second day on the river, they had traveled some fifty miles along currents of the Yarmil, but still they had a long way to go before they reached the Donnor River. Everyone else had fallen asleep, including Rowena. Rowena had slept little the night before, but weariness had eventually caught up to her. She was exhausted from worrying about her brother, and could no longer remain awake. Hollin kept watch as they continued to sail down the river, under the illumination of the waning moon. The river seemed to shine with a glow that lent a solemn atmosphere to the night, making it seem improper to speak for fear of disturbing the eeriness that flowed over the watery road.

Blondor had waken after sleeping several hours. He took up a position at the front of the raft. Sitting with his legs cross, he laid his staff across his lap. His black eyes were alive with thought, as he peered up at the night sky. Blondor's mind was filled with questions. He was disturbed by the fact that he could not see into the future. Neither he nor Arlindor were able to foresee the ambush at Lost Lake. It could not have been the fault of their carelessness. Was it possible that both druids suffered from a lost of sight? He was sure that was not the case. Something had concealed the attack from them, but whom? It could only have been Wargana. This meant that her powers had grown great since the last time he had spoken with her, but how? What sorcery did she command? Blondor was convinced that the trogs were taking the boys to Fennoria. He closed his eyes and let his mind fall free. Before him he could see the shadowy forms running through the trees. They were trogs. He was sure of that, for their essence was black and twisted. But there were others with them. He could clearly make out the images of Palifair and Tom. They were still alive and the White Stone was still in Palifair's possession. It called out to him. He let his mind be drawn into the image and that's when he noticed the other. It was not trog, or half-trog, nor trog-man. It was another Trueman. He was sure of this, but who could it be? He felt its presence before, after the boys were captured, but it was veiled in a dark shadow. He concentrated on this other Trueman. There was something about him that caused his mind to stir, and then it hit him. "I should have realized it all along," he said to himself.

Rowena's sleep was disturbed and she moaned, but did not wake. Blondor could see her lovely face twisted with pain. He placed his hand on her forehead and her face slowly went blank. She once again fell into a deep and restful sleep. Hollin had seen what Blondor had done, and smiled to himself.

Blondor thought to himself how beautiful she looked and thought back to a time when he used to visit her mother and father. She was just a child then, and Palifair was an infant in his mother's arms. But even then he could see that his future was tied-up with this family. Her mother, Tuwena, had known this also. She was the daughter of Hypar Sunbreeze, a servant of the Light, who had lived in Wissenval in his youth. He was once an apprentice of the druids, and could trace his ancestry back thousands of years. He later moved to the Mark, and married Rose Lock of the South Mark Locks. They eventually gave birth to a daughter, who was both beautiful and clairvoyant, whom they named Tuwena. Tuwena seemed to be at home with nature, and animals and birds of the wild did not fear her. She had a way with all living things, and also had the sight. She once told Blondor that she would give birth to a son and a daughter, before they were born, and that the former would be the herald of a new age, while the latter would restore the place of women at Wissenval. She then told him that her daughter would change his life in ways that he could not foresee. Blondor wondered just how much she did know of the events that were now unfolding?

Chapter Two:
A Race Toward Doom

The next day passed uneventful. The banks on either side of the Yarmil River rose until the forest was far over head. The waters grew rougher as they sailed south, but the raft was well constructed and easily handled the rough waters with little difficulty. The Guardians were very capable in maneuvering the raft along the river. Everyone was weary from their trip on the river and anxious to reach the end of the forest. In the evening, gray clouds began to gather and grow thick. They unleashed a light drizzle that lasted into the night. This was followed by a fog that rolled up the river and made their sailing perilous. The four torches had gone out from the rain and had to be refitted with dry wrappings before they could be relit, and provided some light to help guide them on their way. The night passed, wet and gloomy. With the arrival of morning, the fog finally rolled back, and to their surprise, they discovered that they had passed out of the Wolf-Staak.

The Wolf-Staak still grew on the western bank of the river, but on the eastern bank, the trees grew in scattered clumps. Everyone was relieved to be clear of the forest, and decided to sail several more miles before pulling over to the eastern bank and stop. They wanted to make sure that they were far enough away from the dangers of the forest. When they finally pulled the raft to a stop, everyone jumped off, glad to have dry land under their feet once more, and stretch their legs. They built a small fire and cooked themselves a good, hot meal, the first they had in four days.

There was little time to waste, and no sooner had they eaten,

Blondor was rousing everyone again. They refilled their water bags from a small spring nearby and collected berries, wild roots and some nuts and were off once more, sailing down the Yarmil River to the Donnor.

By afternoon the gray clouds overhead grew darker and finally burst into a downpour of heavy rain, filling the sky with thunder and lightning, and causing the river to rise with additional water. The raft was now pushed forward and bucked, as the river became rougher. They decided to pull over to the east bank once more, but found that the river had other ideas.

"I don't like this storm," Blondor said. "It seems alive with a unnatural fury, as if something, or someone was directing it."

Everyone took hold of the poles and tried with all their might to force the raft out of the main current of the rushing river. The force of the running water caused two poles to snap. The raft then hit a jotting rock and buckled, and almost tipped over. Everyone hung on for dear life, as the water carried them on helplessly. There was nothing they could do but wish for the best, all except for Blondor that is, who seemed to be chanting some kind of runic incantation to himself. Anna, who was sitting next to him, tried to hear what he was saying, but the frenzy of the rain drowned out his words.

Rain poured down their faces and waves slashed over the sides of the raft. Suddenly there was a flash, followed by the crackle of lightning that struck a tree up ahead, causing it to fall partly into the river and striking the raft. One of the logs that was tied to the side of the raft came flying off and crashed into the fallen tree, lodging the raft securely to it.

"Everyone! Quickly! Grab the supplies and get off!" Vesten shouted. "We have got to crawl along the tree, to the shore!"

They each grabbed a pack and made their way along the tree, as the river rushed on, splashing them as they struggled not to fall off the log. Twice, a large wave almost knocked them off the log and into the river, as lightning flashed overhead. When a third wave hit them, it cause Hollin to plummet into the waters. He desperately grabbed at the branches of the fallen tree, as Anna called to him. Brim and Hagrim reached out and grabbed him just as the branches broke off the fallen tree, pulling him to safety.

Soon they were all on the eastern bank of the river. They heard a terrible crash, and when they turned, they saw the fallen tree roll over onto the raft, crushing it into pieces. The remains of the raft rushed down the river and disappeared in the racing waters.

Everyone plopped down on the wet grass. They were too exhausted to care about the rain.

"It sure was a bit of luck that the tree fell just before the raft, as it did," Hollin said.

"Luck had nothing to do with it," Vesten said as he looked at Blondor, who was already on his feet. He was supporting himself with his staff as the wind whipped his cape about him. The druid stood there looking off into the distance, as if he was watching something unfolding, without saying a word.

"We can find shelter up ahead," the druid finally said. "There is a rock formation that will provide us with protection from this wind and rain."

As soon as he said this, he was off.

The others followed behind him as the storm thundered overhead. In a little less than ten minutes of walking, they found what Blondor was looking for. He led them into a small dell with large boulders piled up, forming what looked like the remains of some worn down structure. They all huddled into a small opening between two large stones that opened into what was a dugout den. Blondor told them that it was built by hunters that often traveled through this region on their way to the Wolf-Staak, from their homes farther south. Once inside, they lit a fire and dried out. After two hours of resting, and eating a small, but hot meal, they discovered that the storm had stopped.

Blondor pulled a map out from his robes and laid it on the floor of the den, before them. "I'm convinced that the trogs are moving southward through the Wolf-Staak, west of the Yarmil River, and will continue to do so until they reach the Donnor River," he said. "The forest provides them with the cover of darkness, protecting them from the rays of the sun. They hate and fear the daylight. The sunlight robs them of their strength and weakens them. So they will try and keep out of the sun for as long as they can on their journey south. But once they cross the Donnor, they will have to either travel at night and take shelter during the day, or travel during the day and chance being attacked in their weaken state. This will slow them down just as much as if they traveled only at night. If they choose the latter, then it'll become all the more easier for us to overtake them." Blondor pointed to the map. "Here, where the Fenflow River empties into the Donnor River, this is where we'll wait for them. There is a bridge that spans the Donnor River, and we may be able to divide their forces and free the boys."

"It will not be easy," Vesten said. "It's a three-day march to the Donnor, and then only if we march both day and night."

"How far is that?" asked Anna.

"Twenty-five leagues, as the crow flies," Vesten said. "But even if we are able to reach the Donnor in time, we will not be in peak strength, and the advantage, not to mention the difference in numbers, will all favor the enemy."

"But we must try all the same," Rowena pleaded as she turned to Blondor.

"Try?" Blondor said. "That's the least we'll do. I intend to follow them into Fennoria itself, if need demands it. I will not stop until we have rescued Palifair and Tom."

No one said anything. They just looked at each other, contemplating the meaning of the druid's words.

"If Wargana gets her hands on the boys," Blondor said, "that'll mean she will also get her hands on the White Stone. The boys will not live one second longer. If that happens, nothing else will matter. With the loss of Palifair and the White Stone, Vesten will never be crowned the Emperor Returned, and there will only be a collection of divided armies scattered across the face of New Earth to try and halt the rising tide of Allomania. It would not be long before the Shadow of Allomania reaches the borders of the Mark and Wissenval. It will not matter whether the boys died in Fennoria or later, with the rest of us."

"Then we must not delay, not even for a minute," Brim said.

"You're right, old friend," Vesten said. "We must make hast, stopping only a few times a day for short rests and meals."

"But we can't go on like that for three days," Hollin said.

"We must," Vesten said. "The trogs won't be resting much. I doubt if they'll even rest during the day. They'll probably try and run throughout the day, rather than wait for nightfall."

"Then it's agreed," Blondor said. "We'll leave immediately, and head south for the Donnor and the bridge."

"Too bad the raft had to crash in that damn storm," Hagrim said. "We could've made good time sailing down the Yarmil. The damnest bit of luck, I say."

"It was more than luck that crushed the raft," Blondor said.

The druid led everyone south. They traveled in a single file across the open landscape. They each finished what was left of Anna's elixir, and all wished there was time for her to cook up some more. The drink gave them a renewed strength that helped them throw off the chilling effects of the drenching rains, but by nightfall it was wearing off. Once again they were succumbing to fatigue. It was late, and the moon was high in the black sky when they reached a small river and stopped for a short rest and hot meal. Both rest and food were welcomed, but it seemed that no sooner had they fallen asleep, they were being nudged awake by Blondor. They crossed the river, which was only waist-deep, and proceeded southwards once more.

As morning broke they did not stop to eat breakfast, but instead ate some dried meat as they continued to walk. By afternoon the sun was shining bright and hot, which was unusual for the month of Turning. There were now small groups of trees that dotted the open fields, providing little protection from the sun. Everyone was sweating and aching from the forced pace that the druid was setting.

Hollin, strangely enough, was finding it difficult to keep up. He was burning with fever, or at least he felt he was. His head was buzzing and his feet were sore with blisters. He could not understand how the druid could keep up such a pace. It was as if he was unaffected by the elements, walking in another plane of existence. It would have astonished the young aristocrat to know just how close he was to the truth.

Hollin looked over at Anna and Rowena. Both of them seemed exhausted. Rowena's face did not show it, for she was determined to keep up with Blondor at all cost, though she felt like she was about to drop. Hollin could not help but feel a sense of pride in the way his Anna was handling the journey, and especially how wonderfully she was able to win the hearts of the good people of Jassinburg. But at the same time he could not help feel jealous. He felt that he was not doing his share. He handled himself well fighting the trogs and other dangers that the company had to face since they left Middleboro, but any good man could use the blade and do the same. He wondered what his father would say, and felt that he would still have to prove his manhood before he would be permitted to someday take his rightful place as the head of the Hillroller estate. But there was something more. He did so want his father's approval, and prove to his family that he was not just a drifter. He kept these feelings to himself, because it was something he felt he had to work out for himself. He took comfort from the fact that his own problems seemed unimportant when compared to what Palifair and Tom must be facing.

Blondor stumbled as he walked and clutched his staff.

"What is it, Blondor?" asked Vesten, as everyone rushed to see what was wrong with their leader. The druid was staring into the distance, with eyes opened wide. Holding onto his staff for support.

"I have just felt a tremor in the Life-Force," Blondor said. "The hand of the Lord of Darkness has just passed over the face of the world."

Everyone looked at each other, but Blondor said no more about it. "Come. We still have our own troubles," he said. "Let's not delay any longer." He raised himself by gripping his staff and continued marching, as everyone stared in disbelief and fear. They sighed and mustered the strength to continue on with their journey, following the druid as best as they could.

It was late in the afternoon when Blondor called a halt. They found a small clump of trees that provided some shade from both the hot sun and any unfriendly, spying eyes. There they ate a hot meal and were able to sleep for a few hours. When they started off again, the temperature had declined, and a cool evening breeze blew down from the northeast. They felt refreshed from their short but welcomed sleep, and combined with the break in the hot weather, they were able to make good time marching under the star-speckled sky. They had to rap themselves in their walking capes to protect themselves from the cold air that now invaded the landscape. The ground was smooth and not difficult to walk across in the dark, and soon it began sloping downward. Vesten estimated that they would reach the Donnor River within the next twenty-four hours, if they could keel traveling at their present rate.

The next day shined bright and dry, but was noticeably cooler, which was a welcomed relief. It was early in the afternoon when they stopped again for a rest.

Hagrim shouted for everyone to look, as he pointed at the partly cloudy sky.

Everyone turned to see what he was pointing to.

"What is it?" Brim asked.

"There! In the clouds to the east," Hagrim answered.

From a group of low-lying clouds there was a small flock of black crows.

"Crows out of Fennoria, I'll wager," Blondor said. "Wargana has her spies out searching all the lands."

"Are they searching for us?" Anna asked.

"Yes," Blondor answered.

"But how does she know we are making for Fennoria?" Rowena asked.

"She makes it her business to know everything that happens within a thousand miles of her domain," Blondor said.

After the birds flew by, Blondor hurried them up to get ready and move out. "Come! We don't have much time to waste if we want to reach the Donnor by tonight."

"But what about the crows?" asked Rowena.

"There's no use trying to hide from Wargana's spies now,"

Blondor said. "We still have many miles to go, and we'll never make it if we are trying to hide from them."

Blondor led the way with staff in hand, followed by Rowena, Anna and Hollin, with Valenda and Vesten in the rear. Coming up on either side was Brim and Hagrim. When they finally reached the Donnor River it was after dark. They came to a stop under a group of trees over looking the river. When they looked out, over the great watery avenue, they caught their breath in amazement.

The Donnor was a much wider than it was father north, where they crossed it on their way to Jassinburg. The Donnor rose out of the frozen waste lands to the north, fed by the seepage of the melting glacier-covered peeks of the northern regions of the Axis Mountains. All along the length of the river valley, waters constantly flowed down into the great river until its width was almost a mile wide. In the dark it sparkled with the night lights reflecting from the half moon that slowly marched across the blacken sky.

It was not difficult for them to construct a light raft in a few hours and gently sail across the mighty Donnor. The waters were calm and the half moon had disappeared over the horizon, as they crossed under the cover of dark. Once on the southern bank, they hid their raft under some brush, behind a group of trees, and then proceeded inland. The land rose as they reached the area where the Old North Road was located. They had to pass through a thick growth of trees in a single file. It was after sunrise when they finally broke through the brush and crossed a small field. They came upon the road built long ago by the ancient Lothangians. It was constructed in the same way as the Highway, further north.

When they set foot on it, Vesten suddenly jumped forward in excitement. His sharp eyes had spotted something.

"What is it?" asked Blondor.

"Stay!" he commanded. "No one move, not even one step. I think there are tracks in the dust that I must read, and I do not want them trampled upon."

The road was seldom used in these times, and it was littered with dirt and rocks. Vesten stooped down on all fours, carefully examining the footprints. After a few minutes, he jumped up and ran down the road a bit and did the same.

"There are tracks," he finally said after he returned to where the others were waiting. "And by my account, some fifty or sixty trogs passed this way, not more than a hour ago. There's no way we can reach the bridge over the Fenflow before they reach the river."

Everyone fell quiet. They had traveled all this distance only to have failed by no more than an hour.

"Then it's too late to save my brother," Rowena said. Her full lips trampled with fear.

"No! Not yet," Blondor said sharply. "Only an hour has passed and they could not have gone far. We still have a chance to reach them before they pass through the Hole of Fennoria."

"But we'll have to hurry," Vesten said. "They're moving eastward in a great hurry. Wait! Here, see this." Everyone came over to see what he had discovered. "Look here at these tracks. They were not made by trogs. These sets of tracks are smaller and they were made by boots, the kind one would wear in the Mark."

"Palifair and Tom, they're still alive," Hollin declared.

"Thank goodness!" Rowena cried.

Vesten stood over the tracks, fingering his chin as he studied them.

"There is more, isn't there?" Blondor asked.

"I can't be sure, but I think there is another set of prints made by boots that a Trueman would wear, but not a child's," Vesten said. "They were made by a man, a full grown man."

Blondor said nothing at first. He closed his eyes and stood very still for a second. "Come. We have little time to waste if we are going to stop them before they enter Fennoria," he finally said.

"Then we will follow them with the speed of the north winds," Valenda declared.

"My blade needs sharpening, and I can't think of any better way to sharpen it than on trog-necks," Brim laughed.

All that day they followed the tracks, crossing the stone bridge that crossed the Fenflow River. They then turned off the road to the south, onto a smaller, side-road that led to the entrance of Fennoria. The road was of lesser quality than the Old North Road

The sun crossed the blue sky above, and began to set in the west, as night came early in the Turning evening. They were exhausted from their growling pace and had little to eat, except for what they were able to gobble down as they ran along, trying to keep up with their prey. The land about them grew barren and treeless, and the only growth now was thickets, thorn bushes and the grayish weeds that grew in clumps. In the distance, black cliffs loomed up before the peaks of the Axis Mountains. Dark and lifeless they appeared under a black cloud that hung over Fennoria, suspended on the mountain tops like a great black tent that shaded the canyon below, from the sun. Unnatural it seemed, and unaffected it was by the winds.

"It has been more than a year since last I passed into the darkness that lies before us," Blondor said. "You have all heard me tell you of the tale of my journey through Fennoria at the Council of Wissenval, but then I had walked blindly into the witches' den. This time my guard is up."

"Let's hope it will not be necessary for you to pass into that cesspool again," Hollin said, as Rowena looked first at Hollin and then at Blondor, visibly worried.

"As we get closer to Fennoria, it will become more dangerous. The night will not be much of a cover from those who worship the Darkness," Blondor said. He feared the worst, but refrained from speaking more of it to the others, though it was easy to see in Rowena's eyes that she was able to read his unspoken fears better than the druid realized.

"What kind of a place is Fennoria?" asked Anna.

"Do you not remember what I told you all back in Wissenval?" Blondor asked. "It's a land ruled by a cult of witches, who were once druidesses, who lived at Wissenval. They followed their mistress, Wargana, into exile when she was driven out by Gottron. She is vain and hateful, for her mind is filled with hatred and jealousy. Her heart is black with the lust for power. When she rebelled against Gottron, she was spared by him, though some warned him not to be so merciful. But he could not bring himself to destroy her, for he loved all his children, even those who were not worthy of his love.

"Wargana has turned from the Light and now follows the Dark side of the Life-Force. With its power, she has set herself up as the queen of this domain, buried deep within the canyons of the Axis Mountains. Rituals they practice there too horrible to mention. They transformed themselves into hideous, twisted relics of their former selves and hide their true identities under the facade of great beauty. And as with all things that follow the Darkness, they hate themselves and what they've become. They lust for the beauty of the Light, but it is beyond their powers to return to it. Knowing that they can never regain their lost beauty, they hide their ugliness under a cheap mockery of what they have lost forever.

"Wargana has collected under her command a great host of trogs that live within the mountains. She has organized them into armies with which she plans to conquer all of New Earth, with herself as queen of her new order of witches. She has recently begun her abhorrent experiments of mixing the essence of trogs with that of the essence of Truemans. In this way she has been creating the half-trogs and trog-men that I spoke of back in Wissenval. This is her plan—to wipe out the race of Truemans, for she hates them most of all.

"Right now, in that canyon, there are hundreds of caves that house thousands of trogs, half-trogs and trog-men. They've built great underground furnaces that bellow clouds of foul, reeking fumes and fire from their black engines and machines, into the air above. The canyon has become a barren and polluted land with her manufactured breath, and the Fenflow runs brown with muck and foam that her engines vomit into it.

"Deep within Fennoria is a great castle, built on top of steep cliffs. There is a great depression, a chasm, that is several hundred feet deep surrounding the castle that is named Areisten. If Palifair and Tom are brought within Fennoria, it is there that they'll be taken, and it is there that we must go," as Blondor said this last sentence, the memory of the pain that was inflicted upon him the last time he was there caused his face to whence.

Vesten then stopped suddenly, causing everyone to come to a halt. "Never have I come this way before, Blondor," he said. "I fear that we'll not reach the trogs in time."

"What do you see?" Rowena asked.

"See there," Vesten said as he pointed to the ground. "See their tracks? They grow fainter. That means they're pulling ahead of us. They're being forced to run hard and with little rest. That's why we missed them at the Fenflow, and that's why they'll pass into Fennoria before we reach them."

"Vesten is right," Blondor said. He turned to Rowena. "You must have courage. Sometimes things look blacker when you are viewing them from one angle. But the future is always in motion and it's hard to predict how it will turn out. This is not over yet." Blondor then turned back to look at the cliffs in the distance. "Neither those cliffs nor all the trogs in the world will stop us from rescuing our young comrades. If the Life-Force has led us to these gates, then into it we will go."

Chapter Three:
Kidnaped

When Tom woke up, his head was spinning and there was a lump on it. He opened his eyes and found himself lying on his back, looking up at the branches overhead. He tried to move, but could not. He discovered that his hands were bound behind his back, and there seemed to be something on his legs, preventing him from moving them. The sword given to him by Gottron was missing, and so was his backpack. He tried to raise his head to see where he was and what was lying on his legs, but could only do so with great difficulty, as pain raced through his head. Finally, he was able to rest his chin on the green tunic on his chest. This permitted him to see Palifair lying unconscious, across his legs.

He heard voices, intelligible and intermingled with grunts and squealing like those made by pigs. These were followed by the footsteps of people running back and forth. Tom tried to turn his head to see what all the commotion was about, but it was too dark. He could only make out shadowy figures to his right. They were about a dozen yards away, moving in the darkness. It finally dawn on him that he was in the forest and he began to imagine all sorts of horrible creatures in his mind when suddenly, there appeared over him the ugly face of a large, black trog. He put his two yellow tusks close to Tom's face, and his eyes flashed with hate as he examined him.

"Zzzzo youz be-a-waking-upz, little worm?" the trog growled in a badly spoken form of the common language of Daryan. "It's timez you be-a-gettinz-upz." he laughed as he flung a bucket of putrid water on the boys.

Palifair moaned and slowly shook himself awake, as a second trog bent over him. He was board and squat, and he picked the boys up by their jackets with his long arms, lifting them to their feet. Palifair was still groggy and fell to his knees.

"Oh, my head," Palifair moaned.

"Yourz head?" grunted the trog. "Bezzz lucky thatz youz still gotz it on yourz shoulderz."

The other trogs, standing around, began laughing. Then one of them said something in his foul language. *"Yukuauki obubaok orguzu tutotugoak! Lujobubaz gutuguoka ozu tu otugshjo ozu obubaok."*

One of the trogs grabbed the boys by their hair and dragged them a while, as they cried out in pain. This only made the other trogs laugh even harder. The boys were pulled through bushes and then plopped down before a large fire that kept back the surrounding darkness of the forest. Trogs were mulling about, talking to each other in their broken form of Daryan.

"Whyz do we gotz to keeps them bratz alive?" asked one of the trogs.

"Causez themz be de ordaz, youz dunghill!" another trog said.

Tom shook his head and saw a pair of boots before him. He looked up and saw the bent figure of a man standing over him. He was wearing a long, green cape, with a large hood that was pulled down, over his face. He seemed to glow in the eerie light of the fire. The man rubbed his hands together and chuckled in such a way that Tom felt he recognized it. Somehow the man seemed familiar to him.

"Well. It seems that our paths have crossed again, my little friends?" the man said. "Aren't you glad to see me again? Or perhaps you don't recognize your old friend?" With that, he pushed the hood back over his head. Tom and Palifair looked and could clearly see his face leering at him in the light of the campfire.

"Kellium!" Tom shouted. "I might have known that you would

turn up again, and in the company of trogs. Where you find bad apples, you're bound to find a worm.."

"Now, now," Kellium said. "Is this any way to speak to me? Especially after I have convinced my friends here, not to kill you." Kellium bent even lower over the boys. "Confidentially, they wanted to skin you both and make stew out of you."

"It's just like you to take up with trogs and their kind, Kellium," Palifair finally spoke. He was not amused or frightened at the merchant's jesting. "Worms like you can be expected to slither about in slime."

"Brave words, but they can do you no good, Palifair," Kellium said. "It's better to associate with trogs then to take up with robed mystics and highwaymen. They're bad business, you know?"

"Bad business! That's the only type of business you've ever involved yourself in," Palifair said, as his blue eyes burned with hatred. "If I could get my hands free for just one second, you're be sorry for kidnaping us."

Kellium pulled back and stared at Palifair. A shiver took control of his body, and fear made an appearance in his eyes. Somehow, he did not know now, but he felt Palifair's words were not an empty threat. He had changed somehow, since last Kellium had seen him. He was not the same boy he had seen playing in the fields outside of Middleboro, just five months earlier. It was as if he was another person altogether. There seemed to be a fire burning within his soul that caused Kellium to step back in fear, though he tried not to show it.

"Well, then, we'll just have to make sure that we keep your hands securely bound, won't we?" Kellium said. His words got caught in his throat as he spoke.

"Just what is it that you want with us?" Tom asked angrily.

"Frankly, I don't want anything from either of you," Kellium said. "But my mistress has given me strict orders to bring you back to her for a little party, you might say. It would seem that one of you is of some value to her. It was a pity that your two friends, Huck and Rullin, couldn't have join us, but that couldn't be helped. I have a feeling she will be more than pleased with the two of you, though."

You're a filthy traitor, Kellium, and if we ever get you back to the Mark, you'll pay for your treason!" Palifair said.

"You judge me wrongly, Palifair," Kellium said. "To me it's all business. I'm getting paid to bring you to Fennoria alive, and couldn't care less about such ridiculous notions of patriotism and loyalty to those provincial peasants living in that backward pigsty you call the Mark." Kellium's words were filled with contempt. "But I wonder why Wargana is so interested in the likes of you?" Kellium bent over and was about to search the boys when there came a hissing voice behind him.

"Izz won't dozzz thatz, Mas'zer Kellium," one of the half-trogs said. "Youz knowz de ordaz. De mistrezz sayz no seachin' de prisonerz. Must captur' demz and' brinz demz back 'live."

"Gorbug! Mind your own business," Kellium shouted. "I'm in charge here and I will say if these prisoners are searched or not. You just go back and take care of your troops."

Gorbug's eyes flashed with hate. His large, lower, red lip quivered with anger. He clinched his fists and then turned and disappeared into the crowd of trogs.

"Those half-trogs are a pain in the butt," Kellium said as he reached into one of Palifair's pockets. "What is this?" Kellium said as he pulled out the White Stone and held it up in front of him, to examine it more closely. He seemed to be fascinated by its brilliant white light. The trogs around him backed off in disgust and fear. Kellium could not say anything. His mind burned with a fever as he began to tremble.

"Aaaahhh!" Kellium shouted. His face was distorted with pain. The stone fell to the ground. Kellium stood there holding his hand. His lips were curl back, revealing his yellow teeth.

"Thatz will teach youz ta be diz'bayin' de mistrezz'z ordaz," the half-trog said as the other trogs laughed at Kellium's misfortune.

"Shut your mouth, Gorbug, or I'll have you tongue cut from it and feed it to the crows!" Kellium shouted back at him. He grabbed a sword form one of the trogs and tried to lift the stone, but he could not budge it. He kept trying and soon became frustrated, and finally threw the sword on the ground in anger.

"I can lift it for you," Palifair said.

Kellium looked at Palifair for a minute without saying a word. "No thank you, my boy," he finally said. "I have a feeling that it would not be wise to let you touch it. But, perhaps . . .Gugtuk! Come here and untie Tom's arms for me." Kellium pointed to Tom.

A large trog stepped forward and cut the ropes around Tom's hands.

"Come here and pick up the stone and put it back in Palifair's pocket," Kellium said. "And don't try anything, or Palifair here will lose his head."

Tom turned around and saw Gugtuk holding Palifair's hair with one hand, pulling his head back, and holding a knife to his throat with the other. Tom said nothing. He walked over to Palifair and looked into his eyes. Palifair could not speak. Tom bent down before his friend, and picked the stone up and held it in his hand. Gugtuk's red eyes never left Tom, as he put the stone back into Palifair's pocket.

"Very good," Kellium said. "It was fortunate that you didn't try anything foolish. It would seem that we will have to keep you both alive as carriers for that blasted stone. Tie his hands once more."

Just then a small, squat trog came running up to them.

"Mas'zer! Mas'zer! Scoutz report long-robez and light-skinz on de oth'da side of de riv'a. They be-a-movin' east, lookin' forz uz!"

"It would seem that your friends are hunting for us," Kellium said to the boys. He turned back to Gugtuk. "Quickly! Gugtuk! Get your troops ready. We move out, immediately!" Kellium shouted and then walked off, calling for Gorbug.

Gugtuk began shouting orders at the other trogs in their own black speech. *"Jorzuba-zu tub-zuskav glu zugutok! Akokaujokan butugtukak zus tutugo luuki! Gubak butugs! Gubak butugs!"* The other trogs began to move slowly, grumbling to each other. Gugtuk then took out his long whip and began whipping his troops, as he shouted more orders and insults at them until they finally got into formation. He then turned back to the boys.

Pulling them up to their feet, he shouted at them. "Upz! Getz upz! Itz time we be-a-movin' outz, and de twoz of youz muzz' be-a-runnin' witz uz!" He then retied the ropes that bound their hands so that their hands were in front of them, but their arms were tied in such a way that they could not use their fingers. It was impossible for them to reach into Palifair's pocket and grab the White Stone. The trog then shouted at several other trogs, who began pushing the boys into formation. "If I hadz my wayz, I would haf cutz youz bothz into liddle piecesz witz dizz!" he said as he raised his sword up to their faces, while the other trogs around them laughed. "Zo don't be-a-gibben' me any trouble! Undoezstandz?" he said as he walked away from them.

The troops began to move out once more. Tom and Palifair were hustled and bumped by a sea of running black trogs. They could hardly see each other through the running forms. Tom occasionally caught sight of Kellium, who was sitting on a chair that was held up by two poles and carried on the shoulders of eight large trogs. Torches were lit, not so much for sight, since trogs could see clearly in the dark, but to keep away any danger that might be lurking within the woods.

Tom could make out the trogs running along side him. They were wearing dirty, gray tunics that hung over their shoulders and were secured about the waists with a large belt. From the belts hung knives, swords and other weapons. Many also carried long iron spears and small round shields. They wore small, round helmets with horns on their heads. Tangled clumps of black, matted hair hung down from out of the helmets. Few had any form of body armor, since they were expected to run. They were dressed for speed rather than battle. Some trogs carried bows and arrows. They were usually taller than the rest and wore long, gray and brown, hooded, robes that covered themselves from head to toe, except for their faces, feet and hands.

Tom could hear the trogs speaking to each other in their foul language, while others spoke in broken Daryan. Different tribes of trogs spoke different dialects that were so dissimilar that they could not understand each other, so they used a broken form of Daryan to communicate among themselves.

As they moved through the forest, some of the larger trogs ran up and down the formation, cracking their whips and shouting at the rest of the trogs, urging them to run faster. *"Okzusha! Okzusha!"* They shouted. The trogs appeared to be naturally lazy, except for the larger trogs who were terrorizing the rest. These larger trogs appeared to be in charge. The only thing most of the trogs seemed to understand was fear and the threat of brute force.

All that day they ran without rest through the dark forest. The boys found the going difficult with their hands tied. The air grew hotter and heavier as they moved farther south, and it made it even more uncomfortable for them. Occasionally, one of the boys would slow down. When he did, one of the trogs would give him a push with the point of his weapon. They eventually stopped, only once in the afternoon for a short rest. The boys were given dry bread to eat and foul water to drink, while the trogs munched on raw meat, and then they were off once more. By the late afternoon, Palifair was beginning to feel sick. His head was aching and everything around him was spinning when he finally fell over. The trog running behind him jumped over him and shouted , as the rest of the troop of trogs came to a halt.

Gugtuk came running up with a leather bag filled with a brown drink. He grabbed Palifair by his hair and poured some of the drink into his mouth, causing him to cough and wake up. He then poured some water on the boy's head and shouted for him to get up, but Palifair just moaned that he could not.

"Kinnotz? Kinnotz getz-up?" the trog shouted at him.

Palifair just moaned once more. "I need rest," he said.

"Youz getz all de restz youz needz in Fennoria. Youz waitz and zee," the trog hissed.

Gorbug came running up. "Whatz goin' on herez? Why da delay?" He waved his arms about him with excitement. "Can'tz youz even getz thoze bratz on their feetz?"

"Shutz-up, Gorbug! Diz be trog buziness! No place for mixed-up scum buckets like youz!" Gugtuk yelled at Gorbug.

"Watch whatz youz says to me, Gugbuk! You be a-forgettin' daz I be de mistrezz'z appointed agent! Youz just waitz 'till I getz you back to Fennoria. Then we'll be a-seezing who takez care of whoz?" Gorbug hissed back at the black trog.

"Bah! Don'tz you be-a-threatenin' me," Gugtuk growled back at the half-trog. "I be de commander of de mistrezz'z Horgotz, and dez here prisonerz am in my charge. We be de bestz of de mistrezz'z armiez. We attacked de light-skinned thievez backz at de lake and captured de bratz. If youz don'tz shutz-up, I shutz youz up with diz here sword!"

The trog and half-trog began shouting at each other in one of the trog dialects, causing the other trogs and half-trogs to come running to see what the commotion was all about. Gugtuk pulled out his sword and jumped at Gorbug, who just barely got out of the way and fell over. He picked up a fallen branch and leaped at the trog, striking him along the side of his head, causing his helmet to go flying. The other half-trogs began cheering at their leader's blow and shouted insults at the trogs. Gugtuk jumped up, and with his hand, he swung his sword hard, tearing Gorbug's black cape and cutting his arm. Gorbug fell back in pain, holding the gash in his arm with his other hand. It was now the turn of the trogs to jump up and down, waving their arms and hands, and shouting their approval of their commander's skill as a fighter. A half-trog shouted something in the trog tongue, causing the other trogs to pull out their swords from their scabbards, and the two groups were now in the thick of the fighting.

Tom tried to raise himself to his knees to see what was happening. The two trogs that were standing guard over him and Palifair had run off to join the fighting. Palifair was lying down, too exhausted to care what was taking place between the undermen. Tom jumped out of the way, just as a small, fat trog came running at him, followed by a larger, brownish half-trog. The larger half-trog swung his long sword and chopped off the head of the smaller underman, sending it flying through the air with a tail of green blood that came crashing down in front of the boys. Tom and Palifair wanted to try and crawl off to one side, for fear of being trampled by the fighting undermen, but they could not. The best they could do was to huddle together, and try to stay out of the way of the undermen running about. Suddenly, they realized that the noise of the screaming undermen had ceased. They opened their eyes to see what had happened.

Kellium had appeared and restored order.

"I won't have anymore of this bickering between your groups!" Kellium shouted at them. "Don't you stinking dunghills realize that druids and Guardians are hunting us right now? I personally don't care if you all kill each other, but please wait until we reach Fennoria. I don't want to end up in a druid's dungeon, so stop this fighting, or else!"

The undermen seemed to fear Kellium, though Tom could not understand why. Gugtuk began shouting at his trogs to return to their positions, while Gorbug left with Kellium. Tom noticed that there were three trogs and five half-trogs lying dead on the ground. Some were missing arms and heads. Then Gugtuk began giving orders in the speech of the trogs, and his troops began dragging their fallen comrades away.

"Tom, what happened?" Palifair asked.

"Pal. Are you all right?" Tom asked. "I was worried we were going to get trampled."

"Yes, Tom. I'm all right," Palifair said. "This is a fine kettle of stew we got ourselves into, but I feel sick, very sick and I don't think I can go on, Tom. Not another step."

"Well, don't you worry, Pal," Tom said. "If we have to go through another night like this one, there may not be any more trogs or half-trogs left to worry about. They seemed bent on killing each other off, and I think they would have gone on fighting until they had done just that if Kellium hadn't stopped them. Too bad."

Just then Gugtuk appeared with two other trogs. "So. There youz be, youz liddle wormz. I waz wonderin' where youz had gottin' off to? Bothz tryin' to 'scape, are youz now?" the large trog growled as the two other trogs with him, snorted. They dropped the bundles and bowls that they were carrying, onto the ground. "Here. Some good meatz and stew to eatz, and some bread. Eatz well, for wez be-a-movin' outz in a few hourz," he said and then left. The other two trogs remained. They sat down several yards off and began eating some of the raw meat they had, as they guarded the boys.

Tom looked at the meat and immediately recognize it, and almost vomited.

"What's wrong, Tom?" Palifair asked.

Tom gagged for a moment and spit the words from his mouth. "That meat—its part of the trogs that were just killed."

Palifair just looked over at the two trogs munching away on the remains of their fallen comrades, without even the slightest remorse. He threw the meat aside and thumped the cold stew over. He struggled to tear the bread in two, with his arms tied to his side down to his elbows, and gave half to Tom. They discovered that there was some water left in their skins and sat down to a poor, but filling meal. Afterwards they laid down and tried to get some rest.

Tom felt something kicking him in the side and woke up to find Gugtuk kicking him awake. He and Palifair had fallen asleep.

"Up! Getz up!" Gugtuk shouted at them. "It'z time we be-a-movin' on."

Tom got up, but when Palifair tried to stand, he fell over.

"Come'n and getz up, youz liddle roach, or I be-a-stompin' youz good!" the trog shouted at Palifair, as he grabbed him by the arm and pulled him up.

"Can't you see that he's sick?" Tom shouted at the trog. "You can't force him to walk all the way to Fennoria, or he'll die before we get half way there."

Gugtuk was about to slap Tom when Kellium intervened. "He's right, Gugtuk. He doesn't look well."

"They iz only tryin' toz loaf," Gugtuk said. "I makez them walkz. Youz leave itz toz me."

"No! If they die, there will be no one to carry the stone," Kellium said.

"Bah! Allz youz light skinz stickz t'gether," Gugtuk growled. "What I care if de bratz die or notz?"

"You'll care a great deal if you have to carry the stone," Kellium said. With the mention of the White Stone the trog cringed in fear. "How would you like to tell the mistress that it was your fault there was no one to carry it? Well?"

Gugtuk's eyes squinted with hate at the thought of the stone and stumped his feet on the ground and snorted. He then shouted for two of his troops. "Yughu! Ougtog!" Two large, black trogs came running. "Takez them bratz and carryz themz, and don'tz dropz themz or else youz be-a-feelin' de edge of myz blade!"

The two trogs lift the boys. They untied their arms, but retied their hands in such a way as they could not use their fingers. They trogs flung them on their backs, with their arms hooked around their necks. They grabbed their legs in their arms to brace them and prevent the ropes around their hands from choking them. In a short time they were off once more.

The trogs ran most of the way through the dark woods, as their commanders shouted at them, urging them on. Several times the whips that they used liberally on their troops, struck one of the boys. The only thing they could see were the torches that the trogs carried, to keep away uninvited guests. The night passed uneventful, except for the occasional noise they heard in the distance, but they never actually saw any signs of life.

The next two days passed and the trogs ran most of the time. The trogs' foul stench invaded the boys' nostrils. What little sleep that the boys were able to get was while they hung on the back of the dirty trogs that carried them, with their filthy, matted hair in their faces. They ate little, only the dried bread, and avoided any meat that the trogs gave them, especially after the episode with the raw trog flesh. It was always dark in the woods, and they lost all sense of time.

It was in the early morning hours on the third day when the trogs finally called to a halt for any length of time. Trogs can run long and hard when they are compelled to do so with the threat of brute force, especially in the dark. After they rested, they began running all day, though much slower in the daylight.

They had finally reached the north bank of the Donnor River, and had to cross over to its southern bank. The boys were tired and exhausted and their bodies ached. Palifair's fever had broken and his strength had actually returned. Kellium made sure the trogs kept giving him douses of the brown liquid that seemed to have some curative properties.

It was night when they finally reached the river. The trogs had hidden their large rafts along the shore of the river that they used to cross it on their journey from Fennoria. Tom and Palifair were brought by Gugtuk to Kellium, who was already on the first raft, filled with trogs and half-trogs.

"How are you feeling, my little friends?" Kellium asked, standing in the dark. But Tom and Palifair said nothing. "Not talking? Well, maybe you need some medicine to pick you up?" Kellium then waved and a small, squat trog with a large leather bag filled with more of the brown liquid, grabbed each of the boys by their mouths and poured the liquid into them, causing them to gag. It tasted terrible, but immediately they felt a new strength filling and warming their insides, in the similar way that Gottron's golden drink did.

When everyone was aboard the rafts, they slowly floated across the mighty Donnor River. The boys could clearly see that the trogs were uneasy about being on the river. They naturally hated and feared running water. Trogs could not swim or float. The half-trogs could barely swim, and were not as nervous as the trogs were. They also took a great deal of delight in the discomfort of the trogs, as they crossed the river.

The boys actually enjoyed the ride across the river. It felt good to see the stars over their heads once more, and their spirits actually rose by the time they reached the other side of the river. They felt the rich, green earth under their feet once more, and a gentle, morning breeze blew through the trees that grew there, causing the brown leaves to rustle and fly about. But there was not enough time for them to enjoy it all. No sooner did they touch dry land again, they were hustled into a formation of trogs.

Gugtuk put a piece of dry bread in each of their hands for them to munched on as they ran. The trogs gave up giving them raw meat, since the boys refused to eat it, and in the trogs' dark and twisted minds, they did not want to waste good food.

They ran all night and into the morning, and did not stop when the sun rose. The trogs were especially fearful of the daylight. The sun's rays sapped their strength. The boys welcomed the sun and despite the terrible stench from the sweating trogs, they took a great deal of satisfaction from their captors' discomfort.

Once they reached the Old North Road, a quarrel broke out between the trogs and half-trogs. As usual, Gorbug and Gugtuk were having a disagreement. Their argument caused the other trogs and half-trogs to gather around. Kellium had to break them up, as usual.

"I'm getting tired of always breaking up your fights!" Kellium shouted at them. "We're no more than one day's march from Fennoria, but if you two keep this nonsense up, we'll never get there, especially with our enemies lurking about. They could even be waiting for us at the bridge, over the Flenflow."

"Daz whyz I suggested daz I takez de prisonerz and move ahead withz my half-trogz," Gorbug hissed. "De sun will be-a-showin' itz yellow face high in de skyz zoon, and thenz Gugtuk's trogz will be-a-slowin' uz downz, as usual. Butz my half-trogz can run fast in de sunlightz. De sunlightz doesn't bother uz."

"I don'tz trust youz and yourz filthy, watered-down half-trogz," growled Gugtuk. "We be Horgotz. We not be afraid of no long-robez or light-skinz. We be great warriorz. I will makez my trogz march all de dayz long. Even in de sunz. We attacked and destroyed de city of Thilengard and killed and raped many light-skinz. All New Earthz fearz uz, and we fearz nothin'! I, Gugtuk have spoken!"

"Don'tz be a fool, Gugtuk," Gorbog said. "De long-robez can turn yourz Horgotz inta ashez if they ever getz their handz on yourz skinkin' hidez. I will takez de prisonerz to Fennoria and not waitz for youz and yourz lousy trogz."

"Now listen here, Gorbug," Kellium said in a hard but restrained voice. "I am in charge here, and I will say what we will do. I say that we stick together. It'll do us no good to split up. That will only weaken our forces. Besides," Kellium said with a smirking smile. "If you return to Fennoria with the prisoners before the rest of us, you'll get all the credit."

"And whyz notz?" Gorbug asked. "I should have been in charge of diz here company, and notz some light-skinz. But wez will seez what de mistrezz haz to say when we getz back to Fennoria, and I tellz her that youz searched the prinsonerz and tried ta takez de stone for youzself."

"Why you filthy, little, half-breed slug!" Kellium shouted.

Gorbug pulled his sword out and raised it high over his head. Kellium screamed in terror and threw himself on the ground with his hands over his head. Gorbug laughed at his cringing, but his laughter got caught in his throat, as thick greenish blood poured from his mouth. His eyes bulged in shock as he fell over, almost falling on Kellium. The merchant looked up in disbelief and saw, standing over him, the large, black figure of Gugtuk with his sword in his hand. It was covered with Gorbug's blood. The trog's pig-like snout snorted with satisfaction. The excitement of the kill caused the other trogs to begin jumping up and down, while they hooted and howled, and brandished their weapons over head.

Kellium picked himself up from the ground and composed himself. "You're a good solider, Gugtuk," he said. "I won't forget to mention your loyalty when we get back to Fennoria."

"Youz keepz promise. Youz give me man-flesh ta eatz," the trog said as he looked at the boys, sideways.

"Yes. Yes. You'll get your fill of man-flesh," Kellium said. "Enough to fill your belly."

"Good! Gugtuk not forgetz," the trog said as he turned and walked away with a grin on his face. His green tongue licked his two, sharp tusks. He looked over his shoulder at the merchant one last time and grunted to himself.

The boys did not remember much of what happened the rest of the day, except that they crossed the bridge over the Fenflow River. On the other side of the river they turned off the highway and moved south on a smaller road that led to Fennoria. The trogs forced marched through the barren landscape, as the larger trogs curled their whips expertly, hurrying them on their way. The boys were pushed and shoved as they ran along. When they fell, they were dragged by their captors and then beaten. They tried not to remember what happened to them, and were both frightened and relieved when they reached the Hole of Fennoria. The trogs were anxious to get inside the gates once again and began to run the rest of the distance, at double time. The boys could not keep up with the trogs and soon began falling back, when two large trogs gabbed them and threw them over their shoulders.

It was dark when they reached the Hole of Fennoria. The sky was overcast and starless. A black cloud hovered overhead. The air was heavy with a grayish haze that made it hard for the boys to breath.

Kellium called a halt to the company before the black cliffs that rose before them. There were two large towers that seem to be cut right out of the cliffs themselves. They were tall and smooth, as if they were made from black glass. The two towers were connected by a wall of black steel. The wall was one thousand feet high and in it were two large doors. The doors were large enough for an army to pass through them, one hundred soldiers abreast. The boys had never seen anything so large before. They had thought that Gateburg's gate was large, but after seeing the Hole of Fennoria, it seemed insignificant.

The boys were standing on the ground once more, and could see Kellium speaking to one of the guards that patrolled the grounds before the wall, but they were too far in the rear of the formation to hear what was being said. After several minutes, the guard disappeared through a small hole in one of the large doors. Kellium shouted for his troops to prepare to move out. Just then, there was a dreadful clanking noise and the two large doors, standing one hundred feet tall, began to slowly reel open. The company of trogs began to move forward once again, through the doors. The boys passed into the witch queendom of Fennoria.

The trogs and half-trogs grew excited to be home, and began howling and squealing with joy. The Horgots ran up and down the formation, cracking their whips over their heads. Tom and Palifair felt their knees give out and almost fell to the ground with fear.

Gugtuk came running up to the boys and shouted, "Youz liddle slugz! We seez thatz youz getz all de restz you needz in Ariesten, soonz enough." He grunted and cracked his whip over the heads of the boys and laughed. He then ran off once more, shouting at his troops to hurry up.

Once everyone had passed inside of the Hole of Fennoria, the doors slammed shut with a terrible thump that echoed throughout the canyon, and sent shutters through Tom and Palifair with a deadly sense of finality. They moved along the road that took them deeper into Fennoria. Eventually, they came to what appeared to be some kind of village, with a large mill made of black stones. It had three smokestacks which were bellowing thick, black smoke into the air. From a large metal pipe that stuck out of the side of the building, flowed brown muck into the Fenflow River. Around the mill were hundreds of small huts made from pieces of scrap-wood and metal sheets. Behind them, cut into the cliff wall were large caves that housed hundreds of trogs. Before these caves was a huge building made of large blocks of stone, which was covered with black grime and slime. There was a green light shining from its window.

Kellium led his troop passed the mill and around to the large building, where he called a halt. He left the troops waiting on the road while he passed through a metal gate and was greeted by a tall man dressed in green and black armor. He wore a helmet with four horns rising out of it. His face was hidden by the helmet, but they could make out his icy cold eyes that burned with a green light. Kellium seemed to tremble before him. In fact, everyone seem to avoid looking directly at him. The entire troop of trogs and half-trogs grew suddenly calm and silent, like rabbits that freeze when in the presence of a predator.

A few words were exchanged and then Kellium followed the man inside the building, and did not come out for over an hour. When Kellium finally returned, he was accompanied by two small trogs with long arms that almost reached the ground. Kellium ordered Gugtuk to bring the troops into the yard, near a stable that was built into the large building. There the trogs began to mount large boars, which the trogs often rode into battle.

Horses were then brought out of the stable which Kellium and the half-trogs mount. The horses were all large and pitch black, and had an evil look to them. Their eyes burned with a strange green light, as if they were possessed by some demonic force.

Kellium mounted his horse and rode up to the boys, and pulled it to a halt. "Well, my lads," he said. "You no longer have to worry about walking all the way to Arietsen. You will have the pleasure of riding the rest of the way. Oughun! Biluk!" Kellium shouted at two half-trogs who came riding up to him on horses. "You'll ride with them, and don't worry, boys. They won't let you fall or get lost." Kellium smiled as the two boys were hoisted up and plumped down in from of the half-trogs.

All that day they rode along the road with Kelium and the horse-mounted half-trogs. Behind them came the trogs riding on the large boars, squealing in excitement as they rode closer and closer to their destination. They stopped only twice for a few minutes to rest their beasts and then were off again. The boys' hands were still tied before them and they could hardly hang on to the horn of the saddle. They had lost all sense of time or day. That infernal country seemed to be eternally blanketed by an eternal night, due to the black clouds overhead.

Tom knew it was getting late in the day because his stomach was beginning to grumble. They fed the boys only twice; once in the morning and again in the late afternoon. Tom noticed for the first time that he had lost some weight from the lack of good food or drink. But thoughts of hunger were soon replaced by the knife that he noticed hanging from the horn of the saddle. If he could only pull it out of its scabbard and cut the ropes that bound his fingers and hands, he could, perhaps, get the White Stone from Palifair's pocket and place it in his hands. But his rider would stop him if he tried to reach for the knife. He would have to wait for his chance, and he was determined not to let it slip by. He knew he would only get one chance, and if he did not do something soon, before they reached Ariesten, he knew that all hope of escape would be lost.

Outside that black land it was getting late and the sun was slowly slipping down behind the western horizon. Kellium finally called a halt and made camp. The half-trogs dismounted from their horses and led them into the camp that the trogs were making. Tom, who was still sitting on top of the horse, saw his chance to cut his ropes. It was now or never. Bending down, as if he was exhausted and trying to rest, he slowly removed the knife from its scabbard. He stopped dead cold for a second when the half-trog, who was leading the horse on foot, stopped. Tom remained frozen with the knife half-way out. He dared not try to move for fear of his captor turning and catching him in the act.

Then the horse began to move once more, as the half-trog proceeded forward without looking back at Tom. He quickly placed the knife on his lap and cut the ropes, ever-so-gently, by rubbing his hands along its blade. He did not cut them clean through, but only enough to weaken them and then, just as carefully, he put the knife back into the scabbard, a second before the yellowish face of his guard turned and halted the horse.

"Come down from there, my little friends," Kellium said with a large smile. "We must have a little talk." Tom turned around and saw Kellium coming up behind him and Palifair.

The two half-trogs pulled the boys from the horses to the ground, and led them to where Kellium had set-up camp. There was a clearing, surrounded by boulders, and a campfire was burning with several legs of meat cooking over it. The aroma was tantalizing and caused their mouths to water.

"Sit!" Kellium ordered, as they sat down on two small boulders. They just stared at the meat, not caring what beast it might have been cut from. "Ah! I see that you're hungry. Well, never let it be said that Kellium Greengold was a bad host. I'm sure there will be enough to share with you."

Kellium cut three pieces of meat, keeping one for himself and the other two pieces he handed to Tom and Palifair, along with two tankers filled with cool, fresh water. The boys hesitated, even though they were starving.

"Go ahead and eat," Kellium said. "It's good lamb meat, just like the meat your father roasted back in Middleboro, Tom."

The boys could resist no longer, and proceeded to gobble up the pieces of roasted flesh, and washing it down with large gulps of water. They had not felt so good in days.

"I know you're not going to give me any more trouble, because you're going to need my help when you get to Ariesten," Kellium said as he sat down along side them, trying to be as comforting and friendly as possible. "Now that some of the fight has been knocked out of you, I'm sure you realize that I'm your friend and only want to help you." With those words, Tom's ears perked up.

"What do you mean?" Tom asked.

"There will come a time when all that we know will come to an end, and Wargana will be queen of all the western half of New Earth. She will need good people to help her rule. I have been appointed the governor of all the Mark, but I will need some good men to help me rule justly, and both of you are smart and bright lads. You'll be growing up and when you do, you can be a big help to me, and to the Mark. I'm sure you would want only the best for our beloved Mark, just like I do. That's why it's imperative that we convince our friends and neighbors not to resist the force that is already growing and spreading."

"You mean, you want us to betray the Mark, like the thieving pig you are, and join forces with the worms you keep company with?" Tom shouted at the merchant. Kellium's smiling face slowly lost its grin. Tom then spit in his face. "There's you answer!"

Palifair watched Tom with amazement, and was proud of his friend's courage.

Kellium wiped his face clean and stared at the two of them in deadly earnest. "You'll both regret that," he said. "You just wait till we get to Ariesten. I'll have both of you begging for me to put you out of your misery, before I'm done with you." Kellium got up and left the clearing, as Palifair smiled at his friend.

"Well, I guess it will go all the more harder on us for that little act of yours, Tom," Palifair said. "But you know something? I'm proud of you."

Tom smiled for a second and then leaned closer to Palifair. "It might not, Pal," he whispered. "Old Tom still has a trick or two up his sleeve." He then winked and smiled again.

Two black trogs suddenly appeared and picked the boys up and dragged them to where Kellium was waiting. "I just wanted to say farewell for now," he said to the boys. "I'm off to Ariesten, to make sure things will be ready for your arrival." Kellium then smiled wickedly at them. He then jumped on his horse and shouted for Gugtuk, who came running up to him with his long arms swinging, as he hobbled on his short, bowed legs.

"I'll be waiting for you in Ariesten," Kellium said. "Make sure you drive your troops at full speed and reach Ariesten by tomorrow. I'm leaving the prisoners in your charge, and make sure nothing happens to them. The mistress wants them alive. Tomorrow night you will feast on man-flesh, and drink your fill of their blood."

Gugtuk grunted his approval while the other trogs squealed in delight, as they licked their tusks with their tongues.

Kellium then turned back to the boys once more. "Remember, lads. I'll be waiting for you in Ariesten." His beady eyes were almost closed with heavy lids and a wide, crooked smile was sprawled across his thin, pale face. He pulled on the reins of his horse and rode off with the half-trogs, and disappeared into the gray haze.

Gugtuk dragged the boys by their hair and held them close to his foul face and growled at them. "Just be-a-tryin' taz escapez! Just tryz!"

Chapter Four:
To the Top of the World

The trogs remained at the campsite for the rest of the night, with the boys as their captives. They laid along side of the campsite, as two trogs stood guard over them a dozen feet away, talking to themselves in their foul language. Tom could not fall asleep. He was lying on his side with his hands still tied in front of him. His upper arms had been retied to his sides. In the distance he could hear the squealing and grunting of the boars in their pens, occasionally mixed with the uproar of trog noise from the campsite. After several hours, Tom looked over and saw that the two trogs guarding him had fallen asleep. It was now or never. Tom pulled on the cut ropes that easily broke apart. He began pulling at the ropes around his arms and soon loosen them enough to pull them off. He then whispered to Palifair. "Pal. Pal, are you asleep? Wake up."

"I was asleep, but now I'm awake," Palifair said.

"Good. Because if we don't do something fast, we'll be in Ariesten this time tomorrow," Tom said.

"What do you have in mind?" Palifair asked. He could not see that Tom had freed himself in the dark. "Do you have a plan?"

Tom crawled over to his friend and held up his free hands. Palifair's eyes lit up. "How?" was all he said.

"I cut them loose on the knife when I was sitting on that hideous demon-horse, but we can't go into that now," Tom said. "Let me get the stone out of your pocket."

Palifair rolled over so that Tom could reach into his pocket and pull out the White Stone. His small hand closed on the stone that seemed alive and vibrating, as he pulled it out of his friend's pocket and placed it in between the palms of Palifair's tied hands. Bluish-white light began to glow from within Palifair and grew in intensity. Palifair rose to his feet with ease, causing the ropes that bound him to fall to the ground by themselves. Tom sat before Palifair, looking up at his friend. Palifair seemed to grow in size and statue and now appeared as a fierce warrior. His face was frozen with determination, and his eyes burned with the courage of a thousand knights of his race. His long, blond hair blew across his face in a breeze that seem to come from no where. He looked down at the White Stone that he held in his outstretched hand before him. He was totally transformed and became a lightning rod that drew the power of the Life-Force to him.

The two guards suddenly woke and turn to discover where the light was coming from. "Whatz dat? Whatz goin' on herez, and whoz'z dat?" They said as they rose to their feet with swords drawn.

Palifair turned and looked hard at them. He seemed to be encased in a white light and his hard, blue eyes caused them to freeze with fear. They did not see a small boy standing before them, but a warrior clad in bright, sliver armor. Tall and terrible he seemed, with the power of the Light shining about him. The trogs cowered in fear, falling to their knees with their faces buried in their hands.

Palifair stepped forward and brought the stone up to the level of his eyes. He closed his hand around the stone and out of it a beam of pure energy shot, cutting a path through the darkness and striking the two trogs. Their leathery flesh boiled and their ice-cold, greenish blood sizzled as they began melting. Flesh and blood poured down to the ground into a pool of sizzling slime.

Suddenly, a host of trogs, led by Gugtuk, came running into the clearing, wanting to investigate the bright lights, when they ran straight into Palifair. Gugtuk stopped short in his tracks, as the other trogs ran into him, cursing as they fell over each other. Their eyes opened wide and their jaws dropped at the sight of Palifair standing before them, burning with the rage of his entire race. The trogs dropped to the ground in terror and cringed like a pack of whipped dogs. Palifair raised his arm and once again the stone began to shine. This time the light continued to grow until it filled all the clearing. So bright it was that Tom could not see anything, though the light did not seem to hurt his eyes. When the light had finally vanished, he saw Palifair standing alone in the clearing.

Everything had returned to normal. A dead silence seemed to fill the world. Palifair stood before him once again as the simple boy from Middleboro. The power of the White Stone had left him. Tom got up and ran to his friend.

"What in the name of the Mark, happened?" Tom asked. All around them were smoldering piles of ash and charred bones. That was all that was left of the trogs and wild pigs. Palifair seemed dazed by it all. Tom shook him back to his senses.

"Pal! Pal! Come on, Pal! Snap out of it!" Tom shouted.

Palifair just looked at him.

"We've got to get out of here before we run into any more trogs," Tom said.

Palifair looked at his friend, and nodded his understanding.

The boys first went to where the trogs kept their supplies, and began searching for some supplies to take with them. They found their backpacks, which they were wearing when they were captured, and looked around for what they could possibly need to get out of Fennoria. They took no meat, not knowing what kind it was, but they found some knives, water bags filled with fresh water, and a few tools that they might find useful, in a small pouch. They also found some dried bread that they took with them, and they were off. They made their way down the road for several hundred paces until they came to a bend that turned toward the left and upward. The air was heavy and hazy, and made the going more difficult for them. Tom especially found it hard to breathe.

"Come on, Tom," Palifair said. "Let's get off the road. I don't want to run into anyone."

Tom looked out toward the barren landscape and thought for a moment, as he rubbed his chin. "Well? If you say so, but where will we go in this miserable country?"

"Anywhere other than where this road will take us," Palifair said.

The boys climbed over the edge of the road and down into a gully that ran along the side of it and served as a drainage ditch. They landed in a small stream of dirty water, up to their ankles and then proceeded to climb up the other side as fast as possible. They were now on the south side of the road and began moving toward the Fenflow River, which turned westward, and away from the cliffs to their left.

The landscape was almost barren and covered with gray rocks. No grass grew there. Here and there bushes of thorns and thickets pierced the dry, hard surface of the ground. No sign of animal life existed anywhere. The whole scene before them seemed unreal. It was as if they were transported to another world, where there was no sun nor stars. They could not see too far in the distance because of the heavy, dark haze that hung over the landscape.

The land sloped downward, and after many hours of stumbling over rocks and ridges, they finally reached the river. They began walking along its bank, eastward. The river was about two hundred feet wide. Its waters were foul and brown, and reeked with foam and no fish lived in its currents.

As they struggled through the terrain, they were battered and bruised. Tom finally sat down on a large rock.

"I can't go on any longer," he said. "Not another step. We can't go on like this. We can't go back and we can't go forward."

"But maybe we can go up," Palifair said, still standing and looking across the river.

"Up? Up where?" Tom asked.

"Up there," Palifair said, pointing across the river.

"Up there?" Tom asked again. "You mean you can see across the river?" Tom was trying to see through the haze. He squinted his eyes hard.

"Sure. Can't you?" Palifair asked.

"No, I can't" Tom said. "I can't even see across this river through all this confounded haze."

"Well, I can," Palifair reassured his friend. "I think, maybe it has something to do with the stone."

"What do you see?" Tom asked.

"Let me see," Palifair said, as he turned and faced north. "In that direction I see black cliffs. They're about ten miles away and go straight up. It think it would be impossible to climb them." Palifair sad, and then turned and looked south, across the river. "To the south I see the ground sloping up sharply, but I think we could easily find a way up and out of this canyon in that direction?"

"But up to where?" Tom asked.

"Up and out," Palifair said. "That's where. I don't know why, but it's as if something is calling me. Telling me that we should go up there." Palifair then walked over to the edge of the river, still looking across to the other side. "We have to cross the river, Tom. I don't know why, but we must."

"I'm not exactly excited about climbing thousands of feet into the unknown, but I guess anything is better than remaining down here, in this terrible place," Tom said as he lifted himself up to his feet. "And if I'm going to meet my end, it's better to do it high in the mountains than deep in one of Wargana's dungeons. But just one thing, though," Tom said. "How do we get across this foul-looking river? It's plain that we can't swim across this cesspool."

"We'll find a way," Palifair said. "But first let's have a bite to eat. What do you have, Tom?"

"Let me see," Tom said as he opened his backpack. "I have a half a honey cake, some of that dry bread we took back there, and some nuts and three carrots. How about you?"

"I have a whole loaf of honey cake, a bag of nuts and some of that dry bread," Palifair said.

"We'll have to ration what little supplies we have and hope that we find something to eat once we get up into those mountains, and out of this canyon," Tom said. "Thank goodness we were able to find these bags of water."

They sat and ate a few bites of their cakes, dry bread and nuts and then washed it down with a mouthful of water. They then reloaded their supplies and were off once more.

"I wonder what the others are doing right now?" Tom asked.

"I don't know, Tom," Palifair said. "I suppose they're looking for us."

"I hope so, but how in the world are they going to find us in here?" Tom said.

"Don't worry about that, Tom," Palifair said. "I'll bet a druid could make his way through this place better than you or I could. I just hope my sister is well." For the first time in a long time, Palifair's thoughts turned to Rowena, and he wished he was in her loving embrace. He secretly feared that the others were in danger. He had no way of knowing that Blondor was looking for them at that very moment. He tried concentrating on his friends, remembering his lessons in Wissenval and everything Blondor had taught him about using the sight. But no matter how hard he tried, he could not see them. He did not know if he was too weak to use the sight, or if it was being blocked by the Darkness that filled Fennoria. In the back of his mind he could not help but feel that everything that had happened to him and Tom, in the last two weeks, was being directed by some unseen, greater power. He felt sure that eventually they would meet up with their friends.

"I'm still glad that Huck and Rullin weren't with us when we were captured," Palifair said to Tom.

"Look!" Tom shouted, causing them to forget their friends for the moment. "There!" Tom said again, and then ran off with Palifair right behind him. There, by the shore of the river, was the remains of what appeared to be an old wooden pier. Planks of wood were lying about and sticking out of the brown waters of the Fenflow, warped and covered with green slime.

"I think we can salvage enough wood here to build ourselves a small raft that will take us to the other side of the river?" Tom said, as he began collecting several planks of wood.

In a short time they were building a small raft from the planks of wood they were able to get from the pier. They examined each piece of wood carefully, making sure the wood was seaworthy. They would only need the raft to cross the river, so it did not have to be too well built, but just seaworthy enough to get to the other side of the river. In a few hours they were ready and set sail across the Fenflow, using two long planks of wood as paddles. They slowly made their way to the other side of the river. The current was weak, and it was not difficult to cross the river. The craft was wobbly, but it remained afloat long enough to keep them dry. They were careful not to let themselves get too wet by the foul water.

When they reached the other side of the river, they jumped off the raft and pulled it on shore. They found a small depression and tried to hide it within it by covering it with rocks. Then they moved inward, as far away from the river as possible. The ground began to rise sharply and they made their way in between the jagged rocks that dotted the landscape. The going was slow and they found it difficult to climb the slopes. The canyon grew increasingly dark as night descended upon the world. Finally, they came to a ledge with a small hollow that they crawled into for the night. Once inside, they were hidden from the view of any possible spying eyes that might be able to see through the haze.

They huddled together, next to each other, with their capes pulled about them, and munched on a couple of carrots. "I wish we could at least see the moon or stars," Tom said. "I feel like we've been swallowed alive by a great dragon and are traveling through its belly."

"I know what you mean," Palifair said. "Why don't you get some sleep? I'll stand guard for a while."

"All right. I sure can do with some rest," Tom said as he rolled over on his side, using his arm as a pillow and fell fast asleep.

When Tom woke, he found Palifair sound asleep next to him. He had no idea how long they had been sleeping, and could not tell what time it was due to the heavy haze. Actually, better than twelve hours had passed since they stopped climbing, and it was well passed noon on the 6th day of the month of Turning.

"Pal! Pal!" Tom said as he shook his friend awake.

"What is it, Tom?" Palifair asked as he stretched the sleep from his limbs and rubbed his eyes.

"You must have fallen asleep without waking me," he said. "And I have no idea how long we've been sleeping."

"I'm sorry," Palifair said. "But I thought you needed sleep more than I did, and decided to let you sleep while I stood guard. I guess I needed sleep more than I realized."

"Well, that can't be helped now," Tom said. "But don't you think we'd better be moving on? Kellium and his trogs must have figured out by now that we escaped. They're probably looking for us right now. I wouldn't be surprised if the whole blasted Fennorian army is out hunting for us."

"Then we had better continue moving up and out of this cursed land as soon as possible," Palifair said.

They quickly finished the last of the dry bread and took a small gulp of water to wash it down, and were off again. The sloops were becoming steeper the further they went, and in some places they were turning into cliffs. They soon found what looked like a path that whined upward, and began following it. It led them up along a narrow ledge, causing them to hug the side of the mountain.

"Don't look down, Pal," Tom said as they inched their way along, while holding hands. They were now far up, above the valley below. Tom was never more glad then now, that he had lost so much weight over the last few months from all the traveling. It allowed him to hug the wall of the mountain all the closer. Eventually they came to a dead end and had to back-track and try another route. Twice it seemed that the path led down, but they could not be sure if it actually did, or if it was just an illusion caused by the great heights.

They eventually came to a small gorge that cut across the path and had to jump across it. Palifair had no difficulty, but Tom almost did not make it across. Palifair grabbed his hand just in time, as Tom struggled to pull himself onto the ledge. Several rocks were knocked loose from Tom's struggling, and fell down the side of the mountain to the sounds of echoing booms. They stopped to listen for the stones to stop, but it seemed that they never would. The thought of Tom falling all that distance caused them to shiver with fright.

The higher they climbed, the lighter it got, as the haze began to thin. They figured that the sun must be rising above the clouds beyond the haze. Despite the thinning air at the higher altitude, they were able to breathe easier because of the thinning haze, and this raised their spirits.

They finally came to a halt on a ledge overlooking the eastern end of the canyon below. Several huge boulders rose like a fortress on every side of the ledge, but there was no shelter from the haze and wind. It was the best they could find, and since they were tired after climbing all day, they decided that the ledge was a good place to rest. They made themselves comfortable, sitting up against the protruding boulders, and helped themselves to a small meal of a few nuts. They looked out over the brownish haze that blurred the distance, and they could make out reddish lights far below. It looked like the canyon floor was on fire. They had no idea what the lights could be and crawled to the edge of the ledge to get a better look at them. They stared for a while, and when they were confident that the lights represented no threat, they returned to the mountain wall and sat closed together with their capes rapped tightly around them.

They boys did not realize it, but they were watching the great furnaces of Fennoria bellowing fire and smoke into the sky. Wargana had constructed hundreds of them, deep underground, beneath the floor of the valley. Huge smoke stacks rose from the floor of the canyon like a forest of stone poles, bellowing up clouds of poisonous gases into the air twenty-four hours a day, filling the canyon of Fennoria. The gases and smoke had built up over the years until a permanent cloud of brown haze hung over Fennoria. The fires that fed the smoke and ashes into the sky were produced by the vast arsenal of machinery underground, that Wargana used to create great weapons of war. The furnaces were run by the thousands of enslaved Truemans, trogs, half-trogs and trog-men slaves that worked day and night under the cruel lash of the whip.

They spent the night on the ledge, and continued on their way in the morning after a small meal. The day was uneventful, and they slowly climbed as far up the mountain side as they could in their weaken state. They were getting weaker from the lack of food and water. What little they had left, they carefully rationed. They stopped more often now, trying to rest as much as possible. At the altitude of fifteen hundred feet the mountain suddenly grew less steep, making it easier for them to continue their trek upward. They walked along the mountain side, moving in a southernly direction. They continued until they came to a place where they found a path that appeared to be man-made, but there was no sign of life, or any other traces that Truemans ever lived this high up. Soon they were moving right along, following the path that zig-zagged in and out of huge stone fingers that jotted up from the side of the mountain. They were making good time now, and were far up the side of the mountain when it began to grow dark once more.

"I have to stop, Pal," Tom said, as he dropped to his knees. "I need some rest and something to eat."

"All right," Palifair agreed, as he sat down next to his friend."

The two of them sat on a small boulder, munching on the last of their supplies. "We had better go easy on the food," Palifair said. "There isn't much left, and I don't know how far it is until we reach where we're going."

"And just where might that be?" Tom asked.

"I don't know," Palifair said. "I just know that we have to go up. It's as if I'm being called. It's like there is a voice inside of me urging me to climb."

"Well, ask it where we can get something to eat," Tom said. Palifair smiled at his friend's joke.

Neither of the boys realized that the mountain they were climbing was known as Virlon. In ancient times, when Truemans first settled New Earth in their wanderlust from the northern regions, they believed that the Lords of the Light lived on the peak of this mountain. It was their abode on New Earth, and from there they watched over the happenings of the world.

Tom and Palifair started off once again, but it was not long before they were hungry and thirsty once more. Their mouths were parched and their stomachs were empty, but they continued to go on. They were bent over as they walked, climbing up the mountain on all fours. Later in the day they stopped once more and finished the last of their water and honey cakes. They knew that unless they found some food and water, they would not last very long.

All their willpower was turned to the task of going on. They pushed themselves ever upward. Their feet were sore with blisters, and their muscles ached with every step they took. Tom seemed to lag behind Palifair, who refused to give up hope. He would occasionally have to stop and climb back down a short ways to help Tom.

Tom's strength had finally failed him and he could not go on. He slipped out of Palifair's arms and fell flat on his belly, and said nothing.

"Tom! Tom! Are you all right? Speak to me!" Palifair shouted as he spoke to his friend.

Tom moaned. "I tried, Pal. I tried, but I can't go on," Tom said.

"Oh, Tom. What are we going to do?" Palifair said as he sat next to his friend, trying to think what he should do next. He closed his eyes and tried to clear his mind, but nothing came to him. It was no use. He then pulled the White Stone out of his pocket and looked at it. "If only we had some water," Palifair said. Just then, he felt what appeared to be a cool breeze on his face and looked up. There, above him, the brownish haze was rolling back before his eyes. A golden ray of sunlight cut through the haze, and for the first time in days he could see the blue sky high overhead. Palifair was overcome by what was happening and wondered if it had anything to do with the White Stone. The cool breeze continued to blow down from the mountain top. It caused his spirits to rise. Then, for the first time, he saw before him the high mountain peak glistening gold and white with the sunlight dancing on its snowy icecap. A white cloud seemed to be caught on the mountain peak, as if someone had placed a cotton ball on a pointed hat. Below the snow line there grew a blanket of dark, green trees. Tall and straight they stood, and from their ranks there flowed a small stream of water. Clear and fresh it poured gently down the side of the mountain, heading straight for them. It twisted and whined its way until it struck Tom's cheek. Instantly, Tom began to stir.

"Look! Tom, look!" Palifair shouted as he shook his friend. "We've made it! We've made it!"

As the cool mountain water washed the exhaustion from Tom's face, he slowly rose and looked up at the sun and blue sky.

"By my father's inn and all the food and drink in it, we did it," Tom slowly said. The two boys remained still for a while. They were overcome.

"Come on, Tom," Palifair said. "Let's fill our water bags and move up into the sunlight."

In no time they were running up the side of the mountain until they found themselves walking among the trees. The ground was covered with a blanket of clean, white snow. They left the brown haze below, and everywhere they looked they saw only the blue, cloudless sky. They sat on a fallen log and ate some berries and acorns they found in abundance. Soon it was getting dark, and the sun was disappearing behind the mountains in the distance. The eastern sky was turning a dark shade of blue and slowly growing black. The first stars began to twinkle overhead.

"We better find a place to stay for the night," Tom said as he gulped down a handful of berries.

"Let's try up there," Palifair pointed to the right.

Soon they found a small clearing surrounded by tall pines, from there they had a clear view of the haze-filled Fennoria far below.

"This looks like a good place to stay the night," Tom said.

"You're right," Palifair agreed. "I like the feel of this place. We'll stay here the night."

The two boys laid down under the trees with their hands folded behind their heads, looking at the mountains that spread out into the horizon. The sun had disappeared in the west and the sky was now black. The stars dotted the face of the universe overhead. The great belt of starlight stretched across the night sky.

"I wonder what day it is?" Tom said. "I lost all sense of time in that cursed land."

"I'm not sure, but maybe we can figure it out after the moon comes up," Palifair said. "Anyway, it's good to see the stars again."

For the first time in weeks, they felt totally at ease. They watched the sky fill with thousands of points of light. The nightmare of their captivity was now a distant memory that quickly faded into the shadows that lurked deep within a seldom used corner of their minds. They soon dropped off into the world of dreams.

Palifair found himself back in the Mark, under a star-spangled sky and a large, golden, full moon reflecting its rays off the Rill River that lazily flowed between the rolling hills of his homeland. Off in the distance, he could see the mountains of the East Mark. Mount Vigilance was standing tall behind the sleepy town of Middleboro. He then took a closer look and to his horror, he realized that something was terribly wrong with the town. There was black smoke bellowing out of three tall smokestacks on the top of a large, brick building that stood where the apple orchard once stood. Other buildings were missing and in their place were large, gray structures. Most of the trees were cut down, and the fields surrounding the town were fenced in and patrolled by guards.

Palifair wanted to cry out in horror at the sight before him, but he could say nothing. It was as if he suddenly struck speechless. Then he heard a voice. Low and distant it was, but slowly it grew louder and clearer as it called his name over and over. Palifair finally recognized the voice of Blondor, and he looked up and saw the dark face of the druid against the night sky. His eyes shined with a white light, and Palifair knew that he was looking for him. He wanted to call out to him and struggled to find the will to do so. "Here! We're here!" he found himself shouting.

"Who in the world of fairies and hobgoblins are you calling?" Palifair heard someone ask and felt a hand shake him awake. He jumped up out of his dream, and looked at Tom sitting next to him. The morning sun was sitting on the eastern horizon.

"You were shouting in your sleep," Tom said.

"Oh, Tom. What a dream I was having," Palifair said.

"It sure must have been a humdinger," Tom said.

"I heard Blondor calling me," Palifair said. "He's searching for us. I know he is."

"Well, he won't find us up here," Tom said. "Where do we go now that we're up on this mountain?"

"There!" Palifair said as he pointed. "We go there."

Tom turned in the direction that Palifair was pointing. He noticed a tall, natural tower of stone that rose up, out of the side of the mountain. It was about several miles to the south of where they were. Its base was broad and surrounded by a bed of tall pines that were dwarfed by the tower that rose two hundred feet in a cone shape. It stood majestically against the clear, blue morning sky.

"There, Tom," Palifair said again. "That's where we must go."

Tom examined his friend, who was staring at the tower, as if it was calling to him. He wondered why in the world they should climb up there.

"That's an awfully tall tower to climb," Tom said.

"Yes it is, but we must climb it," Palifair said. He then jumped up and began gathering his belongings. "Hurry, Tom. We have to hurry."

Palifair took off, running, with Tom right behind him. They ran through the woods, looking up through the spaces between the branches of the trees, trying to keep the tower in sight as they went. It seemed farther away then they had thought, and it was difficult to run across the snow-covered ground. They slipped more than once.

The tower was known as Hill-Shelf by the druids of Wissenval. It was often said there that if one climbed Hill-Shelf, one could actually speak with the Lords of the Light.

The trees grew right up to the base of the rock tower, and there the boys found stairs cut into its side. The stairs spiraled up the side of the tower and it took the boys several hours to climb to the top of the Hill-Shelf. They were forced to stop and rest several times. The climb was difficult as there was no railing, and the stairs were only five feet wide. Several times the boys feared being swept from the stairs by winds that whipped about the tower.

When they finally reached the top of the tower, they discovered that it was flat and thirty feet in diameter. In the center was a small structure. It had a round platform with four pillars that held up a circular roof made of white granite.

Tom threw himself on the floor. He was exhausted from the climb. He watched Palifair, who stood still for a few minutes, looking at the structure with the wind blowing in his face. He did not seem out of breath. Tom was about to say something when Palifair began walking toward the structure.

Palifair climbed a small flight of stairs that led up to the top of the platform. Once on top of it he looked up at the clouds that hovered high overhead, hiding the top of the mountain. Its white, misty vapors began to descend until they engulfed them. The world below seemed to disappear. Palifair was transfixed. The temple seemed to melt away beneath him and the mist parted. Visions danced in front of him that he could not comprehend. He heard a voice that seemed to come from within him.

"Son of the Mark, look and learn!" it commanded.

Suddenly, the images before him became clearer, and he could make out distinct lands, and saw great armies moving across the face of the world. They came from every corner of New Earth, like swarms of ants. The most terrifying scenes were the armies from Allomania and Fennoria. They were black and horrific and the lands that they crossed were scorched and black with ash and destruction. The armies seemed engaged in a great conflict, where the blood of both Truemans and undermen flowed and mixed with the muddy earth. The vile mixture ran down into the Donnor River, turning its waters red and green that eventually mixed into a putrid brownish color.

Next, Palifair saw the sun, and across its face a black shadow appeared, blocking its rays and plunging the world into darkness.

Throughout New Earth mountains began to crumble and the valleys were filled with ash and smoke. New Earth suffered from great eruptions. Soon the mist grew thick once more and blocked his vision. He heard the voice speak to him once more.

"Son of the Mark, look and learn!"

Once again the mist parted and he looked but saw only darkness. Then, after a few seconds, he saw a small ball of fire that rapidly grew larger until it was gigantic in size. It burned hot like a red sun in the blackness of space. Then out of the distant darkness there appeared a huge piece of ice tumbling through space. It plunged into the ball of fire, causing the flames to flip and leap about until it exploded, sending fire and ice flying in all directions and expanding outward into space. The void of space was filled with steam and mist. Out of the hissing vapors a huge figure appeared. It stretched its enormous limbs wide, filling the void and roared terribly. Then, three white figures appeared. They assaulted the giant and killed him, and began cutting him into pieces. The pieces bursted into fire and ice and the three figures began to take them and rearrange them, forming them into billions of stars. Next they took pieces of ice and mixed them with the sparks from the flames until they coalesced and formed small planets. Around one of these suns, a yellow one, they created a world that Palifair instantly understood to be New Earth. The mist grew once more until it filled his vision only to part once again, and he heard the voice speak to him for a third time.

"Son of the Mark, look and learn!"

Palifair now saw New Earth spinning before him. It was round and around it whirled the moon. Soon the moon began to move closer to New Earth with each rotation until the gravitational pull caused the seas on New Earth to rise and flood all the lands, except for the peaks of the tallest mountains. There, the remainder of Truemandom took refuge and built great cities. From these cities sailed vast navies across the endless oceans that covered the world. Finally, the moon began to break up and its billions of tiny dust particles formed a ring around the planet. For the fourth time, the mist filled his sight and he heard the voice speak to him.

"Son of the Mark, look and learn!"

Palifair now found that he was no longer standing on the platform. He was flying through the cosmos. Darkness surrounded him. When he looked down, he saw a great host of gigantic demons of indescribable horror, coming out of the impenetrable blackness. The vision was too horrible to look at for long and Palifair diverted his eyes, but he could still hear their terrible cries that haunted his soul. He could sense their hatred for everything good and pure. And then he felt a warmth descending from above and when he looked in that direction, he could see a blueish-white light. It grew greater, but it did not hurt his eyes to look at it. It made him feel whole and wonderful and he no longer heard the cries of the demons. He wanted to rise and enter the light.

Then he heard the cries of the demons once more. When he looked down at them once more, he could see that they were twisting in agony as they tried to rise, and entire the light. They were drawn to it. Their faces were distorted with the lust and desire to possess the light, but as hard as they tried, they could not reach it. Palifair could see their faces transformed from lust to hatred—a hatred for what they could never possess.

Palifair looked back up at the light once more and it was then that he noticed what appeared to be a city within it. He could make out great temples and towers shining within the blueish-white halo. Within the structures he could see figures. They appeared to be great lords and ladies. They were both beautiful and wondrous to behold. Never had he seen such beautiful faces. Palifair realized that they were a great army. White and wondrous they appeared, they were clad in brilliant armor, and they held weapons that glimmered with the light of the stars. In joy he watched as they rode through the void on white steeds. Behind them trailed the translucent essence of their purity, and within it rode millions of warriors, all filled with their essence. They joyfully rode behind the great lords and ladies. It was then that Palifair thought he noticed one of the rides. He was a man, who seemed to be watching him. He could not understand it, but for just a moment, he thought he was looking into the face of his father. He smiled at Palifair and then, along with the rest of the riders, he rode on and disappeared into the great host that passed before him.

Palifair knew that he was witnessing some great and final battle between the Demons of the Darkness and the Lords of the Light. He found himself in the midst of this confrontation. Giant forms that dwarfed him whirled all about as he watched from within a white sphere that appeared to be the White Stone.

Finally, the white mist once again filled his vision and the scene faded as he heard a voice speak to him once more.

"Pal! Pal! Look up there! Look!"

The voice belonged to Tom. He had run up the stairs to where Palifair was standing, on top of the platform, at the top of the stone tower. Tom had grabbed Palifair just as his knees gave way.

"Look, Pal! It's him! It's him!"

The two boys stared into the sky and could make out what appeared to be a winged horse flying toward them. It was white and beautiful and it galloped on the rays of the sun, heading straight for them. The sun was behind it and flickered through its flapping wings. On it rode a dark figure that appeared to be encased in a blue flame. Palifair could not see who or what it was for the sun was in his eyes. Tom held Palifair, who was exhausted from his vision. The last thing Palifair heard before he passed out was Tom shouting.

"It's him! It's him!"

Chapter Five:
The Witch's Cauldron

The great, black, metal gates that guarded the entrance to Fennoria stood tall, cold and silent. Seven figures walked slowly up to the black, metal wall and came to a halt. From high up came a voice.

"Haltz and identifyz ya'selvez!"

One of the figures stepped forward and spoke. "I am Princess Valenda of Neutria. I and my two sisters, have come out of the north. We've traveled a long way and have come seeking your mistress, Queen Wargana. We desire to join her sisterhood. We've brought four powerful, male warriors to deliver to her as a token of our admiration for her, and our desire to join her cause. Open your gates and let us in!"

"Waitz there!" the voice called down to them.

Several minutes passed and then a tall, thin window, situated in the wall, opened. A yellowish-brown face with squint eyes popped out of the window to get a better look at the visitors who demanded entry. The half-trog stared at them and shouted.

"Whatz be it daz youz seekz, wench? I havez no or'taz to be on a lookz-outz for youz and yourz prisonerz!"

"We demand that you let us in so that we can deliver these male prisoners to your queen," Valenda answered. "We seek audience with your mistress in Ariesten. When your queen learns of our arrival, and what we have brought her, she will reward you and your wisdom to let us entire."

The half-trog said nothing for a moment while he examined the princess and others, and then disappeared and closed the window. Valenda and the others stood patiently for what seemed like hours, though it was only several minutes, until they finally heard the clanking sound of metal against metal. The huge doors began to reel open before them. Out of them came a party of half-trogs.

"De mistrezz welcomez youz," hissed one of the half-trogs.

Valenda led the others through the gate and into the haze that seem to linger within. Once inside, the monster doors began creaking close until they slammed shut with a terrible thump that echoed off the cliff walls. They were now inside Fennoria and there was no turning back. The only way for them now was forward, toward Ariesten and the witch-queen.

One of the half-trogs approached and came to a halt in front of them. He stood there for a minute, glaring at the northern beauty of the princess. His yellow eyes examined her carefully.

"I be de cap'tin of de guardz," he hissed as he pulled himself up to his full height. "I will be-a-sendin' word ta Areitsten daz youz and yourz captivez will be-a-comin'. Untilz thenz youz and de otherz will be-a-stayin' here and waitz for an answer."

"No! That will not do!" Princess Valenda insisted. "We have not traveled through mountains and forests with our captives only to be held-up by the likes of you. We are expected in Areisten, and Areisten is where we are going, even if we have to fight our way through all the misshapen flesh that dares to stand between us and our destination." The princess grabbed the hilt of her sword, but did not remove it from its scabbard.

The half-trog's eyes opened wide in reaction to the ice-cold determination of the woman that stood before him. He was used to taking orders from women, since Fennoria was ruled by witches. The courage and pride of Valenda's race had caused him to reel back in fear. He cleared his throat and then spoke, barely able to speak the words. "Ifz youz be-a-expected in Areisten, thenz whyz waz I notz told of yourz comin'?"

"I don't know, nor do I care why you did not receive notice of our arrival," Valenda said. "But when your mistress asks us why we were detained, I will tell her that we were held up by the captain of the guard of the gates."

Valenda's threat caused the captain of the guard to back down. The thought of suffering Wargana's wrath and what it meant, caused him to give in. "No . . . uh . . .no, youz may pazz," he finally said as his eyes darted back and forth, as if he was expecting Wargana to step out from some unseen hiding place. "Therez be no reason ta tellz de mistrezz. I letz youz go onz yourz wayz. Yez. Youz go. Now!"

"Good! Then you will provide us with horses so we can ride," Valenda insisted.

"Horsez? We have no more horsez to givez youz," the half-trog said. He decided to try and reassert some of his authority through deception. "Ifz youz wantz ta goz ta Areisten, thenz youz will be havin' ta goz on footz." He then smirked. "I havez no more horsez. No more! All I had waz given to Master Greengold. He too had captivez and waz in a big hurry. Soz ifz youz wantz to be-a-goin' to Areisten, thenz youz must be-a-goin' on footz."

The half-trog slowly began walking away. He suddenly stopped before Vesten and looked hard at him. He put his yellowish face close to the Guardian's face. Vesten could smell his foul breath, but he did not move. He remained frozen and stared back at the underman. The half-trog spat on his face in contempt, but Vesten remained motionless.

"I wish daz I could be dere when de mistrezz getz her handz on youz, youz stinkin' light skinz filth!" he growled.

Vesten's deep blue eyes were now fixed on the piggish face before him. Hard and cold he stared down on the smaller underman. His will burned into the twisted mind of the misshapen creature standing before him. A sudden shiver overcame the half-trog, causing him to shake violently as he stepped back.

"Go! Go! Getz on youz wayz!" the underman shouted as he waved his arms in the air over his head, and then ran back to the barracks, "Getz out of my sightz! Go all ta wayz to Areisten, and into the Yawnin' Void, forz allz I carez!"

The girls led the men along the road, as trogs and half-trogs occasionally stared at them, as they passed.

"Did you hear him refer to Greengold?" Hollin asked in

a whisper. "That bastard must be behind the kidnaping of the boys."

"Quiet We're still not out of danger," Vesten said.

They marched on for several miles along the road that Kellium and his trogs took with Palifair and Tom. They walked slowly without revealing any fear, and left the last black, brick buildings at the guards' compound far behind. Once they had turned a corner and were sure they were out of range of prying eyes and lost in the thick haze that filled the canyon, they turned off the road and climbed a small hill. Once on top, Vesten and the other men removed their bindings. The ropes that were tied around their hands were only loosely bound, and they could easily have pulled them off and use their weapons, which were concealed under their capes, if they had too.

"It was just as Blondor said," Rowena said. "They never expected three women to walk right up to their gates with four male prisoners and demand to be let in. Their thick skulls weren't able to suspect a trick."

"What do we do now?" Hollin asked. "We can't remain here, nor can we walk all the way to Areisten. By the time we reach that witch's den, a message will have reached Areisten that we are on our way. We'll never make it there in time to rescue the boys without horses."

"We'll do exactly as Blondor told us to do," Vesten said. "We'll remain here and wait for him." Vesten showed no concern, though he feared the worst and knew that danger surrounded them. If they were discovered now, there would be no escape. They remained on the hill for several minutes when suddenly, Hagrim gave a shout and pointed into the haze that hung heavy all about them. Everyone stood tense with hands on their weapons. They could make out a dark shape moving in the haze, coming toward them. Vesten pulled his sword from its scabbard and held it out before him, ready to use it if necessary.

"A fine welcome you've prepared for me, considering the gifts I bring you," a voice could be heard through the haze.

"Blondor!" Rowena shouted as she ran to greet him. "You made it."

"Of course I did, my dear Rowena," the druid said. "I've been waiting for you, and was beginning to think that something had happened to you."

"It would have been a black day for all of us if you had not made it through the gates," Vesten said to Blondor.

"It takes more than steel walls to keep a druid from going where he wants and when he wants," Blondor said. "It was rather easy for me to walk by them unseen. I trust everything went well?"

"Just as you said it would," Brim said. "Those undermen are nothing but a bluff. They backed down when confronted with a determined opponent." Brim smiled at Valenda.

"But we learned something disturbing," Rowena said. "It was Kellium who kidnaped my brother and Tom."

"I was wondering when that imp would show up again?" Blondor said. "I've been expecting him to show his face once more, ever since he disappeared on the Woodfields hills. I felt his presence when we were sailing down the Yarmil River, but I wasn't 100 percent sure he was in charge of the kidnaping. We had better hurry and see if we can catch up to him."

"But how can we?" Hollin asked. "They're riding to Areisten. We'll never be able to catch up to them if we have to walk all the way to Areisten, especially in this heat and haze. It must be well over a hundred miles to Areisten?"

Blondor said nothing. He turned and whistled. Up the hill came five, black horses. "I found them in one of the stables. They were taken from farms along the Donnor River by the trog raiding parties. All but the black horses were butchered and eaten. The black horses are saved to be transformed into demon steeds by Wargana's magic. These horse were the only that I could find that were not yet transformed. They were more than glad to have the opportunity to escape that fate."

"But there are only five horses, and there are eight of us," Hagrim said.

"We'll just have to double-up," Vesten said.

"Vesten is right," Blondor said, as he mounted one of the

horses. "We'll have to ride long and hard, if we are to catch up with Kellium and the boys, before they reach Areisten. Let's hope Kellium is not in too much of a hurry, and feels safe now that he is within Fennoria, if so, that'll give us element of surprise on our side."

Vesten jumped on another horse, while Rowena rode behind Valenda. Hagrim and Brim shared the fourth and largest of the horses, while Anna doubled up with Hollin on the fifth horse. They took off, riding down the hill and onto the road with all possible speed. They soon were soaking wet from the hot, hazy air that they felt on their faces as they rode. All they could hear was the thumping of the hooves of their horses hitting the ground, and their heavy breathing. They rode the whole day, stopping several times to walk the horse so that they would not drop from exhaustion. They stopped only once for a short rest and a cold meal in the evening, and then were off again, riding as fast as their steeds could carry them through the night. The horses seemed none the worse for the hard riding, and were actually glad to undergo such enduring hardship, if only to be free from the nightmare fate that awaited them in Wargana's service.

It was early the next morning, on the 5th day of the month of Turning when they stopped and dismounted. As they walked along, they remained alert for anyone who might also be traveling on the road. Several times since they started out along the road, they had to stop and hide off to the side to avoid being seen by travelers going to and from Areisten. They were walking along the side the road when Blondor, who was in the lead, stopped cold in his tracks. He seemed to have frozen in place. Standing motionless, he stared straight ahead. His black eyes opened wide, as if an electrical charge was coursing through him.

Vesten ran to the druid's side. "Blondor, what is it?" he asked.

But the druid could not hear the Guardian's plead. Then, as quickly as it overcame him, it passed. The druid slumped and fell to his knees, holding his staff for support. Brim and Hagrim grabbed him and held him up. They then all sat down on some large rocks alongside the road to rest.

"The stone," Blondor said. He tried to catch his breath. "Palifair has used the White Stone. I felt a shock wave in the Life-Force. He must have used the power of the stone against the enemy? The force of the attack was very strong, and that could only mean that the boys are close by. But if I was able to feel its power, then Wargana must have felt it too."

Blondor jumped to his feet. He seemed to have completely recovered. "Come! We don't have much time left. We have to find the boys before Wargana does. Let's hope that no harm comes to them before we reach them."

Blondor remounted his horse. The others began doing the same. In seconds they were back on the road and riding like the wind.

When they finally reached the campsite where Palifair had used the White Stone, they found only the smoldering remains of the undermen. All about them they saw the black ashes and charred bones that was all that remained of the trogs. Anna was revolted by the sight and held tight to Hollin.

"It was here that Palifair used the stone," Blondor said, as he dismounted and began to carefully step over the debris. "But what transpired here, I cannot be sure. What do you make of it, Vesten?"

"I'll need some time to examine the site and read the signs before I can say for sure," Vesten said. "Everyone, please remain where you are and don't disturb the footprints." Vesten ordered Brim and Hagrim to explore the surrounding area. The Guardians carefully made a thorough search of the area and after some twenty minutes, they regrouped to talk over what they found with Blondor.

"I found what appeared to be another encampment," Brim said. "A fire was still burning, and scattered about the area were discarded weapons, sacks of food and other gear. It seemed that everyone just jumped up and ran off for some unexplained reason.

They must have ran off suddenly. I found the remains of half-eaten meat lying about. Numerous tracks led from that site to this one place. Apparently, whatever it was that disturbed them sent them running here."

"Good work," Vesten said. "What you found, fits in well with what I have read here." Vesten said and then walked over to one side of the clearing, as everyone followed him. "Yes. Here is where the trogs entered the clearing and then stopped. You can clearly see where one of them, most likely their leader, stepped forward and then halted, at this pile of ashes here."

Vesten next walked over to the other side of the clearing. "And over here are two sets of smaller footprints," he said. "They could only have been made by the boys, because they were made by feet that worn footwear found in the Mark. Those prints then run through those bushes and onto the road."

"Then they're still alive?" Rowena asked.

"If anything happened to them, it didn't happen here," Blondor said. "It would seem that Palifair used the White Stone on his captors, permitting him and Tom to escape."

"This fits nicely with what I found," Hagrim said. "The boys came this way and then began walking down the road, in that direction, where I found many prints. They were made by horses that took off down the road."

"In pursuit of the boys?" asked Blondor.

"No. The horses rode away more than twelve hours ago," Hagrim said. "I would calculate that the boys' prints are not more than a few hours old."

"Did you follow them?" asked Blondor.

"Only a short ways," Hagrim answered. "I stopped when I ran into a small herd of boar that ran across the road, the kind that trogs like to ride. So I returned to find out what you discovered and report my findings. But I think the boys escaped without being recaptured."

"Then let's see where these tracks lead to," the druid said.

They walked along the road, carefully following the footprints until they came to where the boys left the road and moved across the country, to the river.

"Here's where they left the road," Vesten said as he examined the tracks. Standing up, he then began looking out across the hazy landscape, but he could see little.

"The river," Blondor suddenly said as he stared into the haze.

"What about the river?" asked Rowena.

Blondor did not immediately answer her. He stood still, staring, as Vesten held her by the shoulders to prevent her from disturbing the druid, as he concentrated.

"Be still and let Blondor see what he can," Vesten whispered to Rowena.

When Rowena could stand the suspense no longer, she pleaded with the druid to tell her what became of her brother and his friend.

Blondor's black eyes looked deep into Rowena's tear-filled eyes. "They're out of danger," he finally said softly. His face seemed to shine with an inner countenance.

"Safe? They're safe! How?" Rowena asked. She could barely get the words out. Tears rolled down her face.

Blondor reached out and held her close. She allowed herself to melt into his black robes. He gently wiped the tears from her face and sat her down on one of the large rocks nearby.

"Dear, Rowena," Blondor said. "You must believe me now, more than at any other time, when I say that you can stop worrying about your brother. He and Tom have passed beyond our reach, and their fate is now in the hands of a greater power than ours. This was meant to happen. I can see that now. All our movements have been directed by forces beyond our understanding, but you can be sure that neither Wargana, nor the Lord of Darkness knew who was really behind our diversion to Fennoria. It was never intended for the boys to fall into Wargana's hands. No! It is we who are meant to go to Areisten and confront the witch."

"Us?" Hagrim asked. "Why us?"

"There is something that needs to be done there, before we are to reach our final destination," Blondor said. "What that is, I'm not altogether sure, but we must go to Areisten before we can go on to Lothangia."

"There is still more," Vesten said. "There is something that you are not telling us. What is it that you saw, Blondor?"

The druid did not answer.

"It's the shadow of death," Rowena said. "Even I can read it in your face, Blondor."

"The boys are no longer in danger," Blondor said. "That much I'm sure of, but we have been brought here, not to rescue them. We've been diverted to Fennoria for another reason. Our fate awaits us in Areisten, and there we must go. I suggest that we concentrate on what lies in store for us there, and figure out how best we can deal with it."

Now that they were sure that Palifair and Tom were safe, they took the opportunity to rest for several hours. They caught up on much needed sleep and ate a small meal before going on to face Wargana. After they were rested, they proceeded down the road that led to Areisten. They no longer feared the possibility of being discovered. They were going to ride straight into the witch's den and let fate take its course.

They finally reached the point where the Fenflow River was formed from the meeting of two smaller rivers; one flowing from the east and another flowing from the north. Both rivers flowed into a small lake from which the Fenflow flowed. In the center of the small lake a large rock rose out of its brown waters. Two small bridges connected the rocky island with the surrounding shores of the lake. A third, larger bridge led straight back from the island to the cliffs, where it ran into a path that cut into the precipices rising over seven hundred feet, straight up.

The path ran on for about a half a mile, leading to Wargana's castle, Areisten, which towered far overhead, half hidden in the haze and dirty air. It was a huge fortress built of great black, stone blocks. Each stone block was so large that it looked as if the castle could only have been built by giants. The only illumination in the castle was an eerie, green light that glowed from behind a large, round, crystal window located over the entranceway. Areisten was nestled inside a wall of stone built on the edge of the cliffs.

The path led up to a great, bottomless gorge that seemed to drop into nothingness.

Blondor led them along the path. They crossed one of the smaller bridges that took them to the rocky island, and then they proceeded to cross the larger bridge that took them to the path that led to Wargana's castle. They could see the brown sludge that flowed beneath the bridge.

"It's hard to believe that once this canyon was teaming with life," Blondor said. "Once those rivers were flowing with clear, mountain water, filled with fish that jumped high into the air in celebration of life. The air was filled with birds that nested on the side of the cliffs, and along its banks there roamed all forms of animal life that lived within the green, lush woods that grew here.

"But all that was destroyed by Wargana and her dark magic. She stripped the earth's flesh of its wealth to feed her engines, which spit up fire and smoke. The air has been turned brown with ash, blocking out the sun and filling this canyon with this haze. She then proceeded to dump the waste and poison from her machinery into the river until it became contaminated, killing all life in this canyon. This is what the Darkness has in store for all of New Earth, if ever it is triumphant."

Once they got to the other side of the bridge, they dismounted.

"Here is where I must leave you," Blondor said. "You must go the rest of the way alone."

"What do you mean, you're going to leave us?" asked Hollin.

"I mean exactly what I said, son of Hillroller," Blondor said. "You must go on by yourselves. I'll join you inside. You, Princess, will lead Anna and Rowena inside once again, in the same matter you did at the gates. Wargana will be flattered if she thinks you have come to join her, but be on your guard. She is not easily fooled for long. And you, Rowena, don't conceal your powers. Let Wargana know that you have some knowledge of the arts. If you can keep her interested in your request to join her, she may not sense my presence. I can then tend to her undoing before she catches wind of my presence."

"And just how will you do that?" Hollin asked.

"Wargana must already know that Palifair and Tom have escaped," Blondor said. "Most of her trogs are probably out searching for them on the southern banks of the river. That's why we haven't run into any trog patrols." Blondor then turned to Rowena. "But don't worry. The boys are out of harm's way. They'll be all right.

"Wargana fears that events are getting out of hand, and she will have to make her move against the alliance of Trueman nations soon. This is what we must prevent, or at the least, delay. By delaying her, we'll provide additional time for us to reach Lothangia and the White Council of Lothar, and awaken the Lothangians to the threat that they face. We'll also be giving Arlindor and the others time to reach Neutria and rally the boatmen of the north. It'll also help the Tillenians, by giving them time to rally their armies. To do this, we must steal the source of Wargana's powers."

"But you still haven't told us what that source is," insisted Hollin.

"I'm not entirely sure what it is myself, but we'll all recognize it when we see it," Blondor said. "I have my suspicions, but until I'm sure what it is, I'll keep my suspicions to myself. If any of you are captured by Wargana, she would be able to read your thoughts, no matter how you tried to concealed them from her, and discover our reason for going on to Areisten, instead of following Palifair and Tom. So do as I say. I'll always be nearby, even though you'll not always see me."

Before the entrance of Areisten, Princess Valenda, Rowena and Anna appeared. They had climbed the path that led to the castle on foot, leaving the horses behind. Before them was the chasm that separated them from the entrance to the castle. Across the chasm was a small, stone bridge that seemed much too narrow, but actually was wide enough for two horses to ride across, side by side with ease. As they across, Rowena looked over the edge. The chasm seemed bottomless. She could only make out its endless blackness below.

They crossed over the bridge slowly, halting before a gate made of steel. Above it were three large gargoyles, perched over the gateway, with eyes that shined with an eerie, green light. Rowena was sure that they were being watched. She could not help feel as if there was some kind of life in those stone carvings. The gate was opened and unbarred, and there was no sign of any guards, anywhere. Since there was nothing to keep them from entering, they did so. But no sooner had they passed through the threshold, their ears were shattered with an inhuman cry that echoed throughout the halls of the castle, bouncing off its walls and cascading through the maze of halls and chambers within. A steel gate came crashing down behind them, trapping them inside and cutting off any hope of escape.

They could hear the sound of many feet running from the hall before them. Suddenly there appeared a host of short, black trogs with gleaming, yellow eyes, blocking their way. They began shouting at the girls in their trog language, and thrusting their long spears at them. The girls immediately drew their swords. Princess Valenda jumped right in the center of the trogs and with two swipes of her sword, she decapitated two of them. Rowena and Anna followed her lead without thinking. They jabbed at the undermen, cutting one of their arms and sending the rest reeling back in shock. They were not used to the display of determined resistance with which the Trueman women defended themselves. Then, as if reacting from an unheard order, the trogs moved back and parted their ranks, as a tall, evil-looking man stepped forward. He was dressed in long black and green robes. Upon his shoulders he wore a green helmet, with four long horns on its top. On the face of the helmet were two eye holes that joined at the center and ran down the length of the face-mask to the chin. The girls could make out no face within the helmet except for two burning lights set in the darkness within. He was the Mount of Fennoria.

The trogs cowered in fear before the Mount of Fennoria, snorting and grunting their submission.

"Welcome to Areisten, maidens of the outside world," he said. His voice sounded like the hissing of molten steel in water. His words, both sinister and menacing, sent goose bumps up and down Rowena's arms. "My mistress has received word of your arrival at the Hole of Fennoria. I've been sent to welcome you and bring you to her." His words came slowly, and his voice seemed to fill the hall. He put out his hand in a friendly matter and bid them to follow. "Come now, with me," he said and then turned. He began walking back through the host of trogs that now filled the hall.

As the women followed the dark figure, they felt an uneasiness overcoming them, as if they were walking in the wake of death itself. He led them through the castle, passing through an open courtyard and then into a large, black building at the other end of the yard. Once inside the castle proper, the Mount of Fennoria led the women up a long flight of stairs. After they had reached the top, they proceeded to walk through several large chambers, which filled the upper part of the castle. Clearly, Areisten was built on monestrous proportions. They could see what appeared to be avenues inside the castle, where a motley mixture of trogs, half-trogs and trog-men hurried about, performing their duties. Occasionally they passed a troop of Truemans who were dress in filthy rages and chained together by their necks and feet. They were pushed along by a troop of large trogs decked in armor and totting whips that they used on their hapless captives, as they shouted obscenities at them. The Truemans seemed in a state of depressed consciousness, as if they were drugged and close to death.

It appeared to Rowena that Areisten was run like a great beehive. She could see and observe the whole fabric of life within the castle in the great marketplaces that they passed through. The air was filled with a foul, reeking stench and they had to hustle their way through a throng of people, as trog guards pushed those in their way aside. Everywhere there were shops and stands where half-trogs and trog-men pushed their way in and out, examining and buying the goods that were being sold by the merchants that were gathered there.

Garbage and waste covered the floors of the marketplaces, mixing with the mud, urine and feces from the undermen that freely relieved themselves whenever they felt the urge. Clouds of gnats and flies were everywhere. There were puddles of putrid, brown water and piles of rotting meats and gray vegetables that were covered with armies of roaches and ants. The air was foul with an overpowering stench that invaded Rowena's nose and turned her stomach.

Rowena took notice of the trog-men and half-trogs. Both were a mixture of Trueman and trog characteristics, but the half-trogs were more trog-like, while the trog-men were more Trueman than trog in appearance. It appeared that everywhere, the trogs were used as guards and maintained order in Areisten. They were too stupid for anything else other than the use of brute force. Their commanders were of the larger and more fierce species of trogs known as the Horgots. The mongrelized half-trogs were more intelligent than trogs, and the trog-men were even more intelligent that the half-trogs. They fulfilled the role as artisans and bureaucrats in Areisten. But by far the most interesting community of undermen at Aresiten were the merchants. They were all of a similar dwarfish race.

Rowena noticed them at once. They seemed to own all the shops in the marketplace, and the other races of undermen all treated them with an exalted state of respect. Rowena caught occasional glimpses of them as they shouted at their customers in their high, rat-like voices. They were short, fat, dwarfish men with dirty, yellowish faces. The head of the dwarfish merchant seemed to be too big for the fat, round body, which was supported by a pair of stubby, but powerful legs. Their eyes glowed with a reddish light from under their heavy eyelids that were crowned with large, pointed eyebrows. Their noses were of different shapes, pointed and thin, or large and crooked and sometimes flat and wide. Their mouths were small, but filled with rows of small, sharp teeth. On their heads were tangled, messy, brown, black or gray hair. Those that were growing bald kept their hair short, revealing their small, pointed ears. Rowena could not help but feel a sense of loading at the sight of them. A dread seemed to overcome her every time one of the rodent-like creatures happen to glance in her direction, and held her stare with their hypnotic, red eyes. It reminded her of the time, when she was a child and was playing with one of the children of the Burntyard family in Middleboro, whose father was the sewer keeper. She spotted a large, gray rat with red eyes that stared at her before it squealed and scurried away. The sight of the rat revolted her, and she always felt disgusted when she saw one of them. Even after she grew up, she always feared rats. The sight of the merchants reminded her of her fear of rats, and every time she spotted one of them, shivers reverberated up and down her spine. It finally dawned on her that she had gotten her first look at the race of undermen that Blondor had referred to as the Kreel.

Rowena was relieved when they finally passed through a wide arch and left the last of the marketplaces behind. The arch led into a long corridor. It was lit by flickering torches that lined the walls. The corridor was empty and no sound could be heard other than their footsteps upon the stone floor. When they finally reached the far end, they were greeted by a small troop of large trogs. They bowed before the Mount of Fennoria. He had not spoken to the women as he led them through the castle, but now he stopped and turned to address them.

"Do not fear our friends," he said in his sinister voice. "They will escort you the rest of the way. The mistress is waiting for you in the Hall of the Covenant, which is beyond these doors and at the top of the stairs." He then turned and without saying another word, he disappeared back down the way they had just come.

"Youz will followz me," one of the trogs growled at the women. The trogs were arrayed in black and green armor and carried spears. They were Horgots, and very disciplined. They passed through the open door and proceeded to climb a flight of wide, stone stairs. Rowena could make out columns rising through the vastness of the chamber, like a forest of stone trees disappearing into the blackness that hung overhead. Rowena tried to find the ceiling, but saw only darkness overhead.

The trogs finally stopped when they reached the top. "Wez

goez no more," one of them said. "Youz goez in there. Da mistress be-a-waitin' for youz."

Princess Valenda led the way between two great columns of stone, and found a door that opened into the Hall of the Covenant. Rowena was overcome by the size of the hall. It was round, like a circle, and topped with a huge dome. Tall, thin windows made of green glass lined the walls. A great fire burned in a large pit, illuminating the hall and sending a column of smoke to the top where it escaped through a round vent. At one end of the hall was a large statue of a demon-cat, made of black stone, finely polished, with eyes that glowed green. The cat rose fifty feet high and dominated the hall. Before the cat was a ten-foot, round, stone platform with a spiral staircase that led to the top. A throne sat on top of the platform. Before the stone platform was a round pool of bubbling liquid from which green vapors rose into the hall.

All around the walls of the hall were rows of pillars. Behind them were archways that led to corridors, running off in every direction. As the women entered the hall, the cauldron seem to come alive, bubbling more violently. High on the throne was seated a woman. She rose and slowly made her way down the spiral stairs. She approached them with outstretched arms.

"I have been waiting your arrival, my dear sisters," Wargana said as she welcomed them to Areisten.

Rowena felt an almost uncontrollable urge to turn and run. There was something about the queen that caused Rowena to flinch. Here was the Queen of Fennoria, who sent trogs against them in the Borderlands, and tried to kidnap her brother and Tom. She had mastered the powers of the Darkness and desired to set herself up as the Queen of New Earth.

Wargana was tall and beautiful. She moved across the hall gracefully. Her long, dark blue gown flowed in ripples, revealing the exquisiteness of her womanly essence and seductive body. Her face was fair, but not childlike. Rather it revealed a womanly beauty tempered with a self-confidence and a truly royal bearing that demanded respect. Her skin was white and her cheeks rosy colored like her lips. Her nose was small and slightly upturned at the tip. Wargana's voice had a musical quality that seem to dispel Rowena's apprehension.

"I am Wargana, the Queen of New Earth," she declared without hesitation. "You have arrived at the most opportune time. "I've received word of your arrival in Fennoria, but I regret that I was unable to meet you or send an escort. The message just arrived, and it was a bit uncomprehensible. These trogs are really terrible when it come to writing."

"I am Princess Valenda of the northern Kingdom of Neutria," the princess said. "I have traveled with my two comrades, Rowena Chestnut, an enchantress from the Mark, and Anna Vineyard, a healer and herbalist, also from the Mark. We've come to Fennoria to seek your wisdom and join your sisterhood. We've decided that women can only achieve their full potential by rejecting the world of male tyranny."

"Then you have made the right choice," Wargana said with a glint of satisfaction. "Everyday, more our of sisters are joining our ranks. They come from every corner of New Earth. Our ranks are growing and soon we will be a force that will challenge the supremacy of the male-dominated world."

Wargana's ruby lips smiled at the three girls before her. "You are all welcome and will be immediately assimilated into our sisterhood. I have a good feeling about the three of you. Yes! You will join us now, for I have called a gathering of our covenant to help capture two escapees." Wargana stopped before Rowena. Her dark, blue eyes stared intensely at the young girl. "Rowena, was the name?" she asked.

Rowena could barely speak. She did not like the way Wargana was looking at her. It made her feel violated. "Yes," is all she finally said.

"There is something about you that intrigues me, my dear," Wargana said. "I can feel the Life-Force within you. You do know something of the arts, don't you?" Wargana gently touched Rowena's cheek as she spoke.

Rowena had to fight the urge to pull back.

"Yes, I have studied and learned much from my mother," she said. "But there is still much that I want to learn. That's why I've come to find you."

"Then you have chosen rightly, my dear Rowena," Wargana said and smiled.

Rowena's revulsion increased as the witch-queen stroked her long, blond hair. "I will take a personal interest in your education. I'm sure that you will learn fast, but first things first." Wargana suddenly stopped and turned. She walked over to a large, bronze gong. She waved her hand before it, and though she did not touch it, she was able to make it boom.

Wargana turned back toward the women. "A day before you arrived, my trogs brought two pup-male captives to Fennoria. One of them was carrying a talisman of great power, but before they were brought to me, the stupid male in charge let the brats escape." Wargana spoke with increasing anger and contempt. "It was my own fault for trusting a man with such an important task." She strut like a peacock as she spoke. "I've called a gathering of my sisters so that we might ask the Demons of the Darkness to assist us in finding these little male-things. It seems that they command the power of the Light, but that won't help them. There's no way in all the deepest pits of the Great Void that they will escape me." Wargana's eyes flashed with a burning hate, and her face became twisted with rage as she spoke.

Wargana once again turned to Rowena. "You said you wanted to learn more of the power of the Life-Force? Well, you are about to get your first lesson. I'm about to show you the true power of the Dark side of the Life-Force. For with it at your command, there's nothing that you cannot accomplish." Wargana laughed as she turned and once more walked over to her raised throne. The girls soon noticed a procession of figures slowly moving in the shadows behind the pillars along the edge of the hall. Hundreds of beautiful women were entering the hall from the many passageways that lined the walls of the hall.

The women were strikingly beautiful. They wore long, silky gowns of different colors that clung to their seductive, shapely forms. Their hair was long and flowed in waves over their shoulders. Around their necks, ankles and waists were silver chains, embedded with rubies, emeralds and diamonds. As they entered the hall, they began singing a soft and melodic tune. The words were in some unknown language, but its effects were hypnotic. Rowena felt as if she was slowly falling into a kind of a trance.

Wargana had climbed to the top of the stone platform and stood before her throne. She looked down into the cauldron below her and stared deep into it. The hall was now filled with thousands of women, singing and chanting in their seductive voices that echoed through the domed hall. Their voices rose and filled the dome, which made it seem as if the castle had come alive.

Wargana suddenly raised her arms over her head, letting the sleeves of her gown slide down her soft, white arms. The hall fell silent, as the witches remained transfixed.

"Sisters!" Wargana shouted. "Tonight we are gathered here to join our souls in a singular force. Give yourselves up to me this night, so that I might call on the power of the Darkness! Let us give glory to the night, and to its blackness! Let us reaffirm our dedication to the Demons of the Darkness, and ask them to do our bidding! We call on the Holy Mother that is the Darkness, to open her dark womb to us! We call on the silver lady of the night, the Moon that shines like a beautiful woman on the side that she reveals to the world, and keeps hidden, her true nature, in the Darkness! It is her dark wisdom that we worship, and call upon for help. Let's join as one and call on the Dark Mother to open her black womb and send us her powers, so that it might do our bidding!"

Drums began to boom. They thundered from somewhere distant, beyond the hall. The witches fell to their knees, still in a trance. Their seductive faces were now distorted with the rapture of the union of their souls in the dark forces that Wargana had called forth. They threw their heads back and began rolling about the floor, flinging their hair about their faces. Their slim, white arms raised upward, and their bodies began to sway and gyrate. As they surrendered to their orgy of swaying, they began to chant.

> *Moon-Mother in the dark sky,*
> *hear your daughters' longing cry.*
> *Queen of Darkness, Ruler of the Night,*
> *bestow on us the power of your might!*

They then rose and began dancing in a wild and erotic fashion, as the drums' beat quickened, creating a hypnotic rhythm. So overpowering it was that Rowena and Anna felt themselves succumbing to its power. They had a difficult time controlling their desire to join in the dancing. Only Princess Valenda seemed unaffected. Her fair face was frozen in determination, revealing the iron will of the women folk of the northern lands of Neutria.

Wargana spoke again, as the witches continued their dancing. "Hear me that which rules the Darkness! Oh servant of the Moon-Mother, hear the pleads of your sisters, who have need of your powers to do our bidding. In return, we once again offer to you our bodies and souls. Our enemies have eluded us and we need your assistance in tracking them down. Find them and destroy them for us! Come to us! Appear before us!"

Wargana then broke into a chanting, in a language not spoken by the nations of Truemans. The cauldron began to seethe more violently and turned blood red, as thick, black smoke rose high into the dome of the hall. Wargana's eyes burned with excitement as the other witches fell once more to their knees, gyrating their shoulders and heads, causing their hair to fly about. Then, from behind the throne, there appeared for the first time a short, fat, hunched figure. It stepped out and stood next to Wargana. On its large head was a wide-rimmed hat that hid most of its rodent-like face. Only its burning, red eyes could clearly be seen as it remained half-hidden behind Wargana's gown. Rowena immediately knew what it was. It was a she-Kreel.

The black smoke began to roll and tumble high above in the nape of the dome. From within its black folds there appeared a huge, black, hulking shape with large, curving horns on its head. Rowena could not make out its form at first, because it was half-hidden by the bellowing black vapors. But gradually, its true form took shape. Rowena could now see what looked like two, slanted, red eyes, as it slowly took on its true form. Black as pitch it was, and it appeared like a hole in the black smoke. Its face was featureless, except for its eyes and what appeared to be a long, forked tongue that slithered between white fangs. Then, from either side, it stretched out two large and powerful arms that reached from one end of the hall to the other. Rowena had never seen anything so monstrous.

"Oh Demon of Darkness, hear my words!" Wargana shouted. "Lend your terrible power to us!"

Then, before Wargana could continue, she heard a cry.

"No!"

Wargana looked down at Rowena.

Rowena knew instantly what to do. It was as if someone was directing her actions. She understood that the apparition was not some Demon of the Darkness, or the servant of some Moon-Mother. It was the King Kreel himself. Wargana had conjured up the Lord of Darkness to ask him to find for her Palifair and Tom. Rowena heard a voice speak to her, and felt a power surge through her like a current. She then heard the sound of metal hitting the stone floor. She looked at Valenda and saw that she had dropped her sword and stood frozen, unable to move. She then looked at Anna, and discovered that she too was frozen in place. Both her friends were transfixed by the sight of the Lord of Darkness. They were immobilized by his power. Only Rowena found the strength to resist, but where that strength had come from, she did not know. She only knew that she had to act.

Rowena ran forward, straight toward the bubbling cauldron, and pulled out her long, silver sword. It was one of the swords given to them by Gottron before they left Wissenval. It had been forged in the fires of Wissenval and bathed in the blue flame in the Cathedral of Light. She stopped at the cauldron's edge and thrust the blade of the sword into it. To the shock and horror of the King Kreel, the smoke changed color, turning snow white. Steam began to rise from the hulking beast. It began to twist faster and faster until it was transformed into a vortex that swallowed the Lord of Darkness. Thunder and lightning filled the hall, and the castle shook. The witches around the hall fell to the floor in horror, crawling on their bellies, begging for mercy and screaming in terror. When the vortex finally disappeared, only Rowena and Wargana remained on their feat. The King Kreel had been sent back to Allomania.

Wargana shriek with rage. "Get that little bitch! Get them all! I'll see them burn before this day is out!"

Several dozen trogs suddenly burst into the hall with long spears. Before any of the girls could react, they were surrounded by a ring of pointed steel.

"So you came to learn something of my powers, did you?" Wargana shouted as she descended the spiral stairs. "Well. You're all going to see that power first hand!"

Just then, Kellium came running into the hall. He had been shaken with fear from the commotion, and was seeking his mistress for protection. When he saw Rowena and the others, his jaw dropped in surprise.

"What in the name of all the gold mines in the East Mark are they doing here?" he cried.

Wargana turned to Kellium "Do you know these wenches?"

"Yes. Two of them at least," Kellium said. "They were members of the convoy that I led out of the Mark to Bridgetown. I told you about them. In fact, this one here is the sister of the brat that carries the stone you're looking for." Kellium walked over to Rowena as he spoke and stared at her with hate. He then gave her a twisted smile and held her chin in his hand.

"Get your stinking hands off me, Kellium, you traitorous pig!" Rowena said as she spat in his face. Kellium was about to slap her with his other hand when Wargana shouted at him. "Kellium! There's no time for your foolishness!" Wargana said. "If they're who you say they are, then I'll have more than my revenge on them." The witch laughed as she stared at the three girls. "Did you really think that you were smart enough to fool me for long? I don't know exactly why you came here, but I'll find out. It can't be to find you brother, because he has already escaped, but I promise that I will hunt him down and when I do, the White Stone will be mine and then there will be nothing to stand between me and my destiny!"

"You'll never find my brother now," Rowena said. "I saw to that. Nor will you never get your hands on the White Stone."

"Did you really think that I would put all my jewels in one chess?" Wargana asked. "I will still find your brother, and I'll use this to help me." Wargana reached for a chain around her neck and pulled out from under her gown, a small, yellow stone that shined with the brilliance of the sun. It was encased in a golden broach. "This, my dear, is the source of my power!"

Rowena instantly recognized the stone.

"Yes. I see you know what this stone is," Wargana snared. "It is the Yellow Stone. One of the three lesser stones from Lothar's Crown, and with it I will find your brother, and get the White Stone for myself. Then I will set myself up as Queen of New Earth."

"I think the Lord of Darkness might have other ideas about that," Princess Valenda said. "A few minutes ago you were begging him to help you. Hardly what the Queen of New Earth would do."

"Watch your tongue, Northlander!" Wargana shouted back at Valenda. "When I'm through, I not only will have destroyed all of Truemankind and that stupid brotherhood of druids, but I'll also have that buffoon of Allomania on his knees before me."

"You're sick, Wargana," Valenda spoke. "As a woman, you make me ill just listening to you. You're consumed by a hatred that has eaten away your soul, and left only the stench of rotting dung within you. You hate men because you are not woman enough to be their equal."

"Equal! Ha!" Wargana laughed. "Woman are the natural superiors of men. It's the natural right of women to rule, and that's why my sisters have joined with me, here in Fennoria, to set up a new order. It is my destiny to rule!"

"Not in Neutria," the princess said. "Men and women stand together to brave the wind and frost. There is no petty jealousy that separates us. We know that if we are to survive, then we must depend on each another. Our women folk are too busy fighting off the hazzards of the northern wilds to compete with our men folk. We have survived as a people because both men and women have put aside their pride and selfishness, and have united in the common purpose of building a better future for our children. The survival of our race is the most holy of holies, and thus we have put aside our greed for wealth, power and fame and have found happiness in the comfort and love of our families. We find spiritual salvation through the union of man and woman, fighting for the survival of our folk. Our common blood unites us."

Rowena listened as the princess spoke, but Wargana snared with contempt.

"Blood! Folk! Family! Children! Bah!" Wargana laughed. "What foolishness? Those things are all illusions compared with raw power!"

"No, Wargana," Anna now spoke. "It is your power that is an illusion. It's rooted in the Darkness, and no matter how hard you try, you'll always be a servant, of either the Lord of Darkness in Allomania, or the nameless creatures that haunt the bottomless pit of the Great Void. Your powers are like a shadow that can easily evaporate with the first burst of the sun's rays."

"So you think my powers are just an illusion?" Wargana asked. "I'll just have to show you just how much pain an illusion can inflict, before I destroy you. I'll see the three of you crying for mercy. You'll be down on your knees worshiping me before I'm done with you."

"That remains to be seen," Rowena said.

"Yes. It does, and I'll begin proving it right now," Wargana said. Her face was a mask of hate. "Kellium! Bring me one of those spears."

Kellium grabbed a spear from one of the trogs and handed it to his mistress.

Wargana took the spear and walked over to one of the torches that hung from the pillars. She held the point of the spear in the flames for several seconds, and then waved her hand over it. Magically, the tip of the spear began to burn until it was white hot.

Just then, the short, fat she-Kreel appeared once more. She stood no more than three feet tall. Her long thin nose stuck out from under the rim of her hat. She looked up. Rowena could see the burning red eyes staring at her from under the gray hair that hung down from under the hat in tangle locks.

"So this is the Trueman filth that ruined our ritual?" she hissed at Rowena.

Rowena could see her face more clearly now, as the she-Kreel glared at her.

"I want to see your stinking blue eyes burned out of that pretty, blond head of your's," she growled. "And then I'll cut your throat and drink your blood in a toast to my lord and master."

The she-Kreel then called to Wargana. "Give me that spear!"

Wargana said nothing as she handed the spear to her. Rowena was surprised at the submissive way Wargana jumped at the she-Kreel's orders. "Kellium! Come here and hold this bitch, while I improve on her looks!"

Kellium immediately ordered the trogs to grab the girls from behind. "Quickly! Do as Kella Kazok, commands! Hold them good and tight, and don't let them move."

Kella Kozok raised the spear to Rowena's face. "You'll be first," she hissed at Rowena.

Rowena could feel the heat from the burning metal hovering just inches before her face, as beads of sweat rolled down her brow. But before the hot metal could burn her white skin, there came a terrible crash from the other end of the hall that sent witches screaming in terror.

"What in the name of the Moon-Mother is going on?" asked Wargana.

Kell Kazok screamed at Wargana. "Don't just stand there! Go and see what it is, fool!"

Chapter Six:
Escape!

Vesten led the men along a small ledge, about three feet wide, which ran along the wall of the castle. Thorns grew on certain sections of the ledge, which forced the men to move slowly. Vesten had the difficult task of chopping the thorns with his sword while hugging the castle wall. Gordonthal shined with a light as it sent branch after branch into the blackness below. The others inched their way as best they could in the dark, until they finally disappeared into the shadow of the fortress. They could barely see where they were going, and if not for the light from Vesten's sword, they would have been completely blind. The castle wall was their only other guide, but it was covered with a dampness that made it difficult to cling to it.

"Wait a minute. What's this?" Vesten said.

"What's, what?" Hollin, who was right behind Vesten, asked.

"There's a rope hanging here," Vesten said. "It seems to have come from no where." Vesten pulled on it to see if it was secured. "It seems strong enough to hold us. When you're inching your way along a ledge, hundreds of feet in the air, and a rope suddenly appears, there's only one thing to do."

"Climb it," Brim said.

"Right you are," Vesten said, as he pulled on the rope one more time to test its strength. "I'll climb up first and see where it leads."

"It leads straight up!" came a voice from high above.

"That sounds like Blondor," Hagrim said.

"That's because it is Blondor!" the voice came again. "So stop dilly-dallying and start climbing!"

One by one they climbed up the rope. Vesten led the way, followed by Hollin, Hagrim and finally Brim. Like spiders ascending their web they slowly made their way straight up, two hundred feet. The walls were slippery and caused them to loose their footing several times. When they reached the top, they found that the rope hung out of a tall, thin window. Brim, who was last, had a difficult time squeezing through the window, and the others had to pull him through. Once inside, they found themselves in a small room filled with nothing but darkness.

"Where are we?" asked Hollin.

"You're in Areisten, young Hillroller," Blondor said, as the room suddenly lit-up with a blueish-white light from Blondor's staff. They could now clearly see the druid standing before them, but before anyone could ask him how he got into the castle, he said, "Come! There's little time to waste. The women have already been taken to the Hall of the Covenant, where Wargana and her witches are trying to summon the Lord of Darkness himself, to help them find Palifair and Tom."

Blondor disappeared through a door. They others quickly followed him. The druid led them down a long corridor that was lit only by the light from Blondor's staff. As they moved along the corridor, they could see doors on either side. The druid moved with a speed that seemed alien to him, causing the others to occasionally run to keep up with him. They finally came to a flight of stairs that led down. When they reached the bottom, they found three doors, which were locked. Blondor began to mumble some words as he held his staff before him. The door in the center opened by itself. They passed through it and once again they found themselves running down another corridor filled only with the flickering light from the druid's staff. They noticed that the hallways of the castle were mysteriously deserted.

They entered a great hall with rows of pillars that held up a high ceiling. The floor was made of red marble and the walls were decorated with tapestries that hung down to the floor. There were tall, thin, green crystal windows that filled the hall with an eerie light. As they made their way across the hall, Blondor stopped suddenly, as if he was listening to something far off.

"Listen," he said. Everyone froze in place. "Trogs," the druid said.

Seconds later, the hall was filled with the echoes of thumping feet. There appeared in the entrance to the hall a dozen large trogs, growling and laughing to themselves.

Vesten pulled out his sword. Gordonthal shined with a white fire. The Guardian charged straight at the trogs before any of them even noticed him. Right behind Vesten followed Hollin, Brim and Hagrim with weapons drawn. The trogs were taken by surprise. Before they could drawn their weapons, Trueman steel and Pure Gold blades began cutting into them, splattering thick globs of thick, green trog-blood everywhere.

Brim's mighty arms swung his sword with such force that he cut two trogs in half, at the waist with one swing. Hagrim and Hollin fought back to back, severing arms and heads, as trogs, who had regained their composure, surrounded them. Trog after trog fell under the blows of the Trueman blades until there were only two left. After seeing the futility of their predicament, they turned and ran back, out the door and into the darkness beyond.

Vesten took off after them, running straight into the darkness. When he finally caught up to the fleeing trogs, he swung his sword, bringing it down on the back of one of the trogs and then jumped over its lifeless body, as it fell to the floor. He came crashing down on the second trog, knocking it down under the weight of his body. But the trog still had some fight left in him. He twisted around, as he fell under Vesten, and with one long arm, he reached around, grabbing Vesten's black locks on the back of his head, causing the Guardian to lose balance. Before Vesten realized what had happened, the trog jumped up and came down on him, trapping him under his weight. The trog reached into its belt and pulled free a short, curved knife. In the blackness, Vesten could see the yellow eyes flashing with hate. He could feel the trog's foul breath on his face, as it grinned and raised its knife over him, intent on cutting his throat. The next thing the Guardian remembered was the two yellow lights that were the trog's eyes, going dim and then out. The trog fell lifeless to one side.

When Vesten pushed the dead trog off him, he noticed three dark figures standing over him. They reached down and grabbed him, pulling him to his feet.

"The next time you go running off into the darkness, you had better not go alone," Brim laughed.

Hollin was standing next to him. He reached down and pulled his sword from the back of the dead trog and wiped the green blood off his weapon on the underman's tunic.

"Thank you, son of Hillroller," Vesten said. "I owe you my life, and will not forget it." He put his hand on the young aristocrat's shoulder in comradeship.

"You owe me nothing, Vesten," Hollin said. "It is reward enough to be permitted to fight by your side."

Hollin was deeply moved by Vesten's words. For the first time since they had started out from the Mark, Hollin felt that he was fully accepted by the Guardians as their equal. A new bond was established between Hollin and the three Guardians. Those who spent most of their lives wandering the Borderlands of the Mark, seldom permitted themselves to get close to the rest of the Marklanders. Eventually, most do fall in love and marry, and then resign from the brotherhood, but while they served, they gave themselves totally to the protection of the land and people they loved. They spend the remainder of their lives living within the Mark, helping the good people of whatever sleepy hollow they decided to settle in to organize their local militia, as old Granpa Crossway did, and others were called to work as agents for the druids or for their brother Guardians, like Olaf Westmorgrove.

The darkness that surrounded them disappeared once more, as the blueish-white light from Blondor's staff drove it out. "I found the way to the Hall of the Covenant," the druid said. "We don't have much time left. I fear that we might be already too late."

Blondor was about to say something else, but before he could, he clutched his heart. Only the support of his staff prevented him from falling.

"Blondor! What is it?" Vesten asked as he grabbed the druid. "Is it Palifair? Did he use the White Stone?"

"No. It's him," Blondor said. There was terror in the druid's eyes. "The Lord of Darkness is in Areisten."

Suddenly the corridors were filled with a shattering cry that echoed throughout the castle, causing everyone to shake in horror. The walls of the Areisten shook, and everything went dark. Blondor's staff blinked as the blueish-white light went out and then flared on again.

"We must hurry," Blondor said. "There's no time to waste. Something has happened, and we must reach the women at once."

They all began running with Blondor in the lead. When they came to a whining stairs, they raced up for three stories and then stepped into a small chamber.

"Through here is the Hall of the Covenant," Blondor said as he stopped. "I fear the worse, but there is no time to be cautious. Come." He ordered the others to follow him as he entered the hall filled with witches.

They pushed through two large doors and down as small corridor. They could hear some commotion in the hall, and when they finally burst into it, the witches began screaming, adding to the bedlam that already existed in the cavernous hall.

The she-Kreel who was holding the spear was distracted and ordered Wargana to go and see what was causing the commotion. The trogs holding the women were also distracted and loosened their grip.

Princess Valenda, sensing her opportunity to act, jumped up, and knocked over two of the trogs holding her, as they turned to see what was happening on the other side of the hall. She then grabbed one of the trogs' spears and swung it at them, tearing off the faces of three undermen and splashing green blood everywhere. The princess then leaped forward and plunged the spear into the belly of the a very fat trog, who charged at her with a sword in his hand. Valenda then rushed to where her sword was lying on the floor. She grabbed it and began hacking her way through the throng of undermen that surrounded her.

Valenda's quick action afforded Rowena the opportunity to raise her hands and shout a spell. With a wave of her hand, the red hot spear that Kella-Kazok held exploded in her face. The she-Kreel screamed and clutched her face as she ran through the hall.

Anna, who was being held on the ground, rolled free and pulled out her sword. She jumped to her feet and leaped to Rowena's side, swinging her sword as it flashed bright. The two women fought back to back, darting this way and that way as they fought off several trogs.

The trogs soon gave up and fled as panic spread through the hall, and when no more tried to attack the women, Rowena and Anna turned and joined Valenda. But then, Rowena caught sight of the short she-Kreel, as she tried to lose herself in the surging mass of panicking people. Her short, fat legs carried her across the floor of the hall. He round body wobbled like a sick duck. She was still clutching her face and lost the power to control the minds of other people because of the injury to her eyes. Her large, green hat flew off as the panicking witches knocked into her, causing her to curse and scream. Rowena took off, running after the she-Kreel. She grabbed a fallen spear and flung it in the dwarf's way, causing her to trip and fall. Kella-Kazok turned and looked up at Rowena. Rowena could see fear in her charred face.

"No! Don't kill me!" the dwarf screamed. The ice-cold determination that she saw in Rowena's eyes filled her with terror. She could see her fate in Rowena's face. "May your stinking souls rot in the Great Void of . . . " she never finished her curse. Rowena had plunged her sword deep into the neck of the dwarf. Green blood gushed up and filled her mouth, and then flowed over her chin as her body spasm in the convulsions of death.

Wargana was wild with rage. "By all the Demons of the Darkness, hear my words and strike down the dung that dares to defile my covenant!" she screamed. The hall thundered and flashed with lightning. "Strike down the Trueman scum!" she shouted, as she waved her arms overhead, causing everyone to fall to the floor. Witch, Trueman and undermen all tumbled as the stone floor beneath their feet seemed to move and wobble like the coils of some monster-snake. Wargana laughed. The cauldron bubbled once more and the eyes of the giant cat statue began to glow with a terrible green light.

Suddenly a bolt of blue lightning crackled and struck the giant stone cat, causing it to crumble. Wargana fell back and cried in horror. "What trickery is this?"

"It is no trickery, Whore of Fennoria. It's the might of Wissenval, come to seek justice for your crimes and treachery," a voice was heard to speak. Before Wargana now stood Blondor. He seem to grow beyond his usual height. His black robes and cape flew about him as a wind rose up from nowhere. He held his staff in his right hand and the globe on its tip was burning bright with a blue light that encased him. The winds increased in force until it swept about the hall. Rowena had to brush her golden locks from her face to see the druid more clearly. She could feel his strength somehow, as if she was linked to him in some unseen way. She felt his will growing in power as he was preparing to do battle.

Like a mighty oak, Blondor now hover over Wargana. He seemed impervious to the winds whipping about the hall. "The time has come, Wargana," he said, "for you to pay your debts in full!"

"Then it was you, who I felt earlier?" Wargana shouted back. "I knew that little bitch could not have possessed such great powers!"

"Yes," Blondor answered. "I used the girl to mask my presence. And you fell for it, witch!" Blondor could not help but mock her, knowing that it would send her into a rage, and thus give him the advantage he needed. The druid's powers were great, perhaps greater than any other druid except for Gottron, but with the Yellow Stone in her possession, Wargana's powers were greatly enhanced. Blondor would have to use more than magic and wizardry to combat her. He would have to outwit her. "Yes,

Wargana, I have come back to Fennoria to put an end to you and your mad dreams. Once I was the hunted, but now I am doing tho hunting!"

Wargana's face turned red and her eyes bulged with anger. She once again raised her hands before her. Flashes of red flame flared from her hands and two great tongues of fire shot at the druid. Blondor was now encased in red fire, but soon it turned purple and then blue, as it was gobbled up by the druid's blue light that surrounded him, until it finally disappeared.

"You'll have to do better than that, witch!" Blondor said. "Your memory is failing you, as are your powers," Blondor chuckled. "You have forgotten that fire and lightning are my elements!"

The druid then extended his left arm and a blue bolt of energy crackled through the hall and struck Wargana. She raised a red shield of energy about her just in time to protect herself from Blondor's attack.

Another bolt of power hit hard at the witch. Wargana seemed to fall back under the fierce assault by the druid. It seemed that his powers were greater than even Wargana had imagined. If she was to defeat him, she would have to muster up all the power at her command.

"Witches of Areister! Arise!" she shouted. Slowly the hundreds of witches began to gather together. They no longer were screaming and running in terror. With arms stretched out, they slowly began to surround the druid. Then, at Wargana's command, the witches began to glow with a red light. Wargana's powers seem to grow. Her will had gathered the collective power of the witches and harnessed it to her bidding. Soon, Blondor found himself wavering under the intense power that Wargana was able to throw at him. The joint powers of the witches of Fennoria was beginning to weaken and subdue him.

Princess Valenda had fought her way through the hall with a fury that was typical of her northern race, but unknown to the trogs of Fennoria. The trogs had all fled before her in terror. She saw the battle that was being waged between druid and witch. Rowena and Anna were right behind her. Valenda could see the horror is Rowena's eyes as she watched the battle unfolding between Blondor and the witches. The princess raised her spear and flung it through the air. It flew straight and true to its mark, toward Wargana. Rowena raised her hands and concentrated her will hard on the spear, guiding it as it flew through the hall, causing it to hit its mark. The spear missed Wargana, but it snapped the chain that hung around her neck, causing the Yellow Stone to fall to the floor. Before Wargana knew what had happened, Anna rushed forward and grabbed the stone. She ran out of the way of the battle, blindly, right into the arms of Vesten.

"The Yellow Stone. Here, take it," Anna could barely speak as she tried to catch her breath and handed Vesten the stone.

Hollin rushed from behind Vesten and took the girl he loved into his arms.

"No!" Wargana cried as she stared at her hands stretched out before her. They were no longer white and soft, but had turned gray and wrinkled. She immediately clutched to where the stone once hung around her neck, and screamed once more in agony when she discovered that it was missing. Falling to her knees, she buried her face in her hands. Her body began to convulse violently and her long black hair had turned white and coarse.

"Look what you have done to me, you pigs!" she cried.

Rowena was taken back in horror by Wargana's transformation. Wargana's face now appeared ancient. Her eyes were two red dots set deeply within two black sockets. Heavy bags hung from under them, and a long crooked nose, covered with warts, protruded from between them. Her face was a mass of wrinkles, and her skin appeared grayish, like that of a corpse. Horrific cries now rose from the other witches. Like their mistress, they too were transformed into ancient hags. They had used the Yellow Stone to harness the power of the Darkness, and used it to mask their ugliness under a facade of beauty, but like everything that comes from the Darkness, it was unreal. It was all a cheat. The witches fell to the floor and began rolling about, trying to escape to the many corridors that lead from the hall, and hide their grotesqueness.

"Get the women! Quickly!" Blondor shouted to the men.

Brim and Hagrim rushed to where Princess Valenda and Rowena were. Hollin followed with Anna in his arms. When they reached them, they all began making their way through the chaos that filled the hall. Now that Wargana had lost the Yellow Stone and the she-Kreel was killed, the hall disintegrated into chaos. "Hurry! This way!" Blondor kept shouting as everyone disappeared through one of the archways. Vesten and Blondor stood by the exit until they all had escaped. Vesten followed them, but Blondor remained behind. He ordered the others to flee and that he would be right behind them. Blondor then turned around, and standing about fifty feet into the corridor, he raised his staff before him and began chanting. "Uruz-Thurisaz! Sowilo-Nauthiz! Fehu-Hagalaz!" Blondor then turned away and disappeared into the darkness of the corridor, following his comrades. He could hear a rumbling rising up behind him that grew until the walls and ceiling began to collapse. Huge stone blocks crashed down from overhead, crushing the witches and trogs that were unfortunate enough not to have escaped from the hall. The tower and throne in the hall fell over, and the cauldron exploded into a fountain of green slime and vapors that filled the hall, as the vast dome overhead caved into the hall.

When Blondor finally caught up to the others, they were already far away from the hall. They had stopped to wait for their friend and leader. He collapsed to his knees, exhausted from the effort of the last spell. Rowena ran up to him, fearing the worse. The druid slowly rose, pulling himself to his feet with her help, as he clutched his staff. It seemed to stand upright on its own power, as its globe glowed with a blue light.

"We were afraid you didn't make it out of there, Blondor," Rowena said.

"I'm all right, Rowena," Blondor said. "But I'm tired. The battle with Wargana took much of my strength from me."

"Then we'll rest until you have time to regain your strength," Rowena insisted.

"No." Blondor said. "There isn't a moment to waste. We must get as far away from here as possible."

"What happened back there?" Vesten asked. "We heard a terrible explosion and crash."

"I used the last of my strength to conjure up a spell," answered Blondor. "I was able to bring the hall down on them before anyone was able to follow us."

"Then Wargana and Kellium are buried under tons of stone?" Anna asked.

"I don't know," the druid said. "Wargana still has much power. Though she lost most of it when we took the Yellow Stone away from her. I fear that she is not out of this game yet. But there is no time to speak of their fate now. It's not safe to remain here another minute." The druid seemed to have recovered once more. "This is the way that will lead us out of Areisten, but we have a long way to go before we are out of danger."

Down the corridor they ran as Blondor led the way. They turned right and continued down another long hallway. They lost count of how many times they turned as they made their way through the maze of passageways, but Blondor seemed to know exactly where he was leading them. Finally they came to a small doorway that opened into a spiral stairwell. Down some seven hundred steps they went in a single file. The stairwell was so narrow that Brim could barely make his way down it. He had to bend low as not to bump his head.

Once they reached the bottom, Blondor stopped for a moment, as if to sniff the air, and then shouted in his usual matter, "Come! This way!" Time seem to stand still for them as they raced through the endless dark hallways. Rowena began to feel that they were lost, but actually, Blondor was making sure they did not run into anyone as they made their escape. She could not remember how long it was since they left the Hall of the Covenant. Except for the fact that they continued to go down, she was not even sure in what direction they were heading. It fell like they were going deeper into the foundation of the castle.

"How are we ever going to find our way out of this web of corridors?" Rowena asked.

"Don't worry," Vesten said. "I have been with Blondor on many such journeys, and he has never steered me wrong before. Blondor has an uncanny sense of direction. Trust his judgement. I'm sure he has some kind of plan to escape from here. He led us into Fennoria to rescue our friends, and he will lead us out again, even at the cost of his own life."

Rowena did not like the sound of what Vesten said, but she did not voice her concern.

"I hope there is more boast than prophecy in your statement," Hollin said.

Rowena heard what Hollin said. A sensation of dread overcame her. Vesten could see it in her eyes and he regretted what he had said. He had come to known Rowena well over the last few months. For an instant, Rowena seemed overwhelmed by something, as if death walked across her grave. He wondered if she might have sense something dreadful that he could not foresee? Did she somehow glimpse into the future only to sense that some unforeseen fate awaited them? The only thing Vesten was sure of was that it troubled him.

"We're almost out of Areisten," Blondor suddenly said. "Just a little way to go and we'll be free of this castle."

Boom! Boom! Two thunderous explosions were heard from far above that shook the castle. *Boom! Boom!* The explosions came again.

"What in the name of the Mark was that?" asked Hollin.

"Wargana," Blondor said. "She must have sounded the alarm? Her trogs will be alerted to our escape. Even without the Yellow Stone, her powers are great. She must have survived the collapse of the hall. I thought we would still have some time left before she was able to rally her forces, but we still have a good head start."

Once again the druid snapped his command. "Come!" They were getting used to Blondor shouting his orders. It actually made them feel confident that he knew exactly what he was doing. There was no hesitation in his voice. He led and they instinctively followed. "The gate is this way," Blondor said as he dashed off down the dark corridor. The others ran after him. They followed him through a large hall and then burst onto the open courtyard that separated the main building from the gate.

The courtyard was filled with all sorts of people. Trueman slaves, who had escaped from their captives, were trying to escape in the confusion. Trogs, trog-men and half-trogs were all pushing and shoving each other as they ran about wildly, without direction. There were some ugly witches in the courtyard. They had lost their beauty and had gone mad when their illusion deserted them. Several Kreel merchants were trying to restore order with the powers of their minds, but they were being overwhelmed by the chaos that was spreading through the crowd.

As they pushed their way along the edge of the courtyard, they ran into a large, fat dwarf. When he saw them, he turned to them and shout something in his foul language, but before anyone could react, Brim leaped at the dwarf. With one swipe of his broad sword, he cut the dwarf in half, sending yellowish humps of flesh splattering. Two other Kreel dwarfs appeared and were quickly dispatched by Hollin and Hagrim in the same way.

They continued to make their way through the crowd. Blondor's staff was burning brightly, causing the multitude to flee before him. The others sometimes had to use their swords to hack at the colliding bodies that ran into them, leaving a trail of bloody bodies as they went. An occasional large trog would try to stop them only to choke on its own green blood, as Trueman steel sank deep into its hide.

They finally made it to the gate and were in luck to discover that it was still open. They made a mad rush for the stone bridge that was still unguarded. When they reached the other side of the bridge, they collapsed with exhaustion and relief, but before they could rest, Blondor was already getting them to their feet. He whistled several times. A few seconds later, five horses appeared out of the darkness. They were the same horses that they rode to Areisten. They were already loaded with small packs of food and supplies.

"I felt we would be in need of food and other provisions," Blondor said, "so I took the liberty of appropriating some from

Wargana's storerooms earlier. I also retrieved these." Blondor pulled out two small bundles from under his robes. When he unwrapped them, the others discovered they contained the two swords given to Palifair and Tom by Gottron. They were taken by Kellium to Areisten. "When we meet up with the boys, we'll return these to them."

"When will that be?" asked Rowena.

"Sooner than you realize," Blondor said. "But first we have to get out of Fennoria."

"And how are we going to do that?" asked Hollin. "We certainly can't just ride up to the Hole of Fennoria and ask the gatekeeper to let us out, and storming it would be suicide. The gates will be guarded well and all the roads will be heavily patrolled."

"Not all the roads," Blondor said. "Wargana will expect us either to go west to the gates or possibly try to climb over the mountains in the north. She will send her troops to patrol those areas, so we must go in a different direction."

"Not farther into Fennoria?" asked Anna. "Where will that get us?"

"No. Not farther into Fennoria, but south," Blondor said.

"But that will mean we will have to climb over miles of mountains," Princess Valenda said.

"Then we are going to follow Palifair and Tom?" asked Rowena.

"No," Blondor said. "The boys are climbing up the mountains and there is higher force guiding their footsteps. We could not follow them, and will not. Instead of climbing over the mountains we'll pass through them."

"And how are we going to walk through them?" asked Hollin.

"By going under them," the druid said. "There is a path that is little known and never used these days. It will take us under the mountains and bring us into Lothangia."

"There is good reason why it's never used," Vesten said. "No one would dare set foot in those dark and forbidden tunnels. Those who are foolish enough to try, are never heard from again."

"I have passed through them, and so have you, Vesten," Blondor said. "And we have both come out alive."

"True, but I do not wish to pass through the Stygian Hole a second time, even if a thousand Warganas were on my tail, in hot pursuit."

"The Stygian Hole?" asked Hollin. "What in the name of the Mark is the Stygian Hole?"

"I have read of such a place," Anna said, "but I thought it was only a place that existed in myth and legend. I never thought it was actually real."

"Oh, it's real," Rowena said. "It's a great complex of tunnels and chambers, built long ago by the ancients, to escape the great fires. It lies under the Axis Mountains, and there are two known entrances that connects Fennoria and Lothangia, though other secret gateways are said to exist."

"Where did you learn about the Stygian Hole?" asked Blondor.

"I read about it in the great library of Wissenval," Rowena said. "There were several scrolls that told of its legends, and there was even a map. I believe you authored one of the scrolls?"

"Yes, I did," Blondor said. "I'm glad that you did not waste your time in that enchanted valley. But you have only told half the story connected with that dark place. Legends say a great dragon lives somewhere within the tunnels. He is suppose to be the last survivor of the ancient race of dragons of the by-gone era. He survived the Dragon Wars of long ago and took refugee within the Stygian Hole. Legends also say he has wings and breeds fire.

"When Vesten and I passed through the Hole, we did not find such a beast, though we did discover some evidence that a dragon once lived there. Perhaps he sleeps in some deep chamber, or he might even have died? Or he might be waiting for the Lord of Darkness to call him forth to join his Dark Alliance?"

"That day might not be far off," Vesten said.

"Perhaps? But what the future holds is better than what the present has in store for us," Blondor said. "Wargana will never think that we would dare go through the Stygian Hole, and so it is that way that is least guarded."

"We'll escape the witch's cauldron, only to be burned alive

in the dragon's fire," Hagrim said. "Hardly what I would call an escape."

"Nor, I," Vesten agreed. "But Blondor has gotten us in and out of Areisten, all in one piece. Though I do not wish to go through that accursed pit, I will follow where he leads."

"And so will I," Princess Valenda said. "If only we had a sage as wise as Blondor in my homeland, then my father and people would not be in the grip of the defeat-fever."

"I'm sure Arlindor will be able to find a way to free your father from the plague that afflicts him," Blondor said. "For now, we have to get out of Fennoria, and reach Lothangia as quickly as possible. Our talk has delayed us for too long, already. We can't remain here another moment without the threat of being recaptured."

Suddenly, from the gates of the castle, a troop of trogs rushed across the bridge at them. Vesten jumped out front and leaped at the approaching horde. His great sword burned with a bright light as it sliced to pieces the lead trog.

Brim and Hagrim, as well as Valenda, were right behind him. They cut down the trogs as they rushed at them. The narrow bridge made it easy for them to dispatch the trogs as they tried to cross it. In a few minutes, the trogs began retreating back across the bridge, but most did not make it back to safety. They fell over each other as Trueman steel sent them falling into the chasm below. Then, from the gates, there appeared the Mount of Fennoria.

"Fools! Pigs! Get up and attack!" he shouted as the trogs falling over each other.

A second wave of trogs surged forward with renewed determination, but they were still no match for the iron will of the Truemans that stood before them.

"Enough!" Blondor shouted. "Mount up and fly!"

Everyone stepped back, as the druid held his staff with both hands over his head. Thunder shook the canyon, and a bolt of blue lightning flashed from higher over head and struck the bridge, causing it to crumble into a hundred small pieces, that sent the trogs falling down into the blackness below. The Mount of Fennoria remained helpless on the other side of the chasm.

The company mount their horses and rode off with Blondor close behind them, down the path and then over the bridge that expand the Fenflow River. They headed south across the dry, rocky plains towards the Stygian Hole.

Chapter Seven:
The Stygian Hole

All that day Blondor led them as they rode south. They continued to ride through the night, stopping only twice to rest their horses. The next day they continued their journey, always on guard for trogs and any other servants of Wargana that might be searching for them. But they saw no one. Wargana's powers were weakened by the lost of the Yellow Stone, and this gave them hope of making their escape. They soon could make out the faint shadow of the Axis Mountains in the distance. The mountains stood tall and black in the brown haze that filled the air. Everyone was now hot and sweaty as they relentlessly rode on. The barren and rocky ground began to rise sharply as they approached the mountains. Nothing grew there except for some thorn bushes and gray-green morse that covered the rocks. In some places the earth was moist and green slime filled the cracks between the boulders. They soon found an old road that had fallen into disuse. The road led them upward into the mountains. Along either side of the road there appeared to be the remains of stone figures, worn down from the pollution and haze, until their shapes became almost formless. It seemed that nature was slowly erasing all signs of previous habitation.

As they drew near to the entrance of the Stygian Hole the road grew steeper. They found themselves standing before a great black cliff. The cliff was split down the center, as if a giant had cut it with a knife. From it a cold wind blew, cutting through their sweat-damp clothing, causing them to shutter with dread. The whole area seemed shroud in a heavy gloom. Only Blondor and

Vesten seemed unaffected. The other members of the company felt themselves alone and alienated from their comrades. Their spirits seem to freeze, and their hearts grew heavy. Blondor sensed what was happening to the others. He caused the globe on the end of his staff a glow with a blue light that seem to return warmth to both their bodies and souls, driving out the chill and dread that had affected them.

"Through that opening lies the Stygian Hole," Vesten said. His words seemed grim. "Through it we will pass, but not unchanged. No one passes through this subterranean domain without being transformed in some way. I fear that the Black Harvester waits for us within."

No one spoke. Vesten's forbidding premonition cut through everyone like an arrow through paper. The Guardian commander reached into his pouch and pulled out the Yellow Stone.

"Then it was for this that we were led into this damnable land," Vesten said.

"Yes," Blondor said. "It would seem that our path was chosen for us long before we had decided which way we would travel. Long ago the Yellow Stone was lost, and Wargana had somehow found it. She never revealed to us at Wissenval that she had it in her possession. She must have found it right before she rebelled against Wissenval. How she found it? I don't know, but it must have turned her against us. She undoubtedly kept it hidden from us, and perhaps intended to use it to defeat the Lord of Darkness, and then conquer the world.

"But in the end, the stone failed her. It's easier to turn evil against itself, then it is to turn good to evil. It didn't help her to learn the true reason for the girls' arrival in Fennoria, nor did she detect my presence. When confronted with our attack, she could not use the stone to repel it. The power of the Yellow Stone failed her because she tried to turn it toward evil ends. The events of the world are passing her by, but she refuses to give up. She is stubborn and will try, yet again, to carry out her mad plans of world domination. What part she will play, if any, is to be seen. Though her powers are greatly reduced by the loss of the stone, she still is a formidable foe, with a great host of undermen under her command, and agents in many lands. I fear she will unleash her armies against Lothangia sooner then she originally planned, because of our intervention.

"There is still a greater danger that we face. Before, Wargana acted on her own plans, now that her powers are reduced, it will be easier for the Lord of Darkness to bend her to his will. Without the Yellow Stone, whatever powers she still possess come from the Darkness, and he is the master of all who worship it. I fear that even though we may have weakened her, we may have inadvertently united the forces that make-up the Dark Alliance, even more than they were, by our actions."

Blondor faced Vesten. "Keep the Yellow Stone in your possession," Blondor said. "It was meant to come to you and it will be your instrument to unite all of Lothangia under your leadership, as the Emperor Returned. No one of good will and pure in heart will doubt your claim to the throne with the Yellow Stone in your possession."

"Then I will keep the stone, as you say," Vesten promised. "But if all you have said is true, then it's imperative that we reach Lothangia with all possible speed."

"And that means the shortest route possible," Blondor said. "We must go through the Stygian Hole."

"I see no other way," Vesten agreed.

"Then let's rest here a while and have something to eat before we enter the Hole," Blondor said. "We're going to need our strength."

Everyone unloaded the horses and distributed the supplies among themselves and quickly cooked a hot meal.

"What are we going to do with the horses?" Anna asked.

"We can't take them inside with us, and I don't think they would come, even if we tried to take them through it?" Blondor said. "We'll have to leave them behind."

"Leave them?" Anna said excitedly. "We can't just leave them behind in this cursed land. They'll be found for sure, and probably butchered by those trogs."

"It can't be helped," Blondor said. "They'll have at least a good chance of escaping the butcher's axe as we have of getting through to the other side of the Stygian Hole—perhaps better." The druid then stood-up and walked up to the horses. He spoke into each of their ears, causing them to whinny and then gallop off down the road and eventually they disappeared into the haze.

"Where are they going?" asked Hollin. "What did you say to them?"

"Just where and how they could find fresh green grass to eat and clear mountain water to drink," Blondor said. "They may just make it over the mountains in time." The druid smiled at Anna and then resumed eating as if nothing had happened.

When they opened the bags that Blondor had loaded on the horses, they discovered sausages and cold pork, cans of butter and honey, baked cakes of seed bread, bags of fresh water and large, red apples.

"Where in all of Areister did you find such food? Asked Hagrim, more delighted than surprised.

"What did you think Wargana and her witches ate? The raw horse-flesh that they gave to their undermen?" Blondor asked. "I discovered dozens of large storerooms filled with all sorts of good food and drink. Remember Kellium and the other merchants that were in her pay? They must have been supplying Fennoria with such good food and drink for years. At first they probably didn't want to do business with Fennoria, but she must have offered them a pretty penny for their wares. Gold and riches are the bane of all merchants, and the promise of wealth is the means by which Wargana was able to seduce them, not only in the Mark, but in many other lands as well. Since they traveled a great deal, it was easy for them to do her bidding. She had enough food to last her through a lengthy siege, even one lasting for years."

"That would explain why Kellium was always sending caravans out of the Mark," Rowena said.

"Damn! It makes my blood boil to think that good Markland food and drink has fattened those she-demons all these years," Hollin said.

After they finished their meal, they reloaded their supplies in the bags and flung them over their backs. They turned and took one last look at the valley behind them. Brown haze hung over the landscape. They turned and moved forward, disappearing within the opening in the cliffs that led to the Stygian Hole.

They made torches from some dried wood they found by the entrance, to light their way as they traveled through the Hole, all except Blondor, who would rely on his staff for illumination. The druid led them into the blackness that laid buried under the mountain. Behind him followed Hollin and the three women. Next came Brim and Hagrim. Vesten came last, bringing up the rear. They soon found themselves walking down a long corridor with a low ceiling and smooth walls. The corridor took them straight into the roots of the mountains and began to slope downward sharply. For hours they marched, until they finally came to a halt in a small chamber.

"It's getting late up above, and we've been traveling for a day and a half, with little rest," Blondor said. "I think this is a good place as any to make camp for the night, and get some long needed sleep before we enter the Hole. We'll need all our strength."

Blondor's proposal came as a welcomed relief to everyone. They made themselves comfortable, sitting down along the chamber walls. After eating a small, cold meal, they unrolled their blankets and stretched out for some badly needed rest. Blondor had the first watch. He needed time to think and remember all that he could about his last journey through the Stygian Hole. No one remained awake for long. They quickly fell into a deep and restful sleep. Blondor had forbidden them from searching the tunnels and corridors that branched off from the chamber to look for wood, for fear of getting lost. So they put their torches out to conserve the wood. The only one who could not fall asleep was Rowena. As tired as she was, her mind was haunted by an uneasy feeling that something terrible was about to happen. Soon her eyes adjusted to the darkness and she could make out the dark figure of Blondor, sitting by himself. Rowena got up and sat down next to the druid.

"You're anxious about something," Blondor spoke softly to Rowena. "Fear and restlessness mixes into a terrible brew within your heart. You dread entering these tunnels." The druid did not present these statements as questions, but rather told her what he felt she was feeling.

Rowena could see his black eyes shining, even in the darkness, as if there was a light behind them. She could feel them looking deep into her heart and she felt naked, and knew that the druid could read her thoughts and feelings. She wondered how much he knew about the way she felt toward him?

"I'm frightened," she said. "I sense Old Man Death hiding some where ahead of us. It's as if he's waiting within the tunnels for us to reach him. I'm afraid to go any farther, and yet I want to go on to Lothangia so very much. You said my brother is well, and I feel as if he's waiting for me on the other side. I almost expect to find him waiting for us at the other end of the Stygian Hole, to greet me."

"The Life-Force has increased your powers," Blondor said. "You see glimpses of what might be, but you will find that you must learn to control your powers so that you can differentiate from what will happen and what might happen. You have to learn to clear your heart and mind of your fears and hopes, so as to let the Life-Force show you clearly, the future. The Life-Force can be a powerful friend. It can help you make the right decisions, because what the future holds often depends on what we decide to do in the present. You should not let your fears interfere with your ability to make decisions."

"I can't help it," Rowena said, trying to control her emotions. "I fear for you. When I look at you I see a dark cloud about you, and fear that you will never see the light of day again. Something will happen to prevent you from leaving these tunnels with us, with me." Rowena lowered her head. She could not hold the tears back any longer.

Blondor put his arm around Rowena and held her to him, and she let herself melt into his embrace. She could no longer restrain the way she felt about him.

"Like your brother, you are strong with the Life-Force," Blondor said. "You are no longer the pretty, flirtatious, young maiden, turning the heads of all those young men in Middleboro. You've been chosen by the Lords of the Light, and you'll never be the same again. You must find strength in that thought. You're made of better stuff than most, as the people in the Mid would say."

Rowena smiled and blushed. She felt that for the first time that the gulf that had always separated her from the illusive druid had been bridged. She hung onto every word he said and wished that she could spent the rest of her life exploring the mysteries of the Life-Force with him. Somehow, it made her feel closer to the memory of her mother, who spent all her life studying the secrets of the Life-Force. But Rowena could not rid herself of the dark shadow that blanketed all her dreams, and the fear that she would never get the opportunity to fulfill her dream, still haunted her.

"Will I really see my brother again?" she finally asked. "He is the only family I have, and if anything happened to him, I don't know . . . " Rowena could not find the words to continue.

Blondor's heart went out to the young woman. He gently held her face in his hands and wiped away the tears from her soft cheeks. Even in the dark he could see her clearly. "I want you to clear your mind of all worries and cares," he whispered to her. "I want you to close your eyes and relax. Make your body totally relaxed and let the Life-Force flow freely through you."

Rowena did as the druid instructed. She had the need to listen to someone she trusted, and wanted so desperately to place her fate in Blondor's hands. She was tired and her mind burned with fears for her brother, for Blondor and for everyone on their quest. She needed peace, even for a short time, to help her regain her strength. As she listened to the druid's words, she felt a surge of energy fill her. It was warm and soothing, and it made her feel as if she was floating.

"Now think of you brother," Blondor said. "Let his image come into your mind, and tell me what you see."

The druid's voice sounded as if it was coming from far off. Rowena concentrated on her brother. "I can see only the darkness," she said. "Wait. There's something in the distance. Yes, I see a light and it's getting larger. It's coming closer, and I can now see what appears to be many men, riding horses. They're clad in golden armor that shines with the light of the sun. And in their hands they are carrying banners and flags with eagles and stars on them. It seems that the darkness is rolling back before them as they ride, and in the lead is—yes. It's Vesten."

"What else do you see?" asked Blondor.

Rowena said nothing for a few seconds, and then her face lit up with joy. "I see Palifair. I can see my brother. He's holding onto a white horse, and he's wearing the same kind of golden armor as Vesten."

"And where are they riding to?" asked the druid.

"Into the darkness," she said. Rowena's face then frowned with fear. "There's something evil within the darkness. Something evil is hiding within it."

"What is the evil?" Blondor asked again.

"I don't know," she said. "I'm too frightened to look."

Blondor put his arm around Rowena and let her rest her head on his shoulder. "Sleep now, Rowena," he whispered. "Sleep and rest, and put all thoughts out of your mind. Let your heart be still and at peace."

It was Blondor who woke the others in the morning. Rowena was rapped in her blanket when she woke. Blondor let everyone sleep for eight hours while he stood guard. They had not slept much since they were attacked by the trogs at Kell Amon.

"What time is it?" asked Hollin, as he stretched the sleep from his limbs. "Time seems to have stopped once again for us, just as it did in the Wolf-Staak."

"It's early morning in the world outside," said Blondor. "The sun must be rising in the east as we speak."

"Morning? You could have fooled me," Brim said. "It feels more like midnight. This place fills me with foreboding. I do not like it here and the sooner we get out the other end, the better it suits me."

"Then we must not dally here long," laughed Hagrim. "It's not good for Brim to be filled with foreboding."

They made their way through the winding passages that took them farther into the heart of the mountains. As they continued their way downward, the air grew progressively hotter and stuffier. Occasionally they felt a gush of cool air that swept down from an air duck in the wall. They could see by the light of their torches archways and corridors that branched off on either side of the corridor they were traveling through.

All that day and well into the evening they continued to walk. They stopped only three times while Blondor checked his bearings. They took the opportunity to gobble down something to eat, holding a piece of dry meat over the torches to warm them up, while Blondor tried to remember which way to go. More than once it seemed that he had gotten lost. Blondor would halt when confronted with the corridor splitting into several archways. He spent some time searching his thoughts, trying to recall every little detail about the way he passed, the last time he entered the Stygian Hole. Several times he left the decision to chance, relying on his instincts and the power of the Light for direction. Blondor proved to be an excellent guide, as all druids are. The power of the Light never seemed to fail him.

They eventually came to a halt before a large stone wall that blocked their way. It seemed that Blondor's powers of direction had finally failed him afterall. They had wandered into a dead end and would not have an easy time of finding their way back to the right passage again. Some were beginning to doubt if they would ever get out of the Stygian Hole, and feared that they were destined to spent the last days of their lives wandering through these endless passageways.

"I heard tell that the Stygian Hole is alive and will deliberately close up passages ways to entrap those who enter, dooming them to wander aimlessly until they succumb to the fate of all those who dare to enter this cursed underground prison," Brim said.

"Not all," Hagrim said. "Both Vesten and Blondor have successfully entered and escaped in the past."

"I hope you're right," Brim said.

"So do I," Hagrim said.

Only Vesten and Rowena did not seem to lose faith in Blondor's ability to navigate through the subterranean tunnels. Their faith in the druid seemed unshaken. Rowena's love for him prevented her from doubting his ability, and Vesten had been on too many journeys with Blondor not to trust to his judgement now.

But Blondor seemed to be having trouble trying to figure out where he had made the mistake. He mumbled something to himself about this having to be the right way. He then carefully began inspecting the stone wall, as if searching for something that could not be seen. Hagrim and Brim followed him about, holding their torches high to give him more light, as he used both hands to inspect the walls. The others remained to the rear and waited. It seemed like hours passed, but it was only minutes when they finally heard Blondor cry out. "Ha! Here it is! I knew it had to be here!"

Carved into one of the stones in the wall was the figure of a small dragon with a long twisting tail that coiled around the edge of the sides of the stones. Blondor pressed his hand over the dragon and spoke. "Nauthiz-Raidho-Thurisaz!" Suddenly, there was clanking noise. The stone was beginning to vibrate and slowly disappeared into the wall of the corridor.

The way was now clear. Blondor did not lead them astray after all.

They were off once more, moving down the passageway as before. After marching for several hours, the corridor began leveling off and twisted around several times. It made them think they were walking in circles, but eventually the passageway straightened out once more and ran straight ahead for several miles. The air began to grow progressively damp and a penetrating cold caused them to shutter. Blondor eventually called a halt where the passageway divided into five archways. After examining them for several minutes, the druid chose the one on the far right and led them through it. After walking for several hundred feet, he raised his staff and its blue light increased in intensity, revealing that they had entered a great hall with large stone pillars carved to appear as if they had grown right out of the stone floor. They looked like stone trees belonging to some subterranean forest. They rose hundreds of feet into the air until they melted into the ceiling high over head. Carved into them were stone figures of warriors and knights, who must have fought in ancient wars now forgotten by Trueman historians.

As they made their way through the forest of pillars, their footsteps echoed through the cavernous hall. Slowly they crept across the gigantic space, fearing what might be lurking within the shadows. They could make out a great deal of rubble in the glow of Blondor's light. The floor was covered with a thick layer of dust and the air was now cold and damp. A chill blew through the immense chamber, but from where it originated they could not say. They appeared like insects making their way through the home of some giant. The loneliness was oppressive and they seemed to have been swallowed by the vastness that engulfed them.

Soon they could make out and endless series of stairs that linked ten highways running the length of the walls of the vast hall. Each highway was higher than the last. Hundreds of archways could be seen leading off from the hall to corridors that ran to every corner of the Stygian Hole. For the first time the size and complexity of the Hole sunk into their heads, and they realized that if not for the wizardry of Blondor's ability, there was no way they could ever have found their way through such a maze of tunnels and underground highways.

The company spent the night in one of the corners of the hall, under a small balcony that provided them protection from the damp and cold air. They were able to make a small fire from some dry wood that they found buried among the rubble that littered the floor. It provided the opportunity to cook a small, but hot meal, which refreshed them immensely. Afterwards they rapped themselves in their blankets and huddled together around the small fire.

Blondor was pleased with himself. "I'm sure that we're going in the right direction," he said to the others. He laid back against the wall with his feet near the fire to dry his black boots and warm his feet. "This hall we're in was once a great city square where thousands of people hurried about conducting whatever business that was needed to be done. In the center was a great market place where just about everything under the sun, or should I say, under the mountains, were bought and sold. This hall is just one of many like it that make up a connecting system that transcends the underground city of the Stygian Hole. Over there," the druid said as he pointed to the far side of the hall, "are the many doorways that were once homes where people lived and conducted their affairs."

"They must have been a race of were-moles to live down here in this darkness?" Hagrim said.

"There was no darkness in here, in those days," Blondor said. "They had discovered the means to bring light into these subterranean chambers. They did it with the use of the precious metal we call Pure Gold. It can be used in many ways, and they had learned to smith it with the greatest skill. Their understanding of that rare metal was far greater than our own metal-smiths. They could hammer it as smooth as silk and as thin as paper. They found ways to cause the voice of man to run through it, so that they could speak to each other across great distances. But most of all, they learned to harness its power for illumination. From a simple rod the size of my staff, made from Pure Gold, they illuminate this entire hall for a hundred years with the brightness of the sun. For Pure-Gold is a great conductor of the Life-Force. It's unfortunate that most of that knowledge was lost, but some of it was passed down to us directly from the people that once lived here, in the Stygian Hole."

"If their wisdom was so great, why did they disappear?" asked Hagrim.

"Do not mistake scientific knowledge with wisdom," Blondor said. "The former is merely the skillful use of the laws that govern the cosmos, while the later is the deeper understanding into the way those laws work. One might have great knowledge, but lack the wisdom to use it constructively."

"What became of them, and how did their knowledge fail them?" Anna asked.

"They dug deep into the flesh of the earth and extracted many precious minerals other than Pure Gold. Gold, silver, iron, copper, coal, diamonds, rubies, sapphires and emeralds are just a few of the valuable minerals and jewels that they mined. Wealth in the

Stygian Hole grew until even the poorest of its citizens could live as kings did on the outside world. But wealth corrupts, and overwhelming wealth corrupts overwhelmingly. Greed became the motivating force underlining their civilization. Their lust for ever more wealth led them to the surface in search of new mines to dig. When they reached the upper world, they found that it had been reborn. But they cared nothing for the rich, green fields, nor did they desire to walk under the lush forests, climb the great purple mountains, nor build ships to sail the blue waves of the new-born oceans. They wished only to burrow back into the earth and extract more wealth. They did not wish to live on the surface itself, but only to rape the world of its riches, preferring to live in underground cities.

"Eventually, as if Mother Nature took her revenge for their insolence, the men of the Stygian Hole happened to come upon another race, one that had once inhabited the surface for centuries. This was the race of dragons."

"Dragons?" Anna said. "I thought they only lived in faerie tales and nightmares?"

"Most of our faerie tales are remnants of the racial memory of our ancestors," Blondor said.

"I have heard of the time known as the Rule of Dragons from my mother, but I thought that was a time before recorded history?" Rowena said. "Dragons were supposed to live so far back in time that it was even before the First Age, and even before the Dark Times."

"You're correct," Blondor said. "The Rule of Dragons was long before the race of Truemans was born in the frozen north. Our ancestors were still living amongst the ice and snow of the lands on the top of the world, while most of the world was still ruled by the were-worms. Our ancestors were protected from the dragons by the cold and ice of the northern lands they inhabited. Dragons hated the cold, which was deadly to them, so they never ventured into the northern regions.

"As for the race of men who lived in the Stygian Hole, they were descended from an older time. Probably, their ancestors and ours shared a common origin that extended back before the great Hell-Fires. We in Wissenval, believe they might have been what was left of the old race of men that survived the death of Old Earth, back before the time when they unleashed the terrible fires that destroyed that ancient world. They survived by burrowing below the surface and in time, they build this domain that we now travel through.

"And while they lived under the earth, protected from the fires that ravaged the surface, the dragon race was born of the poisonous vapors that were unleashed by those ancient fires. Their breath was made of flame and ash, and molten lava flowed through their veins. They grew to enormous size and were terrible to behold. Their skin was like armor plates and their eyes burned with hatred for all that lived.

"There were many different races of dragons. The Blue Dragons were serpents that swam in the oceans and never came on dry land, while the Green Dragons lived in the deepest lakes where some say they still exist. White Dragons possessed wings and lived on the highest peeks of the mountains. This was a time before the mountains were covered with snow and ice. The Yellow Dragons roamed the forests that blanketed the world in those ancient times. The race of Black dragons lived deep within the earth's stomach, and could breath fire, and they came to the surface only under the darkness of night. But the most terrible race of all the were-worms was the race of Red Dragons. Like the White Dragons, they had great leathery wings and could fly, and like the Black Dragons they possessed fiery breaths and bellowed black smoke. They could travel across great distance and inhabited the ash-filled skies before the world was reborn. They were the first of their race and the first to appear. They were the most intelligent of dragons and all other dragons feared them. They waged war against the other races of dragons and came to dominate the world.

"When the Red Dragons discovered the men of the Stygian Hole, they waged war against them, destroying all their colonies. All military and mining parties that ventured onto the surface of New Earth were killed, as dragons attacked them time and again. But once man discovered the dragons' weakness, it was only a matter of time before they were able to turn the tide against them. Dragons, as you know from the legends, are very fierce, but they are not very bright. Even the Red Dragons, the smartest of dragons, could not equal the race of Stygian men in cleverness and intelligence. This permitted the Stygian men to discover ways to hunt them down and kill them through manipulation and cunning, and the use of their great machines of destruction. Through a plan of divide and conquer, they were able to hunt down and virtually kill all the dragons, until they became extinct. In time, all the lands, skies and oceans were free from the tyranny of the dragons.

"The last of the dragons to be defeated by the men of the Stygian Hole, were the Red Dragons. They put up the greatest resistance. Great battles were fought that caused the destruction of whole mountains and changed the flow of rivers. Much of the lands was battered and burnt under the mighty metal machines of the Stygian men. Their machines raced across the land, overcoming all obstacles, even the biggest mountains and the deepest canyons. Their machines could sail the oceans and even dive below the surface of the seas. Other machines followed the dragons into the skies so that the dragons' ability of flight no longer could protect them from the wrath of the Stygian men.

"Then, a time came when only a handful of dragons were left. They decided that they were not a match for the machines of the Stygian men. Their leader was named Gormungtol, and he led them to an unknown land far to the south where they were able to nurse their wounds in the great tropical jungles that grow below the edge of the world. For centuries they lived there and waited until they once again grew in numbers. The Stygian men soon forgot about the threat of the dragons. They believed they had killed them all. Once the threat of the dragons was forgotten, they once again began building new colonies. They convinced themselves that they had killed off the last of the were-worms. The Stygian men grew rich once more and lost interest in making war. They let the thunder of their machines rust and rot.

"Then came the day when the dragons decided the time had come to seek their vengeance on the race of Stygian men.

They left their jungles in the south and returned once more to the lands of the north. The men were caught totally off guard when the dragons struck. The dragons were able to invade their underground chambers and cities, and soon transformed their cities and colonies into an empty, charred, burnt-out holes. One city after another was attacked by the were-worms, as the men tried desperately to defend their homes, but without their war machines it was hopeless. Great battles were fought underground, as their subterranean cities collapsed under the fury of the dragons' attacks.

"Then, the last of the men took refuge in the tunnels of the Stygian Hole. Here they decided to make a last stand and defend what was left of their civilization. When the dragons struck they were confronted with the stiffest resistance that they had yet faced. It was equal to the terrible battles of the first war they fought with the men of the Stygian Hole. The tunnels and passageways of the Stygian Hole were filled with the smoke of burning flesh and armor plating, and echoed with the battle cries of brave men and enraged dragons, killing one another in the most ruthless and brutal fighting ever fought on New Earth. It was in their memory that the men of later ages came to call this place the Stygian Hole, which means 'The Hole of Endless Dying.'"

"But if all the dragons died during the Dragon Wars, what about the legends that some dragons still live?" asked Hagrim.

"Yes. What about the tales of people claiming to have sighted a dragon flying in the mountains, or seeing a serpent in different lakes?" Brim asked.

"What I have told you is what little we know of those long-forgotten times," Blondor explained. "Most of the history of those times have disappeared. What has been passed down to the druids of Wissenval are only bits and pieces of the complete tale. In some lands people transformed these tales into great myths that old men tell to their grandchildren. And you know how easy it is for people to expand and exaggerate when retelling a tale that has already been retold many times over. Many a traveler has claimed to have seen a dragon on his journey. Whether they actually did or not is something we will never know until we have actually seen one for ourselves. But I guest it's possible that some dragons have survived and have remained hidden from the world ever since. If they did they would have taken refuge at the bottom of the deepest lakes, and in the darkness of the deepest holes of the world."

"Like the Stygian Hole?" asked Rowena.

Everyone looked at the girl and then turned to Blondor.

"Like the Stygian Hole," Blondor said. "It's possible that a dragon could have survived in the Stygian Hole, but we are sure that they disappeared from the surface world. That much of which we are certain. When the first Truemans began venturing south from their northern homeland, they did not know of the race of dragons. The world was growing colder, and if any dragons did survive, they either fled south or hid. We druids believe that some of the original men who inhabited New Earth did survive and told the new comers of their wars with the dragons. This is how, what little knowledge we have of those wars, was passed down to us.

"When our ancestors began colonizing New Earth, they came into contact with the undermen races of trogs, trolls and other undermen. It was during those wars that they descended into many different dark tunnels that they found throughout New Earth, including the Stygian Hole, in pursuit of the undermen. Many who did, did not return, but of those who did, told tales of the presence of a fierce dragon that inhabited the tunnels and chambers of the Stygian Hole. In time, the legends grew and many a brave knight went on a personal quest into the Stygian Hole to slay whatever dragon they might find living here. None of them ever returned to tell anyone what they had discovered."

"You said that you and Vesten once traveled through here," Hollin asked. "How did you make it through the Stygian Hole? Did you discover any dragons living here?"

"You are forgetting the power of the druids," Vesten now spoke. "It was over ten years ago when Blondor came to me and asked me if I would join him and go investigate reports of trog movements in and around the mountains near Fennoria. I agreed and we set off at once. We explored all the lands surrounding Fennoria. Then one day, one of the mountain eagles came to us and told us of a large gathering of trogs in Fennoria, near the entrance to the Stygian Hole. We were in Palennoria at the time, and decided to see for ourselves by traveling through the Stygian Hole. For many days we wandered through these dark tunnels and chambers. From the first, Blondor felt a dark presence in the lower chambers, and so we stuck to the upper levels. We discovered that trogs had penetrated into the Stygian Hole, but could not figure out the reason for their being here. We even passed into Fennoria, to see if we could find out what Wargana was up to, but it was all to no avail. When we decided to return the way we came, we discovered that the passages to the upper levels had been blocked. We were forced to descend into the lower chambers once again, but what we found there, I will not tell."

Everyone could see that the memory of his passage through the Stygian Hole troubled Vesten. Vesten refused to speak any more. All eyes turned toward Blondor.

"We made it through to the other side," Blondor said, "but there was something there, in the lower chambers, that caused our hearts to stop cold. Only the presence of the Lord of Darkness himself could have filled us with a greater sense of doom. I sensed that whatever evil there was in the lower chambers was asleep, and so, we made our way back to the upper levels, as quickly as possible, for fear of awakening it. We made our way out of the Stygian Hole, by the way we entered, without being discovered."

Anna was frightened by Blondor's words and moved closer to Hollin, who took her into his arms to embraced her. He gently kissed her on the forehead. As he did, Anna looked at Rowena. She saw terror in her eyes. Anna and Rowena had known each other since they were children, and she knew that her friend possessed clairvoyant abilities. There were many incidents when Rowena had premonitions about things before they happened. More than once Rowena had warned a neighbor in Middleboro of some impending danger before it happened. People came to trust her and take her intuition seriously. Since they had left the Mark, Anna had noticed that Rowena's powers had grown stronger. Because of this, Rowena's fear troubled Anna. She wondered what could possibly have frightened her friend so terribly, but Rowena was not telling anyone what it was.

Blondor fell silent and retreated deep into his own thoughts. Everyone sat wrapped in their blankets, trying to rest and keep warm. Gradually they fell asleep, huddled around the small fire that they had lit to protect themselves from the dampness.

Chapter Eight:
Fire and Darkness

Hagrim had the last watch. It was about 8 o'clock in the morning when he woke everyone up. "Morning already?" asked Hollin as he yawned. "I feel as if I was sleeping for just a few minutes. How can anyone get any rest in this dungeon?"

"If we're lucky and don't waste much time, this should be the last night that we have to spend in the Stygian Hole," Blondor said.

"I sure hope so," Hollin agreed. "It's been too long since I last felt the warmth of the sun on my face."

"I let everyone get a couple of extra hours of sleep last night," Blondor said. "If we can walk through to the night, we might be able to pass out of the Hole and into Lothangia by tomorrow morning."

Everyone gathered around the small fire that was kept burning through the night, and heated some bread and meat. "This will probably be the last hot meal that we'll have before we depart," Blondor said. As the everyone heated their meager breakfast, Blondor and Vesten walked a small ways from the camp to talk privately among themselves.

"I feel that it's time we move upward once more, to the higher levels," Blondor said.

"Do we have to pass through the lost city?" asked Vesten.

"I hope not," Blondor said. "If there is another way for us to go, we'll take it, but I'm not sure I know of one."

"I'm not happy about the way we found the passageway blocked,"

Vesten said. "It forced us to divert to these lower levels. It's as if something or someone was trying to direct our moments."

"I agreed," Blondor said.

"I don't want to enter the lost city," Vesten said. "The stench of death blows from that direction and grows greater with every step we take." The Guardian looked at the druid. His face was grim. "Take care, Blondor. I feared entering that place the last time we passed through the Stygian Hole, and this time I see a shadow lying across your path."

Blondor said nothing, but the Guardian could see a knowing acceptance in his friend's black eyes.

"Then we'll try going around," Blondor said. "We can go through those archways." Blondor pointed to a series of archways on one of the upper levels. "Those archways will take us up and in the right direction, through several large halls like this one, each on a higher level. We should be able to avoid passing through the lost city." Blondor then turned to Vesten. "But even if we do pass through the lost city unharmed, I fear we'll discover that the exit will be guarded. Things have changed here since we last passed through it."

Blondor threw the Guardian a knowing smile.

It was now Vesten's turn to say nothing. He followed Blondor back to where the others were waiting.

After breakfast, they collected their belongings and followed Blondor up the stairs that ran along the wall. They passed through one of the archways and left the great hall behind them. With Blondor in the lead, they walked through the corridor that twisted and turned, for over an hour. The corridor was clearly rising as they walked. Eventually they came to another hall, similar to the one in which they had spent last night. They passed through the hall without stopping and continued on their way, passing through three additional halls, each higher than the previous one. By noon they found themselves passing through what appeared to be a long, straight, underground highway. It was about twenty feet wide and fifteen feet high. After traveling several miles, Blondor stopped and turned into an archway to his right, which opened onto a flight of long stairs leading up. Over one hundred and twenty steps they climbed, and once they reached the top, they were confronted by a wall of rock and stone blocking their way. The tunnel had collapsed.

"What does this mean?" Hollin asked.

The druid slowly sank down. "It's as I feared," he said as he sat on the top step.

"Why did you lead us to a dead end?" Hollin asked again.

"He didn't lead us to a dead end," Rowena said. "It's fate that has blocked our way, and there is no way he can escape what the future has in store for him." Rowena sat next to the druid and placed her hand on his shoulder.

Rowena speaks the truth," Blondor finally spoke. "I had hoped to avoid the lost city by going over it, passing through the upper levels, but it would seem that fate has another way for us to travel. This was not always a dead end. That wall blocks a passageway that runs straight for about five miles and then opens onto the green fields of Lothangia. But now we must retrace our steps and go back the way we came and pass through the lost city. That's the only way left for us."

"We mustn't go that way," Rowena insisted. She trembled with fear as she spoke. "Please, Blondor. We can still find another way to go. We have to."

"There is no time to search for another way," Blondor said as he smiled up at Rowena. "Events are moving faster than even Gottron thought they would. Even now the Shadow of Allomania is moving on Neutria. I fear that the only hope for New Earth and our people, is for Vesten to reach Lothangia as soon as possible."

"But there is danger—danger for you," Rowena said as tears rolled down her cheeks.

"Danger for Blondor? What in the name of the long-tooth cat of the north are you talking about, Rowena?" Brim asked.

"I'm not all that sure, myself," Rowena sobbed. "But I can see only blackness and dread for Blondor, if he enters the lost city. And, I'm not the only one here who sees darkness waiting for Blondor." Rowena looked at Vesten as she spoke. Everyone turned to the Guardian. Silence fell over the small company as Vesten's face tightened with grim expectation.

"Blondor is right, Rowena," Vesten finally said. "We're only pawns in this game. Our lives are not important. What is important is that the game is played out to its conclusion, with the Light victorious. We must resolve to accept whatever destiny Fate has in store for us."

"Besides, Rowena," Blondor said as he rose to his feet. "Your brother will be needing our help. We must reach Lothangia as soon as possible, if we are to be of service to him. If the fastest route to Lothangia is through the lost city, then it is through the lost city that we must pass."

Rowena knew that Blondor and Vesten were right and said no more. The druid placed his arm around her shoulder as he led the others down the stairs, and then along the underground highway once more. They stopped for a short while to gobble-up a quick, cold lunch, and were off again. For two hours they marched on, retracing their steps. Eventually they found themselves moving along another underground highway that ran straight and long, with a high ceiling and many arches on either side. The thoroughfare opened into a gigantic space. It was not until they had walked several dozen yards into the space did they realize the vastness of its dimensions. Blondor once again caused his staff to burn bright with a light strong enough for them to take in the vastness of the chamber. When their eyes finally adjusted, they could not believe the sight before them.

They had entered a domed chamber of such vast proportions that it was hard to believe they were actually underground. The light from Blondor's staff seemed to magnify until they could see right to the ceiling. Great strips of Pure Gold ran upward from the edge of the dome ceiling to the center, like great ribs. The metal absorbed the light and magnified it back, producing light that filled the cavern, so that they could see all the way to its most lofty heights.

It's roof rose three thousand feet from its stone floor. It was actually a natural formation, created long ago when the surface of the world was a great cauldron of boiling, bubbling liquid rock. The dome was formed when a huge air bubble cooled and solidified. When the men of the Stygian Hole discovered the cavern, they built a great city within it.

High above, in the center of the dome ceiling, they could make out what appeared to be a large opening over the city. It was cut into the mountain by the people who once lived there, to let in air and ventilate the city. It was one hundred yards in diameter and led straight up, to the top of the mountain, high above. When the company passed under it, they looked up, but could not see any light through it. They were too deep in the earth for the light outside to reach them.

As they walked through the streets of the city they found themselves surrounded by the remains of stone buildings that had fallen into ruin long ago. Much of the city was made of mountains of rubble, and many of the towers that once rose from the floor of the city, were half-buried in rubble, but some were still standing straight and tall, soaring hundreds of feet in the air. Thousands of years of neglect had taken its toll on the city. Everywhere there were great mounds of bricks and stone blocks lying about. The streets were littered with steel beams, rusted red. Marble and granite pillars that had fallen over were everywhere, broken among the ruins of the ancient buildings. They wondered at what marvelous engineers the Stygian men must have been, to have conceived and constructed such a city so deep underground.

"The people who built this city possessed a level of skill and craftsmanship that is far superior to anything that exists today," Blondor said. "They had the ability to create wonders that our age cannot even imagine. This city was once the heartbeat of their civilization. It's the last remaining monument to the men of Old Earth."

They made their way through the winding avenues and streets that ran in between the fallen buildings. They had to climb over the rubble that filled the streets, and at times they had to detour around a tower that had fallen across the way they were traveling, because it blocked their path. The going was slow and they were in awe of the twisted forms of metal and stone that surrounded them. They imagined that they could still hear the chatter and noise that once must have filled the city, as if the echoes of the past still resonated throughout the great underground dome cavern.

Soon they came to a large clearing. It was once the center of the city. They could make out what once must have been parks and gardens, where the people of the city spent their leisure time. Now it was overgrown with great mushrooms that grew as tall as a house and were green-blue in color. Strange brown leafless vines, with large thorns, grew up the sides of the tower walls. In the center was a small river that flowed through the city from an underground well and formed a small pool. The water looked putrid, and Blondor warned everyone to avoid getting themselves wet.

Across the river was a large stone bridge that was still standing. Blondor avoid crossing it for fear that it was unsafe. Instead, he led them down the banks of the river until he spied a couple of large titanium beams that had fallen across the river, providing a natural bridge for them to cross.

Once on the other side, Blondor called a halt and everyone rested before moving on. Hollin could not help but wonder about the titanic struggle that must have taken place here, long ago. He imagined hundreds of dragons invading the tunnels of the Stygian Hole, and the people who made a last stand in the city. "The battle must have been fierce?" he said.

"It was a desperate, last stand," Blondor said as he looked about. "I can almost hear the terrible cries and shouts of the people who fought here. They were mixed with the horrific roar of the fire-worms. Dragon fire and man-magic filled this city with flames and explosions. It's as if their ghost still haunt the city."

"Here! Come here and see what I found!" Hagrim shouted to the others.

Everyone found Hagrim and Brim surrounded by what appeared to be the remains of a cellar. They had been searching the area while the others rested.

"Here, on the wall," Hagrim pointed.

Everyone had come running with Blondor in the lead. There, standing tall was a pillar of stone. Carved into it was a small maze-like image, with runes written above and below it.

"What is it?" asked Anna.

"They're some kind of runes," Blondor said as he studied the carving. "It's written in an ancient dialect of Daryan."

"Can you read it?" asked Vesten.

"Let me see," Blondor said under his breath, as he continued to study the runes. "This dialect has not been spoken for some time. Let me see if I can remember. Ah! Yes! It says here on top, 'Fear not to go back to go forward,' and below the circle is some kind of code, 'L-3, R-4, L-4 and R-3.'"

"What do you think it means?" asked Vesten.

"This maze-like image is a very ancient symbol that was once used by my order. We haven't used it in thousands of years. It has to do with one's journey through life. Look here," Blondor said as he began running his finger around the length of the circle maze. "If you enter here, you turn left, running the length of the circle until you turn again two more times. You then turn right four times, followed by four turns to the left, only to finish with three turns to the right, which takes you to the center."

"It seems that every time you get close to the center, you take a turn that leads you away once more," Hollin said.

"Yes. You're right," Vesten said.

"Why is this referred to as life's journey?" Rowena asked.

"Because, one usually has to take many detours in the path of life," Blondor said. "Sometimes, it's necessary to go back, before you can continue to go forward."

"But why did the men of the Stygian Hole carve this figure here?" asked Anna.

"They didn't," Blondor said. "I said that these runes are written in an ancient form of Daryan. No Stygian hand carved this. This must have been left by someone who had passed this way long ago. It might be some kind of warning, or a message, but for what?"

"Perhaps someone wanted to leave some form of map, for others to follow if they came this way?" Rowena said.

"Very perspective," Blondor said.

Rowena smiled.

"But what could the maze symbolize?' Hollin asked.

"I don't know," Blondor said. "Perhaps Rowena is right. It could be some kind of map for us to follow. Maybe we will discover the answer to your question further along the way?"

Brim suddenly felt uneasy. "I don't think we should remain here much longer. There's something about the feel of this place that I suddenly don't like. I'm beginning to think that Rowena was right about this place. Evil stalks us, and waits for the opportunity to strike."

"Brim is right," Blondor said. "I suddenly sense something. It's as if death has just entered the city and surrounds us."

Vesten pulled out his sword, Gordonthol. It was burning bright gold, as if it had been placed in a smith's forge. "Look!" Vesten shouted. "Godonthol warns of evil's approach."

"Then let's leave this place with all haste," Blondor said. "Up ahead is a great arch that leads to another great underground highway, like the one that led us here. At the end of it there are passageways that all lead to the exist. We must reach it before . . . "

Blondor never finished his sentence. His voice was drown by an earth-shattering roar that caused everyone to jump with terror.

"*Seeh! Seeh!*" Princess Valenda shouted in her native language. "Look! Look!" Everyone turned and saw the origin of the thundering sound. They were overcome with a fear so great that it paralyzed them, preventing them from reacting.

"Gormungtol, King of the Dragons," Blondor finally said. The words barely escaped his lips as he sang to his knees. "So this is the evil of the Stygian Hole. It's far greater than I, or even Gottron feared or could imagine, even in our most terrible nightmares." Using his staff as support, he raised himself back to his feet and shouted for everyone to quickly take cover, as he distinguished the light in its globe.

They hid behind a broken wall and watched as the dragon made its way through the decaying towers. They could see the dragon's long neck rising high over the city from its armor-plated body. His scaly head was crowned with two long horns. Smoke bellowed from its nostrils. From its jaws slithered a long, red tongue over the rows of raze-sharp fangs that sparkled, as if they were made from pearls. From its cat-like eyes a bright light shined, probing the darkness about it. The entire form of the dragon seemed to glow in the darkness with a translucent light that shined from deep within its form. The dragon suddenly flung its head back and released another roar that echoed off the stone ceiling of the cavern. The beast had not seen them yet, but he had caught hold of the scent of Trueman blood.

They could clearly see the leviathan behemoth before them now. His size was monstrous. His serpentine bulk stretched over two hundred feet, and from its back protruded two large, bat-like sails that were its wings. From his head to the tip of his tail he was covered with a skin of red scales that were as hard as steel. His belly was also armored with golden plates. Four huge, clawed feet slowly dragged the reptilian beast forward, bringing it ever closer to where they were hiding. After crawling for several minutes, it suddenly stopped. Its luminous eyes fixed on the spot where Blondor and the others were hiding. They were found by the nightmare of armor and fangs.

The dragon reeled up on its hindquarters, waving its forelegs before it in a fury of rage and delight. Its neck lift its head high above its body, as its wings fanned out behind it, causing a whirl wind storm of foul air to race about the city.

"There's no use hiding now," Blondor said as he walked out in clear view of the dragon. He raised his staff before him. Its globe began to glow with a blue light. "Worm of Darkness!" he shouted. "I, Blondor of Wissenval, bid you to heed my warning! I have invaded your domain! Come and face me, if you dare? I have come to see if your kind is as cowardly as legends say!"

The dragon stared in disbelief at the boast of the small black-robed druid standing before it. Its eyes turned blood-red with hate. Its scaley lips pulled back in what appeared to be an evil smile. Gormungtol lunged his head forward, opening wide its jaws. A blast of fire burst through the air, engulfing the lonely druid. Rowena cried in horror. It was only due to the quick action of Brim, who grabbed her before she could run out from behind the wall, that stopped her from being consumed by the flames. When the fire cleared, Blondor remained standing, unharmed.

He was encased within a bubble of blue light, and was untouched by the dragon's fire.

The druid raised his right arm and sent a blast of blue light at the dragon, striking it in the face. That caused the behemoth to reel back in pain, as it unleashed a terrifying cry, causing the earth to shake. Stones began dropping from the decaying buildings as it stomp its feet in pain. Blondor had taken the beast by surprise. The dragon had underestimated the power of its opponent. It had been too long since one so powerful as a druid, challenged him.

Blondor's blast had dazed the dragon, blinding him momentarily. His rage grew boundless now, and his flapping wings blew up a windstorm of air, reeking of his stench and sending debris in all directions. Blondor unleashed another blast of blue energy, striking a tower nearby, causing its foundation to give way and collapsing it on top of the dragon.

"Now! Run!" Blondor shouted to the others. "Run while you can! Gormungol is momentarily stunned. So go and fly like the wind!"

Everyone was frozen where they stood, as Vesten began pushing them along. One by one he shook them awake and sent them running down one of the avenues that led away from the square.

Princess Valenda led the way with her weapon ready in her hand. Hollin followed her as he led Anna by the hand. Hagrim and Brim followed right behind them. But Rowena had refuse to leave Blondor, and Vesten had to grab her and hand her over to Brim, who carried her in his arms, as she cried and protested, pleading to him to let her remain by Blondor's side. Lastly, Vesten departed as he shouted for them to run. He turned twice to see if Blondor was following, but he could not make out what was happening. He saw blue smoke mingle with the fiery breath of the dragon. He thought for a moment to turn and go back to assist Blondor.

The dragon slowly dug his way out of the mountain of stone and metal that Blondor had sent crashing down on top of him. Large chunks of debris were sent flying through the air with swipes of his arms and tail, as it shook its head, trying to regain its scenes. When the dragon's eyes cleared, it could make out the small, black figure of Blondor backing off, down the street, shouting to the others.

"Go! Keep running!"

Vesten had remained to see what was happening to his friend. As the smoke cleared, he was stricken with terror at the sight of the dragon, as it stood up once more. Its wings were spread wide and began to flap, lifting the behemoth through the air. It floated like a great balloon as it rose high over the towers of the city, as if it was weightless. It leaped from tower to tower, as it vomited fire from its mouth at the druid. The whole city was now a blazed with a curtain of fire that surrounded the druid, trapping him in the square, preventing him from escaping. The cavern was now lit up like a great oven. Black smoke lingered high above in the hub of the dome and rose through its opening.

Blondor stopped and turned to face the oncoming dragon. For a moment, it hovered overhead, flapping its wings and feeding the flames, causing them to burn with even greater intensity.

"Worm of the Stygian Hole!" Blondor shouted. "Hear my words and take heed! Your days have finally come to en end! You must deal with me, and never before have your faced such an adversary! Worm of the Hell Fires! Prepare to die!"

The dragon seemed hypnotized by the druid's words. There seemed to be some power in them that held his attention, and preventing him from leaving the area of the square. It flapped its wings once more in hope of knocking the druid off his feet, but to no avail. Blondor stood his ground with his staff held high over his head, and then shouted again.

"Go back and return to whatever dark womb gave birth to you!" Blondor shouted. "Crawl back into its dark depths and do not bother the world of Truemans ever again!" A burning light now appeared in the druid's black eyes as he began to chant. "Uruz-

Thurisaz-Hagalaz-Isa-Sowilo!" He chanted the rune-words over and over.

The dragon shot another blast of fire from its throat at Blondor, but the flames were sent back at it. The dragon dodged the fire by flying higher into the blacken air above, and hovered for a minute, hidden in the smoke. Then, it suddenly fell down at the druid, flying over him and knocking him off his feet.

Vesten turned and saw what happened, and began running back toward Blondor, but the druid saw him and shouted for him to go back.

"No! Go back! You can't help me here! You must go with the others and lead them out of the Hole! Forget about me and go to Lothangia, and fulfill your destiny! The others are in need of your leadership! Now do as I say!"

Vesten stopped in his tracks and regretfully, did as the druid commanded. He realized that Blondor spoke true. There was nothing he could do to help him. He began running back to join the others, as his steel-blue eyes were wet with tears at the fate that awaited his friend. When he reached the arch, where the others were waiting for him, he ordered them to go through the corridor, that led away from the lost city. He promised he would join them in a moment. As they did as he said, he turned to see the battle unfolding in the distance.

Blondor got to his feet once again and held his staff with both hands. Raising it high over his head, he called upon every ounce of willpower that he possessed as he repeated his rune-chant. As he did, the dragon tried to grab him, but was greeted with a burst of blue energy that singed its claws. Its wings left it into the air once more, as Blondor continued his chanting.

As he spoke the rune-chant over and over, a wind began to suddenly rise up from nowhere and whirled about the cavern. It increased in force as the blue light that encased Blondor seemed to grow in strength and intensity until it finally filled the entire city. The dragon unleashed yet another blast of fire from its scaley jaws, straight at the druid, but the power of the wind swept the flames along, until they disappeared within its whirling vortex. Gradually the smoke and fire from the burning city was caught up in the druid's hurricane, sucking up stone, wood and metal. The dragon now found it hard to fight the wind and maintain its balance as its great wings fought the power of the winds.

The vortex now increased in intensity, carrying the dragon and everything within it upward and straight through the hole in the hub of the dome ceiling, and disappeared from sight. There was no sign of movement in the city as the ageless blackness once again filled its vastness. The only light that could be seen was the glow of Vesten's sword at the entrance. Slowly the fire in the blade went out. Vesten waited a minute of two and then turned back into the corridor where the others were waiting with lit torches. He hoped that Blondor would come wobbling up to the archway, or perhaps see the glow of his staff, but he did not see any sign of his old friend. He could only wonder how the others, especially Rowena, would take the news of Blondor's disappearance?

Chapter Nine:
Out of the Wolf's Jaws

When Vesten reached the spot where the others were waiting, Rowena came running up to greet him. He could see the tears in her eyes. He reached for her and held her for a moment, as they looked at each other without saying a word. Vesten felt that the girl had already surmised the fate that befell the man she loved.

"What happened?" asked Hollin, who had run up to Vesten with Anna close behind. Vesten looked at Hollin, who was holding a torch. "Where's Blondor? What happened to him?" Hollin asked.

"He's gone," Rowena said with a finality that caused Hollin and Anna to shiver.

"Gone?" Hollin asked.

"Yes, gone," Rowena said as she fought to hold back the tears.

"You knew all along that something would happen to Blondor, didn't you?" asked Vesten.

But Rowena did not answer.

"I felt that something evil was waiting for him in this stinking hole," Vesten finally said. "I think Blondor also knew. But he was willing to face the danger with no fear for his life, because he knew that there are things of greater importance than our individual lives. He gave his life so that we might succeed in our quest."

"What'll we do without him?" asked Hollin.

"He's gone and we must go on," Vesten said. "We must make sure that he did not die in vain. This I swear. Come! We must go."

"But who will lead?" Anna asked.

"I will lead us now," Vesten declared.

From somewhere high above the ground, an explosion shook the entire mountain, causing rocks and dirt to fly down through the hole at the top of the ceiling of the dome cavern. The repercussions vibrated throughout the Stygian Hole. Shockwaves were sent through the corridor, causing it to fill with bellowing smoke. Everyone began running with Vesten in the lead. After sometime, they stopped and shook the dirt and dust off themselves. When they had cleaned themselves off, they used their torches to take a look about and see where they were. In front of them were the three arches that Blondor mentioned.

"These must be the three passageways that Blondor told us about?" Hagrim said. "But which one should we take?"

"I don't know," Vesten said. "Blondor didn't say."

"He did say that all three of them lead to the exit," Hollin said. "But which one is the safest and quickest passageway out of here?"

"I don't like the feel of the one of the left," Hagrim said.

"I don't like the feel of any of them," Brim said as he pulled on his beard. "I have the must unnerving sensation that we are not out of this mess yet."

"Since we cannot decide on which way to go, and all of them go up to the exit, we might as well take the one in the middle," Vesten said. "It leads up and that is the way we're going."

They passed under the stone archway and into the short tunnel that rose sharply beyond. The passageway soon opened into a large hall. They ran across the hall as quickly as they could because they were in a hurry to get out of the Stygian Hole. None of them wanted to remain within its tunnels any longer than possible. It reminded them too much of their loss. Once they reached the other side of the hall, they found a doorway with two large, bronze doors laying on the floor. On the other side of the doorway was a flight of marble stairs that led upward to two large doors made of a white metal. On them were carved two wolf-heads and some runes

"Can you read what the runes say?" asked Anna.

Vesten studied them for several minutes. "My knowledge of rune-writing is great, but not the equal of a druid," he said. "But I think I can make out the meaning of these runes? Let me see. It says, 'Beware, all who enter the Hall of Lost Souls!'"

"The Hall of Lost Souls?" asked Hollin. "What in the name of the Lords of the Light is that?"

"I've heard of that name used in reference to a mazed passageway," Vesten said. "This might mean that we will have to pass through some kind of network of passageways, some kind of maze, designed to trap anyone who tries to pass through it. Blondor once told me that in ancient times, men believed that the souls of anyone who died trying to pass through a maze would haunt the maze for eternity, or when someone discovers its secret, permitting them to pass through it. Until then their souls serve as fodder for demons that feed on them. It's a fitting fate for thieves."

"Well that does it!" shouted Hollin in anger. "After all we've been through, trogs, witches and dragons, and now we're doomed to wind-up wandering the tunnels of a maze for the rest of our short lives, and for eternity as wraiths!"

"Don't give up yet, young Hillroller," Vesten said. "Where there's a will, there's a way, and I've often heard Blondor say that through the power of the will alone, one can achieve great deeds, even when things look the blackest."

"How then are we to turn defeat into victory?" Hollin asked.

"That I haven't figured out, yet," Vesten said. "But this looks as good a time to rest as any, before we go on."

They sat on the steps before the large doors, as they ate most of what was left of their food. They heated some sausages and bread with a small fire they made from some dry wood that they found. They washed down their meal with some water from their water bags. Another day and their supplies would be finished. It did not seem to matter to them. They were solemn about their fate and gloom hung heavy on their hearts. The loss of their friend still weighed heavy, and they were ready to surrender to whatever fate that lied just ahead.

Vesten sat in silence. He knew that everyone trusted Blondor. Now their lives were in his hands. He often had to lead men into battle, but this was different. Except for Brim and Hagrim, who trusted him implicitly, the others were not totally sure of his leadership abilities. His mind was filled with images of all that had happened to them since they left Gateburg. He began to doodle with a stick in the dust that covered the stairs, tying to distract himself from what he had to face. He needed to rest his mind, even for a short while, before they began the rest of their journey through the Stygian Hole. Hard as he tried to concentrate on the figures and circles that he drew in the dust when suddenly, it dawned on him that he had just drawn the circular maze figure that they discovered carved on the stone, in the lost city.

"Of course!" Vesten shouted as he jumped up with excitement. "That's what it meant. It was the key to the maze. It's the way through the Hall of Lost Souls."

Vesten's excitement over his discovery caused everyone to wonder what had happened. "What key? What are you talking about? Have you lost your senses?" asked Hagrim.

"No, I haven't lost my senses," Vesten said. "Remember the circles and runes on the stone we found in the lost city? It was a maze—a puzzle. Well, I think it was the solution to the maze that lies ahead. It was some kind of map through the Hall of Lost Souls. Let me see if I can remember how the runes read?"

Vesten thought for a moment.

It was Princess Valenda who finally spoke. "Do not fear to go back, to go forward," she said, "and then there were the letters and number - L-3, R-4, L-4 and R-3."

"Exactly!" Vesten said excitedly and then bent down and began to retrace the maze in the dust. Brim held his torch over his commander so everyone could see what he was drawing. "Now look," Vesten said. "We enter here and then make the following turns, going around and around, making three turns to the left, followed by four turns to the right. There are then four more left turns and finally three additional turns to the right, which takes us to the center."

"You're right," Hollin agreed, as he pointed to the drawing in the dust. "If we follow the maze, as you said, we move closer to the center, but before we reach it, we have to move away from the center several times. That must be the meaning of the runes? 'Do not fear to go back, to go forward.' Who knows how many men must have gotten lost trying to go forward when they should have gone backward?"

"But where do we go once we reach the center?" asked Brim.

"There must be a way out," Vesten said. "We'll worry about it when we reach the center."

They gathered their things together and climbed back up the stairs to the doors. The men leaned hard against them and slowly pushed them open. It was dark inside and the air was stale. Vesten led the way, ordering everyone to keep close together for fear of getting separated. Once everyone was inside, the doors suddenly slammed closed behind them, locking them in.

"Well, that's that," Anna said. "There's no going back now."

"You're right about that," Brim said as he tried the doors. "Since we can't go back, we might as well go forward."

"Or should we say, backward?" Hagrim laughed, trying to keep everyone's spirits up.

They found themselves walking down the long, narrow passageways. They had only their torches for light and could see an occasional doorway that appeared on either side of the corridor they were passing through. Vesten walked very slowly, not wanting to make any mistakes. It would take just one mistake to get them hopelessly lost. Everyone walked so close together that they were stumbling over each other.

Vesten finally called a halt. They had come to a stone wall and the passageway turned left. "Here's where we make our first turn to the left," he said. "Stay close behind each other and make sure you don't lose sight of the person in front of you. Everyone should try and hold on to the person's walking cape in front of them. If you lose contact, shout 'halt,' immediately. Don't let the torches go out. If any torch does go out, everyone stop, and shout 'halt!' Understand?"

Everyone agreed.

They continued to make their way down the passageways, making one turn after another. The light from their torches flickered, revealing hundreds of archways, all identical to each other. It was impossible to distinguish one from another. Occasionally, they came across the remains of some adventurer who tried unsuccessfully to make it through the maze. They skulls, bones and rusted weapons were all very ancient and littered the floor of the maze. They were testimonies to the fate that was awaiting each and everyone of them, if Vesten had guested wrong about the carvings on the stone in the lost city.

They followed Vesten through the maze for more than two hours. Vesten chose carefully what turns to take before making a decision. Sometimes he spent several minutes thinking about his choice. He seemed to be feeling his way through the tunnels. After several turns, they found themselves moving away from the center.

"Are you sure you didn't make a mistake?" Hollin asked. "It seems as if the circles are getting larger, rather than shorter."

"That's because we're moving away from the center," Vesten said. "Don't fear to go back to go forward—remember?"

Eventually they made the last turn and found themselves moving down a long, straight corridor that brought them to an arch with double, black, iron doors. They were unlocked and the company passed through them by pushing against them. A terrible cold wind greeted them as they entered, and their ears were invaded by the creaking of rushing hinges, bent back on themselves. The doors open inward, into a large, circular chamber.

Statues of kings, long dead, lined the walls. Vesten felt that the eyes of the statues were watching him, and a cold shiver ran through him. He noticed a large spiral stairway that rose up, in the center of the room. It rose through the stone ceiling overhead.

"We made it! Just as Vesten said," Hollin shouted with joy. "Those stairs must lead up and out of the Stygian Hole?"

Hollin leaped forward toward the stairs, but before he could get very far, he was gripped by a terrible dread that sent an icy chill up his spine. There was something else in that chamber. They were not alone. An evil presence could be felt waiting for them. Hollin froze in place just as a large, black, wolf-like creature lunged out of the darkness of the chamber at him. Its huge jaws snapped close, tearing Hollin's walking cape as he leaped backward, out of the way of the deadly fangs, falling to the floor and rolled away to safety.

Anna screamed in terror and the others rushed at the giant wolf, confusing it long enough for Hollin to return to his feat.

They had never seem such a creature as this wolf. Its shoulder reached six feet high and its five-inched fangs snapped at the foul, reeking darkness. The creature's eyes burned red and flashed with a wicked intelligence that revealed its malice for all things that walked in the Light. Around its thick, fury neck was a collar made from Pure Gold. It was attached to a chain made of the same metal. The wolf-demon was securely bound and served as a guard against all those who had discovered the secret of the maze and made it this far. The wolf made it impossible for anyone to reach the stairs and escape.

"It's Fernos," Vesten said. "He is a demonic wolf-creature. Legends tell of three warriors, Laring, Dormi and Gellnor, who were dispatched by the Lords of the Light to hunt him out and place him into captivity. They chased Fernos into the dark cavities of the earth and caught him in the Stygian Hole. They forged that collar and chains and placed him here. It's said that he feeds on the souls of those who have died while trying to pass through the Stygian Hole.

"How are we going to get pass him?" asked Princess Valenda.

"Legends say Fernos can only be killed by the power of the

Light," Rowena said. "He's evil and only good can destroy evil. I remember my mother telling my brother of the legend of Fernos. I always thought it was just a tale that was told to amuse children."

"Most legends have more fact about them than fantasy," Vesten said. "The legends that are passed down to us are racial memories that have been turned to myths."

Rowena looked at Vesten. "You can kill him with your sword," she said. "No ordinary weapon can harm him and no ordinary man can kill him. But you are allied to the Light and your sword was forged in the Light itself. You can kill him, but it won't be easy. Fernos will recognize you immediately and he won't permit you to get near enough to deliver a killing blow."

"Then we must distract him so that Vesten can get close enough to kill the demon-wolf," Brim said.

Everyone drew their weapons and fanned out along the edge of the circular chamber until they completely surrounded the wolf-demon. They began teasing Fernos, taunting him and trying to confuse him, so that Vesten could make his move. But Fernos would not be so easily distracted, and seem to know instinctively who Vesten was. He could smell the blood of Truemans, and knew that the purity of the Light was especially strong in the blood that coursed through Vesten. Fernos' eyes flashed with both hate and fear. He also could smell the scent of his own possible death and it sent him into a panic. His great jaws snapped wildly as he roared frantically and tried to reach Vesten, and the chain around his neck caused him to reel up on his hinge quarters, as his front legs pawed the air before him.

The others grew bolder with every minute. They repeatedly jabbed their swords at Fernos, but their blows were of no interest to the wolf. His black coat of fur was as strong as steel. Brim was determined to give Vesten the chance he needed. He could hear a voice speaking to him, telling him what must be done. Brim knew that if they were ever going to get out of the Stygian Hole, Vesten would have to kill the wolf-demon, and it was up to him to give him his chance.

His face was hardened and his blue eyes burned with determination. His muscles strained by his will, which seemed superhuman. He took a deep breath to fill his lungs and then jumped out in front of the others. The chamber echoed from his battle cry, as he landed right on the wolf's back. The beast reared up and tried to shake Brim off his back, but Brim held on, desperately grabbing the wolf's fur with his left hand. With his right hand, he raised his sword and was about to plunge it into the wolf's throat when the wolf raised his head and snapped his jaws down on Brim's right hand. With one quick toss of its head, it sent Brim flying into the air with his severed hand still in his mouth.

Only Rowena noticed that Vesten seem to shine with a brilliant light. It looked as if he grew in size and stature. She rubbed her eyes, not trusting her sight. When she opened them and looked again, she saw Brim on the wolf's back. It reared up and shook its head, sending Brim flying. Then, from one end of the hall, she noticed Vesten moving with the speed of an arrow right at Fernos. His sword was burning with a golden fire as he leaped at the demon-wolf. He plunged the sword deep into the under side of the wolf's neck just as it tossed Brim off its back. Vesten's sword cut deep into the wolf, as green blood splattered to the floor, bubbling and hissing. A terrible howl filled the hall as the red lights in the wolf's eyes disappeared. The huge body fell dead to the floor.

Brim laid still on the chamber floor. Anna ran to him and picking up his handless arm, she took her torch and placed the severed wrist into the flames, preventing Brim from bleeding to death, while he was unconscious. She then reached into her pouch and pulled out several dry leaves. Crumbling the leaves together, she placed them on the burnt flesh and then taking a piece of cloth, she rapped it around the wrist.

"Brim!" Hagrim shouted as he knelt beside his brother. "Will my brother be alright?"

"Of course he will," Anna said in her soft, reassuring voice. She had a natural way of relieving grief with mere words. It was more the way she spoke then the words themselves that made her a natural born healer. "The herbs that I've applied will prevent infection, but I need to prepare a proper poultice soon."

"Then we can't remain here a minute longer," Vesten said.

Anna took a small pouch out of her bag and opened it just below Brim's nose. The smell caused him to cough back to consciousness.

He looked at the bandage on his wrist, but said nothing.

"Are you well enough to travel?" Vesten asked Brim.

"I can follow you to Allomania and back, with one hand just, as well as with two," he said.

"Now I know that Brim is alright," Hagrim said. "It'll take more than the loss of a hand to keep him down."

Vesten ordered everyone up the stairs. Despite his boast, Brim was weak from the lost of blood, and Hagrim and Hollin had to help Brim by placing a shoulder under each of his for support. They climbed up several hundred stairs that led to a wide chamber above the maze. It was filled with warm, morning sunlight that immediately renewed their hopes and their spirits. High above them were long, thin windows that revealed to them the clear, blue sky in the world outside. It was the first sight of the sky that they had seen since they passed through the Hole of Fennoria.

They began running across the hall and passed through the doors that opened onto a small gate. Once through it, they found themselves outside the Stygian Hole once more, finally stepping out, onto the southern slopes of the Axis Mountains. Below, stretching out before them, were the golden fields of the Lothangian province of Palannoria. From these heights they could see the morning mist that covered the land and clung to the sides of the mountains.

The company found an old road that led down into the valley. They smiled as they walked, enjoying the morning sun, bathing them in its warmth. They all felt like they could properly breath for the first time since they entered Fennoria. In a short time they were far down the mountainside, and surrounded by evergreen tress that grew there. They stopped within the cover of the trees, near a small mountain spring.

"We'll remain here for a while and tend to Brim's injury," Vesten said. "If we should live through the battles that we have yet to face, men will someday remember Brim's unselfish deed forever as the 'Tale of Brim's Deed.' From this day forth, the name of Brim the Bold will be synonymous with unselfish sacrifice."

Anna was busy making two fires with the help of Rowena, while Princess Valenda, Hollin and Hagrim were standing guard. The girls filled two leather bags with water from the spring and set them boiling over the fire. In one bag Anna placed some willow bark and herbs to make a tea that would help to relieve the pain and dull the senses. It would also reduce any fever that Brim might develop. In the second bag Anna dropped some crushed, dried hollyhock roots, Iris roots and alder bark from her healing bag, to create a poultice that she would apply to Brim's wrist. The combination would reduce swelling and inflamation, and purify the injury.

"This will have to do until we get some better medical attention for Brim's injury," Ana said as she wrapped his wrist in a clean dressing. "The tea will make him sleep and he shouldn't be moved for several hours."

"Then we'll remain here for a while to let him rest," Vesten said. "That'll give us all the opportunity to sleep and perhaps find some food?"

Hagrim and Hollin went into the woods to hunt and forage, while Princess Valenda remained on guard. Vesten walked to the edge of the clearing and looked up at the mountains behind him. He reached into his pocket and pulled out the Yellow Stone. As he held it in his hand, he thought about the surge of power he felt when he attack Fernos, and realized that it came from the stone. The stone began to vibrate as he held it in his hand. As he watched it, Vesten's thoughts turned to Blondor. He looked up at the blue sky and spoke. "Blondor, my old friend. You brought us into that stinking hole because you knew that your destiny laid there, but where are you now? How can we continue without you? I don't know the answer. I only know that we must go on."

"I miss him too," a voice spoke from behind Vesten.

When he turned around he saw Rowena standing behind him.

He looked into her tearful eyes and smiled, and reached out to embrace her. She immediately walked into his arms as they closed around her.

"You knew, didn't you?" Vesten asked Rowena. "You warned him several times. I too warned him of the dread that I felt about the Stygian Hole, but he wouldn't listen. I don't think it was out of stubbornness that caused him to ignore our warnings? I think he also saw the shadow of death that awaited him within the Stygian Hole, but he was willing to chance walking into it with no concern for himself. He always put the welfare of others before his own. He knew we had to complete our quest, and if he had to sacrifice himself to achieve that end, he was unafraid to do so. And now he has been taken from us."

Vesten released Rowena and stepped back. He raised his sword and held it before him. "Farewell, Blondor. Your wisdom and guidance will surely be missed. Your ways were hard and often you seemed distant and unapproachable, but you never failed us, not even in death. May we have the courage to live up to your example?"

Vesten then turned and looked down, into the valley below. "Behind us is the past, but before us lies our destiny. Though the past cannot be undone, we have it in our power to make the future a better place for all of us, and for all of Truemankind. Just as Thrangraal predicted. 'The emperor with sword in hand, out of the north, has returned.'"

The two of them looked down into the lands below. The morning mists had disappeared and revealed the majestic spectacle that stretched out before them. Fertile fields and peaceful woods could be seen in the distance with green patches. Down the center of the valley they could see a silver ribbon of a river. The growing sunlight danced on its watery surface like diamonds sprung on a silver chain. The shadows of the mountain slowly shrank as the sun rose in the eastern sky, bathing the thick, lust valley floor with its golden rays. In the distance they could see the purple mountains that surrounded and embraced the valley in its protective arms. A cool breeze blew down from the mountains behind them, and poured into the lands below, as if showing them the way for them to take. The valley seemed to be blessed with a peacefulness that extended across these northern regions of Palennoria.

Book Four:

Fire and Ice

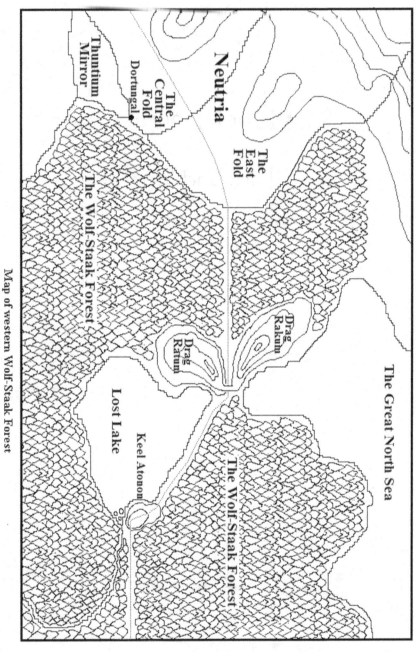

Map of western Wolf-Staak Forest

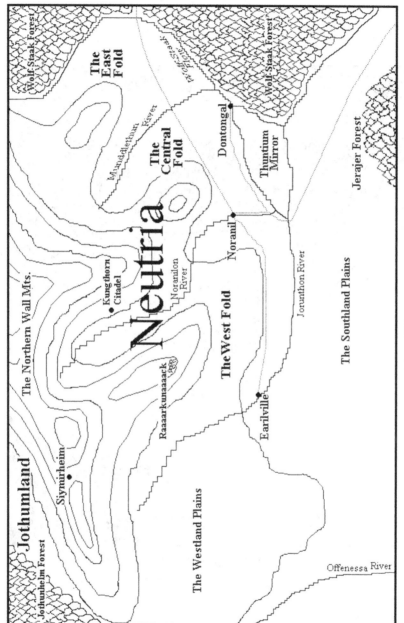

Map of Neutria

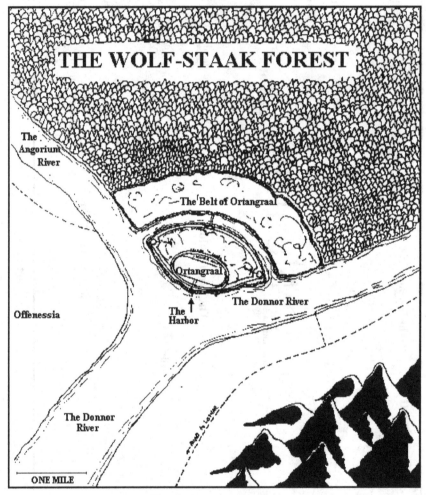

The Ortangraal Fortress

Maxthoium Riders from Tillenia.

Chapter One:
Faerie Hill and Tales

For three days Arlindor led them on the forest road that ran parallel to the shores of Lost Lake. To their right, the forest grew right to the edge of the road, but its branches did not cover it. The trees were large and gray, with huge, twisting trunks and branches that were covered with moss and vines. Behind them, as always, lurked the impenetrable darkness that filled the Wolf-Staak Forest. But the Highway was free from the woods' eternal blackness. The road itself did not pass into the forest, and during the day the warm rays of the sun reflected off the mirror-like waters of the lake. Its surfaced rippled gently against the shore that was no more than a dozen feet from the road. At night they lit a fire, and slept under the star-filled heavens that seemed to ease their apprehension. The weather grew progressively cooler, especially at night, as a northerly wind blew off the lake, causing them to pull out their winter clothing from their backpacks.

It was early in morning and the sun had not yet peeked over the eastern horizon when Magin walked around the small encampment that they had made on the shore of the lake. It was exceptionally cold that Harvestime 30, and Huck and Rullin did not feel much like getting out of their blankets.

"Come on, lads, rise and shine," Magin said laughingly as he nudged the boys, awake. "The sun will soon be up before you, and if you don't get up now, you'll miss breakfast."

The boys rolled over and rubbed the sleep from their eyes. Rullin slowly rose, wrapping his blanket around himself, to protect himself from the morning chill. He got up and sat down next to the fire with Huck right behind him.

Ever since they left Keel Amon, they were moody and depressed because they could not go with Blondor and the others, to rescue Palifair and Tom. They were eaten up with guilt, and felt that they had broken their oaths to stick by Palifair through thick and thin. They often found themselves talking about everything they had passed through, since they found the White Stone with Palifair in the North Mark.

"I wish that we had never left Wissenval," Huck said. "We've proven ourselves to be of no help at all. We're just baggage for the others to worry about."

"Don't talk like that, Huck," Rullin said. "It was Mr. Blondor himself who wanted us to come along, and if Mr. Blondor thought that it was important enough for us to come on this quest, then he must have known what he was doing."

"I hope you're right, but for the love of the Mark, I can't see what possible good our presence has been so far?" Huck said under his breath as he wolfed down his breakfast.

Rullin's mind flashed back to the night in the northern woods, when the night sky lit-up and they found the White Stone. Everything that had happened to them on their adventure raced through his mind: the meeting at the Unicorn Inn, their journey through the Mark and the attack by the Horzugal at Gateburg and again, before Bridgetown. The attack by the trogs and the wild boars, and the council at Wissenval all flashed through his thoughts. He wished he was back in the enchanted valley of Wissenval, or at least, back in the Mark eating a proper breakfast of eggs and bacon with pancakes and hot buttered biscuits. Instead, he was in the middle of the most forbidding forest in all of New Earth, eating burnt bread and month-old, dried sausages, surrounded by danger. Why were he and the others chosen? He kept asking himself. Didn't Blondor say that things just don't happen by chance? That there were hidden reasons for things turning out the way they do. As hard as his young mind tried to ponder the reasons for things turning out the way they did, the less he could understand the events that had unfolded. The druids seemed to have the ability to see things that people like himself, could not. They had the ability to glimpse images of the future. Did they see something in his and Huck's future? If they did, they were not saying. Rullin then felt a warmth on his face and looked up to see the morning sun shining brightly over the trees in the east.

After everyone finished their breakfast and packed their gear, they were off once more. Olaf and Pettin were walking out front, with Arlindor right behind them. The druid had not passed this way in many years. He was not a wanderer like Blondor, and preferred to remain in the Mark. Much had changed about the landscape since he last traveled this way, but the Tillenian woodmen seem to know the woods well enough, even this far west of Jassinburg. In fact, all of Wolf-Staak, east of Dullin's Gate was considered the responsibility of the Tillenians. They were charged with keeping the roads safe, and could make use of the forest's resources, especially the lumber and herbs they found there.

The boys walked behind Arlindor and behind them came Gordon and finally Milland, with his sharp eyes and ears, and his ability to read the language of the forest.

One section of the forest seemed pretty much like the next to the boys. Both the rows of trees and the calm waters of the lake seemed not to change. Despite all their walking, it seemed to Rullin like they were standing still, if not for the blisters on his feet to remind him of how far he had traveled.

Later that morning, a thick fog had rolled in from the lake. They could barely see more than ten feet ahead of them as they walked along the shore. The air was damp and cut through their winter clothing, right to the bone. By late morning the fog began to break up once more, and the sun was soon shining brightly. They walked for the rest of the day, and stopped only for their afternoon meal. They continued to walk until the sun began to sink behind the distant misty shapes of the mountains that could be seen on the western shore of the lake. If not for the rising peeks of the Drag-Ratum, which meant, the Mountain of the Sun, there was no indication that they had made any progress through the forest.

It was late when Arlindor stopped the company. "It's getting late and we had better find a place to put-up for the night," he said. "Tonight is the eve of the Hollow Mass, and it's not wise to travel through these woods on this night."

Rullin remembered the tales that were told in the Mark of the Hollow Mass. It was the night when the spirits of the dead left their graves and walked among the world of the living. The very thought of spending this night in the Wolf-Staak terrified him. Rullin thought about the tale of the headless rider of Timberlandgrove, who was jumped by thieves while passing through the Middle Lawn Woods to Harlinburg, on this night. They cut off his head and buried him in an unmarked grave. The body was eventually discovered and reburied, but no one had ever found where they had buried his head. Ever since, on Hollow Mass Eve Night, it is said that his headless spirit rose from his grave and rode across the country looking for his missing head. He would kill anyone he met out on this night, cut off his head and ride away with it. Rullin shivered as he thought about the story.

"There's as small hill not far from here," Pettin said. "It's about two miles from here and is on the lake side of the road, so it's not inside the forest. It's high enough so that its crown is above the woods' roof, and there is cover on its slopes from unwelcome eyes that might be searching the night."

"That sounds like a good place to make camp for the night," Arlindor said. "We should make for the hill."

"But there's something else," Pettin said. "My people believe that the hill is an Alfen Hill. It's thought to be a home of the faerie spirits of the woods. It's said that the faerie folk gather within such hills, hold great feasts there and made merry. Wild singing and dancing take place at these faerie parties, and they do not like to be disturbed, but they are no friends of the Darkness."

"Then we'll take care not to disturb these forest spirits," Arlindor said, as he turned and led the others up the road.

They continued to travel along the road for another half-hour when the road began to veer away from the lake. The ground began to rise and now they could see the large, dark hump of a hill standing before them in the black of the night. The road curved around it to hill's left slope where the forest edge stopped at the foot of the hill, as if it feared the mount. The hill was not devoid of trees, and a scattering of very old holly, oak and ash trees grew higher up its slopes, close to the top of the hill. They all appeared very ancient and their trunks were thick and covered with moss. The branches seemed all twisted and tangled from the weather that blew off the lake. But they appeared to possess a quality about them that invited one to walk among them. It was apparent from that feel that they were not part of the forest, but that they belonged to the domain of the hill.

As Pettin led them off the road and up the side of the hill, Rullin had an unnerving feeling that they were being watched. He felt as if someone, or something, was aware of their presence. He looked at Arlindor to see if the druid was aware of anything out of the ordinary, but the druid seemed oblivious to the sensation.

When they finally reached the top of the hill, they were standing among a large growth of trees. They came to a halt within a small clearing surrounded by holly trees that overlooked the western slope of the hill. There was a single, large ash tree that was taller and grandeur than the rest of the tress on the hill. Rullin looked up at its dark form in the night. It stood silhouetted against the night sky and crowned with a hallo of stars. Rullin could see the roof of the forest that stretched out to the north and east from where they were on the hilltop. To the west and south the mirror surface of the lake was still and sparkled with the reflected light of the stars overhead.

Huck joined Rullin as he looked out across the lake. They could see the a few clouds gathering in the western sky. The clouds appeared illuminated with the last rays of the sun that had sunk behind the surface of the western horizon. They could see two mountain peaks under the clouds. The larger one was closer and appeared red in color. It appeared as if it was on fire. The smaller peek was further away and had a blueish color. The contrast between them appeared hypnotic.

"That one there, the reddish one, is called Drag Ratum," Arlindor said, causing the boys to jump.

"Oh. It's you, Arlindor," Rullin said. "You startled me."

The druid ignored what Rullin said as he stood, staring off into the west.

"It means, 'the Mountain of the Sun,'" Arlindor explained. "The other peak is named Drag Rakum, 'the Mountain of the Moon.' It was there that the men of Keel Amon built great towers and kept great fires burning. Sacrifices were made to both the moon and the sun. The towers were so large that an entire town could be housed in the base of each other."

"Are the towers still there?" asked Huck.

"No," Arlindor said.

"What happened to them?" asked Rullin.

"The men of Keel Amon were followers of the Light and thus built a great civilization, but there eventually grew among them a cult of priests who were seduced by the Darkness," Arlindor began to explain. "It's said that they had formed a secret alliance with the Kreel priests of Allomania. They took possession of the towers and set-up shrines to the Demons of the Darkness. In time they grew in numbers and caused a chasm to divide the civilization of Keel Amon, between those who followed the Light and those who followed the Darkness. War broke out and civil strife filled all the lands under their rule. Brother killed brother and son fought against father until the lands were drenched in blood.

"Then there appeared a great man by the name of Dullin. He walked in the Light and the Light was strong in him. Many good men looked to him to defeat the followers of the Darkness and put an end to the strife. He called on the Lords of the Light to give him the strength to drive the followers of the Darkness out of Keel Amon. A female messenger was sent from the Lords of the Light and appeared before Dullin. She told him that the Lords of the Light would bestow upon him knowledge that could defeat the Darkness, but first he would have to make a sacrifice. When he asked what kind of sacrifice, she told him to hang himself upon the tallest ash tree that he could find on this hill. He should hang from the tree by tying a rope about his hands and hang from one of its branches for nine days and nights. Dullin did as he was told and after nine days and nights, his followers cut him loose. He explained to them what the Lords of the Light had revealed to him while he hung from the tree. What he learned was the secret knowledge of Rune-writing. He used that great knowledge to defeat the followers of the Darkness in Keel Amon.

"By using the knowledge of the Rune-writing, Dullin was able to cause the earth itself to tremble, causing the hills of Drag Ratum and Drag Rakum to shake. The cliffs between the mountains collapsed and filled the channel that opened into the Great North Sea to the north, creating Lost Lake, as it is now. The earth tremors also caused the towers to collapse and all those who followed the Darkness were either killed or fled. Dullin and his followers then built a great gate and stone wall to control the traffic that moved east and west. In time they were able to build another great civilization on the shores of Lost Lake."

"What kind of people were they?" asked Rullin. The boys were enthralled by Arlindor's story. For the first time the druid's face broke into a smile. He led them back to the others, who had already set-up camp for the night. They were gathered around a fire and cooking their evening meal as Arlindor and the boys joined them, sitting around the fire with them.

"They were a glorious race of tall men and beautiful women," Arlindor said, as he continued his tale. The others began listening to the druid. "They were proud and courageous. Some claimed they were the first of the race of Truemans to settle in the southern lands. Their skin was fair and their hair dark and they possessed eyes that were as gray as steel. They cut the trees of the forest and built great cities along the coasts of Lost Lake and the Great North Sea. The civilization they built was filled with the Light and they waged war against trogs that invaded the forest, and drove the Kreel out of the woods and into the lands to the south. For a long time their civilization flourished, but in time they grew rich and their wealth corrupted them. Their greed made them weak, and eventually, the Darkness returned to the men of Keel Amon. As wealth corrupts and overwhelming wealth corrupts overwhelming, so the men of Keel Amon were corrupted. The richest no longer felt a bound of blood with their fellow countrymen, and used their wealth to acquire power. They used that power to enslave their countrymen and eventually did the unforgiving–they conducted heinous experiments on those they enslaved. They learned to mix the blood of Truemans with the beasts in the wild and in the fields, creating a race of were-men."

"Were-men?" Rullin said. "You and Blondor mentioned them before. Tell us more about them."

"The legends of many lands tell of men who have the power to take on the shape of animals," Arlindor said. "Some use these powers for good while others use them for evil purposes. This was true of the men of Keel Amon."

"Whatever happened to them?" asked Huck.

"The men of Tillenia will tell you that their descendants still roam the darkest regions of the Wolf-Staak. On certain nights one can hear their cries, or so some men say. There are even a few men who claim that they have run into such creatures, fighting them off like one would a pack of wild animals."

"That's right," Olaf said in his gruff voice. "My father once told me that one evening, he and his comrades, while out cutting lumber, ventured deep into an unexplored section of the forest, and there they were attacked by such creatures. Men-like they were, he said, and possessing heads and legs of wild animals, but they walked upright, like men."

"Yes. Even I have heard of such tales," Gordon said. "But never have I seen one, or actually spoke to anyone who had. But there are plenty of tales by Marklanders who claim that they had seen such creatures in the Twin Woods or in the Northern Woods."

"I sure hope we don't run into any of these were-men," Huck said as he piled more wood on the fire.

That night everyone huddled around the fire while they ate their small, but hot meal, and washed it down with the last of the golden drink made by Anna.

"If only we were out of this dreadful forest," Huck said to Rullin. "It seems like there is no end to it."

"It does feel like it's eternal," Rullin said. "It feels like it blankets the entire surface of the world."

"Once it was eternal, or nearly eternal," Milland said. "Long before the race of Truemans wandered down from the frozen regions of the north, and after the great Hell Fires had subsided, and the world was barren of all green life and laid naked to the sun, there was one called Kernunon. He was tall and mighty, like the redwood trees and strong as the oak, and he stood as straight as a cedar tree. He was clad in green and brown, and walked over the barren surface of New Earth. His long legs carried him far and he was able to travel hundreds of miles in a single day. But what he saw caused him great sorrow, for the land was black and gray from the terrible fires that scorched its surface, and from the molten rock that had been vomited up from deep inside the subterranean regions. He lamented long and hard, but eventually Geria heard his cries and brought the rains that filled the great oceans of the world with clear, cool, life-giving waters. Under the heat of the sun, the water vapors rose into the air and caused great thunderstorms that poured down rain on the world. The land was once again cris-crossed with rivers and streams. The waters flowed down into the low-lying areas, filling them with seas and lakes.

"Kernunon was glad, for the waters felt good. He discovered a small plant growing and he nurtured it until it grew into a mighty tree. From its branches he collected hundreds of different kinds of seeds. He wished to spread the green to the rest of the world, and began traveling the whole surface of the world, dropping seeds as he walked. In time, the entire surface of the world was covered with green grass, bushes, trees and flowers. This is why some refer to New Earth as Kernunon's Garden.

"Kernunon considered the trees his children, and he spoke to them and taught them about the Light and the danger of the Darkness. In time, that forest came to be known as the Wolf-Staak, but it was much larger than it is today. It once reached from the east coast of New Earth and stretched as far as the Western Wall

Mountains. Many say that Kernunon still lives, or that he sleeps beneath the Wolf-Staak, and that he is waiting for the time when the forest will shrink to nothingness, and then he will wake once more and replant the Wolf-Staak."

"You said he spoke to the trees," Rullin said. "Do you speak to the trees?"

Milland smiled at Rullin. "Yes, lad, I do speak to the trees. Once most Trueman knew how to speak to the trees. Today, only a few still possesses that knowledge, and even fewer trees know how to speak to Truemans. There was a time, long ago, when Trueman and the trees knew how to converse with each other, but that time is now lost in ancient lore and myth."

"Just as we lost the art of speaking with the stone," Magin said.

"Stones?" asked Huck. "People can speak to rocks?"

"Once we knew how to read the language of the bones of the earth," Magin said. "Stones are also alive with the Life-Force of the Cosmos, in their own fashion. Haven't you lads ever heard of the walking rocks of Harlinland?"

"Yes I have," said Huck. "It's common knowledge among the Locks of Lockland that some stones move all by themselves."

"That's right," Magin continued. "It seems that when the Mark districts were originally drawn-up, the people of Harlinland collected the huge stones that laid about the landscape to create a stone fence to mark the boundaries. It took them a better part of two weeks to build the stone walls. When it was over, the people were pleased with their work. The next day there was a great commotion in the town of Harlinburg. Farmer Tim Groughwood came into town all excited. It seemed that when he went out to his fields, which bordered the stone walls they had just built, he found that the walls had disappeared. The stones laid all about the fields and the walls were gone. All about the fields were long gouges cut into the earth leading away from where the wall stood, as if someone had dragged the stones to where they were originally found.

"When the town folk came to see for themselves, they were shocked at what they saw. All the stones were scattered across the fields, as if someone had dragged them away from the wall. Frightened, they called a council and agreed to rebuild the wall. This time they set a guard over it, both day and night. But when they returned the next day to begin work on the wall, they discovered that the stones had moved even farther away. Many were too frightened to work or rebuild the wall. Some were even too frightened to touch the stones. Supernatural, is what some people said. Wraiths, were responsible for the movement of the stones, others said. The stones were too heavy for just a few people to have moved in one night, and there were no signs of footprints or wagon wheels anywhere.

"The town folk went back to Harlinburg, all except farmer Tim Groughwood and his friend, Danmoor Tumblewind. They decided to sleep out in the fields that night, determined to make sure that no one disturbed their stones even further. They found two long, flat stones lying side by side that they used for beds and soon fell asleep on them. Then, when it was well pass midnight, they each woke and were thrown off the stones they were sleeping on. Something, it seemed, had shaken them off the stones. When they looked up, they found that the stones had moved. Both Danmoor and Tim jumped up and ran as fast as they could back to Harlinburg, and told the others of the moving stones.

"Finally, the good people of Harlinland decided that they would not disturb the stones again, and let them move back to where they wanted to stand. They eventually made new walls from stones that they imported from the quarry that did not mind being used for fence building.

"Today, the stones can be found in their original locations and have never been moved by the people of Harlinland. If you ever get a chance to travel through Harlinland, you will notice the scattered stones throughout the fields of its farms, standing upright. Many of them are located right in the middle of the farmers' fields, or yards, and the folk of Harlinland will rather plow around them rather than try and move them. They even take good care of the stones and treat them like good neighbors. They believe they bring them good luck."

All that evening they continued to exchange stories and

folk tales. The boys loved hearing the stories and never tired of listening to them, even if they heard them before. Gordon began telling them of the tale of the pirate raids of 1999 of the Second Age.

"It was late on a summer night when Ethon Silverbirch was returning from the local tavern, the Silver Dragon. As he rode his horse under the star-speckled night sky, he turned down an old dirt road that led to his farmhouse near the shore. The moon was full that night, but it was setting early. The road took him high on top of the cliffs along the shoreline. Ethon looked out onto the ocean as the gentle waves rolled up onto the beaches, at the foot of the cliffs. It was then that he noticed several small, black shapes on the surface of the water, far out to sea. They appeared to be ships, but there were no fishing boats out that late at night. He stopped to try and get a clearer view, and assured himself that he was not mistaken. After watching them for several minutes, he was convinced that they were indeed ships and were heading toward the Green Towers Bay. He continued to watch them as they sailed closer to shore and soon he could make out, under the golden rays of the moon, black sails that were commonly used by the pirates of the south seas. He had heard about such pirate ships in stories that old sailors told in the town of Seagull Nest, about twenty miles to the south of his farm, but he never thought he would ever see pirate ships this far north. But if they were the same pirate ships that plagued the shores of South Lothangia, he knew he had better sound the warning to the people of the Twin Towers Harbor. The pirates were known to be a fierce and barbaric people, who killed and raped their victims, and sold the women and children into slavery.

"Ethon turned his horse around and rode like the wind. His swift steed took him through one small town after another, as he rode through the peninsula known as the Boar's Tooth. 'Pirates! Pirates! Black sails in the bay!' he shouted as he rode, causing everyone to wake and gather their weapons. For several hours he rode on, shouting and calling the good people of the Mark to arms. By the time he had reached the Twin Towers Harbor, the whole country was awake and about, forming into militias. From

Elmwood in the north, and as far west as Applemorton, and south toward South Corner's Dock, the whole East Mark was up and ready to meet the unwelcome visitors before they ever set foot on Mark soil.

"When the Black Pirates from the south finally landed on the southern coast of the Green Towers Bay, they were greeted by an armed citizenry that ambushed them and cut them down to the last man. The Marklanders then boarded their ships and sank them in the bay. The place is still referred to as the Pirates' Landing.

"Ethon Silvebirch became a hero, and a statue was eventually erected in his honor for his courageous ride through the countryside on that fateful night, long ago. He saved the East Mark from the terrible fury of the Black Pirates of the South Seas, and the people of the East Mark still honor his memory every year on that day."

After several hours of storytelling, everyone turned in, except for Arlindor, who stood guard. Huck looked out toward the lake one more time before turning in for the night. As he stood there watching the still, dark waters, he imagined he could see great ships with blue and gold sails gently floating across its glossy surface. He blinked his eyes, not believing what he saw, and looked over at the druid, who was sitting under a great ash tree. Arlindor gave no hint that he was aware of any ships, and when Huck looked again, they were gone. He quickly returned to his blanket and buried himself under it, next to Rullin, and closed his eyes. He wished he was back in the Mark, in his own comfortable feather bed.

Soon Huck was fast asleep and deep in dreams. He dreamed that the forest was alive with music and song, as thousands of tiny figures, beautiful and pixie-like, danced about the air with wings, like hummingbirds. Huck suddenly woke. He sat-up and discovered it was late. He could still see Arlindor on guard, sitting under the ash tree, motionless and still, as if he was made of stone. Huck rubbed his eyes and then turned to look at Rullin. To his surprise, he discovered that Rullin was missing. He looked about and saw his friend crawling off into a cluster of holly trees, just as he disappeared into the darkness within.

Huck wanted to call out to his friend, but something prevented him from speaking. Surprising himself, he crawled out of his blanket and followed his friend into the darkness, crawling on his hands and knees.

Huck found his friend in a small clearing that seemed to be filled with a yellow illumination that shined brightly before Rullin, who was in a kneeling position. When Huck reached his friend, he saw a small ring of mushrooms on the ground, all a glow.

Neither of the boys could say a word as they stared at the mushroom ring. The light seemed to fill their minds with music that made them dizzy, as it began to twinkle. Once again Huck could hear singing of the most haunting kind. All around them, beyond the light, the world was filled with only darkness and nothing else. They were no longer aware of the hill or the forest. There was only the ring of mushrooms, the light and the music.

The twinkling light began to dance about the toadstool ring, slowly transforming into small faerie-like creatures, like the ones that Huck was dreaming about earlier. The ground within the ring disappeared and they could see a hole. From within the hole rose the sound of merriment and song, as a small pixie appeared before them and spoke. His speech was not in words, but of musical notes. Though the boys could not understand his language, they somehow comprehended its meaning. The pixie stared at Rullin and Huck with its big, bright, green eyes and smiled. His smiling, impish face was rather comical and yet, frightening at the same time.

"Greeting, Trueman youths of the world of earth, air, water, ice and fire," Huck heard him say. "My name is Laurinilin. I am King of the Alfen people of the world of shadows and light. My people live in this hill and we call it Derinilin, which means the hill of the spirits of the forest." He then took off his funny, little blue hat with a long yellow feather in it, and bowed low. "Look and see my merry folk, who live on the winds of the world and dance on the passage of time."

The boys looked into the center of the mushroom ring and peered into the hole. Inside they could see a great hall filled with an inviting light that shined brightly, despite the fact that they could see no lanterns or fires within. They could see a great host of faerie folk dancing, singing and making merrily in all the usual ways that the men and women of Truemandom often did.

"We've been watching your party ever since you entered this forest," the pixie king said. "And we have been especially watching you, Master Ashburn. You did not disturb our mushroom ring when you first saw it in the Woodfields, even though you were overcome with the urge to do so. Most mortals could not find the strength or wisdom to contain their inquisitiveness, but you did. And for that, we of the Alfen Folk of the Kingdom of Tuminrivirimon, wish to reward you by giving you this present."

The pixie king pulled out a small, green gem that was suspended on a gold chain and handed it to Rullin. "Take this and keep it close to your heart, and it may help you to turn the tide when you most need to do so. There is more than magic about it, and it could move mountains if the need calls for it, if you catch my meaning?"

Rullin took the necklace and placed it around his neck. He wanted to thank King Laurinilin, but before he could, the king nodded and smiled, as if he could read his thoughts. He then spoke once more to Rullin and Huck and said, "Remember these words, my friends, and remember it well.

"In long forgotten, ancient day,
    When our New Earth was not yet old.
    Neither north ice or south sea bay,
    Saw deep forest and mountain bold.
    The land was bath in burning fires,
    The skies were black with poison dew.
    Smoldering smoke raged still higher,
    And Old Earth gave birth to the New.

    Wars were fought of knights and men,

Light and Darkness in battle's breath.
And fairies danced on age's end,
Then Truemans welcomed hollow death
As evil approaches, north on fast,
To help the outcome of battle-rage.
In four stones speak souls of wisdom past,
To herald in the coming new age."

The pixie king smiled once more at the boys and again he bowed low before jumping back into the hole. The light slowly disappeared and all had returned to normal, black and dark.

Chapter Two:
Dullin's Gate

The next morning Huck and Rullin woke and found Arlindor standing over them, leaning on his staff. His face was gray and drawn, but he said nothing as he looked down at them. Finally, he broke into a smile. They could see his eyes shining, as if he knew something that no one else knew, but he was not telling.

"It's about time the two of you got up," Arlindor said. "I was beginning to think that you would sleep the day away. But then, you must be extra weary this morning? You had an exceptionally trying night, it would see." The druid then turned and walked back to where the last few flames of the fire were crackling under their breakfast. "Come on, or you'll be eating burnt embers this morning."

The boys sat there staring at each other.

"An exceptionally trying night?" Rullin said under his breath. He was afraid to ask Huck if he remembered the events of last night.

Rullin then grabbed at his chest and felt something under his shirt. Reaching inside, he pulled out the green jewel that King Laurinilin had given him. "Then it wasn't just a dream after all?"

"Do you remember last night?" Huck asked.

"Most of it," Rullin said, as he got up and tucked the jewel back inside his shirt, and then began folding his blanket and put it away. "But I can't remember how we got back to our blankets."

"Neither can I," Huck said.

"Come on, lads! We can't wait all day for you two little pixies!"

Magin shouted as he pulled his beard and his round belly bounced with laughter.

The boys went over to join the others. "Pixies?" Huck said. "I wonder why he called us that?"

"How long will it take to reach Dullin's Gate?" Gordon asked.

"About thirty-six hours if we're lucky and not delayed," Arlindor said.

"Delayed? I don't think I like the sound of that?" Magin said. "What could possibly delay us? We haven't seen any indication of danger since we left Kell Ammon."

"I don't know, but I think I don't like the feel of the forest this morning," Arlindor said. "The Wolf-Staak is not going to let us off as easy as it has, this last week, without some surprise planned for us before we leave this sea of leafy darkness. I fear that Dullin's Gate might be watched?"

"Not by trogs, I hope," Rullin said.

"Maybe trogs, maybe something else? The druid said.

"Something else? What could that be?" Huck asked.

"There are more horrors that dwell under the roof of this forest than you can imagine," Arlindor said with a grim smile.

As they were preparing to depart, Arlindor saw Olaf standing perfectly still, as if he was one of the old holly trees that he was standing under. The druid, accompanied by Gordon and Milland walked over to the man-hulk.

"What's the matter?" the druid asked the huge Tillenian.

Olaf did not stir for a few seconds and then finally spoke. "Don't you hear it? The silence. There are no usual forest sounds, not even the bone-chilling cries of the unknown."

"Yes, it is strangely still," Milland said as he listened with his exceptional hearing.

"When you bring a Tillenian woodman with you, it's wise to heed his warnings, especially when traveling through a forest," Arlindor said.

"The voice of the ancients cries to us, beware and hurry," Olaf said in his deep voice.

"And I like not what the trees tell me, or should I say, refuse to tell me," Milland said. "They are rotten with the Darkness and refuse to give up what they know."

"We'd better take Olaf's warning to heart, and move out at once," Arlindor said. "The sooner we reach Dullin's Gate, the better. This part of the forest is now filled with malice toward all Truemans."

The air was unusually chilly that day. Summer had long departed. As they descended the hill, they found that a damp fog had rolled off the lake during the night, and now it lingered among the trees of the forest and across the road. They walked slowly and closed together, and could only see about ten feet ahead of them. Even the light from Arlindor's staff could not roll the fog back. The day was long and uneventful, but the fog lingered on, to almost the noon hour. They stopped twice to rest and eat along the way, remaining on the road at all times.

The ground gradually rose as they got closer to the mountains, which meant they were getting closer to Dullin's Gate with every step they took. The road was dark, but not as black as the Highway was during the first stretch of the forest road that ran between Jassinburg and Keel Ammon. Arlindor led the way with his staff that burned with a greenish-yellow light, so they could see where they were going.

That night they slept in total darkness on the road and once again Huck and Rullin were overtaken by the gloom and depression that had plagued them when they first entered the woods. They kept thinking about Palifair and Tom, and wondered if they were all right? Did Blondor reach them yet? And were they still alive? That was unthinkable, Rullin thought. They barely slept a wink that night and huddled close to Arlindor for protection from the dark.

The next morning everyone woke, ate and was back on their way, traveling along the road toward Dullin's Gate. They moved more rapidly now, and it appeared that the forest blackness was beginning to break up. Great trees rolled by them on either side and here and there they could make out glimpses of light that pierced the forest roof, lighting up the woods with a greenish glow that lifted everyone's spirits.

No one spoke as they walked. Pettin and Olaf were in the lead. The forest grew progressively lighter the further they went, but it was accompanied by a deadly silence that frightened them more than the howling and growling and other noises that inhabited the darkness. They grew tense with every step they took, and were overcome with a strange sensation that they were being watched by someone or something unseen, hiding within the woods.

It was late in the morning when they finally passed out of the forest. The trees grew increasingly less dense. They grew in small patches between the bramble and brush that covered the ground. The landscape also grew increasingly rockier with large stones lying about in huge formations. They could now clearly see the sky above them in blue patches. The sun kept disappearing and reappearing behind the clouds, overhead. They walked on, passing through a growth of tall birch trees when they stopped cold in their tracks. The air was filled with a nerve-shattering cry that was less Trueman, and more beast-like. It slowly trailed off, but was soon answered by another cry from far off.

No one moved. They were frozen where they stood. Then Arlindor joined Pettin and Olaf and they spoke together for a few minutes.

"Those are not the cries of anything that I have ever heard before," Pettin said.

"They can only be the cries of were-men," Olaf said ominously. "And it would seem that they are on the hunt, and we are the hunted."

"When do you think they'll attack?" Arlindor asked.

"Not here," Olaf said. "They'll probably try and box us in with our backs to the wall, when we reach Dullin's Gate. They'll try and force us to move in that direction, not knowing that is exactly where we're headed."

"Good," Arlindor said. "Maybe we can pull a surprise or two of our own?"

They moved on, increasing their speed through the boulders and birch trees. The arms of Dullin's Gate rose on either side, forming great cliffs, and the road led them right up to and in between them. They could occasionally hear the sounds of movement on either side, but could see nothing through the trees. Sounds of grunts and squealing grew steadily louder, and the cliffs could easily be seen above them, tall and smooth.

They came out onto a clearing, along the northern wall of the cliffs. Arlindor halted the company as they examined the clearing before them. There were no ledges or growths along the walls of the cliffs for the were-men to hide and throw stones down on them. The clearing stretched out about two hundred yards before them. It was grown over with thickets and brush that practically covered the ruins of what once was a small town. The foundations of the buildings and houses could be seen, half buried by the growth. Lying about the clearing was the broken remains of fallen pillars and large blocks of granite and marble.

In the distance they could see, looming up above the ruins, where the two arms of the cliffs joined, two great statues of knights standing two hundred feet tall. They each held in their hands a large sword before them, and though they were worn by time and climate, their faces still displayed the courage and fortitude of the long-forgotten race that built them, frozen for all time in stone. Between them was a passageway, and on each side of the passageway there appeared to be the remains of broken hinges that once held two large doors made of Pure Gold. But the doors were now missing and what fate had befallen them was not known.

"There, before us, you see Dullin' Gate," Arlindor said. "No evil may pass through that gate, for Dullin put into it much of the magic of Kell Ammon when he built it, and that magic was of the Light. If we can make it through them, we'll be safe from that which stalks us."

Suddenly, there were sounds of howling and growling all about them. From behind some bushes, there appeared a creature with the torso of a man and on its broad shoulders was the head of a bull. Its robust form was held up by the hindquarters of the bull. It stood there for a moment, facing them and shaking its head with two, large horns jotting out from either side. It stomped once of its hoofed feet on the ground as its red eyes flared with rage, and its black nose snorted its challenge. Then, moments later, there appeared from the woods other were-men. Some were, part wolf, while others were, part boar, goat, ape and bear.

The half-bull snorted once again and then charged. Olaf stepped forward and raised his great mace above his head and brought it down between the horns of the bull-man, crushing his skull like an egg shell, and splattering its brains.

Seeing the limp body of the bull-man sent the other were-men into a rage. Milland pulled out an arrow and sent it flying into the throat of a wolf-man as it leaped at Rullin, causing it to shriek as it died. This caused the rest of the were-men to charge, squealing and grunting in their animal fury as the steel blades of Gordon, Magin and Pettin struck into their twisted were-flesh.

Arlindor shouted for them to follow him, as he led everyone straight toward the passageway with his staff out in front of him. The staff was burning with a green fire that engulfed any unfortunate beast-man that got in his way in a fireball of flame and smoke.

Olaf crushed the skulls of two more were-men with one swing of his mighty mace. Pettin and Magin brought up the rear with their axes, cutting limbs and heads, and sending body-parts flying in every direction. Gordon's sword was stained with the blood of the were-men. He pushed the two boys along and jumped in the way of any were-men that tried to reach them. Then, from above, out of a tall tree jumped an ape-man. It almost landed on Rullin. It grabbed his arm and just as it was about to twist it off, it cried in pain and dropped to the ground. Huck had pulled out his short, silver blade that Gottron had given him and plunged it into the underside of the were-creature's belly. Milland grabbed Rullin and carried him along with Huck following him close behind.

"Hurry! Hurry!" Arlindor shouted. "Stick close together and make for the gate!"

They were now almost there. Just a few dozen feet more and they would be through the gate. The walls of the cliffs were not far apart, only about thirty feet across. Olaf stood in the rear with Pettin and Magin on either side of him. They continued to swing their weapons before them as the were-men charged in mass. Skulls were crushed and torsos severed. Arlindor reached the passageway and stopped to make sure everyone passed through before him. Milland and Gordon brought the boys through it and then turned. Milland sent a dozen arrows flying into the swarm of were-men, as Magin and the two Tillenians slowly fought their way back to Dullin's Gate.

Once everyone was through the gate, the were-men stood just on the other side. They were jumping up and down in a rage, not daring to pass through the gate. Arlindor stood before them and raised his staff before him, as he began to chant. "Thurisaz-Hagalaz, Sowilo-Isa!" The druid continued to chant over and over until the howling and squealing had stopped. Rullin turned to see what had happened. He could see a sea of stone figures on the other side of the gate. Arlindor had turned the were-men into stone.

"Hurry, now! Away from this place!" Arlindor ordered as he pushed everyone along, down the road that cut into the mountain rock. The arms of the mountains rose straight up from the edges of the road, and they could only see a thin strip of blue sky high overhead, as they made their way down the Highway. The cliffs gradually spread wide as they continued westward, and the ground under their feet began to slope downward. Everyone huffed as they ran. Arlindor wobbled behind, much weakened by his deeds at the gate.

"Why are we running?" asked Huck. "I saw Arlindor turn those were-creatures into stone."

"This is not the time for questions," Gordon said as he ran. "Just keep moving. If Arlindor says we must get as far away as possible from Dullin's Gate, then that is exactly what we must do."

Before Huck could say another word, the ground began to shake and rocks fell from the cliffs above. The boys were knocked off their feet. They had never felt anything like it before. When Huck looked up, he saw the mountains shaking as if they had come alive and began to dance. Olaf then swept the boys up and tucked them under each arm and carried them off as his lumbering hulk moved with a speed that seemed impossible for a man of his size. They jumped into an enclave just as the air was filled with an earthshattering *varoom!* When the ground stopped shaking, everyone crawled out of the enclave that was practically buried by dirt and rocks. They could see a gray column of smoke rising high into the sky, from where Dullin's Gate once stood.

"What in the name of the Mark was that?" asked Rullin.

"That was the black hand of the Lord of Darkness moving across the face of New Earth, reaching out to grab us," Arlindor said as he wiped the dirt from his robes. "I feared that the Lord of Darkness knew that his evil servants could not pass through the gate, and failing to trap us, he would devise some other means to destroy us. Therefore, his plan was not to capture us, but to delay us in passing through the gate until he was able to muster the power necessary to bring the walls of the mountains down on us. And if we had escaped the collapse, the were-men would have been able to cross the buried gate and pursue us into the western end of the forest. That's why I had to transform them into stone while I had the chance, to prevent them from following us any further."

"Then let us not remain here much longer," Pettin said. "If the Lord of Darkness was able to send the were-men to attack us, who knows what other servants he will throw at us before we leave the forest? The forest begins again several miles down the road, and there we can perhaps find some cover from his prying eyes?"

"The forest? I'm not so sure I'm in a hurry to enter those woods again," Magin said as Gordon placed a bandage around his head.

"Nor, I," Rullin said.

"This section of the woods is not as heavy with the Darkness, as the woods we have just passed through," Pettin reassured everyone. "Dullin's Gate kept the evil from fully invading it"

"Then there is hope," Milland said.

"There is always hope so long as there is life,"

Arlindor said. "Come! We still have a long road ahead of us before we finally reach Neutria."

In minutes they had set out once more, moving down the road and away from the Mountains of the Sun and Moon. They had to make their way in and out of the fallen boulders that now littered the road. The arms of the mountains steadily declined as they moved westward. It was late when they reached the edge of the woods and a cold wind blew down from the north.

"Winter is approaching fast," Gordon said.

"It comes early to this part of the world," Arlindor said. "But we will be protected from its freezing winds under the cover of the forest."

"Somehow, I find little comfort in that thought," Magin said.

"Have you ever been inside this section of the forest, Arlindor?" asked Milland.

"Not for many years," the druid said. "What do you know of these woods?" Arlindor asked Pettin.

"Not much, I fear," Pettin said. "My people seldom come this far west, except to trade with the Neutrians. We have little need to travel so far west and less need to venture onto the lands beyond the woods. Merchants are our middlemen, and through them we do business with the boatmen of Neutria. It would have been helpful if Princess Valenda had joined us in our quest. This section of the forest is under the protection of her people, according to the agreement between her people and Tillenia. Though I fear that Neutria has been too preoccupied to patrol these woods of late."

"But Princess Valenda is elsewhere and the part she will play will be more useful to our quest than as a guide through the Wolf-Staak," Arlindor said.

"The trees of this section of the woods tell me that they have not been corrupted by the Darkness," Milland said. "There is still good spirit in them. They have the strength to resist the Darkness, though they weep for their kind to the east."

"That might be good news, but I still don't like walking through this forest," Magin said. "There is something old and ancient in their trunks that does not wish to be disturbed, especially by the thumping of Trueman feet. Our passage disturbs their peace. I'll be glad when we come to the land of rolling hills and open fields once more."

"The road will take us straight through the forest and protect us from any further malice that the trees might harbor for us," Arlindor said. "But as you were told when we first entered the woods, don't leave the road. There is no other way to get to Neutria, unless someone has learned how to sprout wings and fly over the forest? If that is the case, I wish they would reveal that secret to the rest of us. If not, then let us begin and say no more of the lore of trees and stone, or the evil that may lurk within these woods."

"Then lead on," Magin said. "But once we start, let us not delay. I wish to reach Neutria as quickly as possible."

"So do we all, stone-surgeon," Arlindor said as he raised his staff and proceeded to walk down the road.

For two days they walked along the road without incident, stopping only to rest once during the afternoon and then again when it got dark, to sleep through the night. They were making good time, about thirty-five miles a day, and ate most of their meals, which were light due to the shortage of supplies, while they walked. The forest was dark and dreary, but no where as black and forbidding as their first stretch through the Wolf-Staak. There were no unnatural sounds that filled their hearts with horror, or unusual cries in the night. They did spot squirrels and rabbits and an occasional owls at night. There were plenty of birds in the trees, and their songs were a welcome relief that raised their spirits and brighten their hearts. Many of the birds were from the north on their way to the southern lands, seeking to escape the creeping cold of oncoming winter that bit at their tails.

The leaves were beginning to turn different shades of red, gold and brown as autumn deepened. Already, in some places, the road was covered with a light blanket of fallen leaves that rustled under their feet as they walked through them. This made the boys feel like they were back in the Mark, walking down one of its many country roads that cris-crossed their homeland. Occasionally they came across places where the sun broke through the forest roof and filled the woods with a green-golden glow, as the multi-colored leaves drank in the golden light.

It was on the morning of the second day out from Dullin's Gate that Arlindor woke from a deep sleep in an excited state. Milland, who was on guard, was startled by Arlindor, and caused everyone to wake-up.

"Arlindor! What is it? What has happened? Are you all right?" Milland cried as he rushed to his side.

The druid could only mumble. "The stone. It has been used."

"What has happened to Pal and Tom?" Rullin asked, fearing the worst.

"Quiet, lads, and let Arlindor speak," Magin said as he held them in his arms to reassure them.

The druid said nothing for a few seconds. He rose to his feet and stood still with his eyes closed. "For some reason, Palifair has used the White Stone," he finally said. "I cannot see why or where, for it is very dark, but for a moment I saw a light and felt a tremor in the Life-Force that caused great pain in the Darkness, but more than that, I cannot tell."

"What could it mean?" Gordon asked.

"It could only mean that Blondor and the others have failed to reach the boys in time, and they have passed into the land of Fennoria," Arlindor said. "But Palifair and Tom have not fallen into the hands of the witch-queen, and have made their escape. The game has begun in earnest, now. We must make for Neutria in hast, for the shadow of Allomania is moving against the boatmen, and already it maybe too late to help them."

Arlindor pushed the company hard for the rest of the way. He was anxious to reach Neutria as soon as possible. No one spoke much, and everyone was very depressed. The fate of their friends weighed heavy on their minds. Rullin could not contain himself and he found his hand reaching for the Alfen jewel under his shirt, as he walked. They made camp on the road that night, and were glad to rest their weary legs. They had traveled forty miles that day and were exhausted. The night passed and sleep came easy to everyone. The next morning they were wakened early and moved on without incident. The ground began to slope downward as they were nearing the forest's edge.

"Listen," Milland said, as he froze. Everyone stood still, expecting some terrible enemy to attack, and were greatly relieved to see Milland smile. "Do you hear it? It's the sound of rushing water. We're getting close to the river, the Wolf-Staak Flow that marks the western border of the forest."

"I don't hear anything but the rustling of leaves in the wind," Huck said.

"That's because you don't have Milland's ears," Arlindor said, jokingly. "But the air is growing fresh, and the woods seem brighter. We're not far from the edge of the forest and will be on Neutrian soil before the day's end."

"That's sure is good news," Huck said with joy, not able to contain himself. "I almost forgot what the outside world looks like."

Eventually, the forest began to visibly thin out. They could feel a cool wind slicing through the trees that blew on their faces and lift their spirits. It was the cold wind of the north blowing down, out of Neutria. Everyone was tired and their feet ached, but they somehow found the strength to march on in a forced pace, determined to reach the river. After two hours, Arlindor stopped and pointed.

"There," Arlindor said. "We've reached our destination."

Up ahead, they could see the light of day through a clearing in the trees.

"I can see the river!" Huck shouted. "Listen, Rullin! Do you hear it?"

Rullin only nodded, not at all excited. He looked behind him, as he held the green jewel under his shirt. He felt as if he was leaving a part of him behind, in the woods.

"Let's not tarry now that we're just yards from the end of the forest," Magin said. "I'm anxious to see the open fields of Neutria." Magin looked about the trees, half expecting them to take offense at his desire to leave their company.

When they reached the opening, they passed through two marble columns that stood about fifty feet high. Before them was a small, stone bridge that stretched across the twenty-foot width of the Wolf-Staak Flow River. Blue waters rushed under the bridge as they made their way across it to the other side. The fields of Neutria stretched out before them like a golden sea of tall grass blowing in the wind, turned yellow from the rays of the autumn sun. In the gray distance they could see pine-covered mountains. A cold, northerly wind blew across the open fields, as the sky was dotted with gray, puffy clouds rimmed in white, cottony edges that gently sailed eastward. The sun shone brightly, welcoming them back to the world of men. This was the East Fold section of Neutria.

When they had finally set foot on Neutrian soil for the first time, they were overtaken with a powerful sense of the awesomeness of the land. It looked like it had not changed for thousands of years, since the time when the Neutrian people first settled here. Its beauty and wonder hid from them the fact that it was a land plagued by the black specter from the south and burned with the fury of war.

Chapter Three:
Dark Clouds Over Northern Lands

A cold wind was blowing down from the mountains to the north, known among the Neutrians as the Northern Wall. The Neutrians claimed that a race of stone giants lived there long ago. They built the mountain range as a barrier against the encroaching race of Truemans thousands of years ago, after the northern lands were ravaged by war among the giants, Truemans and undermen. Winter was coming early this year to Neutria, and the northern frost that crept down in the month of Hollowtime was arriving a month early.

Arlindor was leading his company of travelers across the open fields of the East Fold. They were following the stretch of road that ran from the bridge they crossed, to another bridge that span the river, Munddlethun, separating the Central Fold from the East Fold. The road continued to run westward until it finally reached the city of Noranil, the capital of Neutria, and where King Amthrin resided.

Everyone was tired, but their spirits had risen since they left the darkness and gloom of the forest behind them. Their supplies were all but gone, but they were able to refill their water bags in the streams that they came across, which ran fresh with clean water flowing down from the mountain springs in the north. Game was plentiful in the countryside of the East Fold, and they were able to hunt rabbits that grew as large as dogs in that region of the world. The streams were jumping with fish, and on several occasions, Milland's keen eye and skill with the bow provided wild geese, which were migrating south for the winter, for a meal. Their strength had soon returned, almost as quickly as their spirits. The boys could not help but smile as they walked across the open fields under the autumn sun, despite the increasing cold. They even broke out into a song on several occasions that caused everyone to laugh. The northern winds caused them to breakout the woolen shirts that they had been carrying in their backpacks, and put them on over their lighter clothing for warmth. The winds slapped them hard, causing their faces to redden and blister, but they did not seem to mind. It felt good to be free from the humid gloom of Wolf-Staak.

It was on the evening of the 9th of Turning when Arlindor called a halt just six miles from the river Munddlethun. "Night will be upon us early this evening, and I'm afraid that it will get mighty cold tonight," the druid said. "I want to reach the Muddlethun before halting for the night, but we won't be able to find game for our dinner if we do."

"We all have some meat left over from yesterday's supper," Pettin said. "I say we go on to Munddlethun."

"So do I," Olaf said.

"And I," Magin agreed. "My legs have carried me across the width of New Earth, into the black forest and out again. I think they'll carry me a few miles more before they give out?"

Everyone agreed that they should go on, even Huck and Rullin, who were dead tired, but would not admit it.

"Then it's agreed," Arlindor said. "We'll go on to the river and make camp along its banks, and eat what's left of our food. Perhaps, in the morning, we can catch some fish or water fowl for our breakfast?"

The sun had disappeared in the west when they finally reached the Munddlethun, and the night air did turn cold, just as Arlindor predicted. Everyone had been traveling long and hard with little rest. The boys wanted to collapse where they stood, but Arlindor would not let them.

"Now what?" asked Rullin.

"Before we rest, we must find a place to make camp for the night," the druid said. They looked about until they found a small hill to the south that provided a good view of the river and surrounding countryside. "Despite the chill, there is little wind so we can camp on the hill. When the sun comes up in the morning, we'll have a good view of the countryside from here. Perhaps Milland will be able to spy out something that will help us in our journey? We still have a ways to go before we reach Noranil."

"How many miles is it to Noranil?" asked Magin.

"About two hundred miles as the crow flies," answered the druid. "Fortunately, the road runs straight and there is little in the way of obstacles to hinder our travel. We still have several days, perhaps a week, of traveling before us."

"Then we'd better get some sleep tonight," said Milland. "In the morning I'll get up early and have a look about the land."

Everyone began searching the countryside for wood. They forced themselves to follow the druid up the hill. Their feet were heavy and dragging, and their legs felt as if they were made from lead. Once on top of the hill, they found it scattered with many large boulders that provided shelter from any cold wind that might decide to pay them an unexpected visit during the night. A watch was set, but no fire was lit. They were close to the war that was waging in the western plains, and there was always the danger that one of the Horzugal might be flying high overhead. Above them they could see the thousands of heavenly, silver lanterns in the northern skies. A sickle moon rose late in the evening, but off in the southwest they could see a darkness that blocked out the stars. When they looked down the hill, on the lands below, there was a stillness that seemed to blanket the sleeping landscape. It was broken only by the reflection of the nightly lights on the gentle waters of the Munddlethun River flowing south to join with the Wolf-Staak Flow River, and together, empty into the lake known as the Thuntun Mirror.

Milland had the last watch. He woke everyone early with his cries. "Boats! I see boats!" he shouted. Everyone jumped up.

"Quickly! Everyone, rise and see the boats sailing south on the Munddlethin!"

The boys fell over each other as they jumped to their feet to see what had caused such excitement in Milland. They had to rub the sleepiness from of their eyes to help them adjust to the bright, morning sun. Milland was standing at the edge of the hill on a large boulder, looking north. Next to him was Arlindor and Pettin, who were the first to join him.

"I can't see anything," insisted Pettin. "Are you sure its boats that you see, and not the reflection of the morning sun on the water?"

"I don't see them either, but I don't doubt the eyes of Milland, nor should you, Tillenian," Arlindor said. "Milland's eyes are unlike all others. He developed his unique sight and hearing from a lifetime spent watching plants grow and listening to them speak. It takes great sight and hearing to communicate with vegetation. Only a tree-farmer could possibly hear grass grow and see a flower open. If he sees boats, then the boats are there, just as he says. Can you tell us something of their make?"

"They're still too far up the river and the sun's glare makes it hard to see clearly, but let me concentrate," Milland said as he stood still for several minutes with his hands over his eyes to protect them from the sun's glare. His sharp, blue eyes did not wink once, and his face seemed to turn to stone as its muscles froze in concentration. Finally, he spoke once more. "I can see the ships more clearly now. Yes, there are three long boats that appear more like serpents then anything built by the skill of man. They are crowned with great blue sails that have a white star on each of them. I count eight points on each star and the black silhouette on the center of each star."

"They belong to Neutrian Boatmen," Arlindor said. "They are known to sail under the blue banner with the shape of the black ship inside the eight-pointed white star. They must be petrolling the East Fold, and are returning from the north country? Can you tell us more about them, Milland?"

Milland concentrated for a quarter of an hour before he spoke once more. "I can now see men dressed in battle gear," he finally spoke once more. "They are tall and cold, like this land. The light of the sun is in their hair, and the color of the sky fills their eyes. Their ships are, maybe, five miles away, with the wind in their sails. They are moving fast. More than this, I cannot say. The morning sun and northern mist blur my vision."

"I wish my vision was blurred like his," Huck said to Rullin.

"They'll be here soon," Milland said. "Perhaps in less then a half-an-hour?"

"Are they friends of foes?" asked Rullin.

"Friends to those who come in peace and comradeship," said Arlindor. "But they fear most strangers traveling through their lands these days, because of their war with Allomania." Arlindor looked at Rullin and spoke more softly. "Don't fear, lads. They are not a hasty folk. Though they are fierce warriors, they possess a strong sense of honor and do not attack those who mean them no harm. They are brave and courageous, but not cruel. They would rather nurse a fallen bird to health just as joyously as they would sever the head of a trog from its shoulders. And though they are little educated in the way scholars are, their knowledge of the ways of the world is unequaled. Keep the memory of Princess Valenda in your minds and hearts and you will not fear those who we are about to meet."

Arlindor instructed the others to build a fire that gave off smoke as a signal for the boatmen to let them know of their presence. They piled some wet wood on the fire, turning the smoke black. In this way the boatmen would see the smoke from a distance. Everyone then went down to the river and waited for their arrival. Soon they could see three large sails in the distance, but the boats were still hidden by the tall grass. As the ships sailed near, they could make out the eight-pointed stars on their sails. Arlindor led everyone out of the trees and stood in sight on the river's edge, as the Neutrian ships came into sight from around the bend in the river.

They appeared just as Milland described them. The bows of the ships were carved into the shapes of great serpents with long necks and horned heads, while the sterns were shaped like curled tails. They seemed more like three great sea worms than boats, swimming down the river. On board the ships were many men. Tall and fierce they appeared, and they wore fur capes to protect them from the cold winds, and helmets decorated with the wings of gulls. Their skin was clear and their faces reddened from the bitting winds. Long beards hung from their chins and their golden hair was kept in braids. The sides of their ships were lined with shields that provided protection for those who manned the ores that helped to propel the wooden ships when the winds were still.

A cry could be heard. "Ho! Ho! Och seh ya sofs!" One of the boatmen shouted in the Neutrian language.

"Everyone show yourselves," Arlindor ordered. "They have sighted us." Arlindor stood in front of the others. He stood straight with his staff in his left hand. He raised the other arm, with open palm, in front of him as a greeting to the boatmen, showing them that he came in peace, and then spoke in their tongue. *"Hul, Nordmanen! Wep comthen en pacesen!"*

The Neutrians pulled their ships to the bank. They ran to and fro and began jumping onto the shore, as planks of wood were extended over the sides of the ships. Before anyone could say another word, several dozen boatmen sprang forward with spears in hand and quickly surrounded Arlindor and the others. Other boatmen began searching the surrounding countryside, looking for any other strangers that might be hiding.

"Stay where you are, strangers," the leader of the boatmen said in the common language of Daryan. All about them stood Neutrians with their spears pointed at them, forming a ring of steel. The boys were frightened by their boldness. They appeared at first, like wild men to Rullin and Huck, and yet, there was a nobleness in all their actions. Their faces were hard but there was no hate or brutality. They noticed a certain something in the way why carried themselves that reminded them of Princess Valenda. Now that they could study them for a few seconds, they recognized the qualities that all disciplined soldiers possessed when they were following orders without questioning them. Rullin and Huck looked at each other, and without speaking, they could agree that there was nothing to fear. They remembered seeing the same qualities in the Tillenian woodmen and they turned out to be friendly.

Arlindor stepped forward and addressed the commander of the boatmen. "I am called Arlindor, druid and member of the Brotherhood of the Order of the Keepers of the Holy Flame of the Light of Wissenval." The boatmen were astonished at the druid's proclamation. A few of them spoke among themselves in their own language.

"I, and my comrades, have journeyed many miles and fought many battles with trogs and other demons to reach your northern lands," Arlindor spoke once more. "We've come to seek a council with your king. We've heard of the war on your western borders with the Beast of Allomania, and we have come to offer what aid that we may render to your people."

"How do we know that you speak the truth?" the commander asked. "How do we know you are not a spy sent to our lands by the Beast, himself, to cause evil among our people?"

Arlindor raised his arms in front of him. He held his staff with both hands. It began to glow with a green light that seemed to surround him in a halo. Soon the light began to turn white. It continued to grow until it encased everyone in it.

"I am Arlindor, follower of Gottron of Wissenval, warrior and servant of the Lords of the Light," Arlindor spoke with a commanding voice. "Search your hearts, brave boatmen of Neutria, and you will know the truth. Not even the Lord of Darkness, with all his evil powers could hide the truth from you."

Arlindor's voice grew louder and more forceful. His words penetrated into the hearts of the men who surrounded them, dispelling their fears and suspicions.

The boatmen dropped their weapons and fell to their knees, but not in fear, but rather in awe of the Light. The commander looked up at the druid and felt a new strength flowing through every ounce of his body and soul.

"Truly, you are what you say," he said. "You can only be from the enchanted valley, and I know that there is no evil within you. My heart tells me these things."

"Then rise and tell me the name by which call yourself,

Trueman," Arlindor commanded. His voice had returned to normal and the light soon faded.

"I am Bolthur, Commander of the forces of the East Fold," the Neutrian commander said. "Let me welcome you to Neutria."

"Thank you, Bolthur," Arlindor said.

"We've been sailing the waters of the East Fold because there have been reports of strange happenings in the Wolf-Staak Forest," Bolthur said. "Once my people traveled freely through those woods, but since the black hand of the Beast of Allomania grasped it for his own, we seldom venture into its leafy realm anymore. We feared that he might have sent some war party through the forest to strike at us from our rear, while we are engaged in battle with him in the west."

"The strange happenings you spoke of were caused by the Lord of Darkness in his pursuit of us," Arlindor said. "He tried to prevent us from reaching your land. We have come to assist your king, for we have been told that he has been struck by a blackness that clouds his mind and heart."

Bolthur's face was grieved at the mentioning of his king's ailing condition. He felt strangely free to speak with the druid about his lord. "For many months now, our king has remained locked up within the Great Hall of Heroes that we call Nuntherdenn, in Noranil. He refuses to leave its dark chambers, preferring to lament the plight of our people and hide in the shadows of past glories then face the reality of the present. It's even said that he has been heard talking to the statues of our legendary heroes that fill the hall. He pleads with them to help him and our people, and refuses to speak with anyone except his closes generals and family members."

"That is why we were sent," Arlindor said. "A great council was held in Wissenval, and there we were told by Princess Valenda of your nation's dilemma."

Bolthur tried to speak when he heard Arlindor speak the princess's name, but Arlindor did not give him the chance and continued to speak.

"With me are good men of the Mark and Tillenia, who have

faced dangers more than once on their perilous journey to help your king and people in their hour of need."

Bolthur looked at the assembled party that accompanied the druid. "I bid you all welcome to my land, and offer you safe passage aboard out ships to Noranil," Bolthur said. "It's the fastest way to our city, and the safest." Bolthur then noticed Rullin and Huck for the first time standing among the others. "Children?" asked Bolthur. "With all respect, my people's plight need more then *kinen*," he said in his native tongue, "to aid us in battle against the black tide of undermen that threatens to roll over our western frontier."

"This is Rullin Ashburn and Huck Lock of the Mark," Arlindor said. "They were brought along not by a decision made by man, but were chosen by forces greater than those that reside among the mortal kingdoms, or even the enchanted valley. They were present when the Thengraal Prophecies were fulfilled, and are the friends of the herald of the Emperor Returned."

Bolthur and the other boatmen looked at the young faces of Huck and Rulln incredulously. They could see in the eyes of those that accompanied the two boys that they believed earnestly and deeply in what Arlindor claimed.

"Tell me, druid out of Wissenval," asked Bolthur, "do you mean to tell us that the ancient prophecies have come true?"

"I spoke clearly enough, good warrior of the north," Arlindor said. "He whose return has been foretold by old wives and wise sages alike has finally awakened. He walks the world, even as we stand here and speak. We've journeyed out of the east with him, but he had to turn south in the company of my brother druid, Blondor, and with your Princess Valenda, and now faces many evils just as dark and terrible as those that plaque your kingdom. They are on their way to the city of Lothar, where the Emperor Returned will reclaim the crown that rightfully belongs to him."

"You speak of things that cause my head to spin," Bolthur said. "Our beloved princess and the mysterious Blondor journey together with a legend out of the past? Your news is of great importance. It has been too long since our princess has left our land, and even longer since Blondor last passed through it. I, myself, spoke with the wandering druid and remember him being filled with great hast and gloom, the last time he visited Neutria. He spoke at great length with our king, prince and our princess, and we have followed his counsel, to prepare for the struggle that was soon to come shortly after his departure. His words were not clear at the time, but now they ring clear like a silver bell, heralding the coming of a storm. The dark shadow out of the south has reached our borders, and the clash between Light and Darkness is taking place on our doorstep. These are truly remarkable times."

"Yes they are," Arlindor agreed. "But we're not the only ones who know the meaning of the signs, and have recognized that New Earth is passing into a New Age. The Lord of Darkness has also realized that the time for the emperor's return is drawing near, and has set into motion his own plans to prevent his return to the throne of Lothar. To do this, he has put together the greatest army New Earth has ever seen. He has united all the races of undermen under his black will, and plans to unleash them against the nations of Truemans before we are able to unite and oppose him. Divide and conquer, is his plan, but if he is to succeed, he will have to make his move soon."

"Then there is no time to waste," Bolthur said. "Come and be our guests. Our sails are ready to carry all of us to Noranil."

Huck and Rullin and the others spent the next several days aboard the serpent-shaped ships of Neutria. The winds carried them down the Munddlethun River with the dark woods of the Wolf-Staak, silently rolling pass them, on their left. Even the natural sounds of birds and other creatures that were normally heard within the leafy expanse were absent. It gave them an eerie feeling and they avoid looking at the forest as they traveled southward. The boys did enjoy watching the green hills of the Neutrian countryside and the golden fields of the open plains that passed before them, to the north. When not watching the scenery, they often watched the boatmen as they manned their ships. How unlike they were to the people of the Mark. Seldom did they laugh like the good people of Jassinburg. Harder and colder they appeared, not always cheerful, but they were polite and dutiful to their guests. It was not difficult to believe that they were born of these northern lands. The wide, open lands of Neutria seemed naked and revealed themselves openly to visitors, but its hard and stoic nature seemed to have imparted those qualities onto the people that inhabited them. The boys did notice that the boatmen shared a comradeship that seemed to be the thread that held their nation together. They worked hard and never complained, and were always ready to give a helping hand to each other, no matter how tired or weary they might seem.

Bolthur spoke at long length with Arlindor, and told him much of what had happened in Neutria since Princess Valenda departed. The boys over heard bits and pieces of what were said, but they were not very interested in anything except relaxing and enjoying the trip after the long and hard trek through the Wolf-Staak. It was the evening of the second day out when they sat down with Magin, Gordon, Milland and Olaf. Pettin and Arlindor were with Bolthur, at the other end of this ship.

"How long will it take, before we reach Noranil?" asked Rullin.

"Not much longer," answered Gordon. "If the winds stay with us, we should be entering the Thuntium Mirror before morning, and cross its length by tomorrow. I think we will be sailing up the Noranilon River by late in the evening, on the morrow."

"You're right, Gordon," Magin agreed. "If we're lucky, we might even arrive earlier than that." Magin had wet his finger and held it up before him to test the winds. "These sails are good and strong and will carry us fast across the waters, untroubled."

"I like these men of Neutria," Huck said. "They seem to belong in this land, as if they are a apart of it."

"I sense that too," Milland said. "Their souls are one with the trees that grow here. They are just as much a part of the land as the mountains to the north, and the rivers that carry us across it. They're Venturian in blood, like Huck and me. The urge to roam runs strong in Venturian blood, and this land. Its wide-open spaces and endless horizons call to me, as it does to the Neutrians. The land is half wild, and there is a similar wildness in these boatmen. They possess a noble barbarism that feels free and refreshing."

"You sound like you would like to live here," Huck said.

"The need to wander that burns bright in their eyes pulls on my soul, but my heart belongs to the Mark," Milland said. "My roots have been planted there for too many generations."

"I know what you mean," Huck said as he looked across the landscape that stretch far to the north. "There's a part of me that would like to go running across those rolling hills and open plains, but at the same time, I wish I was back in the Mark with my family, friends and home."

"It's the same Venturian blood that runs through your veins," Milland said. "But like myself, you too are rooted in the Mark, just as these people are part of this land, and would find our way of life just as different as we find their way of life."

"When a people become one with the soil, their souls mingle with the spirit of the land they inhabit. Folk and land become one," explained Gordon. "You, Huck, Milland and I all have Venturian blood, and yet there is a difference in our nature from that of the Neutrians because of the land that we live in. Just as Magin here is of Fabboian blood, like Olaf and Pettin, and the rest of the good people of Tillenia, and yet, there is a difference between him and the Tillenians. In many ways Magin has more in common with us and even Rullin, who is of Pittorian blood, because we are all united by the same soil-soul of the Mark that has helped to shape our souls and make us a single people."

"But aren't we all Truemans?" asked Rullin. "Aren't we all the same?"

"All Truemans share the same basic nature which is rooted in our blood, but the land we live in will caused different elements within our nature to predominate," Magin said. "A people without a land is not truly a people, but simply a collection of individuals. Their souls are weakened because they have lost contact with the land. This weakens the Life-Force within them, and thus, makes them easy victims of the Darkness. The Darkness preys on people who have lost contact with the land. It can and will seduce those whose bond with the Life-Force has been weakened.

The Darkness can more easily twist their souls into things evil. The poor victims who were caught in the ancient Hell Fires and survived, lost contact with the soil-soul because the earth itself was burnt into ash. They became the deformed and twisted races of undermen that battle with Truemans for the possession of New Earth today."

"You see, lads," Olaf now spoke. "The nature-soul, as we call the soil-soul in Tillenia, is actually the Life-Force of the Cosmos. It's important for people to never lose contact with the soil and the natural surroundings in which they live. My people love the forest. We have learned to make our livelihood from its treasures without destroying the woods. It's our home and our world, and everything one could possibly want to know about my people can be found in the nature of the forest. It may frighten others, but to us it protects us and comforts us."

"Even now, filled with the Darkness?" Rullin asked.

"Yes," Olaf said. "We'll not leave the Wolf-Staak any more than your people would leave the Mark, even though it hugs the Great Eastern Sea, with all the terrors that swim within its vastness. The Wolf-Staak is ill with the Darkness, but my people will not desert it. We would rather stay and fight for the woods we love so much. For our roots are in the same soil that the roots of the trees are planted."

"It's hard to believe that we're more than a thousand miles from the Mark," Rullin said. He stood up and walked to the edge of the ship and stared up, at the night sky. He could see the dancing points of lights against the now velvety, black heaven. The sun had long slipped down below the western edge of the world, as a cold wind blew off the river from the north. Everyone aboard the ship put on fur coats made of wolf skins, to protect them from the nightly cold.

"The sky seems the same as the one over the Mark," Rullin said. "Only this blistering autumn cold reminds me that this is not the Mark." Rullin pulled his wolf's fur coat tight around him.

"Look there!" Milland said as he jumped up and pointed to the river's northern bank.

"What is it you see?" asked Gordon.

"Yes, Milland. Tell us what our eyes can't see," Magin said. "We don't have your exceptional eagle sight."

"It's a town, a dead town," Milland said.

After a few minutes the ships passed what appeared to be a ghost town. They could now make out the frames of buildings made of wood, with tall, pitched roofs. The town was surrounded by a wall made of logs, with tall towers protruding high above the wooden wall.

"That's the town of Dontungal," said one of the boatmen standing nearby. "Once there were more than two thousand of our people living there, but now only shadows inhabit its streets."

"What happened to the people?" asked Rullin.

"They all moved to Noranil, along with the rest of the inhabitants of the East and Central Folds," the boatman said as he stared at the lonely town. "I was born there, and my entire family lived there. We lived a rich and happy life, until the shadow came to the great forest. Once my people patrolled the western part of the woods, according to the agreement we had with the Tillenians. But seldom now, do we ever enter the woods. The Darkness that fills the forest prevents us from entering. As a result, the trogs have grown bold enough to raid our eastern lands by traveling through the woods. It became unsafe to remain in our homes, since we had to move most of our warriors to the western borderlands to hold off the Allomanian armies."

"It would seem that there is no limit to the hunting grounds of the undermen, these days," Olaf growled as his face turned deep red with hate. His bear-like hand came down on the ships' wooden railing with a thud. "Is there no place in all of New Earth that is beyond the reach of the Lord of Darkness?"

"Yes, Tillenian," the boatman said. "Even though all Truemandom is under siege, the beast in the south is unable to reach into the hearts of any Trueman that remains fateful to the Lords of the Light, even if they live within the great woods."

"You know of the plight of my people?" Olaf asked in his deep voice.

"I have heard," the boatman said.

"How do you come by such knowledge? There are no

messengers that travel between our lands, through the Wolf-Staak, these days," Olaf said.

"My name is Huntuheim," the boatman said. "I traveled with a war party of several ships that sailed down the Angorium River and then turned up the Donnor River, a year ago. We were seeking trogs that were moving across the south lands, and into the Wolf-Staak. Blondor feared that the trogs were in the service of the Beast of Allomania, and he asked us to set sail and take possession of the great fortress of Ortangral. If the trogs reached the fortress first, they would have separated the three great Trueman nations of Lothangia, Neutria and Tillenia. Fortunately, we arrived in time and prevented the trogs from taking possession of the fortress, but only after many of my brethren fell in battle. We eventually turned it over to a legion of Lothangians, but not before we exchanged much news about the affairs unfolding in the east and the south. We kept in touch with Ortangral, as Blondor instructed, sending supplies to the garrison that is stationed there."

Everyone fell silent as their ships sailed passed the ghost town of Dontungal. The town appeared eerie. It was still and seemed to be in perfect condition, just as it was left when its citizens departed for Noranil. There were no signs of ruin or decade, or that it was disturbed by bandits. There was only stillness. No sign of movement of life could be seen there, except from the relentless winds. Everyone was glad when the town slowly disappeared, and the ships continued to sail down the river toward the Thuntuim Mirror. The sky was now sprinkled with a billion stars that formed a great bridge, cutting the black heavens in two.

When they finally passed through the mouth of the river and sailed onto the lake called the Thuntuim Mirror, the sickle moon was high in the sky. The gentle waves of the lake rippled with the moon's reflection that gave its surface a dreamlike appearance. Everyone was glad to leave the dark forest behind them, and the cold night winds chilled their bones as they blew down from the north, across the lake. The boys were both fascinated and frightened at once. They had never sailed on so much water before. Even Rullin, who had sailed down the Markway River to the Great Eastern Sea with his father, felt uneasy about sailing across the surface of the lake.

"This lake is filled by the rivers the Wolf Staak Flow, the Munddlethun, the Noranilon and the Jorunthun, which are fed by the melting ice that flows out of the mountains to the north, known as the Northern Wall," Huntuheim said. "Some say the lake is bottomless, or near so. It's supposed to be so deep that no light ever reaches that far down, and is filled with a blackness that haunts the nightmares of men. It is said that within its depths, there live sea serpents. Occasionally some fisherman or sailor has claimed to have seen one of them swimming on the surface of the lake, or bathing in the light of the moon on its shore. I am told they have long necks and great flippers, but I cannot say for sure, for I have never seen one of these creatures, and hope never to have the opportunity."

"I sure hope we don't run into one of those sea worms," Rullin said as he took a quick look over the still, dark waters of the lake. "You don't seem frightened of the possibility of running into one of those monsters." he said to Huntuheim.

"That's because my people love this lake," the boatman said. "We sail and fish its cold waters, and it gives us the substance that we need to live. Its icy waves remind us of an era, long ago, half forgotten now, except for the legends that are told from father to son, about the Wandering Times. The legends of those times live on in our hearts and minds. They are the doorways into our past, and they help us to keep alive our heritage."

"Tell us about them," begged the boys. The Neutrian boatman was pleased at their interest, and could not resist.

"According to our sagas, there was nothing in the beginning except the Great Void," the boatman said. "Within it was a raging conflict between the misty glaciers and the sparkling blue waters in the north, and the burning, black, molten lava pits of fire to the south. There was nothing else in the Great Void—no sun, no moon, no stars. There was just this great Void filled with fire and ice.

"It was out of the frozen north that the Lords of the Light were born, while the Demons of the Darkness came from the burning south. From the center of the void, where the northern ice and southern fires mixed, a great mist was born, and out of this mist was born the world that is called Old Earth. For countless, untold eons, the ice and fire fought over the possession of this world.

"The Demons of the Darkness took the black fires of the south and fashioned such creatures as giants, dwarfs, dragons and trolls upon the world and ruled over them. When the Lords of the Light saw what they had done, they created the race of Truemans and placed them on New Earth to do battle with the servants of the Demons of the Darkness. Eventually, many of the Truemans were seduced by the Darkness and unleashed the Hell Fires that charred the surface of the world.

"The blackness of eternal night hung over the world and burning rock and molten lava charred everything as it flowed in great currents of destruction. But in the north, the great arctic winds of ice and snow, sent by the Lords of the Light, held back the burning destruction. A great sheet of ice grew on top of the world. A great battle between the Light and Darkness was waged between the ice and fire that covered the world. This battled continued for many centuries until one of the Lords of the Light rose from the realm of the dead.

"His name is Boldthor and he is the most beautiful of the Lords of the Light. We refer to him as Boldthor the Beautiful. He placed the sun in the heavens and its rays filled the skies and bathed the lands of the world, causing life to spring up once more. The sun's rays drove the back the darkness that covered the world, causing day and night to appear as the world turned on its axis.

"What was left of race of men of Old Earth, had been saved within the icy halls of the frozen north, far above the present limits of the ice sheets that now cover New Earth. It was Boldthor who appeared in Trueman form and walked among the men and taught them of the power of the Light that shines within our blood. Boldthor told them of the Lords of the Light and how they could call on them for assistance in their fight against the corrupting forces of the Darkness.

"They did as Boldthor said, and one day there appeared great beings who shined like huge pillars of ice, alive with a white light.

Tall as the mighty redwood trees they were, and their skin was as white as snow. Their eyes were the color of the icy, blue waters of the north, and from their heads hung long strands of hair that was the color of the sun, shining like its golden rays of light.

"Wherever they walked, both mountain and forest bowed before their coming, and all of Nature sung their praise. They were not of the race of giants, but were the Lords of the Light themselves. They joined Boldthor, who was one of them, and they lived among the races of men for a long time. They called the race of men, Truemans and taught them all the names of the wonders of the world, and explained to them how to use its gifts. Much of that knowledge has been forgotten, but the druids have sought to rediscover that knowledge, especially the knowledge pertaining to the Life-Force of the cosmos.

"The Lords of the Light departed, but before they did, they told the race of Truemans that one day they would give them a sign that would send them out to reconquer the world. For many centuries the Truemans remained in the north, growing stronger. Then came a time when the Lords of the Light caused the ice sheets that sat patiently for so long on the top of the world, to begin to move south. Down over the land the ice slowly inched, pushing a side the mighty mountains and swallowing up the vast forests that grew in its way. It upturned rocks and changed the course of rivers as it slowly crept over the face of the world.

"The tribes of Truemans living in the north were pushed along with the trees and boulders before the creeping ice. Whole tribes moved south over a period of thousands of years, seeking new lands in the south to settle in. It's said that the people of Neutria were the last to leave the ancestral homelands in the north. We lingered long among the great northern expanses until we finally followed our brothers and sisters who had left before us. But we did not go as far south as they did, and have remained here among these northern folds. We have never forgotten the great Lords of the Light, and especially the beautiful Boldthor. We have fashion the Boldthor Cross and placed them on top of hills, where they are lit during the long winter months as signs of our reverence for the

Lords of the Light. We use them to broadcast our joyous message of the Light and the Life-Force of the Cosmos for all to see."

"Arlindor!" Gordon shouted and then jumped up and rushed to the druid's side. The others followed after Gordon. Gordon had notice Arlindor as he slumped over, as if in pain. Bolthur and Pettin were supporting him and gently sat him down.

"What is it? Are you all right?" Pettin was asking the druid.

"I'm all right," Arlindor said as he grasped for breath. "There was a surge in the Life-Force."

"Like the one you felt in the woods?" asked Magin.

"Yes, but much stronger," the druid said. "Our comrades have passed into the Stygian Hole and there unleashed some kind of great force. More than this I cannot see. I can only be sure there was some kind of titanic struggle taking place under the mountains. How it turned out, I don't know, but we must hurry. I fear events are moving faster than we thought possible, and are passing us by." The druid turned to the captain of the boatmen. "Bolthur. You must make hast. We must reach Noranil as quickly as your sails can carry us. Every minute we delay can spell doom for us and all the Trueman nations throughout New Earth."

They sailed all night and everyone helped to get every bit of speed possible out of their sails. The next morning dawned bright and clear, and the sun's first rays danced across the mirror-like surface of the lake. Sea birds were flying overhead, singing their morning songs that welcomed the arrival of a new day. The wind was still cold and the warmth of the rising sun did little to drive the chill from their bones. To assist the sails that propelled the ships along, the strong arms of the boatmen strained to push wood against water.

That afternoon their lookouts spied a darkness looming on the southern horizon. It did not seem to be moving northward, and not even the eyes of Milland, with the help of a looking glass, could pierce the blackness that lingered in the distance.

By late afternoon the ships swung north and set sail up the Noranilon River, passing golden hills on either side. The trees were bare this time of the year, except for the evergreens that grew in increasing numbers, as they sailed north. The ground was covered with a blanket of red, gold and brown leafs that had turned color and fell early this year.

Arlindor stood on deck with Pettin at his side. Arlindor was staring at the darkness in the distance. "Tell me, Arlindor, can you see into the darkness to the south?" Pettin asked the druid. "Even Milland could not see into it with his sight."

"Yes, Pettin," the druid said. "I can see into it, but not with the vision of my eyes. I use the power of the Light to see through the darkness. But it takes a great deal of concentration."

Pettin understood what the druid meant. "It seems to fade into the distance as we sail north. What is it?   Is it a storm? I understand that storms sometimes appear rather suddenly in these lands, and can be very violent, forming great vortexes of twisting winds."

"Yes. A storm it is, but not the handiwork of Nature," Arlindor said. "It's a storm out of the south. The Lord of Darkness is moving across the land, once more. I fear doom is approaching, and the fire of war will soon be burning its way through the world once more."

"Those are grave words," Pettin said.

"These are grave times," answered the druid. Arlindor then turned away from the darkness in the south and looked north. He felt the cool, refreshing wind blowing against his bearded face.

"With men such as these Neutrians as allies, we have as good a chance to make a stand against all the evil that the Lord of Darkness can muster against us," Pettin said. "They are strong of bone and heart, and fear little that walks across the face of New Earth. Together, with my people and the men of Lothangia, we will make a formidable alliance. I would not wish to be among the ranks belonging to the armies of the Lord of Darkness."

"It will take more than strong hearts and bones to roll back the blackness that the Lord of Darkness can send against us," Arlindor said. "Even the power of the blood-purity that flows in our veins might not be a match for his power." Arlindor turned and looked into Pettin's face and smiled. "But perhaps the eternal optimism of your race will burn bright enough to drive out the darkness that invades our hearts? It's said that your people even laugh in the face of death. How can we but be victorious with such men as Tillenians and Neutrians in our ranks?"

Chapter Four:
In The Hall of Heroes

The ships sailed up the Noranilon River until they came to a great wall constructed out of great logs standing upright, like sentries on duty. The wall was lined with watch towers and built to protect the city of Noranil. A bell began to ring as the ships sailed near to the city, heralding the return of the patrol.

The wall extended around the limits of the city of Noranil with two great arms stretching out into the river, creating a harbor. Once the ships were within the wall, Huck and Rullin could see other ships lingering along the banks of the harbor. Further up the shore were many rows of houses, built long and flat with pitched roofs. They were made of long logs, like the wall, and there were several smoke stacks on each house. There were several rows of small windows that lined the sides of the houses. On either side of each house is a small garden or pen filled with goats or hogs. Stables and barns dotted the town and water towers, loomed overhead. They could also see several larger buildings that towered over the lower buildings. These were the long halls that the town folk used to house their armaments, conduct business and other commercial activities, used as beer halls and for other forms of indoor entertainment. Further into the city was a large hall that sat on a small hill, where the King of Neutria resides.

The ships sailed up to the docks as men rushed to and fro, guiding the ships with the ease of riding a horse. On the docks, crowds of people gathered. They were made up of family members—fathers, mothers, wives and the children of the warriors on the three ships. Huck and Rullin could see old men and women dressed in furs and skins over finely embroidered clothing, who wore their age with grace and pride. No matter how old they appeared to be, they still stood tall and straight and not bent over. The older women kept their silver hair in braids that were wrapped about the head, and on the chins of the men hung long, white beards. Along side them stood tall, graceful women, with faces both handsome and beautiful. Their long golden locks of hair varied from the color of honey to a bright yellow. Their skin was fair, and one could read both feminine charm and strength of character in their faces. But it was their eyes that united them all, young and old. They shined with a blue or gray brilliance. All who saw them could read their determination never to surrender, in those eyes. All about them were the children who ran up and down the piers, waiting anxiously with their mothers for their fathers to return. The air was filled with their chatter and hails.

The ships docked among many other boats of various sizes. There were both war ships and vessels used for fishing and commerce. Ropes were thrown to the men on the docks, who grabbed them and tied them fast. The ships were then pulled close to the piers. Planks were laid over the side of the ships, and the men rushed ashore into the outstretched, welcoming arms of their loved ones.

Bolthur went ashore with Arlindor and the others. "I'll lead you to King Amthrim," he said. "He resides in the great Hall of Heroes atop the hill. I'm sure the king will want to speak with you as soon as possible." Bolthur said as he looked into the druid's face. Arlindor could read the distress and concern in the captain's eyes. "Arlindor, he is not the same king that my people have always loved. He has been stricken with a madness that blinds him to the reality that we face, and it has sapped his will to fight. I know our people. They will not fight if King Amthrim does not will it."

Though Bolthur did not ask, Arlindor could read the question in his eyes. "I will do what I can to cure your king of his madness," Arlindor said. "Lead me to your king, and let's not delay with more talk."

Arlindor followed the Neutrian up a flight of steps cut from half logs that led up from the river bank to an avenue that took them into the city.

Huck and Rullin were intrigued by the Northmen. As they followed Arlindor and Bolthur through the streets that snaked between the long houses, they passed through throngs of tall men and women. The womenfolk moved with a majesty that was the equal of the high lords and ladies of far off Lothangia. Their fair faces were frozen in expression of determined stoicism. There was little to smile and laugh about during the times they lived. Proud and beautiful they appeared, clad in wolf furs and the skins of the wooly steers that roamed the northern plains, over their fine clothing. The streets were also crowded with the children of this northern land. They ran and played whenever they could find the time in between their many duties. Huck and Rullin felt like running off with them more than once, and several of the Neutrian boys and girls they passed, stopped and stared at the foreign lads.

The city was overcrowded, and whole families had to be quartered in tents set up between the buildings. These were the many families that fled the western settlements and sought refuge in the city. There were also many who gave up their farms and villages in the eastern folds, in answer to the call of arms. Men, women and children were all preparing for war, determined to stand and fight and even die, if the need demanded, in the defense of their homeland and way of life. It was not just their sense of duty to their king and people, but their love of their liberty and freedom that was bred into them by the land they lived on that motivated them to make whatever sacrifices were necessary to defend their way of life. Never had they been enslaved, neither by a conqueror, nor by a domestic tyrant. They preferred to die fighting as free men and women, then to live on their knees as slaves.

Bolthur led them up a large street, made from logs cut in half, to protect them from the mud. The sounds of the city filled their ears. They saw wagons, pulled by great beasts known as wooly steers. Six feet tall they stood at the shoulder, with a thick growth of black, curly hair and two long horns measuring two to three feet in length which grew out of either side of their heads. Along the sides of some of the long houses were hung the skins of various animals. They were stretched out to dry. They also passed stockades filled with great rain deers standing six feet high at the shoulders, and were covered with great coats of fur. The boys were struck with wonder at these great beasts. Not since they saw the maxthoiums of Tillenia did they see an animal so impressive. The two shovel-like antlers that grew from their heads looked like huge hands with extending fingers. A growth of white fur hung from around their necks and chests like huge manes. Like the maxthoiums, these deers inhabited the cold environments of the northern regions of New Earth that hugged the southern edges of the great glaciers to the north.

As they moved along the wooden streets of Noranil, everyone stopped and stared at the strangers from the east. News traveled quickly among the Neutrians. The arrival of the travelers from the east, who had come to speak with their king, had spread rapidly through word of mouth. Soon, everyone in the city heard of their tale about traveling through the Wolf-Staak Forest, and battling with trogs and were-demons. It pleased the Neutrians that men should travel so far and face such dangers, as those which lurked in the dark woods, to come and face death at their sides, in these dark times.

Soon they found themselves in the center of the city. Before them, was a small hill, and on its crown was built a great hall. It was made of long logs and rested on a foundation of stone. Around its sides were rows of stone pillars that held up the overhanging roof that pitched upwards at a 45-degree angle for five stories, and then the roof pitched upward at an even sharper angle of 75 degrees. Built into the lower section of the roof were long, thin windows that let light invade the interior of the hall. Bolthur led them up the long flight of stone stairs that took them to the hall's front doors.

On two large doors made of steel, and overlaid with emeralds and rubies, were shields and crossed spears. Carved into the doors and decorated with silver and gold, were images of warriors in battle with giants. Rullin remembered the tales of battles between the Neutrians and giants told to them aboard the ships by the boatmen. Over the doors was a great, eight-pointed star made of gold and implanted with diamonds along its edges. In the center of the star was a carving of a ship with a great sail. Over the doors and below the star were three wooden carvings. One was of a white-headed eagle with spread wings that represented the blues skies that roofed the land of Neutria. To the eagle's left was a great woolly steer with long horns that symbolized the open plans of Neutria, which provided food for the north men. On the eagle's right was another carving. This one was of a large bear that fished in its clear rivers on which their ships sailed.

This was Heldonhuller, the Hall of Heroes and it was said by the people of Neutria, that within its walls, the souls of Neutria's most honored heroes would come speak to their kings in times of crisis. It was considered a hallow place, where people came to give offerings to their ancestors, request favors from the Lords of the Light, to grant them victory in battle, or good fortune in their lives.

When they reached the top of the stairs, they were greeted by two guards. Each one stood next to a great bronze pot, carved with runes. The pots were filled with alcohol, especially brewed, and lit with fires that were kept burning day and night. Rullin looked hard at the flames and a strange sensation caused him to shake for an instance. He instinctively clutched his jacket and the Alfen stone underneath. Rullin could not help but feel that he was being watched by unseen eyes. Huck looked at his friend with concern and knew that something was troubling him.

"Hey, Rullin," Huck whispered. "You're holding the jewel."

Huck's words had a sobering effect on his friend. Rullin opened his eyes wide with surprise and immediately released the jewel and lowered his hand. Neither of them said anything further about it.

The two guards stepped forward. The strong chiseled features of their faces were expressionless, but their eyes revealed that they recognized Bolthur. In their left hands they held their spears. They brought their right hands, clinched in fists, to their chests and placed them over their hearts. They then extended their right arms before them, with their hands open in a sign of peace, and saluted Bolthur.

"Welcome, Captain Bolthur," one of the guards said, "Prince Sagtrim has returned from the western settlements and is waiting your arrival, and those of your companions."

"The prince has returned?" asked Bolthur. "When did he return?"

"Last night," the guard answered. "He's inside with the king. Word of you return, with your guests, has reached him just moments before."

Bolthur turned to Arlindor, who bid him to lead on. The druid and his companions followed Bolthur through the doors. They entered a hallway. To one side was a small chamber. Bolthur looked inside and then entered. The others followed him. They could see a flame burning on a small altar. It was kept lit in memory of all who have fallen in the defense of Neutria. Next to the flame was a bundle of oak and ash leaves, acorns and mistletoe. Behind the flame was a sword made of iron with its blade turned upward, pointing toward the heavens. Above the altar, on the wall, was the blue, white and black banner of Neutria. There, before the altar was a warrior standing with arms stretch out, in meditation. His swan-winged helmet sat on the altar. Everyone stood and waited, not wishing to disturb his meditation. Suddenly, he lowered his arms and turned to face them.

The boys could clearly see the warrior standing before them. He was tall, well over six feet. His shoulders were board and his body was clad in armor and furs. A cape hung from his neck, held in place by a large iron ring. Under his outer fur garments was a suite of mail, and from his waist hung a long, heavy sword, sitting in its scabbard, which was the traditional weapon of the Neutrians.

His face was frozen hard in a mixture of woe and determination. His handsome features were worn by the hardships of warfare, though his blue eyes sparkled with an energy that was common to his race. His hair was long and yellow, kept in braids, as all the men of this northern land did, and a heavy growth of a honey-colored beard hung from under his chin. His face looked familiar to the boys, and then it dawned on them that he looked very much like the Princess Valenda. Both this man and the princess held themselves in the same noble manner, and yet there was nothing arrogant or vain about them. Truly they were born of the same womb. But there was a quality about this warrior that the boys had not seen in the other Neutrians, though it was not unfamiliar to them. Everyone recognized it. It was the noble spirit of one who was destined to rule. They could see he was a natural born leader whom men could follow without questioning. Only once before did they see such a quality, and that was in their friend and comrade, Vesten. They knew instantly that standing before them was, Sagtrim, Prince of Neutria.

One day Sagtrim would become the leader of this northern people, who loved him dearly and would gladly follow him into battle, even if he led them into the Yawning Void. Sagtrim was more than just a prince, destined to be their king. He was their leader and good comrade, and always could be found at the head of his men, when they charged into battle, and he never left the field of blood and steel until the last of his men had departed. On his bronze arms, they could see the multitude of scars attesting to this. It was a testimony to his bravery and leadership.

"*Hul Nordtheim!*" Arlindor said in the Neutrian language, as he greeted the prince. "I am Arlindor, the green druid of earth and alchemy. I have traveled from Wissenval to offer what assistance I can to your people. With me have also traveled good men out of the east. Pettin and Olaf are from Tillenia, and from the Mark has come Magin, Gordon and Milland. Also, from the Mark are these two lads, Rullin and Huck."

"Long have we waited for help from the enchanted valley," Sagtrim said. "It has been many months since my sister, Princess Valenda, has sailed east to seek help from Wissenval. We've almost given up hope of her return. Has she not returned with you?"

"The Princess Valenda had arrived at Wissenval, and represented your father at a great council that was held there," Arlindor said, as the prince carefully listened to him. "She joined us on our quest, and set out from Wissenval on foot. But she did not return with us. Half way here, several of the members of our fellowship were abducted by trogs, out of Fennoria. Princess Valenda chose to join those of our party, who were sent to try and rescue them."

"To Fennoria?" Sagtrim asked. His eyes flashed with concern about his sister's fate. "If anyone could enter that accursed land and return from it with her soul intact, it is she. But I still fear for her, for in these dark times no one is safe."

"Your concern for your sister is understandable," Arlindor said, "but she did not go alone. She walks alongside many who are counted among the high in bravery and skilled in wisdom, including my brother-druid, Blondor."

"Blondor?" asked Sagtrim. "We've expected Blondor to return to Neutria. He said he would, and we dearly have need of his advice. It is a great regret that our halls will not echo with the sounds of his footsteps once more."

"I have come in his place,"Arlindor said. "We've traveled long, hard miles to reach your land, and I offer myself in Blondor's place."

The prince looked at the tall druid. He thought how unlike he seemed from the wandering druid whom he called, friend. "Then we welcome you to our land, friend Arlindor," the prince finally said. "My father sits inside. I would wish that you would speak with him. In these times he finds the darkness that lingers behind closed doors more appealing then the light of day. Ever since he was stricken by the winged demon's black breath, his heart has been heavy with grief, and now he wails for death's embrace. His distress is contagious and spreads throughout the land, like a plague among my people. It took all our efforts to convince my father to send Valena to Wissenval in search of help. Since then, things have gotten worst, I fear."

"Your sister told us much of the plight of Neutria, at Wissenval," Arlindor said. "We hurried to you, to provide assistance. If I'm to help your king and father, then you must first fill me in on what has transpired since your sister left Neutria."

Prince Sagtrim told Arlindor of the events that had taken place, briefly referring to the attack on his father by the Horzugal. "We have seen many black days in the last few months. Shortly after my sister departed for the east, the High Caliph of Alfienia and Greater Allomania, as the Kreel overlord calls himself, appeared once again before the walls of Earilville and demanded an answer to the question he put before us on his last visit. But when we refused to give an answer to his ultimatum, he spat his hatred at us and threatened to avenge the insult. It was less than twelve hours when his armies, brandishing spears and scimitars, laid siege to our city. We burnt the bridge across the Jorunthon River and took up guard, refusing to surrender. Great boulders were catapulted over the walls of Earilville. The boulders would burst into flames as they sailed through the air, fueled by some dark magic that made it almost impossible to extinguish. Most of the city was burnt to the ground, but still we held out, refusing to abandon the black and charred walls.

"Across the Jorunthon River was mustered a great host of trogs, Aflienians and trolls. So great were their ranks that we could barely make out their numbers. Their eyes were filled with burning hate that shined red under the darkened the sky. When last I left the western settlements, there were more undermen joining them each day. We were able to hold the city and prevent them from crossing the river, but I fear, for not much longer.

"Then one day there appeared a great eagle with feathers as white as the virgin snow on its head and wings. I knew that it could only be one of the enchanted birds that resided in the far off Axis Mountains. It landed before me and held me transfixed with its gaze, as if it took possession of my will in its talons. I could hear it speak to me, though no words passed through its mouth. It was as if I heard a voice within my head. It then flapped its great wings and flew off once more, but I knew that I had to return to my father at once, here in Noranil. So it was fated that I would arrive just when you and your comrades arrived. It would seem that my prayers to the Lords of the Light have been answered."

"The eagle might have been a messenger from Gottron," Arlindor said. "It was his way of telling you that you were needed in Noranil. But now you must tell me of what you can about your father's illness."

Sagtrim's face changed as fear and terror appeared for the first time, melting the frozen expression of determination. It was as if the mere mentioning of the illness infected Sagtrim. Arlindor looked into his cold eyes and asked him, "You spoke of the black-winged demon that men called the Horzugal. Tell me, has there been any other sightings of it?"

"No," Sagtrim said, as if he was relieved to hear his own answer. "We've seen no further signs of that foul demon, and I pray that we never see it's like again."

Arlindor said nothing. He seemed to be deep in thought.

"What is it?" asked Milland. "You don't seem pleased about what the prince told you. What does it mean?"

"It could only mean that the demon has fled," Magin interrupted.

"No, Magin, not fled," Arlindor said. "This is black news. Think for a moment. If the Horzugal is not here, then where? His absence during the attack on Earilville can only mean that the Lord of Darkness has changed his plans. Unable to gain possession of the Red Stone, he has decided to divert our attention by his siege on Earilville, while his main forces are moving to strike else where."

"But where?" asked Magin.

Arlindor did not answer the stone breaker and turned to the prince. "I think it's time that you take us to the king."

They followed the prince into the main hall. As the doors opened, a cold chill rushed out like an animal, long trapped, delighted at its liberation from its confines. It cut through them, causing them to shiver. When they stepped inside, they found the hall filled with dark and gloom. Once, where the echoes of hearty voices sung of heroic sagas and brave warriors celebrated and feasted, there was now only an unbearable melancholy. What little light that could be seen in the hall revealed rows of columns on either side of the hall. On them were hung shields and spears. Between the columns, were statues of warriors clad in armor, neglected and gathering dust. Along the walls were torches that long since lost their fire because no attendant was permitted to keep them burning. Dark curtains were hung over the windows high above, to keep out the light. The only illumination was from a fire that burnt brightly on a pyre at the far end of the hall. Behind it the boys could make out a great altar of stone. On it were candles unlit, thick as a log and four feet high, rooted in solid gold candlesticks holders and draped in dried flows of melted wax. Over the altar the banner of Neutria hung on the wall. On either side of the banner was a dragon's head carved from wood. Placed on the altar was a great sword made from the finest craftsmanship. Runes were cut into its blade and its handle was made of silver and ivory and studded with diamonds and rubies. The sword was called Ructhon, the Sword of Kings. It was passed down from generation to generation in the long line of Neutrian kings.

Ructhon was usually displayed with the blade facing upward, so as not to permit its power from draining from it. But now the sword's blade was placed upside down by the king, after he was stricken by the Horzugal. Resting before the sword, on a white cloth, was a solid gold arm. It stood upright with an open palm. In the center of the palm rested the Red Stone, given to Neutria for safekeeping by Lothangia long ago, to cement the alliance between the two nations. The stone was set in a gold chain that the kings of Neutria wore around their necks when they rode into battle.

Amidst the shadows and flickering lights sat a sunken man. He appeared old and feeble, as his body slouch in a large, wooden chair. His white beard rested on his chest, and his face was hidden by his boney hands. He wore long, gray robes and the Iron Crown of Neutria rested on his silver hair.

Sagtrim slowly led them to his father, King Amthrim. They came to a halt before him, but the king did not seem to register their presence.

"Father. It's I, Sagtrim, your son," the prince said in a soft, but commanding voice. The king made no sound or movement. "I have with me that which we have hoped for. Help from the enchanted valley has arrived. They have traveled far under the command of the druid, Arlindor."

King Amtrhim lowered his frail hands, revealing his tired and worn face. Kingly, he seemed, despite the effects of the black illness that plagued him. His blue eyes shined like a clear, wintery sky under his heavy, white brows. He slowly rose to his feat, grasping a wood cane for support. The boys saw a man who appeared old and bent in the figure of King Amthrim, but one who has retained his royal bearing. They could understand why the men of Neutria loved their king and trusted him. Despite appearing old and bent, they felt that he was once a great leader, who fearlessly led men into battle. But now, Amtrhim's spirits seem broken, just as the spirit and will of Neutria seem broken.

Amthrim rested his eyes on Arlindor. "You've come a long way," the king finally spoke. His icy eyes held the gentle dark eyes of the druid. "But I fear that even a druid from Wissenval cannot change the course of events that have been placed into motion. These are black days, druid. A great darkness is moving across the world that not even a thousand sun lamps burning brightly on every hill in all of New Earth, day and night, could hold back. I fear we're doomed to pass into the growing darkness."

"If you really believe such a fate awaits us, and there is no hope of holding it back, why then did you send your daughter to Wissenval to seek our help?" asked Arlindor.

With the mention of Valenda, the king's eyes awoke with a new light.

"Valenda? Yes. My child. A maiden born out of the northern gales. Hard as steel and cold as ice she can be when the need demands it, and yet there is a warmth like that of the summer sun, and as soft as a doe's tail, that any man would give his right arm to know," the king said, more to himself than to the druid. His eyes flashed again and he took a few steps toward Arlindor. "What can you tell me of my dear daughter? Did she reach Wissenval? And if so, why has she not returned with you? It has been months since last her beauty and grace has charmed my tired eyes, and her laughter filled my halls with its sweet song. How so very much like her mother she is. Tell me, druid. Tell me where she is?"

Arlindor stood tall before the king, pulling himself to his full height. "Princess Valenda arrived in Wissenval last Eremid and took part in the council called by the head of my order, Gottron. She was your representative at the council, and counted among the great who sat there. She told all who were gathered there of the plight of your people."

Arlindor proceeded to tell King Amthrim of all the events of the council and all that was decided by those who were part of the council. He then continued to tell the king how the princess joined the company and traveled through the Wolf-Staak Forest, and how they were ambushed by trogs, who took Palifair and Tom captive. He then told of Valenda's decision to join Blondor and the others in their rescue attempt to save the boys, and how she asked him to come to Neutria to help her people and her father. Amthrim listened with fascination at what Arlindor told him and seemed transfixed by the news the druid brought him. He never once blinked an eye as he listened.

"Tell me, Arlindor," the king finally spoke. "How will the end of this year see this war unfold? Is there any hope for the race of Truemans?"

"So long as there is life, there is hope," the druid answered. "What the year's end holds in-store for New Earth and our race, not even Gottron can see. We stand at the doorway to a new age. What that age will be like depends on what men decide to do in the present. The threat is great and with the passing of each hour it grows even greater, but all is not lost. So long as there are Truemans who are still free from the domination of the tyranny of the Lord of Darkness, freedom remains alive. But freedom will surely die if Truemans do not stand up and defend what belongs to them. For freedom can only live in the hearts of men and women who are determined to fight to remain free. That is the hope that we still have."

"But we're few and scattered by my count," King Amthrim said. "I've seen their armies. They're like locusts blackening the fields and eating everything in their path. Nothing can stand up to them, and worse—I've looked into the face of one of the demons that serves the Beast of Allomania, and I know that there is no hope. There's only the vain pride of our people who are too stubborn to accept the reality of the situation that confronts us. Perhaps it would be better if we all fall on our swords, to save our souls from being taken by those blasted, winged demons back to

Allomania, to be tormented in the next world. I don't fear for my own life, druid. I'm an old man and have lived my life as I saw fit. I have always tried to do what is best for my people. No! I fear for the young, my son and daughter, and the children of all my people. When I look into their young faces, especially the youngest, I wonder what will become of them?"

"The danger that we face is truly great, but I too have looked into the face of the Horzugal, as have those who walk with me, and we have not only survived with our souls intact, but have triumphed on the demon," Arlindor told the king. Amthrim looked at him in disbelief. "Believe me when I tell you that there is still hope," Arlindor said. "The mere fact that you care more for the fate of the young proves to me that your heart is still strong, but you must understand that their fate will be determined not by the might of the enemy, but by what we decide to do in the struggle against him. The times we live in demands action, and men with strong hearts that burn with the warrior's flame. I don't fear the times we live in. I welcome them. The Thrangraal prophecies are coming true, and that means there is great opportunity to rid the world of the evil that lurks within Allomania. I tell you, King Amthrim, that hope exists and it has taken Trueman form. It walks the world as we speak, for he who was prophesied to return has done so, and your daughter walks at his side."

"The Emperor has returned?" asked Amthrim. He could barely say the words.

"Yes, he has," Arlindor said. "The time has come. The White Stone has been found by a youth, just as the prophecies foretold. It was found in the far off land to the north and east, which Truemans call the Mark."

King Amtrhim's eyes turned toward Huck and Rullin, who were standing beside Arlindor. Before he could ask the question, Arlindor spoke.

"No, my King," the druid said. "They are not the one, but they were present when the stone was found by the chosen youth. They are his friends. His name is Palifair, and it was on his shoulders that the fate of the world has been placed. Only a lad, and yet he and his friends found the courage to face the dangers that tried to stop them on their quest. They also have looked into the face of the Horzugal and done battle with them, and survived."

Amthrim's blues eyes were now filled with tears. He rose and walked to the boys. He touched each on the cheek and smiled. Turning back to Arlindor, he spoke, "How could I have let myself remain hidden in the darkness of this hall, while I let these children fight my battles? Too long have I let the young face all the dangers. My son does battle in the western folds, leading my armies, while my daughter now faces nameless dangers at the side of the Emperor Returned. And now, these lads are brought before me to remind me of my foolishness."

Amthrim straightened himself up. No longer bent, he turned and faced the boys once more. "Tell me, lads, what are your full names?" he asked.

"This here is Huck Lock and Rullin Ashburn," Arlindor answered for the boys.

"At your service," Huck was the first to speak and bowed at the waist.

"You servant, sir," Rullin also said and bowed.

"Come here, lads," Amtrhim said as he sat on his throne once more.

As the boys approached, the king's eyes examined their young faces. King Amthrim seemed moved. The wrinkles on his long, sad face were drawn back.

Prince Sagtrim, noticed for the first time in many months, the sparkle of joy returning to his father's eyes. "These lads must be pixies who possess great magic, for they have returned by father to me and our king to his people," Sagtrim said.

"It is not magic," Amthrim said as he looked at his son. "The thought of these two lads traveling so far from their homeland, leaving the safety of their families and homes, to come and offer their services to me, and their aid to our people, that has rekindled the fire of our race, in my heart. Their unselfish bravery has driven the darkness from my mind and I can see clearly once more. If that is magic, then perhaps, they truly do possess it?

"Tell me, lads," Amtrhim spoke once again to Rullin and Huck.

"Have you really seen the White Stone? Tell me of the wondrous talisman."

Huck and Rullin looked into Arlindor's face, waiting to know what they should do. The druid's dark face lit up with a smile and nodded his approval.

"Well, sire, Huck and I were camping out in the Mark, that's our homeland, with two friends, Tom Applekean and Palifair Chestnut," Rullin began to speak. "It was last Eremid of the calender of my people. After dark we turned in, but before we had dropped off, into sleep, a great fire ball streaked across the sky and crashed into the side of a mountain."

"Weren't you afraid?" the king asked.

"Well, yes, we were," Huck now spoke. "But our friend, Palifair, wasn't. He got up and without saying a word, began walking over to where the fire ball had crashed. We all followed him and he led us to the exact spot where it had come down."

"He found it because of the Light," Rullin interrupted. "That's what Mr. Blondor and Mr. Arlindor told us."

When Rullin mentioned the Light, Amthrim's face seemed to change its expression, as if he was trying to remember something.

"And that's when we found the stone," Huck said. "At the bottom of the mountain was a great deal of rocks that had been unearthed by the impact of the fireball. The stone was lying there, all shining and glowing with a strange, white light. Palifair wasn't afraid at all. He went right up to it and picked it up."

The king looked back up at Arlindor. "Tell me the full story of this lad, Palifair," he said to Arlindor.

Arlindor began telling the king the entire tale of their plight. He told him about the meeting in the Unicorn Inn, their journey to Gateburg and then their flight toward Wissenval, and the council that was held there. Amthrim was extremely interested in everything the druid said, and clung to every word, especially those concerning his daughter. He was very moved when the druid told him of the attack by the Horzugal at Gateburg and before Bridgetown, and how Palifair, with the power of the White Stone, was able to fight off his attackers. When Arlindor had finished his tale, Amthrim just stared at the boys in wonder. He was amazed that such young lads could muster the strength to face the servants of the Lord of Darkness and survive, while he had done so poorly in just one conflict.

"I must be truly feeble?" the king said. "A young child was able to succeed where I failed. Am I not able to find the courage of a child?"

"Don't try to compare yourself with the valor of the stone bearer, sire," Arlindor said. "Even the bravest warrior, in all the nations of Truemandom, would have fallen before the Horzugal without the aid of the White Stone. Even with the Red Stone in your possession, it was no equal to the weapon that young Palifair possessed. With the White Stone, Palifair was able to muster the power of the Light to fight off the Horzugal. Even the Lord of Darkness is no match for the White Stone. Sire, you faced the winged Servant of the Darkness and came through it still alive, which is more than what most mortals could have done. Come and walk with me, and let me speak to you of things that are meant for only a king's ear."

Arlindor took the king by the arm and helped him to his feet. The others watched as the king walked alongside of the druid through the darkened hall. They could not hear what the druid was saying, not even Milland with his exceptional hearing. Several times the king would stop and stare in amazement, as if the druid's words were like that of a healer's waking potion. When they had made a complete circle around the hall, they returned to where the others were waiting by the throne. Alongside the druid was no longer the feeble, ailing king that they found hiding in the dark, but a king that seemed transformed. King Amthrim stood tall and straight and towered over everyone else. He no longer needed the support of the druid's arm, but walked with a brisk step of a much younger man. The wrinkles on his face had disappeared and his eyes now burned with a blue fire. Before them stood King Amthrim, King of Neutria, Lord of the Northern Folk and Soldier-Warrior of the Boatmen of Neutria.

"Father?" The word barely escaped Prince Sagtrim's lips. The prince was both amazed and surprised by the transformation in his father. "Father, you have returned to us."

"Yes, my son," the king said. "The smell of war is in the air and the Beast is at our door. It's time that we stop lamenting over our plight, like old women, and take control of our destiny."

Amthrim's voice echoed with a new life. His beard sparkled like silver and his cheeks grew pink. "Captain Bolthur," the king called for Bolthur who was standing in the back. He came running to his king and kneeled before him.

"Yes, my Lord," Bolthur said.

"Go and ring the war bells," Amthrim command. "Let all know that the time to fight is upon us. Then call my war lords together and tell them to make ready the city, and all Neutria, for battle. All able-bodied men are to answer the call, and arm themselves for war. Then tell them to make ready the womenfolk, children and the old and injured, who will be evacuated from the cities and fields. They are to leave in three days for Kungthorn, and there they are to prepare for the worst. We will sail to war. There is only one of two fates that awaits us, either victory or death. If the latter is our fate, then they are to make a last stand in Kungthorn. Go now and tell my children that their father has returned to them."

Bolthur rose and hurried from the hall, calling to the guards as he left. Amthrim watched and then turned to Arlindor and his son.

"It's good to be alive once more, even if it's only to meet a glorious death in battle," the king said.

"Better to die fighting as a free man, then to live on one's knees, like a slave," Arlindor said.

Amthrim turned to his son and placed his hand on his shoulder. "You have proven yourself more than worthy to be king and commander during my illness," Amthrim said. "Now, I must ask you to once again take command, but this time it will be on the water. Make ready the fleet. We will set sail in three days."

"Set sail?" asked Prince Sagtrim. "In what direction will the winds of war take our sails?"

"South. To Ortangral," answered the king. "We must reach Ortangral before Caliph Kharz-Zish reaches the fortress. As we speak, his entire army is marching to the fortress. I think the attack on Earilville was meant to divert your attention, while he sought to capture his true objective. Since he could not convince Neutria to join with Allomania, he was ordered by his master to take Ortangral. Once taken, the armies of Neutria and Tillenia will be blocked from sailing south to join with the Lothangians. Do you agree, Arlindor?"

Arlindor did not speak at once. His dark eyes stared into the darkness that filled the hall, as if he was looking for something.

"I can see a great darkness moving across the world, to the south of Neutria," Arlindor said. "It's like a black fog that hides what is below it. There isn't an hour to lose. We must set out for Ortangral and reach it before Kharz-Zish does."

"But can we stop that horde, even if we reach Ortangral in time?" asked Sagtrim.

"Now whose words speak of doubts?" King Amthrim laughed. He smiled at the prince and then said, "My son, we can only do that which is in our power to do, and with you leading my armies, and Arlindor advising us, as well as the help of our new friends from beyond the great woods, we can hope to dare great deeds, and nothing more."

"But, will that be enough?" Sagtrim asked.

"Only the Lords of the Light can tell," Amthrim said "If we begin preparing now, we can leave on the third day and reach Ortangral in three days from then. It will take the Beast's armies seven days to reach Ortangral, at the least, which means we will have twenty-four hours to prepare our defenses once we arrive."

"We will not reach Ortangral unprepared," Arlindor said. "A detachment of Lothangian knights stands guard at Ortangral. They are from the best their armies have to offer, though they are not enough to hold the fortress for long. Hopefully, if we are delayed, they will hold the fortress long enough until we arrive."

"That is good news," the king said. "Then our strength will be even greater, and our cause not so hopeless."

Arlindor walked over to where the Red Stone was kept, without saying a word. Everyone watched in silence as the druid lift the stone and brought it to King Amthrim. He placed the chain around his neck and let the stone rest on the king's chest.

"King Amthrim, Lord of the Northerners, the time has come for the Truemans of the north to take their place alongside their brothers, in the struggle that is taking place in the south. All that is good and noble in this world is threatened by the Lord of Darkness. He has unleashed his armies, which march at this very moment against our brothers in Lothangia. All that stands between him and the fulfillment of his black dream of domination, is the purity of the blood that courses through our veins. That purity is the Light that shines within it. It is a gift given to us by the Lords of the Light, and we must use it when the times become perilous. If we fail, then there will be no more tomorrows and the world will be covered with the endless blackness of the Darkness. If we fail, then those who survive this struggle, well do so as slaves of the Beast of Allomania, and will suffer the most horrible torments that his black mind can conjure-up."

Arlindor's voice grew forceful as he spoke, and his words thundered throughout the hall, like a great war horn calling them to arms. Everyone raised their weapons and shouted. "Hail to the Light!"

In the next three days, Neutria came alive once more. It was as if a new confidence surged through the land. Everyone's spirits were uplifted at the news of their king's recovery. King Amthrim made sure that he was seen by as many of his subjects as possible, in and around the city of Noranil. He wanted his people to see that their king had returned to them. He had faced the black breath of the Beast of Allomania and survived. He knew that his presence would make his people feel that they could face and defeat the King Kreel, no matter how great Allomania's power was, or how large its armies. And wherever he went, the people of Neutria saw the tall, green druid from Wissenval, ever at his side. Many of the people began to joke that their king cased a green shadow.

Everyone was busy preparing for the war that was coming. Iluck and Rullin spent most of their days with Magin, as they explored the harbors and watched the ships coming and going. Dozens of serpent ships were being readied by the boatmen, supplies were being loaded and their sails were overhauled to make sure there were no tears or holes in them. Many of the ships had already left Noranil and sailed out onto the river and down to the Thuntium Mirror. There they would wait for their king to lead them the rest of the way to Ortangral.

"Never have I seen such magnificent boats," Rullin said. "I'm sure that my people in the West Mark would love the opportunity to sail in such ships. With just a few ships like these, the fishermen of the Markway River, could easily haul in enough fish to feed the entire Mark for a year, in just one week."

"Such ships are not for fishing," Magin said. "At least not these ships, though there are others that they use for fishing. Let's go and see if we can learn more about them?"

Magin led the boys along the piers, where ruby-cheeked men with yellow, braided hair, hurried back and forth. Soon they came to a tower made of wood overlooking the harbor. They proceeded to climb the tower and when they reached the top, they discovered they could see the wooden gate at the far end of the harbor that cut it off from the river. There were all types of boats in the harbor. Most looked like the serpent ships, but they were of various sizes and shapes. The longest were the war ships, but smaller versions of them were used for fishing and transporting goods by Neutrian merchants.

"What type of ships are they?" asked Huck. He pointed to the northern shore of the harbor where twenty, large, flat boats, about three times as long as the war ships, were docked. They had barrack-like houses built on them.

"Those are the boats that will carry the elderly, the women and children up the Noranilon River to the Kungthorn Citadel," Magin said.

"King Amthrim mentioned the Kungthorn Citadel," Huck said. "What is it?"

"I believe I heard Arlindor say it was a great redoubt built into the side of the mountains to the north of the Central Fold," Magin said. "It was built long ago, as a refuge for the families of the men who sailed off to war. The people of Neutria will await the outcome of the war there."

"When are we leaving for Ortangral?" Rullin asked. "It frightens me, something terrible, to think about what is going to take place there."

"Me too," Huck agreed. "I've read a great deal about war and heard the stories told by my father and grandfather and others, about the trogs when they attacked the South Mark. Even after facing the trogs in the forest and on the borderlands, I'm still not sure I've gotten used to the idea about going to war?"

Magin looked at both boys. "The boats will sail on the morrow's dawn, and should arrive at Ortangral in three days. Even now the ships are assembling in the Thuntium Mirror. But enough about ships and war. We have to get back to the Hall of Heroes. Arlindor is waiting for us. The sun is setting and it will soon be dark. Let's go," Magin said as he began climbing down the tower.

Back at the Hall of Heroes, the boys found Arlindor waiting with Gordon, Milland and the Tillenian woodmen.

Rullin had a strange feeling when he saw Arlindor. It was a premonition of some bad news. Arlindor seemed gray and quite. His black eyes no longer shined with the warmth that the boys had come to expect to see, whenever they turned to the druid for help.

"Tomorrow we set sail for Ortangral," Arlindor began to speak to everyone who was present. "All Neutria is aroused and ready to live up to its alliance and obligations to their friends in the south. Their king is well once more and leads his people, as he should. It would seem that I have fulfilled the purpose of my mission to this land. You who have aided me on this quest are no longer bound to continue to follow me any further. I say to you that if anyone who wishes to remain behind or return home, by whatever means possible, I will think not ill of you. I will never forget any of you and will always hold you all close to my heart as comrades."

"Perhaps our obligations to you have been fulfilled," Milland said, "but we have made a vow to the stone bearer, Palifair. That obligation has not yet been fulfilled. I think I speak for everyone present, when I say that there is no place we will not follow if you lead us. I, for one, am determined to ride with the men of this land to Ortangral, and do what little I can to resist the dark legions of Allomania, if it may help Palifair and our comrades?"

"Milland is right," Pettin agreed. "Though my brother and I did not take an oath to Palifair, we do take one now, that we will never abandon our comrades who are with us here, and those who followed the stone bearer. Our only hope lies in Palifair crowning Vesten the Emperor Returned in Lothar. I am more than willing to give my life, if it permits them to fulfill their destinies. Besides, there is no place to go other than south. Our nation is at war with Allomania, so we will go with you to Ortangral. All the world is in flames, or soon will be. We will follow you, Arlindor."

Olaf nodded his agreement with his brother.

"Pettin speaks the truth," Gordon said. "We know you are going south with the Neutrians, so we will all go with you."

Arlindor looked into the faces of everyone present. He studied them for a moment.

"I expected no less from each of you," the druid said, "but I wanted to give you the opportunity to make the decision freely."

"You should have known what our answers would be, Arlindor," Rullin said.

Arlindor turned to the boys. "Do you both also want to go to war?" he asked them.

The thought of going to war frightened them. "Yes, we do," Huck finally said, as he fought to get the words out. "We gave our word of honor to stand by Palifair, and if that means going to Ortangral, then that is where we will go."

"Fortunately for both of you, it does not mean that," Arlindor said.

"What?" The boys each stammered.

"The two of you will accompany the people of Neutria to the Kungthorn Citadel," Arlindor said.

"You can't mean it?" Huck said. "You can't leave us behind. It's not right. We're not luggage to be discarded at the first stop."

"Huck is right," Rullin agreed. "We've been through too much together. We want to see this through to the end. We promised Palifair that we would not desert him. When he was captured by the trogs, you and Mr. Blondor wouldn't let us go after him, and now you would abandon us in this northern land, while you all go south. Besides, you and Mr. Blondor said that we were chosen by the Light to go with Palifair, that we were chosen to be part of this struggle against the Lord of Darkness."

Rullin seemed determined to convince the druid to take them along. His eyes blazed with desperation, and his face turned deep red with anger.

Arlindor's dark eyes stared hard at Rullin, as if he was able to see something within him not visible to the rest of those present.

"You speak strong words for one so young," Arlindor said. "Perhaps you are forgetting whom you are talking to?"

Arlindor's voice seemed earnest and grave and frightening to the boys. Immediately the druid's face grew soft once more.

"But I can understand your disappointment, even though you have no understanding of the dangers that await us in Ortangral," the druid said. "But without realizing it, you are right about one thing. You were chosen for a purpose, but what that is may not seem apparent to you right now, but it will, in time."

The druid touched Rullin's cheek with his finger. Rullin instinctively stepped back, clutching at the Alfen Jewel under his shirt and blushed.

Chapter Five:
Ironbone

Huck and Rullin felt depressed as they sat aboard one of the barges loaded with people and their belongings. The fleet slowly made its way up the Noranilon River to the Kungthorn Citadel, where the Neutrian people sought refuge, while their menfolk sailed off to war. Everyone was busy manning the oars, to move the barges upstream. At certain points they had to unload oxen, mules and horses on the river bank. Ropes were tied to them so they could pull the barges along through those parts of the river where the currents were too strong for them to row against. Since everyone was busy most of the time, there were few people, Huck and Rullin could talk too, which made them feel forgotten and abandoned.

Huck and Rullin tried to help whenever the opportunity arose, but their depression at being left behind, made them feel miserable, and everyone who came into contact with them felt their pain. They so desperately wanted to go south and find their friends. They felt terrible because they were convinced that they had broken their oaths to Palifair.

As the boats made their way farther north, the mountains that bordered Neutria in the north, grew larger. Rullin felt himself drawn to the looming mountains, and could not shake the feeling that they were calling to him. He often clutched the Alfen Jewel under his garments. Huck began to fear that Rullin was becoming obsessed with the jewel.

West and then north the fleet of flat boats sailed up the Noranilon all that day. When night slowly began to claim its

247

lordship once more over the world, they had traveled seventy-five miles upriver. The boys were told that they would reach the place of disembarkment on the next day They would then proceed on foot along the road that ran up into the foothills of the mountains, where the Kungthorn Citadel was located. It was a great fortress dug deep into the earth thousands of years in the past, as a refuge to protect the Neutrians during the times of the War of the Races. Those were years of constant warfare against the fierce, flesh-eating Alfeinians, who lived on the wild plains to the west.

In those times, Truemans found friendship among the races of stone giants, who lived to the north, in the land of Jothumland. The giants never loved the foul, carrion-eating Alfeinians. Neutrian legends tell of an alliance between Neutria and Jothumland, long ago. The two nations waged war against the carrion-eaters and drove them out of the folds of Neutria. It was agreed that all the lands north of the mountains would belong to the stone giants, while the lands to the south, between the rivers, would belong to the Truemans. To cement the friendship between giants and Truemans, the giants dug out a series of halls deep into the base of the mountains, for the Neutrians to use as a refuge during times of war.

That night the boys were unable to sleep. They stood on the deck of the barge and stared up at the kaleidoscope of stars in the black heavens above. They pulled their fur hoods over their heads to protect them from the cold winds that swept down from the icy mountains to the north.

"You couldn't sleep either?" Huck asked Rullin.

"Not a wink," Rullin said. "It gets colder the farther north we travel. I never thought it could get so cold this early in Turning. I wonder what day of the month it is anyway? I seemed to have lost all sense of time up here."

"I know what you mean," Huck said.

"It seems so long ago since we left the Mark," Rullin said. "It feels more like years than months since we set out from Middleboro. That's probably because we're all along. Right now my father must be gathering together the town masters for the annual meeting of the West Mark Council. The fishermen must be going down the Markway River with their fleet of ships, to the Great Sea for the autumn catch, before winter comes and freezes over the river. How I wish, I was back home."

"I too miss the Mark," Huck said. I bet it's harvest time on my father's estate. We would often ride together to the fields, as my father explained to me everything that needs to be done. He would scold me if I wasn't paying attention, and then explain that I must learn everything that is required to run the estate, if I'm to someday take his place, when I grow up. I used to be bored with the lessons, but right now, I would give anything to be back home, riding with my father.

"Do you think we'll ever get back?" ask Huck.

"I don't know," Rullin said, and sighed.

The boys watched the dark landscape roll by in the night as they sailed ever northward, heading into the cold winds that blew down on them from the mountains. The rivers were calm and the people of Neutria decided to row as far as they could during the night. They wanted to reach the northern retreat as soon as possible, and decided to row in shifts during the night, so long as the currents permitted. The calm waters of the Noranilon River sparkled dreamily with the reflection of the stars dancing on their surface. After several hours, sleep finally overpowered the boys, They surrendered to its welcomed embrace, and turned in for the night.

The next morning the boys woke to the sight of the Jothumland Mountains looming hugely before them on the horizon. Two great arms of stone and rock jotted south from the mountain range proper on both sides of the Noranilon River. The source of the river flowed down from the mountains between the arms, where it was fed from melting ice.

"We should reach the Kungthorn Road in less than an hour, lads," said Freytheron, the boat master of the barge. He placed a hand on the shoulder of each boy. Freytheron's wrinkled, red face was worn with his age of one hundred and ninety-years. He was the oldest citizen of Neutria. From his face hung long, white whiskers that reached down to his belt. He was a ship's captain, and in charge of the Neutrians, now that their king was away. Huck and Rullin were placed in his charge. He was given the seal of Neutria, which gave him the authority to rule in place of the king, while he was gone. As a veteran of many wars, he served Amthrim's father, King Brimthrim, well. Now, in his old age, he led those unable to fight in the war.

In the last two days, since they left Noranil on the 15 of Turning, Freytheron took charge of the *Markins*, as they Neutrians called the Marklanders, Huck and Rullin. He felt their disappointment at being separated from their comrades. His heart was also heavy at being left behind. He was far passed his prime and too old to sail off to war with the others, and thought of being condemned to the fate of a straw death made his heart heavy.

"How far is Kungthorn from the river, sir?" asked Rullin, as his dark eyes looked up into the old man's gray eyes.

"Not far, lad," he said in his deep voice, speaking the common language of Daryan. "It's no more than a five-hour march. It lies up there, some three hundred feet above us, over those cliffs. They offer protection, making it impossible for any enemy to reach us there, even under a full scale siege. We always make sure that the citadel is well supplied with everything we will need for a long stay.

"Tell us about it," asked Huck.

Freytheron began to tell the boys of the origin of Kungthron. "Long ago, when this land was still wild, and my people were in a constant state of war with the Alfeinians, our legends tell us that the race of stone giants who live beyond those mountains, came down to see what all the fighting was about. They hated the Alfeinians, and soon became friends with the Truemans. When the last of the Alfeinians were driven from our lands, the giants dug out tunnels that reached deep into the mountains. Great chambers, with high halls there are there, that is strong enough to protect us from any attack. Many times in the past we have taken refuge there, and it has never failed us. I hope it will not fail us now."

"What about the stone giants?" asked Huck. "We heard about

them, but everyone we asked said they had never seen any giants. Do you think they really exist?"

"Our legends say they do," Freytheron said. "I have never seen one, and I know of no account by of my people having any contact with them in the last thousand years, though there always are a few individuals who claimed to have seen one from time to time. We call the giants, the Jothunthum, and they call themselves the Yomiron. We believe that they still live in these mountains, and the lands further northern, especially in the great woods that grow there. We call these mountains, the Teeth of the World. There is supposed to be a great city on the other side of the mountain, where the giants live. It's called Symirheim, by my people, but no one has ever been there. They seldom venture south of the mountains anymore, and their numbers are supposed to have dwindled, not by death or war, but by sleep. Many have laid down and retreated from this life, and have returned to the Great Mother World."

"What is the Great Mother World?" asked Huck.

"The giants believe the world is alive and gave birth to their race," Freytheron said. "When they become tired of this world, they return to their Great Mother World by falling into a deep sleep and thus become one with her once more. Many of my people believe you can see them sleeping in strange rock formations. Occasionally some hunting parties will return from these mountains with stories about seeing some great stone giant walking, or claim to have seen one sitting on a ledge or on some high peak in the mountains."

"Are any of them in league with the Lord of Darkness?" asked Rullin.

"I think not," Freytheron said. "They have withdrawn from the world of Truemans and undermen, and no longer care what happens to us, though I pray that will someday change."

"Which are they? Trueman or undermen?" asked Rullin again.

"Neither," Freytheron said as he pulled on his long, white beard and stared at the wall of stone and trees that lined the river. The boys watched him as the northern winds blew through his white whiskers.

"They are a much older race," Freytheron said. "Some say that they existed even before the Great Hell Fires, of long ago. They are even reputed to have seen the inferno of Soltar, in the very beginning of time, before the birth of Old Earth."

"I wonder if we will see giants," Rullin said.

"One never knows," Freytheron said as he looked at Rullin and smiled.

Huck and Rullin listened with great interest to everything Freytheron told them. From one of the boats they heard a roaster crowning, as the first warm rays of the sun rose in the eastern horizon, lighting up the morning sky. The mountain peaks caught the rays as they raced through the Turning sky. The golden rays sent the winking brightness of the nightly stars into hiding once more, until they were needed once again to aid travelers that dared to journey at night.

Everyone was deep in their own thoughts as the barges finally came to where the people of Neutria were to disembark and make their trek up, into the mountains. There they would wait for the return of their king from war and welcome them back to their home, or until the shadow of doom came knocking on their threshold and take them away to the realm of the dead, Hellunheim.

When the first of the barges docked, several dozen men on horses rode ahead to the citadel and make it ready for those who would soon follow after them. Planks of wood were laid over the sides, as people began to disembark and prepare for the trip to Kungthorn, Many feet hurried to dry land, with arms filled with supplies and personal belongings, too valuable for their owners to leave behind. Wagons loaded with goods were unloaded from the flatboats. Old women, the injured and children rode on many of the wagons. Everywhere people were alive with the din of necessity. Huck and Rullin were bewildered and overwhelmed by so many people rushing about. The chatter and shouts in the Neutrian language mixed with the sounds of animal noises, creating a whirlwind of confusion, or so the boys thought. Freytheron had left them to supervise the work of unloading the boats.

The boys were soon placed in a wagon with several of the wounded warriors that had fought in the western regions of Neutria. It was then that Huck began to notice a queer change in Rullin. He seemed to suddenly withdraw into himself. Gone was the inquisitive nature that was characteristic of him. Huck noticed him staring into the trees that grew on the foothills of the mountains, as if he was looking for someone or listening to something that they could not see. Huck also noticed Rullin clutching the jewel under his shirt. He had done this more and more since they left Noranil. Several times Huck had to remind Rullin not to draw attention to the jewel or take it out from under his garments.

"Is there anything wrong, Rullin?" Huck asked, concerned for his friend. "Why are you always clutching that jewel?"

"What?" Rullin asked, as if he was suddenly shaken from a deep sleep. "Did you say something?"

"I don't like the way you've been acting," Huck confessed. "It's not like you at all."

Rullin's dark eyes stared, trance-like at his friend for a moment. He then broke out into a smile and chuckled.

"I'm sorry," Rullin said. "But ever since we set out from Noranil, I've had the funniest feeling that—well—it's as if someone was singing somewhere off in the distance. It's not as if I can hear someone singing, but it's as if I can hear a song in my mind, far away, but it's compelling and calling to me, telling me to follow."

"Follow? Where to?" Huck asked, not liking the sound of it all.

"Up there," Rullin pointed to the mountains towering over head. "There, listen."

Huck listened, but heard nothing. He turned around to tell his friend, only to discovered that Rullin had jumped off the wagon and was running off, into the woods without having said another word. Without thinking, Huck jumped off the wagon and ran after his friend.

"Rullin! Wait! Wait for me!" Huck shouted as he ran after Rullin. Before anyone could see what all the commotion was about, they had disappeared into the woods.

Huck pushed his way through a wall of pine branches that pricked him with an assault of needles and bristles. He was barely able to keep up with his friend, who seemed to pass through the woods, unhindered. He shouted and shouted, but Rullin seemed unaware of him. It was as if he was in another world. Huck thought back at the way Palifair acted, way back on that night that the White Stone was discovered, and it reminded him of the way Rullin was now acting. He shook the thoughts from his mind and fought to concentrate on keeping up with Rullin. He was afraid of losing him in the darkness of the woods.

The ground soon began to rise sharply under their feet the farther they traveled into the woods. Huck realized they were climbing up the side of the mountain range, as they melted deeper and deeper into the forest. The trees were mostly pines and spruce, and the floor of the forest was thickly covered with a layer of fallen cones and pine needles, mixed with snow that did not melt in these higher elevations.

At last, Rullin stopped and fell to the ground. His knees buckled under him. Reaching into his shirt, he pulled out the jewel and held it in his hands, as puffs of white vapors floated from his mouth.

"What is it?" Huck asked his friend when he finally reached him. He was concern and out of breath. He feared that the jewel had taken control of his friend's mind.

"Does it have something to do with the jewel given to you by the Alfen King?" Huck asked. "Rullin! Please speak to me!"

Rullin slowly looked up at Huck, straight into his friend's eyes, and said in a voice that seemed altogether strange. "Don't worry, Huck. I'll be all right."

"All right?" Huck said, not altogether sure that he believed him. His heart was still pounding hard from chasing after Rullin.

"For a minute there, I thought you went off half-cocked," Huck said.

"It's the jewel," Rullin said. "It had some kind of control over me–directing me. It compelled me follow the song, but it has released me now."

Rullin stared hard at the green jewel that he held in his hands. His forehead frowned. "Now I know how Palifair must have felt that night in the North Mark, when he discovered the White Stone," Rullin said. "Remember when he ran off in a trance?"

"Oh, I remember," Huck said as he knelt down next to his friend. "How can I ever forget that night? I was beginning to think that the same thing was happening to you. But tell me, what did you hear?"

"Nothing really," Rullin tried to find the right words to explain what sensations coursed through him, but failed. "It was more like I was being pulled along, up there, in that direction." Rullin pointed up at the mountains.

"Up there? What for?" Huck asked.

"I don't rightly know, but somehow I felt that I had to go up there," Rullin said. "There's something up there, waiting for me, I think?"

"What's up there? What are you talking about? You're frightening me." Huck was becoming more concern for his friend as he listened to him. He did not like the direction the conversation was heading.

Finally, Rullin turned to his friend and smiled. "Let's find out. Come on," he said to Huck, and then jumped to his feet and was off once again, maneuvering his way through the rocks and trees.

"But? Rullin! We haven't got any supplies! No food or water for the hike!" Huck shouted after his friend. "How are we going to survive? We've got to get back to the road and try and catch up with the Neutrians!"

Huck pleaded with Rullin, as he fatefully followed after his friend. They scrambled up the rocky landscape that rose still higher. The snow grew deeper in some places where it clung between the larger boulders. The trees grew thinner in the higher altitudes and soon they were high above the tree line. They could see the tops of the woods, down below them, as they continued their climb ever higher. The boys could also see the valley, far below, with the Noranilon River flowing ever southward. They stopped and looked at each other for a few minutes, trying to catch their breaths. Rullin seemed himself once more.

"Well, Rullin," Huck said. "Which way do we go from here?" Huck did not expect an answer, and Rullin did not give him one.

Rullin was busy trying to catch his breath, and trying to figure out what in the world ever possessed him to run off the way he did. As he pondered the reason for his strange behavior, he realized that he was still clutching the green jewel, and began examining it. Huck looked at it and then at his friend's face. Rullin was studying it intensely. Rullin then looked up to their right and saw a shelf of stone carved into the side of the mountain. He began climbing once more, slowly made his way toward it. Huck jumped up again and followed his friend, mumbling to himself.

"Here we go again," Huck said.

When they reached the ledge, they discovered a stairway cut into the mountain wall. Old and worn it was from constant punishment of the weather and winds that swept up from the plains to the west, over the centuries.

"Come on, Huck," Rullin said, and waved his arm as an invitation for Huck to follow him.

"We have to go up," Rullin insisted.

"We do? Why?" Huck asked.

"Because that's where I'm going," he said and then suddenly turned and began climbing up the stairs.

The stairs winded up the side of the cliffs, first taking them up and south, and then turning north until it proceeded up the side of the ridge that extended out of the mountain range. The stairway became less steep, as it took them further up the ridge. Soon they were able to see before them, in the distance, looming up, great cliffs over a plateau. The cliffs began to take on shapes and forms, the closer they got to it. Trees grew at the base of the cliffs from the plateau. Their roots clutched the piles of boulders and earth that were sprawled about the foot of the precipice. High above, the boys could see what appeared to be forming before them, four great faces carved into the stone cliffs. Their features were cracked and partly overgrown with weeds, vines and other vegetation. The ravages of time and weather had disfigured them, but Huck and Rullin could now clearly make out four distinctive faces staring out, over the world.

The boys walked slowly, as if afraid that the sounds of their footsteps might awaken the four giant stone gargantuans from their slumber. They walked across the length of the plateau and sat down on a large stone that stuck out from a still larger boulder. There they sat, saying nothing for a while, examining the magnificent aberration that towered over them.

"What do you think it is, Huck?" Rullin asked finally, still looking up at the faces.

"I don't know for sure, but it looks as if someone carved four faces into the cliffs a very long time ago," Huck said.

"Whom do you think carved them?" asked Rullin again.

"They were carved by the hands of those who lived before the Great Hell Fires," said a strange, deep rolling voice above the boys.

The stone that they were sitting on all of sudden began to move, causing the boys to jump up in fright. They ran a short distance, stopped and turned around to discover that they were sitting on the foot of a large, stone figure. It was manlike and yet it was so like the rocks scattered about the plateau that they thought it was just another boulder.

They could not find the courage to move, and felt as if they had been transformed to stone, as they watched and listened to the stone giant that looked down at them.

"Yes. I believe that is what the legends say concerning the origin of the great Mountain Fathers, who sleep here," the stone giant said, partly to the boys and partly to himself, as if he was trying to dig deep into the memories he had buried in his mind from long ago.

Huck and Rullin still had not yet adjusted to the reality of the situation that confronted them. They had trouble believing their eyes and ears. What they had thought was a pile of boulders turned out to be a living being who was sitting so still that they could not accept the fact that it was alive. They looked around them for a second, expecting the other rocks that laid about to come alive any minute.

"Crack!" the throat of the stone giant made the noise that sounded like rocks breaking against each other, as he cleared this throat. He still sat on a stone, though it was hard at first to distinguish him from the stone he was sitting on. It was only when he stood up to his full sixteen feet that the boys could clearly make out his actual shape. His head was large and roundish, but not like a ball. It sat on his broad shoulders with no neck that could be distinguished. His face was hard to make out at first, but gradually it took form as he spoke. His mouth was little more than a crack. His skin, if you could call it skin, was a dark, grayish color that sparkled like iron graphite. His body seemed like a large, broad, vertical slab of stone, supported by two long legs. When he stood standing still, the legs and body seemed to form one large piece of stone, similar to those that made up the High Senate in the Mark. The only thing to disrupt its form, were the two large arms that extended from his shoulder. They were made of the same material as the rest of his body, though they were slightly smoother. But it was his eyes, most of all, that revealed to the observer that the spark of life existed, within this living monolith of stone. They appeared like Trueman eyes, but shined with the glimmer of some beautiful diamond.

"Crack! Ruck! You two don't look like Neutrian pups, but you are Trueman children, I'm sure of that," the stone giant said as he now examined Huck and Rullin. "Where do you come from, and why are you up here in this place, so far from the lowlands that your race likes so much?"

As frightened as Huck and Rullin were, they felt deep down that the giant would not harm them. It was something about his eyes that gave them the courage and confidence to finally speak.

"We didn't mean to disturb you, sir, or sit on your foot," Rullin said. "You see, we're lost and tired, and only wanted to sit and rest a while."

"Sit and rest, lost and tired," the giant said. "Yes, you should not be running loose in these earth-teeth without your parent-folk. "Pups like you could easily become a meal for a mountain lion, or some great bear. Yes, but where do you come from? How did you get here? Come now and answer my question, young pups. A rolling stone cannot wait."

"I'm known as Hucklin Lock, but everyone calls me Huck, and this here is my friend, Rullin Ashburn," Huck said as the boys bowed low. "And we're from the Mark. Have you heard of it?"

"Why? Should I have?" asked the giant.

"Well—no, I suppose, not," Rullin said. "It's a long way from here, far to the east."

"How far is far?" the giant asked.

"About twelve hundred miles, as the crow flies, I think?" Rullin said as he thought about it. "It's way on the other side of the Wolf-Staak Forest."

"Well, now that is a very long way off," the giant said. "I should like to hear more about your story, especially how you got here, and why you have come all this way? But first let me introduce myself. I am called Ironbone, in your language. In my language I'm called Gunt-thur, and my people are known as the Yomiron. We live in Jothumland, to the north of Neutria, where we're referred to as stone giants."

"A stone giant?" Rullin said. "I've heard of stone giants in the tales that the Neutrians told us. May I ask you just what are stone giants? Are you Trueman or underman?"

"Trueman or underman?" Ironstone said to himself out loud, as if trying to recall if either word fit the description of his people, as he cleared his throat. "Crack! Why, we are neither," he said. "My people are descended from a time before New Earth was born. We walked the world before it was new and lived through the Great Hell Fires of long ago, or I should say we slept through it all. My people claim a descent that goes far enough back to when Old Earth was new. Yes. That sounds about right. We dug deep into the earth and laid there buried and slept until the ashes had disappeared. This is how we survived those terrible fires. It was only after the world was cleared once more, did we wake from our long slumber.

"We were originally spawn out of the hot, molten womb of

the Great Earth Mother herself. Muttina, she is called by some. Erdina, she is called by others. But my people know her as Bodina, which means "Our Mother," in our language."

The boys listened to the great stone man as he spoke with such love and emotion that his crackling voice took on an almost musical tone, like golden bells chiming a lovely song. He eventually stopped talking and looked down at his two, uninvited guests, who seemed so enthralled by his storytelling that it moved him.

"Well, now," Ironbone said. "I think, before I go on talking, and a stone giant can talk long into the night and right through the next day once he gets started talking about the Great Mother Earth and her treasures, I think, perhaps, you should tell me more about yourselves. But not here, I think."

"You're not going to take us prisoners, are you, Mr. Ironbone?" asked Huck.

"Prisoners? Why, no," Ironbone said. "But I do think that you should come with me. It's not safe for you to be up here in the mountains all alone, especially after dark. The mountain lion and great bear that I warned you about, are still hungry."

Ironbone then bent down and gently lifted the boys up, holding each one cradled in the pits of his elbows.

"We can be more comfortable in my campsite. It's not far from here, and there you can tell me your story in full. And I might tell you more about my people, if you wish to hear more about them, while I give you both something to eat, if I can still remember what Truemans eat?"

Ironstone turned and began walking up the side of the mountain ridge toward the cliffs. His great, bulking form moved with a grace that seemed alien to one made of stone. As he moved over the rock floor, his feet locked into place with the stones. In this way, he was able to move through the most difficult terrain with all the confidence of a mountain goat.

He soon entered the small woods that grew on the spine of the ridge, under the ever watchful eyes of the four great stone faces high over heard. The boys sat silently, as he carried them. They felt strangely at ease in his arms. Eventually, Rullin, who felt the need to speak to Ironbone. "Please, Mr. Ironbone, may I ask a question?"

"You just did, but you may ask another," Ironbone said as he looked down at Rullin.

"Why were you sitting up on that ridge?" he asked. "It seemed strange that you should be sitting there just as we came along."

Ironbone did not speak at first. He made a cracking sound deep in his throat.

"Strange? Indeed," he said. "I was waiting for the arrival of a friend who asked me to meet him there, on this very day, or at the least, send a message if he was delayed. He asked me to meet him there and wait for him, long ago, when I saw him last. Let me see when this was? Crack!"

His throat made the cracking sound once more.

"It was over a year ago, I think?" he said. "It's hard to measure time in Trueman reckoning. Yes. That was the last time I spoke with Blondor."

"Blondor!" Both Huck and Rullin said, almost shouting the druid's name.

"You know Blondor?" Huck asked.

"Doesn't everyone?" Ironbone said. "He's called Cuurunk in my language. It means, the rolling stone. We call him that because he's always traveling here and there, and occasionally ventures into Jothumland. I remember him asking me to wait for him on this very day. Last year it was. He said, 'Ironbone. I have a favor to ask of you, and it's of the utmost importance. I want you to wait for my arrival before the four faces, on the 17th of Turning, on the next year.' Well, Blondor never asks anyone to do something unless it's very important, and never has to say it is very important, unless you don't know him very well, and I've known Blondor for centuries.

"So without asking why, I agreed, and he told me that if he could not make the appointment, he would send someone else in his place. I was surprised to hear Blondor say that he might not be able to keep his appointment. If he has doubts about something, then it must not only be important, but incredibly dangerous.

"So that's why I was sitting up on that ridge, when you two

pups came stumbling along instead of Blondor," Ironbone said. "And when you told me that you came out of the east, twelve hundred miles, all the way on the far side of the Wolf-Staak Forest, I knew that you must have been sent by Blondor, in his place. Am I correct?"

"Yes, in a way," Rullin said. "We started out traveling with Blondor and Arlindor, but we got separated and both of them went off to the south, to fight in wars. In fact, everyone has gone and left us behind."

"Yes. Well. Crack! Don't be too disappointed that you weren't asked to join them in fighting their wars," Ironbone said. "Wars can be a down right bloody business for Trueman adults, not to mention how dangerous it can be for their pups. But enough talk for the moment. We have reached our destination."

They came out of the wooded region and into a clearing below the cliffs. High above them were the four, staring faces that towered overhead. Their silent vigil was undisturbed by their presence. The clearing was positioned between two small ridges of rocks that stretched out from the cliffs in a 45-degree angle, and rose one hundred feet high on either side. Series of large steps were carved into them, worn by time and weather. They climbed up to the tops of the ridges, giving them the impression of a stadium.

In the center of this strange stadium were several large stone blocks that Ironstone used as a table and seats. High over head was an outcropping of rock that acted as a natural roof.

"This is the Raaaarkunaaaack, the gathering place," Ironbone said as he sat on one of the smaller blocks and placed the boys on the large stone that he used as a table. It stood six feet high and the boys sat with their feet dangling off the edge.

"Now, there, I want you two pups to remain here while I'm away," Ironstone said. "You'll both be safe here, so long as you don't go wandering off."

"Away? You're going to leave us here all alone?" asked Rullin.

"Only for a short time," Ironbone said. "You don't seem to have any supplies, so I'll wager that neither of you have anything to eat or drink. You must be getting hungry about now? I think

I'll go and try and find you some Trueman food. I should not be long. At least I will be back before the others arrive."

"Others? What others?" Huck asked.

"The others of my kind, of course," Ironbone said. "There's going to be a gathering of the Yomiron tonight, so don't go and get yourselves lost or one of my people might accidently step on you without realizing it until it's too late."

The giant then turned and lumbered away and soon disappeared into the trees, leaving the boys alone, to ponder the situation that they found themselves in.

"More stone giants?" Huck said as he looked over the stadium, trying to imagine what it would look like filled with the large stone men? "Well, Rullin, just what kind of stew have you gotten us into? Five hours ago we were safe with the Neutrians, on our way to the Kungthorn Citadel with plenty of food to eat and warm beds to sleep in, and then you go running off, half-mad, like a cock-a-jay, and lead us into the middle of a gathering of stone giants. I swear by my grandfather's beard, Rullin Ashburn. What in the name of the five Marks has gotten into you?"

"This," Rullin said as he pulled out the small, green jewel that hung around his neck. "It was as if something or someone, was talking to me. It told me to come up here, and I couldn't resist."

"I knew you shouldn't have taken that jewel from the Pixie King," Huck said.

"I don't know about that, Huck," Rullin said. "Remember what Blondor said back in Wissenval, about there being a reason for us being with Palifair, when he found the White Stone? He insisted that we come along, even when everyone else at the council meeting thought otherwise. Now this Ironstone tells us that he was waiting for Mr. Blondor, when we just happen to come along in his place. Do you think that Blondor knew that he wasn't going to keep his appointment with Ironbone?"

Huck scratched his head, trying to get straight all the facts that Rullin had laid before him.

"Well, maybe he did?" Huck said. "Druids can see into the future sometimes. It's possible that he knew he would have to make a detour, and that we would come here in his place. But what about the jewel? Did the Alfen King give you the stone so that it could lead you here? Did he know about Blondor?"

"I don't know, but maybe the Alfen King did know Blondor, and gave us the jewel so that we would be led to this place?" Rullin said.

"You may be right, but perhaps you shouldn't tell Ironstone about the jewel," Huck said. "At least wait until we know more about him."

When Ironbone returned after being gone for several hours, he was carrying a long tree trunk in his arms that he had cut and carved out. It was filled with fresh water from a nearby stream, as well as chestnuts, roots and several fish that he caught.

When the stone giant walked, he kept his back straight and the upper part of his body remained fixed. All that moved were his two, large, pillar-like legs that pound the ground under the weight of his bulk. The look on his face was frozen like that of a stone statue. Yet, for all his cold exteriors, the boys could not help but notice the life that shined within his two eyes, as he approached. They were filled with a timelessness, as well as the wisdom of his race. It made him seem a contradiction of hard stone and gentile warmth.

The boys were starved and gobbled down the chestnuts and washed them down with great gulps of clear, cool mountain string water. Ironbone piled some dry leaves and wood together within a small circle of stones, and lit a fire by snapping his hands together, sending sparks flying. Once the fire was lit, he cleaned the fish and began roasting them for the boys to eat.

After Huck and Rullin had their fill, they laid back with filed bellies, resting on the table top, as Ironbone stomped out the fire and cleaned up the stone stadium. He then returned to the boys and sat himself down on one of the stone seats.

"Crack! Ruuuck! Well, my little pups, I see that you have drunk and eaten your fill and are rested. Perhaps now we can talk? Let's see? Raaarkunaaak! The gathering," he said as his stone vocal cords grind together in his throat. "Let's start with the gathering.

It's a special place for my people, where we can come and meet whenever we must call upon the spirit of the Great Earth Mother to help us make important decisions. These great faces you see high above us are her children, who, if they are pleased, will intervene for us to seek her assistance."

As the giant told the boys about the gathering place, a cold wind blew up from the western plains far below, causing Huck and Rullin to pull their fur hoods on their coats over their heads.

"Are your people going to meet here tonight?" Huck asked.

"Yes, they are," Ironbone said. "They're on their way here as we speak. I came ahead to meet with Blondor, but he never showed up, and I was getting worried when you came along. I can only assume that he sent you two in his place, to represent him at the meeting."

The boys looked at each other and then up at the giant.

"Blondor never told us about you or the meeting," Huck confessed. "Actually, we came up here by accident, or by chance, if you want to call it that? We were on our way to Kungthorn with the Neutrians, but we separated from them."

Ironbone stared at Huck and then at Rullin. His eyes sparkled. Rullin felt that the giant could see right through him and knew what he was thinking. He instinctively clutched his chest.

"Now. Now. Don't you worry? You keep it where it is," Ironbone said.

Rullin's mouth dropped at hearing the giant's assurance, but before he could say anything, Ironbone began to speak again.

"But now, you must tell me your full story," the giant said. "Tell me how you got here and why. And please don't leave anything out. No. You mustn't. Craaaack," an especially long cracking sound emanated from his throat. "You see, your friend, Blondor, is also a friend of the Yomiron. He sent word by way of the big-winged birds of Wissenval. Oh, yes. And they told us much about the discovery of the White Stone in a faraway land to the east, and about the return of the Emperor, and the war that is unfolding between Allomania and Lothangia."

"You know?" The boys both jumped to their feet in surprise.

"Yes, of course I do," Ironbone said. "That's why I was waiting for Blondor. He wanted to speak to my people, and convince them to join the alliance he's forging against the Lord of Darkness. He and I felt that the Yomiron would be more inclined to do so if the Emperor and the White Stone were presented to them in person, at the meeting tonight."

"But Blondor and Vesten are not here," Huck said. "They went south after the trogs who kidnaped our friends–Palifair and Tom."

The giant watched the boys, studying them carefully. "I think it's time you told me the whole story," he said.

The boys no longer seemed frightened of the giant anymore. He could have killed them at any time if he was under the control of King Kreel. It was nothing that he said, that convinced them that he was a friend. It was more in the way he spoke. Despite his formidable appearance, there was a kindness and gentleness that pervaded his mannerism and everything he said and did. It could not be faked by someone who was in the service of the King Kreel.

All that afternoon the boys told Ironbone their tale, from the beginning to the end. They left nothing out. They described how they found the stone and were pursued by the Horzugal, Kellium's treachery, the council of Wissenval and everything that happened since they left the enchanted valley. Ironbone listened very carefully to everything the boys told him, and had to stop them with questions to make clear some points in their story, as the boys constantly interrupted each other. Ironbone was immensely interested in the ambush at Lost Lake and everything to do with Fennoria. When they told him about the war between Allomania and Neutria, Ironbone's ears, if he had any, would have stood up, on end.

Ironbone was especially concerned with the events as they unfolded in the northern regions of New Earth. The shadow out of the south had grown great indeed, and he realized that the Yomiron were becoming anxious. They had debated among themselves about what they should do about the growing danger, and had not come to any decision.

When Huck and Rullin finished telling their story, Ironbone

said nothing for a long while. He had a far away look on his stony face that gave him the appearance that he was just a block of stone with no life within, except for his eyes, which betrayed a great wisdom that dwelled behind them. His mind was filled with concern. He needed time to digest everything the boys told him. They watched him without saying a word. They felt at ease, at least around the stone giant in the short time they had spent with him. But he was still strange and they wondered if he could be unpredictable and do harm without meaning any, just like the earth itself. Then, suddenly, he lived up to their apprehension and stood up to his full height. His stone body crackled like thunder from his sudden jerk. It reminded them of the rumbling made when the earth quaked.

"Gruuuunaaaack!" he roared as anger exploded from within him. "By all the jewels within the crust of the earth, we cannot let the Lord of Darkness take possession of Bodina! No! I must convince the Yomiron to move against him and his slaves, this evening!

"Come! Now we must fix up the place. The Yomiron will arrive soon. Eat your fill of what is left of the refreshments I brought you, and then make ready. You'll see tonight what mortals seldom ever dreamed of possibly witnessing in a hundred lifetimes."

Chapter Six:
Rolling Stones Go to War

Ironbone began clearing away the branches, vines and brush that grew over the stone formation. Even for the long-lived stone giants, it was a very long time since the stone giants had gathered at the Raaaarkunaaaack.

Huck and Rullin had just finished the last of the food and washed it down with the mountain spring water. They watched Ironbone move with a speed that seemed unnatural for someone of his bulk and size. By sundown the gathering place was spotless. He had freed it of the overgrowth of vegetation, and discarded rocks that had collected there over the centuries.

As twilight descended over the northern lands, the boys pulled their hoods up and capes about them to protect themselves from the approaching cold. The winds blew and whistled, whipping through the dancing trees, and about the cliffs, singing their winter song. The forest grew black, as the night covered the world, like black waves rolling against the night sky in the twilight breeze.

Ironbone brought more wood to feed the small fire he had lit earlier, to cook the fish he had caught for the boys. The rising flames drove away the relentless night. Its flames jumped and leaped high into the air, trying to escape the inferno below, and filling the stone amphitheater with an eerie illumination. Off in the distance the boys could hear the rumbling of what sounded like distant thunder that grew progressively louder. It was like the sound one heard during a mild earth tremor. The ridge that they sat on shook with just the slightest vibration, that seem to rippled throughout the mountains.

The sound grew in intensity, as its source continued to approach. The boys imagined they could make out a rhythm, as it rumbled.

Ruuur-ra-on ruuur-ra-on, ra-on ra-on, on-ra on-ra ruuur! Rum-ra-roo rum-ra-roo. Ruuuuuum. Ra-rooooo roooooo-ra. Ruuuuuum!

From the western edge of the ridge the boys could barely make out a long procession of stone giants, making their way up through the darkness, as a half-moon waxed in the velvety sky. As they continued to snake closer, their rumbling chant grew louder. They marched with long strides, as they filed up the ridge with ease. Nothing could stand in their way. The boys could hear the sound of trees crashing to the ground and rocks cracking under their feet, as the stone giants pushed their way ever closer. Soon they had reached the top of the ridge and were marching into the stadium. They continued to parade around the cliffs until the gathering place was filled with them.

The boys could now see them clearly in the light from the fire. They expected them to all look very much like Ironbone in appearance, and were surprised to discover the great variation in their size, shape, color and texture. There was nothing uniform about the Yomiron. So sharply were the differences that each individual could easily have been mistaken as a member of a different race of giants. They differed as greatly as rocks did, and when they were seen up close, one would be startled by their beauty. Some seemed to shine with different colors. Some were of different shades of emerald green, ruby red and sapphire blue, while others appeared dull gray or milky white, and still others possessed colors that ranged from light tan to dark brown, gray or black. Even the texture of their skin varied from smooth like crystal-quarts to rough, jagged and craggy.

Their sizes and shapes also contributed to their variation. Some were tall, even taller than Ironbone, while others were short. There were giants both thin and broad in shape. Some appeared manlike in form, while others seemed to look more like irregular piles of rocks.

As Huck and Rullin watched the stone giants file into the stadium, and finally finding seats to rest on, they noticed that all the eyes of the giants remained fixed on them. They were still sitting on the stone table. Ironbone was standing motionless next to the table. He appeared to be like a lifeless statue. Huck kept looking up at him, though he could not be sure, he felt that the giant was, in some unspoken way, greeting his people. The silent salutations were exchanged with their brilliantly vibrant eyes that all seemed to share. Their eyes shined with a wisdom, both ancient and timeless, which was the one trait that bound them all together, as belonging to one race.

In all, there were more than three hundred giants seated in the stone stadium. The attention of everyone had suddenly shifted from the boys to Ironbone, who had moved to the center of the stadium. A silence filled the gathering place. The light from the roaring fire danced on the stone faces that concentrated on Ironbone, waiting for him to begin the meeting.

After remaining silent and motionless for some time, Ironbone began to chant in his own language. To the boys it sounded like rocks cracking. The giants rose and turned toward the cliffs and took up the chant. They were praying to the spirits of the four faces that were chiseled into the earth's breast.

The rumbling continued for several minutes, echoing off the cliff walls and bouncing into the twilight. The boys could not understand what the giants were saying, but they intuitively knew that they were engaged in some solemn ceremony, praying to the earth spirits, calling for guidance and wisdom in the decisions that they were about to make. The sounds continued until it finally stopped with such suddenness, that the abruptness startled the boys.

Huck and Rullin watched as the giants took their seat once more, and turned their attention back toward Ironbone. Ironbone stood in the center of the stadium without moving. He was waiting for the Yomiron to settle down before he began to address them. When he finally did speak, it was once again in his own language.

"I wonder what he's saying to them?" Huck said.

"I'm not sure, but considering how they were examining us when they arrived, I would not be surprised if he's telling them about us," Rullin said.

"Did you ever see such a wide assortment of beings, all belonging to the same race?" Huck said. "If I had come across them one by one, I would never have taken them for members as the same race of beings."

"I know what you mean," Rullin agreed. "I thought they would all look pretty much like Ironbone. He looks like his name–like iron graphite, while that one there looks like slate and that one looks like a piece of quartz."

"They remind me of your rock collection," Huck said to Rullin.

"I wish I had a rock collection like them," Rullin said.

"They are beautiful to look at," Huck said. "I'd hate to face them in combat."

"I'm glad Ironbone knew Blondor," Rullin said.

Rullin seemed nervous, or Huck thought so as he watched his friend clutching the Alfen Jewel under his coat. "I'd hate to think what would have happened to us if Ironbone had been hostile," Rullin said.

"I know what you mean," Huck said. "Just look at them. They could easily wipe out a whole army, if ever they had a mind to do so."

The boys lapsed into silence as the stone giants continued their discussion. After a while they lost interest all together in what was being said because the sound of the stone giants' language sounded too much like rocks cracking. They eventually laid back and began to fall asleep. Ironbone eventually stopped talking. Another stone giant stood up and continued to make the same cracking sounds, as the attention of those gathered there turned toward him. He was taller than Ironbone, but not as massive in built. He appeared to be made of green limestone and his skin sparkled with tiny specks of crystals that shined in the glow of the fire. His voice was not as rough as Ironbone's and sounded more like pieces of slate being rubbed against each other.

After about ten minutes of uninterrupted talk, he sat down and was replaced by another giant who was sitting in the rear of the stadium. He could hardly be seen in the shadows that lingered out of reach of the fire's light. The boys quickly woke up when he spoke in a deep, clear voice. They could see his eyes shining like two pieces of burning coal. Several other giants began to make rumbling sounds as they nodded their heads. Ironbone looked down at the boys.

"I can't understand a word that's being said, but I think you're not convincing them?" Rullin said to Ironbone.

"You're correct, Rullin, but all is not lost," Ironbone said and gave him a look as if he still had a trick or two that he could play to win over his people to his argument.

"Just what is it you're trying to convince them to do?" Rullin asked.

"Why, I'm trying to convince my people that the time has finally come for the Yomiron to become involved, once again, in the affairs of the world," Ironbone said. "Our isolation must come to an end, but they have grown passive, like boulders that have fallen in a valley and remained in the same place for centuries, without moving. They prefer to let the dust of time bury them deep within the protective stealth of Mother Earth. We are becoming like fossils, just images in stone. Many think they can hide in our mountain home and remain safe from the darkness that is spreading out of the south. They are not convinced that the Lord of Darkness wants to rule over all living things, and that his madness would be satisfied with the domination over undermen and Trueman races. They say they can hide as we once did, to escape the ancient fires of old. As I told you, during the Hell Fires, our race buried itself deep within the bosom of Mother Earth and woke only after the world was reborn. Many believe that this would be the best course of action for us today. But I'm convinced that the Lord of Darkness will not stop until he has reduced the very rocks themselves to slavery.

"You must convince them, Ironbone!" Huck jumped up so

excitedly that several of the giants sitting nearby turned their heads to see what happened. "Right now the Neutrians are sailing south to Ortangraal, to do battle with the Allomanian armies. Arlindor and King Amthrim both thought that they had only a slight chance of defeating his armies. To make matters worst, we expect that the witch, Wargana, is sending her armies west to attack Ortangraal from the rear. If Ortangraal falls, they'll march together on Lothangia. I don't know if they can stop them without the Yomiron? Your help is greatly needed if they are going to have any chance at all."

Ironbone said nothing as he listened to the passionate pleads of the Trueman child, but he was moved. Moisture, like morning dew that gathers on rocks after a damp night, formed about his eyes.

"Don't worry, Huck," the giant said. He used Huck's name for the first time. "No decision has been made yet. Nothing is final, and I still have a hidden gem of an idea, to pull out, that has not been used yet. Isn't that right, Rullin?"

Huck and Rullin looked at each other in surprise. They both knew the giant was referring to the Alfen Jewel, though they did not understand why he referred to it the way he did. Huck noticed that Rullin was still nervously clutching the jewel under his coat. Before either of them could say anything, the stone giant turned to face his people once more and begin speaking to them, making the cracking noises in his throat.

The Yomiron had been talking among themselves in an informal way, everything that had been mentioned so far. It was their way to mingle formal debate with informal discussion. They once again grew quiet as Ironbone spoke to them once more. He started to chant, mixing both the cracking and rumbling sounds. The others soon joined in the chanting. After doing this for some time, everyone stopped and Ironbone continued with his formal way of talking. The boys listened to this long rumbling oration, as if they could understand what he was saying.

The stone figures sat on the edges of their seats, listening intensely to everything that he said, not wanting to miss even one word, as the sounds rose into the cold, night air and echoed of the cliffs. Ironbone seemed to be transformed. Like any good orator, he saved his most impressive argument for his final ovation. His rumbling took on greater force, as the momentum of his speech increased. Rullin and Huck watched the large, gray figure, silhouetted against the black night, standing motionless and yet vibrating with emotion. The boys could feel the vibrations that emanated from Ironbone in stone on which they were standing. They noticed the intelligence in his eyes, which seemed to flash with the emotional emphases as he spoke.

Ironbone appeared dark and mysterious as well as gentle and understanding, and this made the boys think of how much Ironbone seemed like Blonder. Rullin, in particular, felt drawn to him, much in the same way that he was toward Blonder. Suddenly a thought appeared in his head. He felt that he should pull out the jewel, but he hesitated. He was waiting to pull the jewel out, or so he thought. He knew Ironbone was aware of the jewel and that it was a source of secret power, but what type of power? Why did the Alfen King give it to him? What did it have to do with the stone giants? Why did he run off the way he did? He tried to remember what he felt when he ran off into the woods and up the ridge, but it was all too confusing. He only knew that he was compelled to go forward by some unseen force from deep within his soul. The same force that led him up to these heights, was now causing his hand to take out the jewel.

Rullin's hand pulled out the Alfen Jewel, just as Ironbone's oration reached a climax.

"Hold up the jewel and face the cliffs, where the spirits reside," Ironbone suddenly said as he faced Rullin.

Rullin looked at Ironbone and then at the jewel in his hand. Without asking why, he turned and faced the cliffs, just as the stone giant ordered. The cliffs appeared black against the star-filled night. As Rullin held up the jewel, a light began to shine against the stone wall. Its intensity grew, lighting up the four faces that could now be made out clearly in the green light. They appeared to be peering down over the top of the trees that grew along the bottom of the cliffs.

A voice could be heard that seemed to come from every direction.

It has been a long time since we have spoken to the Children of Bodina, and never was the need to do so, greater. A shadow is growing out of the south that now threatens to unleash the ancient fires once more. All New Earth is in grave danger. The shadow of war is moving across the face of the world. The Children of Bodina must decide on which side they will fight.

A second voice could now be heard picking up where the first voice left off.

Yes, my brother, it's time that the rock children move. Children of Bodina, you can no longer remain detached from the cosmic rhythms that push and pull against the fulfilment of history. Even stone and rock must eventually give way before the pull of the tides of the sea and battering of the winds. You! The Yomiron! You must decide how you will ride out the whirlwinds that threaten to engulf the entire world.

When the second voice faded, a third voice began to speak.

Can it be, that the wisdom that is as sound as the mountains themselves, now falters before the darkness that rushes up from the foul pit? Are you so old and feeble that you cannot see what fate lies in wait for you as a people, if you do not act? This jewel that the Trueman child holds before you, the Coruuumble, has come back to you so that we might speak as we once did in the time long since forgotten. The rocks and stones of the earth speak to you, Children of Bodina, to warn you of the danger, and lay before you the paths you may follow. But you must decide which way you will walk. So take care, for how you decide will determine the fate of Mother Bodina. Will she continue to give life that is beautiful, or will she be reduced to ash and cinder? Will she remain green and rich with life, or burned black under the scorching heat that will melt down mountains and turn the land into a sea of molten rock?

Finally, a fourth voice echoed through the night air.

Children of Bodina! My brothers speak the truth. You must decide, but the choice is really not yours to make. We, the four who have sat on the crown of the world, have watched over you since before the world you now know took form. We have seen the fires,

*and had the foresight to send you back into the bosom of Bodina,
to sleep until it was time to rise again. But we witnessed the pain
and suffering inflicted upon her during that terrible time, and we
cannot sit by and permit her to suffer under another onslaught by
the black fires. This time she might not have the endurance to come
through it, and once again be reborn. This time there is no safe
refuge to hide. This time we must be moved to act to prevent the
fires from burning her black and barren. This time the Darkness
must be turned back to the pit from whence it crawled out. This
time the might of the Yomiron must be counted among the numbers
of those who dare to take up arms against the Darkness, or stand
idly by and let Bodina die. I put the question to you, Children of
Bodina, how will you decide?*

A silence now filled the ridge, as the green light retreated back
into the jewel. The night once again claimed dominion over that
small part of the world. Ironbone's voice broke the stillness, as it
rose in the cold, night air, and mixed with the sounds of the wind
that whipped down from the north. Once again he spoke to his
people in his own tongue, but this time it was with a passion that
he had not yet revealed till now. His speech was short and to the
point, and when he was finished, the Yomiron rose to their feet and
began marching out of the stone stadium. They began chanting
as they marched, making sounds that blend into a crackling song.
They were now worked up into a frenzy of excitement, moved by
a war frenzy, and sang a war song, as they march off to war in an
avalanche of chauvinism.

Ironbone turned back to Rullin and lowered his huge stone
head until he was eye to eye with the boy. He said nothing, but
Rullin could see tears of moisture in Ironbone's eyes. The giant
reached out his large, stone hand and into it Rullin placed the
jewel and the chain. Ironbone slowly lifted the chain and placed it
around his neck. He then reached down and picked up the boys,
one in each hand, and cradled them in the nap of his arms with
loving care.

"Ironbone. What's happening?" Huck asked. His voice was
filled with emotion.

"What's happening?" the giant said as if he was asking himself the question. He looked at the slowly unraveling assembly of giants that were making their way, like a great parade, down the side of the ridge and into the darkness that filled the lands below.

"My people have been moved by *the Avalanche!*"

"Avalanche? What does that mean?" Huck asked.

"Why, it means the Yomiron is going to war," he said. "That's what's happening."

The boys could see his eyes flashing now with a red light that burned hard and bright from the depths of his soul.

"War? Against whom?" asked Rullin.

"Against Allomania, of course. Who else?" Ironbone rumbled. He stepped out in long strides until he was now out in front of the column and took up the chanting.

Ruuuummmmbllllle-ram, Rooooccccl-roooaaack roooruuuck!

The boys did not ask any more questions for a long while, as they listened to the rumbling chant that rose in intensity, as the column of stone giants made their way down the side of the ridge and into the forest below, moving as fast as a rock-slide. They moved with all the speed and force of an avalanche, knocking over trees and stamping down brush and anything else that was unfortunate enough to get in their way, as they went. Animals fled before them and birds escaped through flight. Nothing could stop them as their fury and wrath mounted, burning red hot like the belly of a volcano. The rumbling chant grew louder and cracked with greater force, filling the night with the dread of their coming. It made anyone or anything that might have overheard them, think that the very world itself was breaking in two. The pounding of their heavy feet sounded like the thunder of an earthquake that split open the surface of the world, taking everything in its wake with them as they went.

After about an hour, the giants had made rapid progress along the spine of the ridge. They had traveled about ten miles. The boys could see other giants all about them. Their long, thick legs pumped up and down like great steam engine plunging deep into the earth and kicking up stones and dirt, high into the air, creating clouds of dust. Their great forms swayed to and fro, their arms swung about them as they marched, smashing wood and bark that dared to stand in their path. All the time they marched, they continued their rumbling chant.

The green jewel that hung from Ironbone's neck shined brightly, as he walked. The chain that had hung loosely around Rullin's neck was pulled tight about Ironbone's neck, like a collar.

"It was the Coooorumble that turned the minds of the Yomiron," Ironbone said. "It woke the spirits of this land and allowed them to speak to us."

"We know," Rullin said. "We also heard the voices speaking to you."

"You heard the voices? And you understood them?" Ironbone asked, surprised. "I did not know that you understood the language of the Yomiron."

"We don't," Huck said. "The voices spoke in our own language."

"That's right," Rullin agreed. "'We speak the common language that all Truemans speak. It's called Daryan, which is still spoke in Lothangia."

"So, I see," Ironbone said. "I did not know that the spirits had spoken to you as well. The voices I heard were in my language, which is the speech of the Yomiron. But I suppose the spirits of the mountains could speak to Truemans, as well as the Yomiron, if they had a mind to do so."

"Ironbone. You said you were going to war against the Lord of Darkness," Rullin said.

"That's right," Ironbone said.

"Does that mean you are headed to Ortangraal?" Rullin asked.

"Yes, that's also correct," Ironbone said. "We'll reach it in five days. We're moving fast, and have not moved this fast in such a long time. So long it has been that I'm not sure how long it actually has been. But I think that we'll make it in five days, as I said. Yes. Five days, sounds right, not six. I'm very certain that we'll be in time to help, that is if I can remember what Blonder said. We're dearly needed there. The eagle from Wissenval told me that the hordes of Fennoria are also on the march. They are also headed toward Ortangraal. They plan to link up with the Allomanian army and destroy the boat warriors of Neutria, and they will, unless we can come to their aid in time."

"I'm sure glad you're going to help," Huck said. "Some of our friends are there."

"Well then, we must hurry," Ironbone said. "We've far to go. It's a long way to Ortangraal, but you'll see just how fast the Yomiron can travel. Our speed increases the farther we travel, and we never stop to rest, just like an avalanche."

"Ironbone," Rullin said his name with hesitation.

"Yes, Rullin. What is it?" the giant spoke his name with a tenderness that seemed unnatural for one of his size and bulk.

"You knew from the very first time we met that I was carrying the Alfen Jewel, didn't you?" Rullin asked.

"Well, no," Ironbone said. "Not from the very first, as you put it. But I was expecting someone to bring something with them to the assembly. The last time I spoke with Blondor, he said that he had spoken to Lurinilin. He told me that the little king had told him that his people had found something that once belonged to my people—something that is precious to us and has been lost for thousands of years. I told Blondor that if he was able to retrieve it, and returned it to the Yomiron, they would be grateful. It would be useful in convincing them to join the alliance. Blondor promised to bring it here and present it to my people at the assembly, but when you showed up in his place, I suspected that you might be carrying whatever it was that the Alfen King gave him. And I had an idea that it might be the Coooorumbllle, or the Alfen Jewel, as you called it."

"What exactly is the Coor. . .," Huck could not pronounce the Yomironian word. ". . . the Alfen Jewel?"

"Well, the Coooorumbllle is one of the many jewels that once made up the treasure of the Yomiron, that we called the Tumrrrriiilllor," Ironbone said. "It was given to us by the little people of the forest in ages long ago. We are an old race, as you already know. Once the Yomiron numbered in the hundreds of thousands. But our numbers have dwindled, and our race has declined, as all races must do in time. As a result, much of our strength has been lost, though I dear say we are still a formidable force, compared to most.

"It was in the Tumrrrriiilllor that our powers resided, and wars were fought by my people over their possession. Many of the Yomiron were killed in those wars, and most of the Tumrrrriiilllor were lost or destroyed. It was the lost of our treasure that accelerated our decline. That happened before the First Age, as your people count time. It happened during the Dark Times and permitted the rise of the dragons, who ruled the world before the rise of the Truemans. For a long time we searched for the Coooorumbllle, which is the last of the Tumrrrriiilllor that was unaccountable, but eventually, even a mountain is worn down by time, and so we gave up the search and withdrew to our northern domain.

"Since their disappearance, many of the Yomiron have gone to sleep, and if a stone giant sleeps long enough among the rocks in one place, he becomes part of the landscape. His sleep is a way of telling the Great Mother that he is tired of this life and wants to return to her womb. The Life-Force seems to have lost much of its hold over many of the Yomiron, ever since we lost the Tumrrrriiilllor."

Huck's forehead frowned with troubled thoughts.

"What troubles you, Huck?" Ironbone asked.

"You said you were expecting the Alfen Jewel, or something," Huck said. "But if that's the case, why didn't Rullin realize he had to bring the jewel to you? And why didn't the Alfen King simply tell him?"

"I think Rullin knew, deep down inside of him that he had to bring the jewel to me," Ironbone said. "The little people are a mysterious and strange folk. When they talk to someone, they do it in two languages at once. They speak with their tongues and with their minds at the same time. The Alfen King told Rullin that he was supposed to bring the jewel to me, but he told him with his mind. The message was implanted in Rullin's mind or his subconscious, I think is the word? That's why he ran off the way he did. He wasn't conscious that the little king had told him to deliver the jewel to me. That's the way the little people do things. They use the larger races for their own ends, without them ever realizing it."

Rullin's face turned red. "Somehow I knew I had to bring the jewel to someone, but I didn't know who or where."

"Let me see if I can remember," the giant said, as if he was trying to remember something from long ago. "Did the little king sing a song when he gave you the jewel?"

"Yes, he did," Rullin said. "Now that you mention it, I do remember him singing a song. It went like this.

In long forgotten, ancient day,
when our New Earth was not yet old.
Neither north ice or south sea bay,
saw deep forest and mountain bold.
The land was bath in burning fires,
the skies were black with poison dew.
Smoldering smoke raged still higher,
and Old Earth gave birth to the New.
Wars were fought of knights and men,
Light and Darkness in battle's breath.
And fairies danced on age's end,
then Truemans welcomed hollow death
as evil approaches, north on fast,
to help the outcome of battle-rage.
In four stones speak souls of wisdom past,
to herald in the coming new age.

"Yes. Yes, that's an Alfen song, if ever I heard one," Rumbled Ironbone. "It's a song that sings of the birth of New Earth, the spirits of the stone giants, war, doom and gloom. But hope is also there, and where hope still lives, there is always a chance—only a chance, mind you—that good will triumph in the end."

The Yomiron marched on at an ever increasing pace. Their lumbering forms took on a strange gracefulness, as they plowed their way through the woods. They were heading down to the plains that stretched out below, known as the West Fold of Neutria. The land grew flat as they traveled. It was covered with a thick carpet of tall, rich, golden, autumn grass. Here and there the plains were dotted with patches of trees that grew in low dells, where water tend to congregate. If anyone still remained on these open lands, they would have heard the thunderous rumbling and cracking of the Yomiron's song.

The next morning, as the new day woke from a restful sleep, it drove away a gray mist that had covered the lands during the night. As the day wore on, the sky got darker with gray clouds, and soon white flakes of snow raced about on winter's northern winds. A storm had heard the giants' compelling song, and answered their call to arms. It followed their trail as they traveled south.

The boys snuggled closer to Ironbone, as they pulled their fur coats up and over their faces to protect themselves against the snow. Ironstone sensed the boys were cold and he caused his body to generate an inner heat, as if lava was boiling just beneath the surface of his rocky skin. His body grew warmer, just enough to keep the boys protected against the falling snow and whipping winds.

All that day and into the next they marched, with Ironbone stopping only to get the boys something to eat and drink. By the middle of the next night, they had crossed over the Jorunthon River and disappeared south into the lands beyond. They followed the road that ran from the bridge that spanned the river. The road ran along the western banks of the Angorium River to Ortangraal, and the fate that awaited them there.

Chapter Seven:
A Final Stand - A Family United

The sun was rising in the east as one hundred dragon-ships turned south onto the Angorium River, leaving the Thuntum Mirror behind. A thick layer of heavy, gray clouds moved south out of the northern reaches of the world on a blast of winter's icy breath, filling the bright blue, white and black sails of the Neutrian ships. The winds pushed the ships along the silver, watery road that flowed south toward Ortangraal, cutting a passage between the countless green sentries of the Wolf-Staak Forest and the Jerajer Forest to the west. The ships sailed down the Angorium without stopping along the way. A great need drove them on. They were engaged in a race to reach Ortangraal before the Allomanian armies arrived.

The ships were weighed down with the tools of war and supplies needed to support the ten thousand men that rode within the ships. Among those who rode on the ships were the travelers from the east. In all, the Neutrians were a fierce group. They were tall and fair and possessed eyes the color of the sky, blue and gray. Cold and determined their hearts were set in the killing fever, that filled their minds and souls like a hardy wine. Their wills were bent toward one desire—to kill all undermen that they came across without regard to their own lives.

Strong arms and muscular backs rippled as they pressed against wooden ores, which propelled the ships along the river when the winds failed them. Gruff voices were transformed into bitter sweet songs about war and battles, women and love, as the men sang to help make easier their burdensome task.

On the third day out, the Neutrians passed under a great darkness that blocked out the sun during the day, and the stars at night. A gloom seemed to linger within the darkness that invaded even the strongest hearts of the boatmen. Fires were lit to drive away the shadows that filled the world and invaded their thoughts. Backs were once again bent even harder to hurry them on their way to their appointment with the *Rundergron*, the Neutrian name for the final battle between good and evil that will take place when the world ends.

The Allomanian hoards that had attacked Neutria were now moving south under the command of Kharz-Zish, the Caliph of Alfeinia. The denizens that made up the army of the King Kreel were driven on, under the unmerciful whips of their Kreel masters. They were the instruments of their master's evil will. His will was their's, and it enslaved the hapless undermen caught in its unbreakable grip. The will of the King Kreel burned with a hatred for everything that was pure and good and filled with the Light. Brutish trolls and trogs grunted and squealed, mixing their cries with the howls of the carrion-eating Alfeinians and the bloodthirsty war-crazed wails of the dwarves of Aixia.

The King Kreel had united all the different races of undermen in one great single orgy of hate, fed by his black will. The King Kreel's mad dream of ruling the world and enslaving all living things under his tyrannical domain, was intoxicating and inflamed the minds of the slow-witted and feeble-minded brutes that made up his armies.

To dominate such creatures as undermen, was an easy task for the King Kreel, but he was never able to enslave whole nations of Truemans. It was possible for individual Truemans to be caught in his web and forced to succumb to his will, but the collective spirit of whole Trueman nations was too strong with the power of the Light, for him to overcome. Collectively, Truemans drew enough strength from each other to resist his powers of domination. Only those individuals who were alienated from their own kind could be seduced. He had decided that those who could not be seduced would have to be destroyed.

The dragon-ships soon passed out from under the blackness that laid oppressively over part of the world. Only the presence of Arlindor and the Red Stone that King Amthrim carried, gave the boatmen the fortitude and resolution to push on toward their destination. They were less than two days from Ortangraal when they saw, once again, the shining sun overhead. Its yellow face, bright and beautiful in the clear blue sky, welcomed them back to the world of light, congratulating them on their success, even if it was only fleeting and temporary.

Arlindor joined the king at the bow of the lead ship. They were soon joined by Prince Sagtrim, Milland, Magin and Gordon. A warm tropical wind blew up from the south, warming their souls.

"How long before we arrive at Ortangraal?" the king asked Arlindor. His regal eyes were fixed on the river that flow beneath their ship.

"We should reach its fortification in the morning of the day after tomorrow, if we don't delay," Arlindor said.

"To delay before battle is not the way of my people," King Amthrim said. His white beard blew in the warm breeze. "Will we have enough time to make ready the defenses of Ortangraal? I did not like the darkness that we passed through, and I like less how close it was to the fortress."

"We'll have at least one full day to prepare for battle after we arrive at Ortangraal," Arlindor said. "If luck is with us, perhaps we might have some additional time, if we continue to sail at his pace."

"But will it be enough?" Prince Sagtrim said. "Our people are good fighters, but even ten thousand pairs of arms could not make ready the battlements or Ortangraal in one day."

"I wish we had a troop of Fabbroughian diggers with us," Magin said. "They could work all day and through the night with stone, when the mood moves them. They could build a fortress that might put a thorn in the side of the Allomanian Army."

"Your folk in the East Mark are renown for their skill in shaping earth and stone, but we are a long way from the East Mark," Arlindor said. "I would not worry though. Ortangraal is not unmanned. Blondor convinced the White Council of Lothai to dispatched a brigade to occupy the fort last year. I'm sure that they have not spent all that time in idleness. Lothangian legionaries are renown for their engineering skills, especially when it comes to the construction of fortifications."

"A brigade? How many is that?" Magin asked.

"About a thousand," Gordon asked.

"Including a hundred Knights of the Silver Swan," Arlindor said.

"Knights of the Silver Swan—that is good news," the king said. "They are worth a thousand times their numbers on the field of battle. This will make our task all the easier, if I could use such a word in these times?"

"Use it, my Lord," Arlindor said. "Such a word can be used even when referring to the way men die. And if we do die at Ortangraal, let us do it in such a way as to inspire men, if any survive the struggle that is swelling up around us, to sing a song to remember how we die."

"Then let all who might see the golden gates of *Vorulha*, and hear the sweet songs of the *Farales* before this battle is at an end. Now give us a song to steel our hearts and lighten our cares," Prince Sagtrim said as he turned to the men of their ship. "Your King wants a song full of war and glory!" he shouted. "Sing it loud so the Lords of the Light might hear it and send the *Farales* to come and follow us into the battle that awaits us, and take those of us who will die to *Vorulha!*"

Voices now rose in joyous verse.

Look to the east, see the dawn of day,
a new age on New Earth is a'rising!
We stand fast together, come what may,
against the Forces of Darkness!
Truemans to arms!
Truemans to arms!
With steel helmets on, and battle swords drawn,

we rush into battle cheerfully!
Through our struggle, we shall be reborn,
and enter Vorulha joyfully!
Truemans to arms!
Truemans to arms!
May the Farales ride hard and fast,
and Balthor bless our heroic fight!
We will stand together, to the last,
and fight for the Lords of the Holy Light!
Truemans to arms!
Truemans to arms!"

It was in the early hours of the morning of Turning 20 the Neutrian ships finally reached the fortress of Ortangraal. The call to arms rose up among the holders of the fort, as the ships sailed into view. The Lothangians recognized the Neutrian ships, but prepared for battle in case it was a deception by the enemy. When the ships drew closer, the Lothangians could clearly make out the eight-pointed stars with the images of black ships on the blue sails. Now the ships were close enough so that they could see the thousands of tall, blond warriors in battle gear on board. They knew that it was their ancient allies and friends from the north coming to help.

A blast of trumpets greeted them as their ships, like a flock of great swans floating down the river Angorium, turned east where the river flowed into the Donnor River. It is here that Ortangraal was built over four thousand years ago by the ancient Lothangians, during the First War of the Races, in the First Age. It sat on the top of steep cliffs that rose more than one hundred feet, out of the river. The waters that flowed by it were turbulent, swirling with hard currents that were treacherous, and made any attempt to scale the heights by an invading army, virtuously impossible. The cliffs were like a heel of rock that rose straight up on three sides, but gently slopped down on its northern side, toward the forest edge for two miles, forming a great plateau. At the northern edge of the plateau was a twenty-five-foot drop. The forest grew right up to the northern edge of the plateau.

The fort was built at the southern edge of the plateau, and on the northern bank where the two rivers joined. The fort was oval in shape and three quarters of a mile in length and one half of a mile in width. A great wall encompassed the fort and a two hundred-foot tower ascended from the center of the fort above the cliffs, to the south. The tower could be seen for miles in every direction, and thus made it impossible for an attacker to sneak up on the fort.

The plateau ran two miles along the banks of the Angorium and Donnor Rivers, and cut through the forest in a semicircle shape. Long ago the men of Lothangia cut an enormous semicircle canal through the plateau, connecting the Angorium and Donnor Rivers and transforming Ortangraal into an island. The canal was wide. Its width stretched about one hundred feet, and its walls were impossible to climb. A wall was built along the edge of the island that ran around its entire length. There were two smaller towers, located at both the eastern and western edges of the island. A bridge of stone stretched across the width of the canal, in the center, right up to a gate in the wall. This was the only way to reach the island. From the canal to the northern edge of the plateau, the surface was treeless and open, so that no enemy could reach the canal unseen. No enemy army has ever taken the fortress in forty centuries since it was first built.

Long ago a great city had grown up within the walls of the fortress, inhabited by Truemans. They had burrowed deep under the feet of Ortangraal, and there they constructed a great underground harbor. The harbor once housed hundreds of ships that sailed up and down the rivers of New Earth, which served as watery highways for the old empire. This had made Ortangraal a great commercial and trade center in the old empire. The harbor still existed, but had not been used for centuries. The entrance to the harbor was a large hole, like the entrance to a cave, but it was clear that the entrance was man-made. It was cut in the shape of a perfect arch, fifty feet above the surface of the water. Its passageway was blocked by a metal gate, with five inches thick bars made of Pure Gold, and spaced five inches apart, so that no man could possibly swim between them.

The Neutrians returned their welcome with a chorus of trumpets. A volley of cheering and saluting from the Lothangians rose to welcome the arrival of their northern allies. The white, red and blue eagle and stars flag of Lothangia waved in the wind from overhead, on top of the tower.

As the ships reached the cliffs, the heavy gate was hauled up by the men who manned the fortress. The Neutrian ships gently disappeared into the heart of Ortangraal until the last of them had entered the harbor. The gates were then lowered once more. The ships passed through a short tunnel that opened into a large subterranean chamber. Within the chamber was an underground pool with piers and docks along its sides. Fifteen ships were already docked there, all Lothangian. They were larger than the Neutrian ships and were used primarily for deep water sailing. They were heavily armored, but not used much now by the Lothangians, except to defend their coast. Once Lothangia was a great sea power with possessions on foreign coasts, beyond the seas, but now her domain was restricted to the original thirteen states. Lothangia no longer had much use for a large navy.

Along side the far wall of the underground harbor was a series of rooms cut into the rock, which once served as warehouses filled with supplies and goods needed to withstand a long siege. On a stone platform were several men in gold battle armor and red capes, waiting to greet the Neutrians as their ships pulled up to where they stood.

When King Amthrim's ship finally docked, he and his son, Prince Sagtrim, Arlindor and those who came with the druid, plus several Neutrians, stepped off the ships and onto the docks. They walked down a wooden plank and were greeted by three Lothangian knights.

One of the knights stepped forward. He placed his right fist over his heart and then extended it out before him with an open palm and spoke in Daryan. "Hail, boatmen of the north and friends of Lothangia. I am Caratium Countius, Commander of Ortangraal and colonel in the Order of the Knights of the Silver Swan. I welcome you to Ortangraal."

Arlindor placed his fist over his heart and returned the salute in the same manner. "Hail and greetings, Commander Caratium Countius," Arlindor said. "I am Arlindor, druid from Wissenval. I have traveled with King Amthrim, Lord of Neutria and his son, Prince Sagtrim. With us also travel others from Tillenia and lands to the east of the woodmen. We've all faced great peril and worst, to come and stand by you and your men and help you in your defense of Ortangraal against the Forces of Darkness that is rapidly marching on this fortress."

Arlindor's pronouncement was more than the Lothangian commander had expected, and it showed in the look of surprise on his face. Caratium was a tall and healthy looking man with dark brown hair, cut short in the Lothangian style, and possessed warm, dark brown eyes. The fine, chiseled features of his face were browned from the southern sun, and his figure was clad in the traditional armor and robes that all Swan Knights wore. The armor was made from the extremely strong and very light metal known as Pure Gold. He was covered from head to toe in the armor, but it did not weight him down, and was no heavier than a suite of cloth clothing. From his shoulders hung a long and flowing red cape. His body was clad in robes of the same color that hung down to his knees, and strapped tight about the waist with a heavy, brown, leather belt. From the belt hung a long sword made of the same metal as the armor. He held in his left hand a helmet also made from Pure Gold with a large, red plume on it.

"King Amthrim and Prince Sagtrim," Caratium said as he turned to face the king and his son, "I welcome you and I am honored by your presence at Ortangraal. My life and the lives of those who are under my command are at your service." Caratium fell down on one knee as he spoke these words. He had taken his sword from its scabbard and held it before the king in both hands.

"Rise, noble knight of Lothangia," King Amthrim commanded. "You honor me more than words can describe, but it is we, who are at your command. Command us as you will. We've sailed long and far to aid you in your defense of this fortress. It is you who command here, and so you are our commander. Come and tell us what we can do to help. I have ten thousand men strong, who have faced the danger that is coming, and we are ready to face whatever destiny fate has in store for us."

"Come then and let me take you to better quarters, where we can talk," Caratium said as he returned his sword to its scabbard. He then led them up the stone stairway that was cut into the rock, rising up into the fortress overhead. They came to a large room with a huge fireplace. A heavy oak table stood in the middle of the room. Servants were already filling the table with refreshments. Everyone sat about the table and wasted no time in discussing the matters at hand.

"Neutria is at war with Allomania," Prince Sagtrim began to tell Caratium of the events that had transpired in the north. "We've already faced their forces in the north, and we've followed them south, to continue the battle here, at Ortangraal." The prince broke a loaf of bread and dunked it into a meat broth. "We were told that you have one thousand men here."

"Yes," Caratium said. "One hundred of them are knights, and the rest are made up of the finest men that Lothangia could spare. Your arrival is timely and news welcomed. I think that our task, to defend Ortangraal, is no longer hopeless. Our combined forces will put up an able defense."

"It will take more than numbers to halt the black tide that comes to Ortangraal," Arlindor said. "We've brought the means to fight the enemy, with us. I am speaking of the Red Stone."

With these words, Arlindor looked at King Amthrim. His dark eyes spoke unheard words. The king reached under his garb and pulled out a small, perfectly round red stone that shined with an unreal life of its own in the king's old, but strong hand.

"The ... Red ... Stone," Caratium almost whispered the words, moved as he was with awe at the sight of the legendary stone.

King Amthrim rose to speak. He never looked more kingly. His pride and the power of his will, had returned to him, after months of being stricken by the black breath of the Horzugal. All eyes naturally turned in his direction, as Arlindor spoke of the battle between the Neutrians and the Horzugal. The king's stately form and icy blue eyes glowed with a royal strength, not pompous and ostentatious, but lordly and hard like the northern winds that called out and commanded men's hearts and mind to follow his lead. They could see that he was truly King Amthrim, Lord of the Neutrians, Father of the Northmen, born of the race born out of the snow-covered plains and icy blue waters, within whose veins flowed the inner strength of the noble barbarian blood, unpolluted and uncorrupted by over domestication, that was so typical of so many who were considered "civilized."

"As the King of Neutria, I have kept faithful the pledge of my fathers by the alliance they made with your Empire," King Amthrim said. "In this time of darkness, I and my people, have come out of the noth to join you in taking a stand against the Forces of Darkness that now threatens all of Truemandom." As the king spoke these words, he raised the Red Stone before him. "By this ancient talisman, I do dwear the loyalty of my folk to that of Lothangia."

All the Lothangians in the room rose and stood in amazement and then broke into a storm of cheers. "By the Lords of the Light, the prophecies are coming true," Caratium said.

"These are times when prophecies do come to pass," Arlindor said. "More then the Red Stone is coming to the south. As we speak, The White Stone, which has been found, as well as the Emperor Returned, are on their way to Lothangia."

Arlindor's pronouncement had the effect of a thunderbolt on the men in the room. Riotous shouting and joyous turmoil once again exploded. Caratium rose and raised his arms, as the shouting soon subsided and order was restored. When the thick brew of men's outpouring of excitement, disbelief and joy that had filled the room evaporated, Arlindor began telling the full story from the beginning, as quickly as he could. As the druid told of their adventures, the earnest expressions of the words that flowed from his lips cause men's hearts to lightened. Though they realized that the evil that still plagued their lands had not been defeated, the flames of hope once again rekindled in their hearts. They understood for the first time that they were living on the doorstep of a new age, and what the nature of that age would be, would be determined by how they braved the struggle that was about to unfold.   How they fought and died would decide whether the next age would be one belonging to the Light or Darkness.

"Tell us now, Commander Caratium, of the news that may help us in our fight," Arlindor said after he finally completed telling the events that led up to their arrival in Ortangraal. "What news can you tell us of events that are unfolding in the south?"

"Last year, after Blondor visited Lothangia and convinced the White Council to reoccupy Ortangraal, we detached the forces that you see here now," Caratium said. "We made hast to Ortangraal, and began making ready its defenses. It has been too long since this fortress guarded the cross roads of the old empire. We set about doing what could be done to make the fort ready for battle. But we still hoped that the White Council would send more than just one thousand men to man the fort. We eventually received word that no reinforcements would be coming. We would have to defend the fort with what men we had, which was not even a full legion. They considered it too costly to maintain Ortangraal for a prolonged length of time. If it had not been for General Tyrilon and prince Fayrilon, no knights would have been included in the one thousand who presently occupy this fort."

"It was wise of Fayrilon and Tyrilon to include knights in the detachment sent to Ortangraal," Arlindor said. "Not only does their presence stiffen the resolve of those who man the fort, but their presence ensures a continuous flow of supplies from the knightly order."

"Your praise honors us," Caratium said. "Our order was able to ensure that the fortress would be supplied. Without the knights here, they could not have justified sending supplies, and the fort would have been abandoned long ago. This last year has been quiet and uneventful, but we have managed not to fall into idleness. We've sent out patrols regularly in all directions, and have kept these parts free from thieves, trogs and other vermin. We've received reports from the south, north and east. Much of what you told us about Tillenia and Neutria, we have already heard, though now we know the full story and understand much that was not clear to us before. But we've received no instructions from the city of Lothar. What goes on there we know very little, but I must confess that the news you have brought us of the Horzugal is new and very black. I was unaware of just how black the times that we live in are."

Many of those who were in the room agreed with Caratium.

"Dark the time might be," Arlindor said, "but as you said, Caratium, hope still lives, and hope can be a hardy crop when planted in the blood that courses through the veins of Truemans."

Everyone agreed

"Though the task that we must face is formidable, we can face it with those forces at hand and backed up with a courage that is fueled with moral righteousness. If we remain resolved with iron wills and fixed determination to defend our homes and way of life, we may still triumph in the end."

"It's said that druid's words are filled with good medicine, and I must say that I agree," Prince Sagtrim said. "There is more than the healer's magic in what you say."

Caratium resumed telling in full, the happenings of this part of the world.

"Reports have come to us," he said, "and they've been mostly bad. Fennoria's black gates have opened more than once. Wargana has sent her armies to the north to kill and burn out the people of Tillenia, who live in the northern lands. They've laid siege to the city of Jassinburg, but the Tillenians are not about to surrender the freedom that they loved so much. They're resisting with every ounce of strength that they can muster."

Caratium's eyes fell on the two woodmen seated at the table. Pettin and Olaf rose at hearing the news from their motherland.

"What evil is this you tell us?" cried Pettin. "Our kinsmen are under siege, while we are stuck here? What evil has led us so far from our city, and deny us the right to die among our blood-folk?"

"Fear not, Pettin, for it was not evil that led you so far from your city," Arlindor said. His words had a tranquilizing effect on the troubled hearts of the woodsmen. "War's shadow laid across the doorway of your country, when we left Tillenia. This you both knew, and yet, you chose to come along with us, on our quest.

But if you still wish to fight along side your kinsmen, you still might depart before the battle that is racing down on Ortangraal overwhelms us?"

"What do you mean, druid?" Olaf asked. The ends of his mustache wiggled as his face frown with thoughts over the words that Arlindor spoke.

"Only that your land is not the objective of Fennoria's aggression," Arlindor said. "The invasion of Tillenia is a facade, meant to pin down the Tillenian armies while Fennoria sends the vast majority of her hordes west, along the Donnor River, against this fortress. In this way, they hope to prevent Tillenia from marching to Ortangraal and link up her armies with both the Neutrians and the Lothangians, in a common effort to halt the advance of Allomania."

"Ha! If that witch thinks she can frighten Tillenian men and women, she is in for one mighty big disappointment," Olaf said. "We'll teach her a costly lesson before this war is over." Olaf lift his giant mace and swung it over his head with such a force that it could be heard cutting through the air.

"Aye!" Pettin said. "My brother speaks the truth. We will show the black mistress how Tillenians fight." Pettin's eyes flashed with pride.

"No doubt you will," Caratium said as he watched the mountainous hulk of a man and his little brother. "And I'm glad that Ortangraal has at least four Tillenian arms to wield weapons in her defense."

Everyone agreed with Caratium.

"But what of your brother druid?" Caratium turned to Arlindor, asking about Blondor. "You said that Blondor and rest of your company had followed the youth, Palifair, who carries the White Stone and was taken captive to Fennoria. If they're in Wargana's hands, then all is lost."

"I have no way of saying for sure what fate has fallen them," Arlindor said, "but if Wargana had gained possession of the White Stone, I would've felt a disturbance in the Life-Force. Since I have not, I can only surmise that the stone remains beyond her reach."

Caratium was pleased at Arlindor's words.

"I think the rest of the company has passed through Fennoria, but not unchanged," Arlindor said. "If my guess is correct, and a guess it only is, they should have reached Lothangia by now." Arlindor searched his feelings for a second. "Perhaps it's safe to say that they have left that foul land with more than they entered it with. The Life-Force that emanate from Fennoria seems to have weakened considerably."

"Then Fennoria might not go to war against us?" asked Magin.

"No, Magin," King Amthrim said. "The opposite is probably true, I fear."

"King Amthrim is right," Arlindor said. "If Wargana has been robbed of some of her powers by Blondor and the others, she might panic and unleash her armies prematurely. But this might lead to her downfall. If she sends her armies west against Ortangraal before she has made sure that Tillenia will not intervene, then the Tillenians could strike at her from her rear while her armies are storming this fortress. This might very well be her undoing."

"If this witch-queen is going to send her armies against us while the Allomanian forces are moving on Ortangraal from the west, then I suggest we talk less and begin to prepare a welcome that they won't expect," King Amthrim said. "Centurion Caratium, we're all waiting for your orders. Tell us what must be done."

Everyone worked around the clock to transform Ortangraal into an even more formidable barrier. They poured all their strength into the effort of placing the ten thousand Neutrians into the best possible defensive positions, and prepared a plan for the defense of the fortress if attacked from two different directions. Everyone hurried, knowing that in a day's time the dark hordes from Fennoria and Allomania would reach Ortangraal.

Neither star nor moon shined that night as black clouds rolled in from the west. The air became thick with a heavy, oppressive haze that made it hard for men to breath. All that day and through the night everyone worked without rest. They were driven on by the encouragement of their leaders, who appeared everywhere, giving support and help where needed and trying to keep up the morale of their men. There was no time to complain. The knowledge that the fate of New Earth, including their families and loved one, laid on their shoulders was always in their thoughts.

They would defend the Ortangraal on the outer walls, but if they were breached, they could retreat to the inner walls, which were bigger and stronger. The inner walls were twice as high as the outer walls, and twice as thick. They rose fifty feet from the ground and five men could walk abreast along its top. Its parapets were six feet tall with slots through which archers could shoot their arrows. There were pipes built into the walls in which boiling oil could be poured through, and down on the heads of those who tried the scale the walls.

A skill lost to Truemans long ago, was used in the construction of the fortress. Its walls were made of huge blocks of stone, and fitted together in such a way that not even a sheet of the finest paper could be fitted between them. The outer side of the walls were polished until it was as smooth as ice to prevent foot, claw or hand from climbing its heights.

Magin walked with Gordon and Milland along the outer walls, inspecting the craftsmanship that went into the building of Ortangraal.

"I've never seen such an example of stone craft, but I've heard tell from tales told to me by my father, of this lost craft," Magin said to his friends. "He walked these walls once, and so he often described them to me and others, of their quality, in such detail that I almost feel as if I've been here before. But I must admit that deep down, I always thought that he exaggerated his description, just a bit, to make his stories more interesting. Now that I've had a chance to see the walls for myself, I realize that his words fell far short of the truth. When I return, I must apologize."

Milland and Gordon listened to the younger man's excited words. They were filled with his love of the Fabbroughian skill of stone crafting, and they could understand the passion he felt for his craft. They each shared a similar love for their own skills.

"If Fate is kind enough to allow us to live to see this war to a victorious conclusion, I will return to Ortangraal with a troop of my friends from the East Mark, so we could study the art of masonry that went into the construction of this fortress," Magin said. "Yes. Even if it took a lifetime to master, I would do it. What a master craftsman of stone-shaping I would become."

"Milland and Gordon smiled at hearing Magin's dream.

"I do not doubt you could do as you say, Magin Strongbone," Milland said. "If you can pile stone as good as you swing your axe in battle, then I hope that I will live long enough to hear you called, Magin Strongbone, Master Stone-sharper."

The three comrades soon came upon Pettin and Olaf, as they walked along the turrets.

"Ah! There are our three comrades from the Mark!" Olaf shouted in his deep, gruff voice, sounding more like a drum roll. His wide, round face was stretched with a broad smile as he leaned on his battle mace. His huge size easily allowed him to see over the parapets. "Come and join us in an early breakfast, before the battle disturbs our peace on this morning." Pettin was cutting slices of bread and cheese as Olaf invited them to join him and his brother.

The five comrades ate their meal, which tasted all the better in the company of friends, tried and true.

"I can't help but miss Huck and Rullin," Magin said. "I hope they're safe with the Neutrians. I feel guilty about leaving them behind."

"We all feel the same," Pettin said, "This is no place for children, though they are both as brave as any man I ever met. In the morning we'll be consumed by war, and they are better off in the north. I only hope that Palifair and Tom have been rescued by Blondor and the others."

"I think that Arlindor had a hidden motive for leaving Huck and Rullin behind," Olaf said, as he washed down the bread and cheese with several gulps of rich, red wine. "Druids seldom say what they really mean and everything they say has a double meaning, as we say in Jassinburg."

"Tell us, Milland, can you see into the darkness that surrounds us?" asked Gordon. "Do you see any signs of the enemy?"

Milland peered over the turrets, into the dark landscape to

the west. His keen eyes were as sharp as those of an eagle. "I can see little through this eerie darkness," Milland said. "There is movement beyond the river, to the northwest, but I can't tell if it's from the gloom and wind, or from the movement of the enemy. I have never seen such thickness of haze before."

"It's unnatural," Pettin said. "I've heard it called the Beast's breath, in Tillenia. Legends told among my people, describe such a darkness, thick and black that covers all the land and blocks out the sun, used in the War of the Races long ago, but I never thought that I'd live to see such a thing. It makes me feel mellow in my heart–no, woeful."

Pettin's right," Gordon said. "This gloom is filled with a melancholy cooked from a demon's brew. Now I know what they mean by the Shadow of Allomania."

"I think we have not long to wait until this gloom is lit up with the fires of war and filled with the sounds of battle," Magin said as he stared into the blackish horizon.

Waiting made the time pass slowly, and caused an anxiousness to penetrate everyone's hearts. The darkness did not lift as the morning hours wore on, and made everyone fearful and jumpy. Soon, fires could be seen in the distance, to the west of the Angorium River. The flames grew and seemed to flow over the horizon, like a sea of lava. Men stared in silence as the torches, like a vast army of fireflies, crawled closer. For hours, the advancing enemy made its way along the western bank of the river. From high on top the tower of Ortangraal, a bell rang out its warning song.

To arms! To arms! Voices were heard. *The enemy has come from the west!* Men shouted as they hurried to the walls and prepare for the coming assault.

"The waters of the Angorium are wide, a half of a mile wide," Arlindor said to the king and Caratium. "They'll have to cross it by boat. They'll probably do so up the river there, beyond the Belt of Ortangraal, as the plateau to the north is called, and pass through the forest. There they'll assemble their ranks and then march on the outer walls."

"We'll be ready for them when they do," Caratium said. "My men have been diligently waiting for just such an attack. There is more than one surprise waiting for our uninvited guests, along the belt."

"I'm sure you're right, Centurian," the king said. "But perhaps we can make their crossing of the Angorium less easy?" The king turned to the Prince Sagtrim. "Might we send a few of our ships up the river and make them pay a heavy toll for their crossing?"

"It won't stop them from crossing the river, father," Sagtrim said, "but perhaps it will knock some of the fighting spirit out of them, and delay their attack on the outer walls? And besides, the fish in the river need to be fed."

"I see no reason why not," Caratium laughed.

"Then I'll go and make ready the ships," the prince said and departed.

"He's a brave warrior, your son is," Caratium said to King Amthrim as he looked after the prince. "You must be very proud of him? Neutria will be fortunate when he becomes king."

"Aye. No better son could have been produced from my loins," the king said as tears of pride swelled in his eyes. He fought to hold them back.

"He's very much like his sister," Arlindor said.

"He is that, druid," the king said. "They are both so much like their mother. A fire burned hot in the frozen north when I first laid eyes on my dear, departed queen." The king turned and stared into the dark waters below. "How I wish my dear daughter was here with us now, so that we might make a final stand together, as a family united."

"You speak as one who does not expect to live to see the end of this conflict, my Lord," Caratium said.

"Victory might be our's, good knight, but I think that the royal House of Neutria will not come out of this conflict unscathed. I think I hear the song of the Farales calling?"

Chapter Eight:
The Siege of Ortangraal

In the dark, three ships sailed out of the cliffs under the Ortangraal. Their floating bulks sailed effortlessly across the black waters of the Donnor, and turned up the Angorium River, as strong arms pressed wood against the fluid surface and sails filled with the foul winds. The ships sailed low in the water. They were heavy with men clad in armor and arms. In their readied hands were spears and swords, carved with runes that called on the Lords of the Light to guide them so that they will hit their targets.

The ships made their way silently up the river for four miles, masked from view by the enemy's own gloomy blackness. As they approached to where the enemy was crossing the Angorium, they could make out the sounds of alien chatter in foul tongues, mixing with the clang of metal against metal. Their fires were like beacons drawing the Neutrians to their location.

The armies of Allomania made their way across the Angorium river with the intention to melt into the woods of the Wolf-Staak Forest. There they would mass their countless numbers under the cover that the forest provided, and then strike against the Ortangraal. Thousands of shapes, short and stout, tall and thine, large and hulking, hurried along as the larger trog overlords lashed them under the stinging bites of their leather whips that whistled and cracked, while Kreel masters shouted commands at them. Their grunting and growling could be heard far over the deep waters of the Angorium, as the complaints and whining laid thick in the heavy air. Their foul speech was filled with hundreds of unintelligible curses at their masters' orders.

The most numerous of the undermen were the trogs of various shapes and sizes. The most plentiful were the Oolugs. These were the short race of trogs that were most common. But mixed among their ranks were the taller and thinner Tarkuz. Fewer in numbers were the larger and more powerful Horgots. They held mostly positions as overlords, shouting their Kreel masters' commands to the other undermen.

There were also just as many Alfeinians as there were trogs. They were tall and lean and covered with a very thin layer of fur. They lived in tribes on the western plains, warring among themselves, but the King Kreel had convinced the many tribes of Alfeinians to join his Dark Alliance in his war against the Truemans. They leaped and jumped as they hurried along, wearing multicolored feathers, beads and even scalps taken from Truemans, they killed. The scalps were often fashioned into hoods or even capes that they wore in combat. These carrion-eating undermen howled with lust like coyotes baying at the moon, and their large ears twitched in anticipation of killing more Truemans.

Also among their ranks, were large, lumbering grayish-green trolls. Their numbers were the fewest of all undermen within the Allomanian army. Their scaley hides were dressed in armor and they carried great maces and mattocks, which were their favorite weapons, since they enjoyed crushing their opponents, rather then cutting them with swords or impaling them on spears. They had large eyes that burned red with hate over their long snouts that made them appear elephant-like. Their small trunks hung down, over the lower, pig-like lip. Their mouths were filled with razor-sharped teeth. Dark green bristles grew on the top of their heads and ran down the back of their necks and under their chins. They stood towering over the rest of the horde, standing between seven and eight feet tall. In general, trolls were slow-moving dullards, but once under the control of their Kreel masters, they are transformed into formidable warriors.

The vast multitude of countless undermen stretched far back into the lands to the north and west, like a great field of waving black wheat. They were herded onto hundreds of small rafts and boats that would ferry them across the Angorium River. Their minds were locked within the all-pervasive psychic grip of their Kreel masters, who sat within large carriages guarded by troops of the largest and most fierce Horgot trogs. They would peer out at their armies with their red, rodent-like eyes that glowed with their master's indomitable will.

A great clamor rose from the river. Those on the shore could see fires burning high into the black sky. The boatmen of Neutria struck with the swiftness of wolves. Under the cover of dark they snuck up to the large armada of rafts and boats, undetected, they unleashed a hailstorm of flaming arrows onto the underman boats. Boats and rafts were set on fire and caused thousands of trogs, trolls and Alfeinians to fall into the cold, dark depths of the Angorium River.

A shout of cheers rose from among the Truemans of Neutria, as their ships rammed into the flotilla of small crafts like great timber wolves into a flock of deer. All about them smaller boats were set a blaze with burning undermen, as they sank into the watery grips of death. Many of the rafts and boats were capsized by the larger ships that rammed into them, and cutting into the line of ferrying crafts that were taking undermen to the other side of the river. The Neutrians guided their ships with great skill, but eventually, even an elephant will be overwhelmed when it attacks an army of ants. He may kill thousands, even millions, but soon the sheer weight of their numbers will overpower him and bring him down.

As the Neutrian ships cut through the line of underman boats they soon found themselves surrounded on all sides by swarms of the smaller boats, filled with undermen. Their numbers were too great for them to destroy them all. No sooner did the Neutrians send the smaller boats to the bottom of the Angorium, hundreds of other crafts sailed out to take their place. After the success of the initial attack, the Kreel dwarves were able to collect their thoughts and regroup the panicking undermen under their control, and urged them on to surround the Neutrian ships until they were unable to maneuver. It was as if their ships were caught in ice that freezes up on the surface of a lake in sub-zero temperatures, causing them to stall in place.

Prince Sagtrim ordered his men to cease the barrage of flaming arrows, because the fire they caused might spread across the enemy craft and leap onto their own ships, as they became enclosed by them.

"Swords and spears!" Sagtrim shouted to his men as hundreds of undermen began boarding their ships.

Neutrian swords rose and fell like so many butcher's knives, cutting into trogs as they tried to climb up the sides of the Neutrians ships. Several dozen large trogs made their way up the bow of Prince Sagtrim's ship with swords drawn. Their red eyes glowed in the dark. Sagtrim and several others jumped at them, bringing their swords down on them, severing their heads from their necks, and sending thick green blood flying. They fought with a fury that propelled to fight on until they had repelled the invasion.

The prince stood there panting as he surveyed the carnage around him and lift his sword over his head and shouted to the other ships. "About and tight formation!" he ordered. He knew that they could not hold out much longer and had to retreat. They had sent thousands of undermen to their doom and now it was time to withdraw.

Just then, a large Horgot trog jumped up and onto the deck of Sagtrim's ship from behind and flung himself at the Neutrian prince, swinging his sword at him. A shout of warning from one of his men caused the prince to swing about while ducking and plunging his sword up and deep into the large, round belly of the trog. The prince's sword cut open the trog's stomach, causing an eruption of green blood, gray organs and gore. Two other trogs, who had followed their leader on board, fell under the bitting edges of Neutrian blades, as Sagtrim's men swung their sword and decapitated them.

The prince brought his ships around into a triangular formation that cut its way through the sea of undermen crafts, capsizing them as they made their way back to Ortangraal's underground harbor. The three ships cut their way through the carnage of sinking crafts and floating corps, guided by the light from the tower of the fortress, back to the protective walls of Ortangraal, as the men of Neutria rowed hard through the waters.

They reentered the Donnor River and turned Into the harbor's entrance when their ears were filled with the sounds of flapping wings overhead, in the darkness. It was followed by a soul-chilling scream that caused even the bravest and strongest Truemans to fall to the floor of their ships in fear and freeze with terror.

Prince Sagtrim looked up and saw, swooping down on him out of the darkness, the most terrible sight he had ever saw. There, above him flying down with burning red eyes, was one of the winged-servants of the King Kreel.

"Horzugal!" Prince Sagtrim shouted.

His voice was filled with dread at the sight of the demon, as it flew low over the ships. Its claws cut into the sails of the ships as it flew over them and then ascended into the darkness above once more. They could hear a terrible laugher from the creature. It flew up and around only to descend once more on the ships. As it swooped down, tongues of fire shot at one of the ships, causing it to burst into a blossom of flame. The men on board jumped into the dark waters, as their ship was transformed into a flaming inferno, rapidly sending it beneath the dark waters of the Donnor.

As the two other ships slowed to give help to their comrades struggling in the cold waters, arms reached out and pulled their countrymen into their ships. Just then, the Horzugal turned on one of the other ships. It swooped down for the kill, but before it could unleash another deadly bolt of fire, it was struck from high above by a green bolt of light that sent it reeling in pain, causing it to fall into the waters below.

A cloud of hissing steam rose up as the winged servant disappeared into the river. A cheer rose up from the two remaining ships, as they sailed through the entrance of the harbor and the gate of Pure Gold close behind them.

Then, from the far side of the river, the Horzugal rose once again into the air from beneath the waters and made its way back to the Allomanian armies, licking its wounds as it flew off into the darkness.

For the rest of the morning, the army of Allomania continued to cross the Angorium River, as the Wolf-Staak filled with undermen.

Trees were felled under their cutting axes. There rose up smoke from far within the woods, as the undermen worked at building some kind of devilry.

It was shortly after noon that the assault against Ortangraal began with a distant, but gradually increasing, booming of drums. The booming was eventually joined by the sounds of thousands of voices singing some unholy song in the black speech of Allomania.

The Allomanian army began climbing up the cliffs to the top of the plateau known as the Belt of Ortangraal. Black figures could be seen moving across the plateau, carrying banners and burning torches as they swarmed through the ruins of what was once a fair city. They spread out across the plateau. Their torches lit up the dark. Their deep, growling voices sang with a terrifying beauty, like a flock of vultures excited by the sent of rotting flesh.

Hundreds turned into thousands as undermen crossed the mile width of the plateau. Like an army of ants they march closer to the fortress. Ever closer they were driven on by the black will of their Kreel masters. The sounds of their feet stomping on hard ground, mingled with the rolling drums, causing a thunderous dirge to reverberated over the fortress, calling down the Darkness on those who manned the walls of Ortangraal.

The Allomania horde was greeted by a storm of arrows that leaped down on them from the archers' bows, from the walls of the fortress. The flying wood cut down hundreds of oncoming undermen, but still the enemy moved on, taking no notice of their fallen comrades. They climbed over the bodies of the dead and marched forward, as the archers unleashed one volley of flying death after another.

The undermen continued to march until they finally reached the edge of the canal. The drums ceased and the chanting died down, as silence descended over the plateau. The archers halted their assault and waited, bewildered at the spectacle before them. Minutes seemed like hours as the waiting became unbearable. Finally, the suspense was broken by the blaring of trumpets. A deafening roar of cries rose from the thousands of undermen as they unleashed a terrible outburst of rage. The multitude began jumping about, waving and brandishing their weapons, shouting curses at those who stood upon the walls. Then, as if acting like some great beast, the horde surged forward, across the single bridge that spanned the canal, right up to the gates in a frenzied state. They threw themselves at the closed gates that barred their way. Over and over they came in the useless display of disregard for their lives, as if telling those who manned the fort, they care not for their own lives.

Once more a hail of arrows fell down on the ranks of undermen, cutting down trogs, trolls, dwarves and Alfeinians under the assault of killing missiles. A volley of black arrows now ascended from the ranks of the undermen. The black projectiles rose from the plateau into the air and over the walls, cutting into Trueman flesh and spilling red blood on gray stone.

The men on the battlements took cover before the onslaught of flying death. Trogs shouted and squealed in delight, as the cloud of arrows rose over the walls. Just then the air was filled with a rumbling noise, as thunder bellowed across the sky and flashes of lightning lit up the black canopy overhead in fiery flashes. No rain fell and the Truemans who held Ortangraal wondered at what kind of magic could cause the sky to cry without tears?

Trumpets blared once more, which was followed by the rolling of drums, as huge trolls hurried to the forefront with logs tied together in bundles of six. They were cut from the tallest trees that could be found in the forest. The trogs laid them across the canal in such a way as their tips were lodged securely in the rocks at the foot of the walls of Ortangraal. Trogs surged up and ran across the make-shift bridges, carrying long, wooden ladders that were hoisted against the walls. The largest trogs, the Horgots, were mustering in great numbers. They would be the first to scale the walls.

Within the walls, Truemans from north and south rallied together, shoulder to shoulder, they stood as comrades-in-arms against the undermen that were preparing to assault the fortress. They jumped at the commands of their superiors, and quickly brought forward huge stones that were hurdled down on their uninvited guests, who were climbing up the walls of the fortress.

Trueman voices rose and echoed in cheers at the sounds of trog skulls being crushed by the falling rocks. Many tumbled into the canal far below, and into its cold waters, while others reached the top of the walls, only to be cut to pieces by Trueman steel.

It was not difficult keeping the undermen from successfully scaling, but the task was its toll. The men were becoming exhausted. Their numbers seemed inexhaustible. For everyone who was repelled, two others jumped up to take its place. The defenders fought with fury of the frozen gales of the northern storms, but they were growing weary from the endless waves of undermen that continued to climb the walls.

Soon the defenders were covered in sweat, and their muscles ached. Breathing became harder in the thick, hazy air that hung over the land and filled their lungs. But no man slacked in his duty. They ran back and forth, repelling again and again, sending thousands crashing down into the canal below.

Another storm of arrows began to fly at them, and many found their mark in the flesh of those who manned the walls. But most bounced off the steel shields that were held high overhead like a great roof of dragon scales protecting those underneath from the killing rain of arrows.

Now, far below, a troop of trolls was mustering. They carried a large battering ram made of steel and shaped like a boar's head. They pulled it to and across the bridge that led up to the doors of the outer walls of Ortangraal. Boom! Boom! It slammed again and again against the locked doors, pounding its demand to open for them to enter.

It was then that the trolls stopped the pounding and listened, as if they were trying to make out some familiar, but as yet still unrecognizable sound. Finally they heard a crackling sound from beneath their feet, as the bridge gave way and collapsed under them, sending the trolls and the battering ram into the dark, watery death below. There was heard a cheer rising up from high on the walls of the fortress.

The rejoicing was cut short by the bells of the Ortangraal tower that cried their warning once more. All heads turned, as men shouted.

Beware of the east winds, was the shout.

Trueman and underman mouths opened in fear when suddenly, the word went out–the Mount of Fennoria had come!

"Arlindor! What has happened?" asked King Amthrim.

The druid joined the king and Caratium. His face was gray and long. "The jaws of the enemy are closing in on us," Arlindor said. "From the east has come Wargana's armies. They will join the Allomanian army and complete the encirclement. We will be surrounded."

"Fennoria has come," Caratium said. "Then the tide of battle goes against us. But I swear here before you all that we Lothangians, will fight to the end if necessary, and we will make such and end that its memory will someday inspire a tale to be told among men, for all the ages."

"Then let us make sure that there will be Truemans living to tell such a tale in ages to come," Arlindor said. "Come with me and together we will make sure that if Ortangraal falls, it will at such a cost to the enemy that it will not help Allomania's invasion of Lothangia."

From out of the valley of the Donnor River, a great host of trogs, half-trogs and trog-men spread across the lands to the south and east of the great river. Their numbers transformed the landscape into fields of fire and steel. At the head of the Fennorian army rode the Mount of Fennoria. He was clad in black armor and wore a green cape. On his head laid a helmet of green and black metal with long horns reaching up and over like tongues of black fire. From within the helmet his eyes burned bright green with a hate for all that was pure and good in the world. He rode upon the back of a black steed that was nurture with the malice of Fennoria.

Along the old road built by the ancient Lothangians, he rode to the river's edge. Once a bridge stood there that crossed the expanse of the Donnor River. He called his demon horse to a halt. His eyes flashed with a green light at the tower that rose over Ortangraal. His mouth opened and a terrible cry emanated from it and rose through the air, calling for all that was in the service of the Darkness to come and witness what he would do this day.

Caratium and King Amthrim watched all that afternoon as the Fennorian army ferried itself across the Donnor River and melted into the forest.

"Come evening, I would wager we will see the attack on Ortangraal renewed," Caratium said to the king. "In the morning, we will either be victorious or dead."

"That may be, but if so, we must try and delay the enemy from departing to the south too soon," King Amthrim said as he turned to the Lothangian commander. Caratium could see the king holding the Red Stone. "But remember, we are not without weapons of our own," the king said.

The king then turned north, as if listening for something.

"What is it you hear, my Lord?" Caratium asked. "You act as if something hidden has made itself known to you."

"I feel a breeze out of the north that has the taste of snow on its winds," the king said. "It's the herald of a storm that we in Neutria call the *Harsbiddenbors*. It means, the bitting cold. I think there is help approaching from a corner of the world that we have long forgotten. Perhaps some of us might yet live to see the light of the sun once more?"

Caratium looked at the king and watched him, as he stared into the north and said no more.

Time passed slowly throughout the afternoon. It was late in the evening when Arlindor found them still watching the progress of the Fennoria army crossing the Donnor River to the east.

"Where have you been?" the king asked Arlindor. "We have not seen you for some time."

"I have been deep in the looking-vision," Arlindor said. He seemed exhausted.

"What did you see?" Caratium asked.

Help is coming from the north and east," Arlindor said. "I

cannot tell for sure who they are, or their strength. The Life-Force is blurred by this darkness. It blocks my sight, but I have an idea who might they be that march to our assistance."

The king and commander waited for Arlindor to tell them who was coming to Ortangraal, but Arlindor said nothing more.

All that day and into the evening, the Allomanian army remained on the belt of Ortangraal, and kept up the barrage against the fortress. Huge catapults flung boulders at the fortress walls. Arrows flew through the air seeking Trueman flesh to pierce. The day's gloom continued to hang heavy over everything. Night was coming to that part of the world, though those within the blackness could not tell the difference, when something seemed to stir the ranks of the enemy to a new fever pitch. The armies of Allomania and Fennoria had joined up. Together they were going to make a final assault against ancient Ortangraal. Lightning once again crackled across the black sky, and thunder rumbled from deep within hidden clouds high above. A surge of grisly faces rushed forward in a nightmare scene on the plateau north of the fortress.

The good men of Ortangraal readied themselves on its outer walls for the coming attack. Their hands clasped spears, swords and shields. Bows were pulled tight, waiting to send their arrows singing through the haze that filled the air between Ortangraal and the armies spread out to the north. They could see great wooden towers on wheels, built from the trees of the Wolf-Staak, pulled to the top of the plateau by the slaves of the King Kreel. There was ten such structures in all. The towers were pulled ever closer, like giant, wooden monsters that towered over the walls of Ortangraal. Their drawbridges, once lowered, would allow the undermen to rush across the running waters for below, and over the walls, right into the fortress.

As the towers were brought to the edge of the canal, a call went up and archers unleashed a storm of fire and wood that transformed several of the towers into infernos. The flames ate at the support beams until they came crashing down under their own weight. The other towers extended their arms over the watery chasm and rested on the top of the walls. The enemy rushed across the ramps in a mad fury as others climbed up the towers behind them.

Trueman defenders fought to halt the onslaught, but they were eventually over powered by the vast swarm of undermen that continued to climb the towers and cross the ramps onto the walls. Several more towers were pulled down by hooks and ropes, but enough undermen had crossed over into Ortangraal to force the defenders to abandon the outer walls. The Truemans fought bravely and spilled a great deal of blood on the walls, but they could not stem the tide. Two more towers were sent tumbling down into the canal, in an avalanche of fire and wood, by blasts from Arlindor, but even his efforts could not repulse the attack.

Ropes and grappling hooks were now flung up to the walls like so many spider webs for the undermen to climb. Many were sent crashing down into the canal as ropes were cut where the walls were still defended by Truemans, but many more made their it over the walls. The Truemans continued to fight where they could. Their resolve not to surrender an inch of ground still burned in their hearts, but the weight of the attack was too much for even them. Every inch of wall that the undermen took was paid dearly with blood as the Truemans spirit was strengthened by the power of the Red Stone. Like mad men they cut and hacked at the multitude that stormed the citadel. Their shouts of fury and screams of the enemy mixed with the continuous thunder and lightning that roared overhead.

The battlefield shook with an explosion that caused everyone to collapse from the shockwaves that danced across the plateau. Truemans and undermen alike fell beneath the earth shattering concussions. When finally the smoke cleared and the combatants regained their composure, they looked with wonder and fright at the sight that stood before them. There, on the eastern bank of the Angorium River they saw a cannon made of bronze and black metal. It was forged in the fires that burned deep beneath the earth of Allomania. Its barrel was long and decorated to look like a dragon. It was gigantic in size and dwarfed the hundreds of giant trolls that pulled it along. From its great barrel smoke smoldered and rose into the air. It wheels left deep tracks in the ground.

When the smoke and ash from the explosion cleared, to the amazement of all present, they saw the steel doors that barred the entrance through the outer walls, lying broken and open, hanging impotently from their hinges. They were no longer able to prevent the tide of undermen from swarming through the outer walls and flooding the courtyard within.

Trolls rushed forward carrying huge logs that they placed across the canal, creating a platform for the underman army to cross. Hundreds and thousands of trogs, half-trogs, Alfeinians and trolls poured through the broken entrance and into the courtyard beyond the walls. The Truemans within retreated into the inner walls of the fortress.

Madness griped the undermen as they stormed through, swarming over those that could not escape to safety. They tried to halt the tide, but no matter how heroically they fought they could not stop the stamped that eventually over whelmed them.

Lothangians and Neutrians archers now mounted the inner walls and unleashed their arrows upon the surge of undermen, in an attempt to help their comrades make it to the safety of the inner fortress. The wooden darts cut down thousands of the enemy as they surged forward in a frenzy of excitement. Again and again the arrows flew through the air and cut deep into undermen flesh, but nothing seemed capable of halting their advance.

Those Truemans who were still on the outer walls made an orderly retreat to the two smaller towers that stood where the canal met the Donnor and the Angorium Rivers. On the western portion of the wall, Gordon, Magin and Milland made their way back with a group of Neutrian warriors and Lothangian legionaries. A young centurion by the name of Turahium shouted for them to give each other cover as they retreated.

Magin stood his ground as trogs fought their way along the wall. He refused to retreat until all his comrade had retreated in safety. Gordon saw Magin standing alone and shouted a warning. Magin heard the warning from Gordon and swung around in one quick movement. His axe sliced the head off the shoulder of a large trog that had just climbed over the wall behind him. Gordon jumped to his side and thrust his sword through the throat of another trog that rushed along the wall at Magin.

"Thank you, Gordon," Magin said as he smiled at his friend. "I owe you one."

"Time enough for that later, boys!" Milland shouted as he hurried to both of them. He held his long silver knife in his hand. He was out of arrows and resorted to stabbing the enemy as they climbed over the wall.

"Out of arrows already? The hunting must have been good?" Magin laughed as he followed him to the tower.

"If we're to cut down every tree in the Wolf-Staak and turn them into arrows, I fear that it would not be enough to turn the tide of enemy," Milland said. "There seems to be no limit to their numbers."

"We have to get back to the tower!" Turahium shouted as he hurried his men along. "There we can make a stand."

The Truemans on the walls held off the undermen heroically as the share weight of their numbers pressed them back. As the last of the defenders retreated to the tower, a large trog leaped over the wall and onto two of the last Neutrians retreating, causing them to fall backwards, as three other trogs rushed forward along the wall. Two of the trogs were cut down as Turahium rushed forward, but the large trog dodged his sword and then, with a cry, he raised his axe and was about to bring it down on Turahium when the his head flew off its shoulders.

Magin instinctively acted and stepped in between the Lothangian and the trog. With all the strength of his two powerful arms, he flung his axe before him and sliced its blade through the neck of the large trog. Thick, green blood splattered every where as the red lights in the flying head of the decapitated trog went out.

"I owe you my life, Marklander," Turahium said as he laughed.

Magin's eyes shined with delight as he succumbed to the Lothangian's contagious joy. His round belly bounced and his cheeks turned red as he bellowed his laugher.

"There may yet be opportunity for repayment before the day

has run its course?" Magin said. "In the meantime, we had better follow your own orders and seek the safety of the tower."

They grabbed their wounded comrades and fought back towards the tower and closed the door behind them, shutting out the war that was still being waged outside, for the moment.

When the gates in the outer wall were blasted open, Sagtrim had rushed down from the walls to take charge of the collapsing situation in the yard below. Right behind him followed Olaf and Pettin, close on his heels. When they finally reached the yard, they ran right into the thick of the fighting. Swords, axes and battle maces rose and fell like pile drivers, cutting and pounding screaming trogs and Alfeinians to the ground as they invaded the yard. Olaf held his giant battle mace in his two, thick hands, whirling it about him and smashing down rows of undermen like so much black wheat in his path. Heads were sent flying in every direction as trails of ice-cold green blood sprayed everywhere.

A dozen large Hogot trogs brandishing scimitars, suddenly made a mad rush at the prince and the two woodsmen. Their eyes were filled with the malice of their master's will. They screamed foul curses in their trog language as they attacked in a frenzy of berserk fury.

Prince Sagtrim came to a halt, and with his two feet planted on the ground, and flung his sword before him in a wide swipe that struck one of the Hogots in the back of its neck, and brought his sword down on the side of the neck of another large trog, severing its head from its shoulders. The prince jumped over the lifeless bodies and thrust the blade of his sword into the gut of a third trog.

Pettin was behind the prince. He swung his axe, cutting open the bellies of two trogs, causing their guts to spill open in gush of green organs. The upswing of his axe then split the throat of still another trog, causing his death screams to drown in an up-rush of green liquid that poured out of its mouth.

Olaf lumbered right into the wave of trogs that charged at them. His great mace crushed three trogs in a split second. The sounds of their skulls being smashed and bones cracking, could be clearly heard over the roar of battle. He then pulverized the shields of two other trogs with one swipe and then severed their heads with the return swipe, transforming them into green mush. Grabbing the last of the trogs, he lifted it by its arm and flung it into the air. It came crashing down on two Alfeinians that were trying to join the battle.

Like a stampeding herd of cattle, the undermen continued to rush into the yard of Ortangraal. The retreating Truemans maintained their discipline as they fought their way backwards to the inner walls. The undermen in the front of their armies were caught between Trueman steel and the ever on coming weight of their comrades that pushed forward, crushing them under the force of their stampede, as they tried to escape the cutting bites of Trueman steel.

Prince Sagtrim and the two Tillenians found themselves and a group of Neutrians being separated from the main body of Truemans that were making their way back to the inner walls blocked by the on rushing flood of undermen. They flung themselves at the tide of undermen, cutting down trogs and Alfeinians. They fought with a ruthless determination as they leaped into the undisciplined ranks of the invaders. But soon the very force of the uncountable numbers of the enemy coming through the outer walls like a flash flood of rushing water, caused the tide to turn against the defenders. The prince realized that they would soon be separated from the rest of the defenders. He called to those Neutrians and Lothangians that were nearby to him and the Tillenians, and together they made a last effort to fight their way through the ranks of the invaders and to the security of the inner walls. If they did not, they would eventually be overwhelmed by the seemingly limitless numbers of the enemy that pushed ever forward.

Instinctively, the undermen were in pursuit. They tried to use the weight of their numbers to overpower the Truemans as they fought to break through their ranks. The undermen now seemed to be driven by a fury that was demonic. They leaped and flung themselves through the air at the Truemans, killing many without regard to their own lives. But the Truemans fought on, making the enemy pay dearly for each of their comrades that fell in their efforts to reach the inner walls. Twisted flesh and fur was hacked and cut by Trueman weapons, covering the floor of the yard with a foul slime of dirt and green blood.

Though half of the Truemans fell in their efforts to break through the undermen ranks, they finally reached the inner walls and the gate that led into the inner sanctum of Ortangraal. The entrance was still open and Prince Sagtrim took up a position at there, refusing to enter until the last of his men had gone through before him. With him stood Olaf and Pettin.

"Within! Hurry, men!" the prince shouted as he stood with his cape flying about him and his winged helmet on his head. His eyes flashed with the determination of his northern breed as he continued to shout. Only after the last of his men entered the gates, did he then order Olaf and Pettin to enter before him. He followed the woodmen and disappeared through the gate just as an axe flew passed his head, missing his face by inches. The doors to the gate were slammed closed with a thud as scores of twisted and furry bodies crashed into the doors. Their shouts of anger quickly turned into cries of pain as hot oil was poured down on them from heights overhead. The scorching liquid burned and killed those that it drenched, charring flesh and searing fur, as those who pushed from behind forced their comrade into the curtain of liquid death.

The court yard was filled with undermen. Their cries of frustration rose in a symphony of hate directed at the defenders of Ortangraal. The Truemans within the fortress, who stood on the inner walls, and continued to pour burning oil and arrows down on the undermen. Suddenly and without warning, a hush overcame the invading army within the court yard. The multitude parted as the Mount of Fennoria rode through the gates of the outer wall, riding his black horse. Behind him marched four of the largest trolls, carrying a wheelless coach draped in red and black. Within it sat a short, fat Kreel dwarf dressed in the finest garments of silk and furs. On its thick fingers were rings of such beauty that they shined like stars. They were made of gold and embedded with diamonds and rubies. But their glow faded in comparison with the fire that burned with hate from the Kreel's two rodent-like eyes, which were fueled by the dark will of his lord and master.

Drums boomed and trumpets blared as a trog-man, who stood on the coach before the Kreel dwarf, called up to the inner walls.

"Truemans! Truemans! Goz an' fetchz your leaderz! De most gloriouz an' noble Caliph of Alfeinia, Kharz-Zish, an' de highest of de high Mount of Fennoria would parley diz day withz themz!"

From above closed gates, there came a voice.

"What does the slaves of the Beast of Allomania and the Bitch of Fennoria want with free men of the Light? What could we possibly have to say to your masters?" Arlindor said. His voice no longer gentle and soft, but instead it rang hard and sharp like war bells.

The dwarf that sat in the chair of the coach rose to full height of four feet and three inches. His round belly protruded out in front of him. From within his balding head the fierce will of his race concentrated all its power as he spoke.

"Who speaks thus to Kharz-Zish and his allies?" he asked with indignation. Those who stood upon the inner walls were surprised to discover a surge of sensation that elicited sympathy for the dwarf as he spoke.

"Who dares to speak so, to us?" the dwarf asked again. "You remain hidden. Do you fear to show yourself, because you're ashamed of the foul words out speak? Show yourself so that we might talk, and perhaps discover if this war is a mistake? Let us see if this war is but a mere falling out, perchance, among friends who should be sitting around the same table, feasting together in merriment and brotherhood?"

"You speak of brotherhood?" Arlindor spoke once more to the Kreel. "But you and your evil brew, who have killed many of our blood this day, are no brothers to us. Through our veins flows the essence of the Light, while there is nothing but liquid hate flowing through your's. If you wish to talk, then talk! But don't waste your strength trying to bend wills to your end, and don't waste our time with useless promises of brotherhood. We have much killing yet to do this day!"

"You misjudge us and our intentions," the dwarf said now, almost crying. "Your words sting worse than your arrows. We don't want to spill your blood this day. We ask you to come down from your hiding place and join us in bringing order and peace to the world. Once again I besiege you to look to a brotherhood that could bridge even the void that separates us, for no void is too great that cannot be bridge with the willingness to live in peace. After all, why shouldn't Truemans and undermen work together to build a better world where we can all simply live side by side as simple men?"

The Trueman defenders, who heard the Kreel's word, began to wonder if it would be better to throw away their weapons and clasp the hand of friendship that was now extended to them? "Yes! Why fight? For what? The Light? The Darkness?" the Kreel continued to speak. "These are mere words used by druids and magicians. They have nothing to do with the doings of everyday life of the common man. Kreel and trog already live together with Truemans in these times. Do they not live in peace within the very walls of the city of Lothar? Kreel merchants trade with the good people of Lothangia. It's their commerce that brings the people of Lothangia and Allomania together. Why shouldn't the same be true between Allomania and Neutria?"

The men within Ortangraal could not help but agree with the dwarf's logic, but then they heard the voice of Arlindor once more. His laughter rang like a bell, loud and clear, driving the confusion from the their minds.

"You missed your calling, dwarf!" Arlindor shouted. "Instead of Caliph, you should have been a court jester to your master. Your words do lighten my heart with merriment. I have never heard such foolishness before. Peace? How could there be peace between the Light and the Darkness? You cannot mix oil and water. You ask us to come down and talk with you. We will let our steel speak for us. We war against your master and mistress because we choose to remain free men. Even if we can only find freedom in death—so be it! It's better then living in servitude, on our knees, to the likes of you."

The men of Ortangraal unleashed a chorus of cheers upon hearing Arlindor's words. The cloud that plagued their minds was lifted. The Kreel's lips curled with hate as he watched the Truemans cheer.

"If death is your choice—so be it!" the Kreel shouted. "But if we must fight, why not let us see who it is we do battle with? Have we not shown ourselves? Do you not have the courage to reveal your identities?"

With that, Arlindor stepped in sight upon the wall, so that everyone below could see who he was. On his right and left stood King Amthrim and Caratium. The three men, druid, king and centurion, stared down at the messengers of the Darkness. The Kreel's face was twisted with hate. His red eyes glowed with malice at the sight of the three men. He fell back into the seat of his chair, and clutched its arms with his twisted fingers, as he spit out his contempt for the men who resisted the power of his will.

"I thought I smelled the reek of Wissenval," the Kreel dwarf said. "But not even the spells of your accursed valley can stand against the power that faces you now, even though you have been able to turn our friends from Lothangia and Neutria against us. Victory will yet be ours. But I will offer those that stand with you for the last time, to come down and join us."

The old king threw his gray head back. His white beard waved in the wind, before him. His eyes were fixed on the Kreel far below. Their wills were locked in a contest of strength. For seconds that seemed like hours, the two stood as if on the abyss of time and space, until finally, the king pulled out the Red Stone and held it before him. At the sight of the stone, the Kreel dwarf reeled back in terrible pain. Screams emanated from his twisted lips, as he clutched his eyes with yellow hands.

"What matter of sorcery is this?" the dwarf cried.

The Mount of Fennoria sat upon his horse which he struggled to control. His green eyes flashed with terror. No words came from within his helmet, but he listened as his ally spoke.

"What power does that old fool have?" the Kreel asked.

"It's the power of the Red Stone, maggot of Allomania," Amthrim said. "I have broken free from the dark chains your master has woven in my mind, and now I carry the stone that was entrusted to my people long ago, as a symbol of our alliance with Lothangia, against you and your master. The prophecies of old shall be fulfilled. The three stones will be united with the one, and all the wrongs of the world will be set right once more!"

As cries of such terror and fear rose, the combined armies of Fennoria and Allomania shook with fright. The Mount of Fennoria reeled back on his steed and shouted in its foul tongue, trying to keep his undermen under control. He understood the implication of the words that the king spoke. His mistress has lost control of the Yellow Stone. Without waiting for his Kreel ally, he wheeled about and rode without haste, back through the outer wall and into the depths of the his army beyond.

Chapter Nine:
The King and the Demon

The Caliph of Alfeinia hurried away on the heels of the Mount of Fennoria. His dark mind was filled with fear of the power that his opponents possessed. Somehow, in the wider scheme of the cosmos, the balance of power had shifted in the favor of the Light. King Amthrim seemed to have recovered his strength of will. He was no longer stricken by the King Kreel's foul breath, but the Horzugal were still around and could be called upon to assist in the siege of Ortangraal. The Kreel's mouth twisted in an evil smile across his wart-ridden face, as he rode back to the safety of his army.

In the skies beyond the black clouds that hung over the battlefield, the sun had just descended behind the purple horizon to the west. Its energy-giving rays no longer radiated with the power of the Light that could weaken the Children of the Darkness, even under the protection of their master's shadow. The night was their element. It was a time that traditionally filled men's hearts with dread of the unknown. The night is when all the evils that haunted men's dreams were given free reign to run amok. The dark half of the day was when the forces of the Darkness were at the peek of their strength.

It was now in this twilight time that the armies of Allomania and Fennoria chose to unleash their most formidable attack against the fortress of Ortangraal, with a viciousness that is alien to the soul of Truemans. As if with one mind, thousands of pairs of legs marched forward to the boom of drums and the blaring

of trumpets. The red and black banners of Allomania mingled
with the red and gold flags of Fennoria, flapping in the hot haze,
like waves upon the back of a great tidal wave, rushing forward to
crash upon the walls of the Ortangraal.

As they came, they seemed undisturbed by the devastating
hailstorm of arrows that the archers rained down on them. The
black legions raised hundreds of ladders against the walls and
began climbing. Fire-crested oil was poured down from high,
setting undermen on fire as they tried to climb the stone walls.
More and more oil fell with dancing flames until rivers of black
liquid flowed down the court yard, under the feet of the undermen
surging forward. Fires spread, engulfing the invaders in their
purifying embrace. Hundreds of undermen tried to scurried
away without direction. The pain and panic temporarily freed
them from the clutches of their master's will. The roasting lumps
of flesh ran into their comrades, who were coming up behind
them, setting them also ablaze. The night seemed to come alive
with a red light, crowned by bellowing columns of gray smoke
that silhouetted against the black clouds overhead. The stench
of burning flesh laid heavy in the air and caused the men of the
Ortangraal to wrench with disgust.

The Kreel overlords bent their wills to regain control of the
situation and drive their slaves forward. They set them marching
straight into the thick curtain of fiery oil with no regard for
their welfare. The lives of those that served the King Kreel were
unimportant. The only thing that mattered to him was the
fulfillment of his orders. In his dark mind all the creatures of
this world were placed on it to serve his wishes. They were mere
pieces in a great chess game, and if he had to sacrifice a pawn or
a million pawns to win the game, then he would do so without so
much as a second thought.

Grappling hooks attached with ropes were flung over the
inner walls of the Ortangraal. Wooden ladders were raised again,
as undermen continued to climb like apes, upward toward the
waiting steel blades above. Alfeinians howled and hooted and
fell to the earth below, as their ropes were cut. Trogs screamed
in terror as they were sent flying over the sides of the walls and

crashing into the courtyard far below, by the defenders of the wall.

Prince Sagtrim was directing the men on the inner wall that included Olaf and Pettin. They were cutting ropes, knocking over ladders and slicing undermen who tried to storm the walls. Half-trog archers sent a wave of flying death at the Truemans manning the walls, killing many and wounding even more. Again and again the slaves of the Dark kingdoms climbed up the heights of the walls only to be beaten back, but each time less and less Truemans were left standing to repel the next assault. This war of attrition was beginning to take its toll on the defenders of Ortangraal.

At the foot of the tower stood King Amthrim and Arlindor.

"I don't like the turn of battle," the king said to the druid. "We're losing too many of our men—more than we can afford to lose. At this rate, there won't be any of us left to continue the battle in the morning. The way to Lothar will then be open for the enemy."

"I like not the situation any more than you do, my Lord," Arlindor said. "But perhaps we may take out the combined armies of our enemy? We command enough power to do this, if we so choose, but it will mean our destruction as well."

"What power do we command that might do such a deed?" the king asked. He was visibly up set at the druid's suggestion.

"The power I speak of lies within the Red Stone," Arlindor said. "But to do it, I must unleash its full power. It will destroy all living things for miles."

"Will it destroy the stone?" the king asked.

"I don't believe it will," Arlindor said. "But there won't be anyone left to take the stone to Lothar, to be united with its sister-stones."

"Do you have the means to do this?" King Amthrim asked.

"I know the secrets of the stones," Arlindor confessed. "Everything within a ten mile radius will be leveled, including us."

"If that be the only way to stop the enemy, then I'll gladly welcome death," the king said. A cold, dark look caused his face to freeze in a grim mask. "If we don't do this thing that you speak of, then the Red Stone will surely fall into the hands of the Lord of Darkness. This way, it might be loss again, but there is still a chance that our friends might find it before the enemy does. Do not mistaken my intent. I do not wish to die, nor do my men, but if we have to, I would wish only one thing. I wish I could see my daughter, Valenda, once more before death claims me."

Arlindor watched the king, but said nothing, permitting Amthrim to be alone with his memory of his daughter for a few moments.

"There is a chance that the Red Stone will be destroyed," the druid finally spoke once more, "If that happens, then the prophecies will never be fulfilled. The three lesser stones will never be reunited with the White Stone and this means that the Emperor will never return."

"Then we must not destroy the Red Stone," the king said. "We must try and cause as much mayhem as possible, and in this way, cause such harm against this dark army that it may come too late to aid the attack on Lothar. But if we must die, we must make sure that the Red Stone does not fall into the hands of the enemy and reaches the city of Lothar. Where is Caratium? I wish to speak with him concerning a plan," the king said.

"I am here, my Lord," Caratium said as he approached. His armor of Pure Gold was stained with the green blood of the enemy. It was cut as thin as paper, and yet its strength was still greater than steel and it had no dents or cuts in its metal skin. The red plunges that hung from his helmet was partly torn, and his red cape and robes were also in shreds, but he was unharmed, protected as he was by his armor.

"If a plan you have, then please tell it to me?" Caratium said. "The battle is not going well, for our numbers are dwindling, though my knights suffer few casualties due to the protection of our armor. But we are losing too many of my legionaries and your Neutrian warriors. If the attrition continues at its present rate, we will be force to retreat into the fortress itself and make what last stand that we might make within its chambers."

"If the need demands it, we will," the king said. "But, I think we might be able to gain additional time, and perhaps let the Red Stone escape to Lothar, by an attack on the enemy."

"An attack? Where to, my Lord?" asked Caratium.

"Into the jaws of death, if we must," King Amthrim said. The look on the king's face was as hard and cold as the ice that laid on the top of the world. If we gather our forces and make a run through the enemy's forces?"

Caratium could see the resolution in the king's eyes.

"King Amthrim's plan might work," Arlindor said. "I suggest we lead a charge of what forces that we might muster and charge into the middle of the enemy's ranks and do what damage that we might. If we concentrate all the knights in the lead, like the head of an arrow, they can cut a hole through the enemy army with the aid of their superior armor. This will give us the advantage. With the outer walls working to our advantage, the enemy will not be able to concentrate the full strength of its forces against us, and we might be able to cut their forces into little pieces."

"It might work, but to what end?" asked Caratium.

"I have said that aid is on its way," Arlindor reminded the Caratium. "I can see a storm approaching through the haze of the blackness, and it will arrive soon. Our attack could give us additional time that is needed for its arrival. But if this aid does not arrive, then perhaps we might be able to cut a hole through the enemy's ranks and permit someone to flee to Lothar, taking the Red Stone with him? If we achieve nothing else, this would be worth all our lives."

Caratium thought hard for a moment. "It would be an honor to ride at your side, my Lord," Caratium said to the king. "And if Lothangia last another millennium, men will sing of the ride of the Knights of the Silver Swan at the side of the King from the North. And with the Red Stone in your possession, we might just make a glorious end to this battle, whether we live to see its end or not?"

It was late now, well passed the midnight hour. The battle had raged all evening. With iron firmness the defenders fought off one assault after another in the enemy's relentless attempts to take the inner walls. Finally, the blare of trumpets went up from somewhere within Ortangraal, and the doors of the fortress opened. Thousands of undermen in the yard froze in place, as all heads turned like a field of dark wheat bowing under the force of a foul wind. Then from within the walls rode a force of eighty-six knights clad in their golden armor and red caps. Within their ranks rode King Amthrim and Caratium, and behind them rode several hundred of Neutria's best horsemen. The knights carried their lances low and shields upright, and the horsemen held shields and spears and swords. As they raced into the enemy, they impaled all who were foolish enough not to get out of their way.

The thunderous pounding of heavy, iron-shoed hooves on hard ground, caused the earth itself to shake. Fear and panic shot through the ranks of undermen that filled the courtyard. The charge was fierce. The knights rode out front with the Neutrians riders following behind them. They sliced through the enemy ranks, as the undermen tried to escape. The undermen collided with each other, as the Trueman riders cut them down. The undermen were gradually broken up into small groups by the charging horsemen, thus making it easier to kill them.

When Caratium and King Amthrim came to a halt in the center of the courtyard, they could see their men fanning out to the left and right. Two standards were held high. One of them was the red, blue and white banner of the stars and eagle of Lothangia, and the other standard was the blue, black and white banner, of the ship in the star of Neutria.

"Remember, Knights of the Silver Swan!" Caratium shouted to the knights. "Your lives have already been given in the service of the Light, so fear not the death that might claim you this day! If you die, then you will be reborn once more, to walk within the fair halls if the Lords of the Light on Virlon, just as all who have died before you, in the service of the Light, do!"

Caratium sat tall on his white charger. He seemed to glow with a golden aura. His brown eyes were filled with the fanaticism that the Knights of the Silver Swan had been weaned on for over a thousand years: loyalty, honor and self-sacrifice.

Next to Caratium was King Amthrim, sitting straight and upright in the stirrups of his steed. He held over his head the sword, *Ructhron*, of the House of Neutria and cried aloud. "Men of Neutria! Born of the northern winds! We ride to battle on this day like the *Fingingothar* of legend, on the Winds of Death! When this battle be done, and we are united in death, then let it be written upon our epithet that we inflicted such injury upon the enemy that they could not march beyond Ortangraal!"

As the Truemans did battle in the courtyard, they could hear the words of their leaders ring across the battlefield.

The Kreel was able to eventually regain control of their panicking undermen. They caused them to turn and stand their ground against the Truemans. The courtyard was now transformed into a scene of hand-to-hand combat. The Truemans continue to fight their way through the courtyard with a vengeance. They fought with no regard to their lives, throwing caution to the winds. They went at the enemy with a berserker's determination, cutting down trogs, half-trogs, trog-men and other undermen as they fell upon them from all directions. The Truemans laughed at the whirlwind of hate and steel that was directed at them. Their comrades who watched them from the inner walls began to sing a song of war in their honor as they slaughtered the harvest of foul underman weeds. The song rose into the air and it was both sweet and terrible to hear.

Upon this field a battle does rage
While all the world, its breath to hold,
To decide the fate of the new age.
While Truemans fight, as brothers bold!

And if our bodies, are cut and scared
Fighting for the Lords of the Light,
may the Light our souls to take unmarred.
So our children's future, might be bright!

So we throw ourselves, into the fray
To death! To death! In battle's breath,
we gladly give our lives, this day.
And live on, in the Light, after death!

From the gate in the inner wall, several thousand Neutrian foot warriors charged out onto the battle field to assist the knights and horsemen in the courtyard. With them came Olaf and Pettin. They joined their equestrian comrades in battle.

The king and the centurion soon found themselves surrounded by a wall of ten trolls. Each stood over ten feet tall, with skin of green scales and caked in filth. They swung their large mattocks before them. Their eyes blazed with a mindless rage as they screech their Keel-induced hate at them. Drool dripped form their long, red tongues that hung from their mouths filled rodent-like teeth. They were on top of them in seconds, and only the intervention of the massive form of Olaf saved the king from the troll's deadly swing. Olaf knocked one of the monsters down by bashing him in the groin with his battle mace, and then brought his weapon up and down on the head of a second troll, as they rushed by him toward the king. Pettin jumped in between the legs of another troll and cut his battle axe deep into the thighs of the troll. He swung around and then plunged his axe into the back of the leg of another troll. Both giants fell to the ground, and causing those pushing up from behind them to fall over them. Pettin was able to cut into the necks and severing the heads of two other trolls that were climbing over the bodies of their dead comrades, still jerking in their death throws. Olaf continued to swing at the trolls, as they now scrambled over each other in a vain attempt to escape the fury of the Tillenian woodsmen. His battle mace found its mark time and time again, sending green blood and gray guts flying about in a vortex of death and destruction.

Caratium pulled his sword from its scabbard and proceeded to hack and swing at the legs of several large trolls. His first blow hit with the force of an avalanche, crushing the knees of one troll, causing it to buckle and fall. Before he reached the ground, Caratium swung again and severed its head from its armor-plated shoulders. The next troll Caratium struck was cut in two at the waist. Caratium's sword was made from Pure Gold, which cut easily through armor, flesh and bone as if they were made of paper. When Caratium swung his sword, neither steel armor nor underman flesh could withstand its cutting blade. Metal ripped and green blood gushed, mixing with gore and gray organs that poured on the battlefield and stained the golden armor of the knights.

"To war! To war! Onward, my knights! To war!" Caratium shouted. He could hear a cheer rise all around him from his fellow knights, who were fired with a heroic zeal. Though heavily outnumbered, they threw themselves at the enemy, cutting and ripping, crushing and stabbing their way through a field of twisted un-humanity. No barrier of flesh and armor could slow them down, but not without a price. Many in their ranks died as they fought, but for each one that fell, hundreds of the enemy were dispatched. Right behind the knights fought the Neutrians, protecting their flanks and fighting with equal determination.

King Amthrim held the reins of his horse with his left hand as a world of slaughter whirled about him with a force of a hurricane. In his right hand, his sword was unsheathed and already stained green with the blood of many trogs. He sniffed the air and thought how long it had been since last he warred against the force of the Darkness. For too long he let his bones and limbs grow old from non-use. Like an old woman he hid in the shadow-filled rooms, hiding from the world outside. For too long he let others govern in his name and fight his battles, but now he was reborn. He was king, a leader to lead his people in the service of the Light. He knew that this would be his last hour on New Earth, but the dread of death did not frighten him. It was not into the Pit of Darkness that he would be flung, but instead, he knew he would take his place among the Lords of the Light.

Then Amthrim saw, over the pulsating sea of bodies, a large carriage pulled by several great trolls dressed in black and green armor. The coach was draped in black, and the trolls were desperately trying to carry it through the melee, away from the advancing columns of Truemans, killing even their own soldiers in their attempt to escape,

Without waiting, King Amthrim knew instinctively, as if the Red Stone he was carrying endowed him with a deeper sense of knowing, he must reach the troll-pulled coach. He pulled on the reins and his steed galloped up and over the mountain of fallen bodies. Like a flash of lightning, the king rode toward the black carriage. He cut a path through the enemy, who hurried out of his way despite the power of the Kreel's willpower that drove them on. Like the Wind of Death that his people spoke about in whispers behind locked doors, he rode on, filled with the bitting force of the winter storms of his fatherland. He seemed to those that chanced to watch, to be some apparition of some unearthly force that men feared more than death.

Trogs fell and Alfeinians whimpered as his blows cut them down. Trolls were smashed bloodied if they ventured to interfere with the king's onslaught. He was driven by the power of the Red Stone, which endowed him with a superhuman determination and fighting fever that dropped all who tried to stand between him and his intended target.

When the king finally reached the coach, he quickly dispatched the trolls carrying it with several swipes of his sword, severing arms and cutting throats. The trolls seemed helpless before the power of the Red Stone, which sapped them of their master's will. The wheelless carriage fell to the ground with a thud. Just then, two knights rode up beside the king, holding lances. The black box was smashed open by the knights, splintering wood as steel lances pierced the ruins of the carriage. Inside were three short dwarves with glowing, red eyes. Small, pointed ears protruded from their gray, matted hair on their large, bulbous heads. Red tongues jotted over rows of sharp teeth that filled their mouths, as they spat and shrieked their hatred of the knights. The knights plunged their lances deep into the fat, round bellies of two of the dwarves, causing them to erupt into fountains of blood and guts.

The third dwarf crawled to the far corner of what was left of his wooden box. His gleaming rat-like eyes glared up at the configurations of shining armor that stood before him. He shouted something intangible in his foul language, and then changed over to the common speech of Daryan.

"You'll never live to see your precious sun again, Trueman filth!" the dwarf shouted. "You'll all burn in the blackest pits of my master's belly before this war is ended. I'll see . . ."

Thick green blood and grayish slime splattered all about, as the cold, hard steel of the king's blade came crashing down and split the Kreel's skull in two.

With the death of their Kreel masters, the undermen were now leaderless. There was no one to direct them. Panic quickly spread through their ranks. Trogs began running in all directions and Alfeinians jumped on the other undermen that were in their way, bitting them as they tried to escape from the avenging Truemans. The chaos spread like a storm among the undermen. Trolls began stampeding in every direction, crushing undermen and Truemans alike, killing all who were unfortunate enough to be in their way.

For the first time, the battle seemed to turn against the Dark Alliance. King Amthrim raised his sword in hand, high over his head and shouted, "To me! To me! We will yet snatch victory from our enemy this day! To me and onto victory!"

Then, from high above, coming out of the black roof of bellowing clouds overhead, there could be heard a soul-shattering cry that sent tremors through the hearts of even the bravest men present. It was followed by another cry of a different pitch. Everyone looked up and saw flying against the clouds, two bat-like, winged creatures circling over the battlefield. They were slowly coming ever down in wide spirals.

"Horzugal!" one of the knights shouted as he dropped his lance and threw himself to the ground. Dread and fear overcame him as the bat-like things grew ever closer. As the Horzugal descended, they screamed their demands of submission and capitulation, filling hearts with terror and clouding minds with doubt, as all who heard them, cowered in fear. One of the Horzugal swooped down, over the inner walls, and then flew about, tormenting the walls' defenders. The other Horzugal flew even lower into the courtyard. Its great shadow caused the spirits of the dark armies to rise once again with the hope of victory. Suddenly, something caught the eye of the winged servant of the Lord of Darkness, and drew its attention like sweet honey draws ants.

The Horzugal turned and flew in the direction of King Amthrim, who was sitting tall upon his steed. It shrieked a terrifying cry, causing the king's horse to rear. The king struggled to remain in his saddle, but the power of the King Kreel's servant was too great. Amthrim was thrown to the ground as everyone cowered in fear.

The Horzugal landed and leered at those few knights and warriors, who found the courage and will to tried to come to the king's aid.

"You dare to challenge the power of my master?" it sneered, as it rose to its legs. Its black wings flapped, blowing foul, reeking air about, causing a cloud of dirt to rise. It looked down at the king and laughed. "You stinking old bag of bones. Did you really think you could escape your destiny? I'm going to rip your heart out of your stinking chest and bring it back to Allomania, where your soul will suffer everlasting torment at the hands of my master." The demon's eyes flashed red with a fire that burned hot with hate for all that was good and filled with the power of the Light.

The Horzugal's eyes flashed with flames. From its eyes two beams of energy burst and struck at the king, but they were stopped by a ball of light that surrounded him. The power of the Red Stone was protecting him. The Horzugal concentrated until the globe of light that surrounded the king flashed, causing the Horzugal to cease its attack. The king was weakened, but so was the demon. The Horzugal shook its head. He could smell the king's pain and a terrible grin appeared on its hideous face, as it prepared to deliver a death blow.

The king struggled to rise. He felt the dark, tormenting will of the black servant burning into his mind. He remembered a pain that he once suffered not too long ago. The memory of his weakness shamed him and he fought to find the will to resist. He refused to submit to it. With every ounce of his strength, he fought against it, clutching at the Red Stone that he held in his hand, drawing on its power for help.

Just then, Caratium crawled from where he had fallen, when the Horzugal had landed. He was now situated behind the beast, and fought with all his strength to crawl closer to it. The winged-servant was about to lunge at the king when the Lothangian knight rose to his feet, reached for a lance that lay on the ground next to him, and grabbed it. He raised the lance and held it before him. Drawing on what strength of body and mind he could muster, he threw himself at the Horzugal from behind. The weight of his body caused the lance to plunge into the demon's back. It burst forth from its chest in an explosion of green slime.

The Horzugal cried out in pain and turned toward his attacker. His hatred now flared white hot. He reached around and pulled the lance from his back and crushed it over the fallen body of Caratium with one blow. It was then that the Horzugal turned back to the king. Fear now flashed in its eyes, as he saw the king rising to his knees with the Red Stone held out before him in his left hand, while he supported himself with his right hand.

The king wobbled. The winged-servant could see that he was still weak, and this restored his self-confidence. "Now you die, Trueman filth!" Its laughter was cruel and cold. Its eyes burned bright like two pieces of hot coal. It raised its clawed hand, but before it could strike, it reeled back in pain, clutching its horned head. It was struck by a green bolt of light from the walls where Arlindor stood. Before the Horzugal could react to the druid's attack, it was engulfed in a red light that sent pain cutting deep into its very being. Sharp and nerve-piercing, burning and bitting agony filled its black soul, and then suddenly, there was nothing. The Horzugal had disintegrated.

King Amthrim stood before a pile of black ashes. Arlindor's attack gave the king time to use the Red Stone. From it a red bolt of energy struck the Horzugal, destroying it.

Far over head the other Horzugal cried out in anguish. For the first time in a thousand years that which was made of evil was destroyed. The six servants were no more. Now they were only five, and their power, though still great, was diminished.

The world seemed like a blur, spinning about the king as he fell over. Knights and warriors rushed to the king's side. Caratium laid still, next to the king. Amthrim could barely hear a distant voice crying out, "Father! Father!" Prince Sagtrim was now kneeling by his father's side, trying to call him back from the world of shadows. The king opened his eyes and looked into the face of his son, who was staring down at him. He could see the hurt and grief in his son's eyes.

"My son," the king struggled to speak. "Don't grieve for me, for I am going to live with the Lords of the Light. I die a hero's death. Mine is a death that would be the envy of all our people."

"No, father," was all that Sagtrim could say.

"Do not speak, my son," the king's face winced in pain. "My body is broken, but my soul is stronger than ever. I am saved. I have destroyed one of the servants of the Darkness, and broke the hold that that creature had on me. Perhaps this deed has erased the long months of weakness that I suffered under the beast's foul breath from the memory of all Truemans?"

"I should have been with you, father," the prince said. "Perhaps then I could have saved you? Better it be I lying here than you. Our people need your wisdom and leadership. You must not die."

"Your words ease my pain, my son," Amthrim spoke once more. "But I am the past and you are the future. You'll now lead our people, and your reign will be one better remembered than mine. What is needed now is strength and youth." The king struggled to reach up and touch his son's face. His eyes were filled with tears and there was a far away look in the king's eyes, as if he was looking through the prince, at someone or something standing behind him. Sagtrim turned and saw the druid standing over them.

"You must look after my son, druid," the king said. "He's young and has need of your sage wisdom."

"The House of Neutria will always be welcomed in the halls of Wissenval," Arlindor assured the dying king. "We"ll look after the new king and the people of Neutria as we have in the past."

"Thank you, druid," the king finally said. His face now revealed a serenity, as if some great burden was lifted from his soul. "Now I can go without care and walk among our fathers, in the Halls of Vorulha. But before I give up my spirit, you must promise me two things, my son."

"Anything, father. You have only to ask," Sagtrim's voice almost broke with grief.

"First, give your sister my love," the king said. "You and she have always been more important to me than all the treasures in the world. Tell Valenda that I am proud of her to have gone on such a quest, as she did, and that I always held a special place in my heart for her."

"I will tell her, father," the prince promised.

The king now grabbed his arm, struggling not to surrender his soul until he had said what he wished to say. "Secondly, you must swear to me that you will lead our people south, if you come through this battle, and give what aid you might to the Lothangians, in their war against Allomania." The king looked over at the broken body of Caratium. "He fought mightily to try and save my life, and prevent my soul from being taken by that carrion-eater of souls. His people and our people are both born of the same womb of nations. Promise me you will never let the alliance between Neutria and Lothangia fall apart."

"I promise, father. I swear it," the prince said.

"Thank you, my son," the king said and smiled. "Now I can take leave of this world. I hear your mother calling me, I think?"

The king's hand still clutched the Red Stone as he raised it and placed it in his son's hand. The king's eyes closed and he slumped into an eternal sleep, one from which he would never wake. A wind suddenly blew over them, cold and chilling as if something flew pass them. Then, from above, the first flakes of snow began to fall upon the battlefield. Everyone looked up and saw great white clouds pushing away the black veil that hung for too long over the world.

Chapter Ten:
The Battle of Six Nations

All heads now turned toward the sound of galloping hooves, as a rider approached. "My Lord!" a Lothangian rider shouted, as he rode to a halt and dismounted.

Before Sagtrim could speak, Arlindor spoke, "Listen!"

Everyone could hear the bells from the tower ringing.

"An army from the east is attacking the Fennorian army on the southern bank of the river," the messenger said. "There are maxthoiums among their ranks."

"Tillenia has come," Arlindor said. "They have come at last."

"Victory may yet be ours?" Pettin shouted. "Long live Tillenia!"

"There is something else," Arlindor said.

"What else is there?" Pettin asked.

"This snow," Arlindor said as he let the white flakes land on his face.

"The snow comes from the north, but it seems queer," Olaf said. "It's as if there is a hand that guides it on its course."

"And so there is," Arlindor said. "The Lord of Darkness has forgotten the race of Yomiron. But I think he is about to be reminded of them, before this day is out."

Suddenly, everyone was aware of the war still raging all about them. The tide seemed to have turned once more. A fear seemed to have come over the undermen and everywhere they looked they saw Truemans putting them to the sword, as they were reduced once again, to an uncontrollable mob. Sensing the moment at hand, out from the western towers charged the Trueman defenders led by Turahium, who had held it against the rising tide of undermen, storming the walls. With him came the three Marklanders, Gordon, Milland and Magin.

Everyone now fought with the tenacity of madmen filled with the lust of the berserkers. They hacked and cut their way, slashing at trogs and Alfeinians in a mad frenzy of hate. Then suddenly, there was a blast of trumpets. A song was heard that filled the courtyard.

Turahium could see the spreading ranks of the knights before him. He rallied his men and led them in their direction. Trueman met Trueman as they rejoiced in their song of battle. After the Horzugal was destroyed, and its terrible hold over the hearts and minds of the Trueman warriors was destroyed, Turahium and his three Marklander companions fought their way through the panicking horde of undermen, and reach the spot where Arlindor and Sagtrim stood over the body of the fallen King of Neutria.

In the east an army numbering some four thousand men and two hundred wooly maxthoiums had come to the end of their great march, south from woods of Tillenia and on the heels of the Fennorian army. The Council of Elders in the city of Jassinburg had sent their army to aid their allies. They had to keep the bulk of their forces at home to defend their towns and farms from any army that Wargana might have held back in Fennoria. But even the fear of a Fennorian sneak attack could not prevent the Tillenians from living up to their word.

With a force of a tidal wave, the Tillenian woodmen, decked out in armor and horned helmets, carrying battle axes, lances and maces, rammed into the rear of that part of the Fennorian army that was still on the southern banks of the Donnor River. Led by a phalanx of two hundred maxthoiums, the largest animal that walked the lands of New Earth, their riders drove them into the rear of the Fennorians, who were completely unprepared for the assault, as they were still crossing the river Donnor.

The great mountains of hair and muscle trumpeted their arrival with raised trunks and backs loaded with Tillenian archers. Trogs and half-trogs turned and saw a wall of great curving tusks, like huge shovels that could rip into flesh and metal with deadly results. The maxthoiums steamrolled into the Fennorian army, blaring their charge. Behind them came thousands of Tillenians, swinging their axes and maces, jabbing long lances into the ranks of the enemy, causing them to scatter in all directions.

The attack was successful. The Fennorian army was devastated. as the maxthoiums that thundered their fury. The great beats ripped and crushed anyone or anything unfortunate enough to fall beneath their stampeding legs.

On the lead maxthoium sat Tharokon, the Commander of the Tillenian army. Before him, he could see the endless multitude of undermen, screaming in panic and throwing away their weapons, running in every direction, as Tillenian foot soldiers mopped up the flanks of the maxthoium phalanx.

"Vengeance! Vengeance for the atrocities committed against Tillenia!" Tharokon shouted as he led the charge.

Thousands of undermen jumped into the river in a vain attempt to escape the massive phalanx of stream rolling muscle and tucks, only to be swallowed up by the whirling, icy waters of the mighty Donnor River.

Then a cool, fresh wind blew down from the northwest, across the face of Tharokon.

"What is this?" he said to his sub-commander. Then, pointing across the river, he shouted, "Look! Do you see it also, or am I going mad?"

"No Tharokon. You're not going mad," the sub-commander said, staring in disbelief. Before them, approached a wall of white and gray, coming ever closer until it overtook them. All about them was a whirlwind of snow flakes that began to pile higher and higher on the battlefield.

"Snow? Here and now?" Tharokon stammered in disbelief. "What could this possibly mean?" He had only to look about the battlefield and see the trogs and half-trogs freezing and falling in the soft bed of white death that was rapidly overcoming them.

The snow storm blew south from the frozen north, giving cover to the Yomiron, who were marching south to war against the Army of Allomania. For five days and nights they advanced along the road that ran from Neutria, southwest toward Ortangraal. But before they reached the fortress, they turned off the road and marched up the Offenessian Hills. More than one hundred and fifty stone giants marched behind their leader, Ironbone, who carried the two Marklander children, Huck and Rullin, warmly tucked in his arms.

"We've come a long way," Ironbone said as he came to a halt. The whole company of giants came to a stop when he did, and stood as still and silent as the great stone megaliths that dotted the landscape of the Mark. "We're now just a few miles north of the Allomanian Army. They must have already begun crossing the river and attacked Ortangraal by now."

"I hope we're not too late," Huck said.

"I think not," Ironbone said. "But I can't take you any farther."

"Why not?" Rullin asked.

"Because, I need my arms free to smash and kill trogs and Alfeinians, that's why," Ironbone said. "But don't worry, you'll be left in good care."

Ironbone made a rumbling sound and then up stepped a shorter, heavier-set giant. He was light gray in color and possessed smooth skin. Lines ran along the length of his body, as if he wore a pin-stripped suite. His face was broad and flat, but his eyes radiated the same gleaming Life-Force that shined in Ironbone's eyes.

"I'm known as Slatstone, in you tongue," the shorter giant said as he slightly bowed his head and took the boys from Ironbone. "I'm young by the count of time according to my people, and so Ironbone thought I would be good company for you two Trueman pups."

"Take good care of them," Ironbone said to Slatestone. His

voice was hard and sharp like diamonds. "We're about to attack the dark army." Ironbone then looked at Huck and Rullin. "While we fight, Slatestone will watch over you. I will lead the attack, but don't worry, I'll see you both safe at the end of this battle."

Ironbone made his farewells to Huck and Rullin. He had grown fond of them and instructed Slatestone to remain on the Offenessian Hills and wait until the battle was concluded. He was then to bring the boys down to him when he received word from him.

Snow continued to fall all about the land, and the Allomanian Army began to panic. Snow had always been something to fear for the trogs. Alfeinians were used to it, covered as they were with a short, thick coat of fur. They could easily survive the cold winters on the great plains of their homelands, but trogs were unlike Alfeinians, and could not survive the cold. They lived in a hot, ash-filled environment, deep under the earth and close to the veins of volcanos. Their blood was green, thick and icy-cold to the point that it actually provided a natural cooling system for such creatures that were born in the molten rock and flame-filled environment that existed right after the terrible Hell Fires of the past. Thus their blood was incapable of providing body heat to warm them. Trogs could not stand the cold and would freeze solid in temperatures that dropped below freezing.

It was under the cover of the falling snow that the stone giants attacked the Allomanian army. First they moved silently and with stealth. They slowly crept up on the horde of undermen, who were unaware of any movement among the rocks and stones that gathered at the foot of the hills of Offenessia. The Allomanians were blinded by the heavy curtain of white frost that fell over the landscape. Many guards deserted their posts, to huddle around the fires that were lit for protection against the advancing cold.

While the battle for Ortangraal raged on as undermen scaled the inner walls, and the king and the centurion led the charge of knights and Neutrian warriors into the mist of the enemy, across the river, the Yomiron rushed through the blinding snow like an avalanche. Everything exploded into chaos as the wall of living stone swept across the fields and into the camp grounds, crushing and smashing everything and everyone under their terrible charge. Trogs, Alfeinians and trolls, along with wagons, camp tents, shields, spears and racks of weapons were all reduced to broken bodies and wreckage in the fury of their attack.

Stone fists, slammed down like great battering rams, crushing steel armor and breaking bones, shattering twisted flesh and leathery hides, splitting skulls that blossomed into grayish-green fountains of brains and gore.

The Yomiron surged forward in waves, battering, crushing and smashing all undermen, as they went. Nothing could stand against them. Even the largest trolls were no match against the berserking stone giants. Their rock-hard arms easily deflected the steel maces and axes that were aimed at them. Their stone feet crushed through armor and flesh. They rolled over the dark legions like boulders bouncing down the side of a cliff. Nothing could stop them once they began their attack. As a race, they were slow to start, but once the war fever possessed them, they moved with the growing force of an avalanche. They could no more be stopped than the earth, when it began to tremble with quakes.

The alarm was sounded and Kreel wills bend toward restoring order to the ranks of their armies. The undermen were slowly returning to their master's control. The charge of the giants was an awesome and frightening spectacle to behold. The Yomiron were kicking up snow in clouds of white powder as they stormed their way into the enemy. The cold soon began to have its chilling effects of the trogs. Many were freezing up and unable to obey their master's will. The Kreel struggled to maintain control over their army of slaves. The dwarfs summoned every ounce of their will power to halt the flight of their legions, and turned them around to confront the invading force of stone giants. Eventually, the Kreel were able to rally their forces once more and send once last wave of undermen across the snow-covered fields, toward the stone giants. The twisted forms of undermen rushed at the giants despite the freezing effects of the snowstorm. The dark horde of black, green and brown forms were driven on to meet the oncoming wall of living stone, like rats driven forward by the scent of rotting flesh.

Upon the white fields, time seemed to cease as the wall of rampaging stone slammed into the dark wave of twisting, leaping, lumbering, mail-covered bodies, brandishing spears and swords, wielding battle maces and hurtling clubs. Under a curtain of white snow that whirled and swept about them, the undermen crashed into one another as the stone steamroller pulverized the flood of mutated humanity.

Stone and flesh smashed into each other. Trogs and Alfeinians flung themselves at the stone giants, shrieking with pain as stone, hammer-like fists flatten them under their smashing weight. Trolls were crushed under slamming blows of whirling, rock limbs, sending fountains of blood splattering into the air, and staining the newly fallen snow green with their blood. Undermen convulsed and fell, their broken bodies, a testament to the earth's fury, were quickly buried under the falling snow. Wave after wave of dark, twisted forms slammed into the stone giants, not even slowing down under the assault, until finally, the counterattack faltered and was thrown back by the stone giants. Again the Kreel concentrated all the strength their minds could muster, and sent another surge of fangs and claws at the Yomiron, who were determined to get at the dwarfish overlords. But this attack was feeble compared to the previous assaults.

Again and again stone limbs rose and came pounding down, sending fountains of guts and blood into the air to the sounds of cracking bones and splintering steel, as the stone giants ceaselessly moved on, until finally, after an hour of endless slaughter, they had reached the inner camp, where the Kreel were located.

Kharz-Zish had returned from the courtyard of Ortangraal and now sat on top of a platform located on the western banks, where the Angorium River joined the Donnor. From this point he could observe the battles raging on the other side of the Donnor, as well as the progress of the siege of Ortangraal. And from this point he could direct the combined wills of his brother-Kreel in a renewed assault against the defenders of the fortress. But now, the Caliph of Alfeinia, found himself the object of another invader. The other Kreel had gathered with him and together they expected to repel the charge out of Ortangraal, but now they found themselves surrounded by the ever-enclosing wall of living stone, making its way toward them, like the irresistible flow of molten rock. The hearts of the stone giants were fire with the force of a volcano, and could not be stopped by the muscle of all the undermen that the Kreel could send against, nor by the combined force of their collective willpower.

The Kreel Caliph sent thousands of his slaves to their deaths in a senseless, mindless and futile rush against the Yomiron. The power of the Kreel minds bent the lesser minds of their slaves to do the will of their dark master, the King Kreel, which was to send wave after wave of undermen into the fighting wall of stone, had now faulted. How easy it was for the Kreel to force the races of undermen to rally under their black and red flags and blindly attack, like lemmings, rushing to their doom. But now they were faced with an opponent that defied even their paralyzing power of their minds. All around them they were surrounded with the dark shadow of death.

A last stand was taken by the Kreel, who had held back several hundred of their largest trolls. They were almost as large as the Yomiron. Some were as tall as twelve feet in height. Clad in armor and carrying great maces, battleaxes and mattocks, they formed a ring around their Kreel masters. All about them was a field of snow, mixed with heaps of their fallen comrades. Mixed among the bodies were disembodied limbs and heads, laid about partly buried by the falling flakes.

As the ring of stone enclosed on the wall of trolls, from within their ranks, great balls of fire were catapulted from a large sling-shot machine manned by Kreel commanders. The fire balls exploded on impact, causing chips of stone to fly as they hit the giants. Several stone giants were stopped in their tracks, as the fire balls struck, causing them to cry out in pain. Soon more flaming balls began to fly at the Yomiron, forcing them to withdraw out of range.

The trolls began to shout and swing their battle weapons about, as they jeered at the giants, who now stood strangely silent. They did not move or speak. Only their eyes betrayed that there was life within the stone figures. Within them the Life-Force burned hot with the force of an eruption. Their eyes flashed with an anger as great as the pressure that builds up long and hot, deep under a mountain, until finally the earth's crust is unable to contain it any longer, and it finally explodes in a volcanic fury, spewing out fire and molten rock.

The Yomiron now began to pound their feet upon the earth beneath them with such force that it shook the ground, causing the trolls to fall as the wind and snow whirled about them. Then, to the surprise of the trolls and before they could regain their footing, the Yomiron began breaking up the earth and hurling great chunks of stones and boulders at them. The rocks flew through the curtain of falling white frost, crushing and killing trolls as they impacted.

Ironstone ordered his people to keep up the bombardment of boulders until the last troll had fallen under the tons of flying rock. Now the stone giants stared at the hundred or so Kreel dwarves that remained within the crater of broken flesh and rocks piled high about them. The eyes of the stone giants flashed with a white-hot anger, fed by the recent memory of the bitting fire balls. Slowly they began to move in on their rodent-like victims.

Ironbone stepped forward, as the ring of stone close tighter. Some of the Kreel began screaming in fright, running about helplessly in circles, desperately looking for a way to escape. Other Kreel fell on their knees, in the snow, begging for their lord and master, who had suddenly abandoned them now that they were no longer useful, to come and deliver them from the fate that was enclosing in on them. Large, stone hands reached down and grabbed at them, crushing the life out of their small, round bodies like eggs. Blood oozed, eyes popped, tongue hung loose and gore popped out of the sockets and ears, as all life was squeezed out of them under the pressure of tightening stone fingers. Other Kreel were stumped to death like bugs under the slamming weight of stone feet. One by one the Yomiron killed the Kreel until only one, fat dwarf, with a balding, round head, was still alive. He crawled on his knees in the center of the ring of stone giants. He looked up and hissed defiantly at Ironbone, who stood towering over him.

The giant just stared for a moment at the small, wizened, hunched form of Kharz-Zish. His large, red eyes burned with hate. His small, pointed ears barely stuck out through the mess of matted, gray hair that hung down from around his balding head.

In a futile and desperate effort, the dwarf rose to his feet and stared at Ironbone, directing all the power of his will at him, but to no effect. The realization that he had no power over the stone giant caused him to whirled about in terror, looking into the eyes of each stone face, trying desperately to find a recognition of the power of his will, but to no avail. Finally, his eyes locked once more on those of Ironbone.

"Do you think you can stop the Lord of the World?" he shouted the words at the stone figure before him. "You can't stop Allomania from obtaining its rightful destiny. Today we will conquer Ortangraal, tomorrow Lothangia. Then we will bring all of New Earth under the rule of its rightful lord and master—the King Kreel. And you and all your kind will pay for your defiance. You have condemned your race to complete extinction. My master will melt your entire race down into molten rock, in the furnaces of Allomania, before this war is finished. You will all . . ."

Kharz-Zish's tirade was cut short, as a massive, stone foot was brought down with crushing force upon the pimple of a man, that was known as Kharz-Zish, silencing him forever.

Chapter Eleven:
The Winds Blow South

A large, dragon-shaped ship set sail down the Donnor River with a large, blue sail filled with the northern winds, pushing it along the mirror-still waters. On the sail was the Neutrian star with a black ship in its center. From the top of the mass flew the blue, white and red, stars and eagle banner of Lothangia. On board the ship laid side by side the bodies of King Amthrim of Neutria and Caratium, Commander of the Knights of the Silver Swan, dressed in his Pure Gold armor and red garments. Many fair things belonging to both men were laid in the ship, as well as the gear that they took with them into battle.

Both men had died together, in battle with the Horzugal. Caratium gave up his life to aid the king, and so it was agreed that they should journey together to the next world.

Men of Lothangia and Neutria gathered and stood along the banks of the Donnor River. Knights stood with arms raised in salute and red capes waving, as their commander and the king sailed passed them. As men gave their last respects, flaming arrows were launched and flew across the river, striking the ship. In a short time the ship was transformed into a fiery swan. It continued to sail, as smoke and fire jumped from its decks. Its blaze consumed the two bodies on board, as the ship slowly sank into the embrace of the cool waters of the great river, baptizing them in the elemental forces of fire and water.

On the eastern bank of the Donnor River, across from Ortangraal, stood Arlindor. Next to him stood Prince Sagtrim, holding his father's sword, and Turahium, in his armor of Pure Gold. Behind them, standing tall, were the three Marklanders, Gordon, Milland and Magin. With them stood the two young, Marklander boys, Huck and Rullin. Next to them were Olaf and Pettin from Tillenia, as well as Tharokon, Commander of the Tillenian Army. Others also had joined them in saying farewell to the king and the centurion. They included Bolthur, Huntilheim and Junthunor from Neutria, who wished their king a good journey to Vorulha, and standing behind them, towering over all, standing erect and motionless, was the stone giant, Ironbone, of the race of the Yomiron.

The sky was clear blue. The snow clouds of yesterday had already broken apart to let the sun's rays bathe the world in their warmth. The cloud of black malice that had hung over Ortangraal for so long, had been driven away. Golden rays reflected off the snowy white ground like a great fire lighting up all the fields with joy. Trumpets blared and flags from the three nations waved alongside each other, as Truemans stood victorious with the Yomiron.

"Farewell, King of the North," Sagtrim said as he fought to contain his grief and pride over his father's departure. "I hail thee as you go with the Farales to Vorulha. Someday we will ride together on its green fields, and sail its blue waters. But for now, you go to join your fathers."

Next, Turahium raised his arm in salute. "Hail Caratium! Knight of the Silver Swan, and like the swan of legend, you will never truly be dead. You will live forever within our ranks, so long as our order lives, just as the swan is reborn. You are a Warrior of the Light, and now ride with the Lords who rule over the Light, on top of Mount Virolon."

Then, as one, the voices of all who were assembled, rose in unison. *Hail Amthrim! Hail Caratium! Hail the Lords of the Light!*

When the funeral ceremony was over, there was a meeting on the banks of the Donnor, on a field of melting, white snow.

Arlindor and Prince Sagtrim were joined by Turahium and the commanders of the Knights of the Silver Swan. The number of knights had been reduced from 100 to 68, and of the original 900 Lothangian legionaries who were sent to occupy Ortangraal, only 610 had survived the battle. With them there were 8,610 Neutrian Boatmen, who were still fit to travel of the original 10,000 who set sail with their king from Noranil. They busied themselves, collecting the bodies of their fallen comrades and preparing their funeral, as well as tending to the wounded.

With them were gathered the Tillenian commanders, as well as Ironbone.

"Strange things have happened this morning," Prince Sagtrim said. "I have lived through the labor of battle and witnessed the legends of old come alive." His eyes turned toward Ironbone. Everyone else also looked in his direction.

Arlindor smiled and looked at Ironbone, whose eyes flashed with recognition.

"It has been a long count of years since last we spoke together, Druid of the Earth," Ironbone said to Arlindor. "And even longer since stone giants and men of flesh and blood have parleyed. Yes, it has been too long, Prince of the Folds." Ironbone looked at Sagtrim.

"It has, indeed," Sagtrim said, trying to look tall before the towering giant. He pulled himself up to his full height of 6' 2". "It has been so long that the memory of it has turned to legend, and the legend in time turned to myth. We must make sure that man and rock do not wait so long between councils, in the future."

"The legends of old have become the reality of today," Arlindor said. "Much that is happening in these times are legends come true. When have the nations of Lothangia, Neutria and Tillenia last fought together as allies? I ask you all to tell me. The memory of such an even, escapes all our recollections, lost in the fog of the distant past.

"But the time for talk of such things has not yet come. There is still much fighting that needs to be done, and your men are weary. Let us go back to our armies and prepare them for the departure that must come tomorrow. All should sleep well tonight, so that we will be refreshed for the journey. In the morning, the Neutrians must sail with their ships, loaded with as many men as they can carry, while the Tillenians will ride as they might on their maxthoiums, along the banks of the Donnor River, to the south."

"And what of the Yomiron?" asked Sagtrim.

"We will not go south," Ironbone said. "My people will stay here a short while longer, and help clear the battlefield of the dead." Ironbone pointed to the east. "See, even now we burn the dead."

Everyone turned and could see a great pillar of smoke rising into the air from across the Donnor, where the Allomanian army was destroyed.

"My people are gathering the remains of the undermen across the river," Ironbone said. "Their carrion was too great to bury, so we are burning them first."

"We will do the same with the remains of the Fennorian army, on this side of the river," Tharokon said. His round face was still frowning hard with the effects of battle.

"There is little time for your army to deal with the dead," Arlindor told Tharokon. "In the morning, we must be readied to move south toward the city of Lothar. I will not remain here even a minute longer than is necessary. We must move south, down the Donnor River, if we are to arrive at Lothar before the Lord of Darkness is able to invade Lothangia, and take the Lothangian capital."

"But we must at least see to our dead," Tharokon said.

"We will see to your dead," Ironbone. "We will remain here and assist those Truemans who will also remain behind to man Ortangraal, and make sure that the dead are honorably disposed."

"Thank you," Tharokon said. "We will be in your debt."

Ironbone bowed his head silently. "When we are finished, I will lead my people west to Offenessia. We will then travel along the river until we reach the Wold River, and then move south to the Kil'org Pass. There, we will stand guard and stop whatever foul things that might try and pass out of Allomania to the north. Afterwards we will return to our lands in the north, by way of

Alfeinia. There is a score that we must settle with these evil, carrion-eaters."

"Then you will have the gratitude of all Neutrians," Prince Sagtrim said. "The Alfeinians have for too long raided my realm— my realm?" The prince repeated the last two words to himself, as their meaning sunk in.

"Yes. Your realm, King Sagtrim," Arlindor said. "All hail King Sagtrim!"

Everyone joined in the cheering as Sagtrim held his head high proudly, and had to fight to hold back the tears for his father.

All that day, everyone worked hard to make their ships ready for the journey south. The ships were loaded with what supplies they could gather. The men of Ortangraal collected the dead and separated Truemans from undermen. Lothangians, Neutrians and Tillenians were buried together in a common grave. A great hole was dug into the Belt of Ortangraal, and the burned remains of the dead were placed inside by the Yomiron. They would eventually pile a huge hill of stones over the grave, marking the spot until after the war, when they hoped to return and build a great monument to their memory, if anyone survived the war.

The stone giants continued to burn the dead undermen that they collected from the banks of the Donnor and the Angorium Rivers. All day long, pillars of black smoke climbed high overhead, and could be seen for miles in the clear sky. The smoke continued to rise throughout the night and when morning came, the smoke continued to bellow overhead. The fires were being fed by trees taken from the Offenessian Hills. The giants were cutting and hauling the trees down to the river bank.

That evening, Arlindor visited the Yomiron, and used what magic he commanded, to heal the wounds the giants had incurred in their fierce battle with the Allomanian army. None of them suffered such injury that would cause them to lose their lives, but axe, mattock and mace had inflicted chips and cracks on the stone giants that demanded attention. Fortunately for the giants,

Arlindor, the Earth Druid, as he was referred to by the Yomiron, possessed such healing skills.

While business was taken care of by the high, a reunion was held among friends elsewhere. When the battle was over, Ironbone sent for Slatestone and the boys. Rullin and Huck were brought down to Ironbone by Slatestone, after the battle. They had watched the battle unfold, as best they could through the raging snow storm from a high hill, just above where the Yomiron attacked the Allomanian army.

"You must tell us about these stone giants, and how you fell into their company?" Magin insisted, as he and the other two Marklanders, Milland and Gordon, along with Pettin and Olaf, sat around a small fire, and cut some meat that they had just roasted. His round, bearded face sparkled with joy and interest as he laughed with delight.

Huck and Rullin were sipping some hot willow bark tea to warm themselves.

"Yes. You must tell us, lads," Olaf said. "How in all the trees of the Wolf-Staak did you whine up with these stone giants?"

"When we last saw you, you were sailing north with the people of Neutria to Kungthorn," Milland said.

"It's a long story," Huck said as he swallowed a big mouthful of tea. "But first I would like to know how many trogs you've killed with your axe, Magin?"

The East Marklander threw his head back and released a hardy laugh. "Seventy-one! Plus twenty-two Alfeinians, and eleven trolls," he said proudly as he rubbed the blade of his axe.

"Trolls? Really?" Rullin asked.

"Now, now, boys, you're not going to change the subject by appealing to Magin's unique talent of boasting," Gordon said as he patted Magin on the shoulder. "You must tell us about the Yomiron."

"Yes. Tell us, and hurry," Pettin said. "I'm most curious about what happened to Gordon, Milland and Magin after they retreated to the west tower, with Turahium, so tell us quickly how two youths were able to tame the race of the Yomiron?"

Huck and Rullin looked at each other for a moment. "I think

Rullin should begin, since it really began with him, long before we actually reached Neutria," Huck said.

"What? What is this?" Magin asked as he leaned forward, as if not wanting to miss even a single word of the tale he was about to hear. "Before you reached Neutria?"

"When exactly was that?" Olaf asked.

"When we were still traveling through the Wolf-Staak," Rullin said. "After we were ambushed and loss Palifair and Tom, I believe it was. We were traveling around Lost Lake and had not yet passed through Dullin's Gate." Rullin continued to recant his encounter with the Alfen King and how he was given the Alfen Jewel by the faerie king. As he told everyone of what happened that night, he began to sing the Alfen song to them.

"So you were carrying the Alfen Jewel with you all that time and we didn't suspect?" Milland said. "Only you two little scamps knew about it and kept the secret all to yourselves? A private little secret all your own."

"That's not exactly true," Rullin said. "On more than one occasion, I felt that Arlindor knew about the Alfen King and the jewel, and now I'm sure that he did, though he never once admitted it. Later, Ironbone told us he was expecting to meet with Mr. Blondor, but he never showed up. Apparently, Blondor was suppose to meet with the Alfen King and get the jewel from him, and bring it to Ironbone. It was instrumental in convincing the stone giants to join us in the war against the Lord of Darkness. It was lucky that we ran into him when we did."

"Or, perhaps the Alfen King intervened and gave it to you because Blondor was forced to divert from his original plan?" Pettin said. "Since he was unable to meet with the Alfen King, the king of the little people gave it to you, so that you could pass it on to Ironbone?"

"Perhaps?" Rullin said, thinking to himself about what Pettin's speculation implied. "But why didn't he give it to Arlindor?"

"Because Arlindor would have to go south with King Amthrim," Milland said. "And that's why Arlindor wanted you to go north with the Neutrians. It all makes sense."

"Druids are able to read the future, though not always clearly,"

Gordon said. "Remember when Blondor defended your right to come along on this quest, at the council in Wissenval?"

"Yes, that's right," Huck said. "It's as if he knew we would play some part in all this, didn't he?"

"It seems so," Magin said. "But now, get back to the story."

Huck and Rullin now told them about their boat trip up the river to Kungthorn, and how Rullin took off, running up the side of the mountain. They sometimes interrupted each other to fill in parts the other missed. Other times one of the listeners interrupted their story to ask a question about a point that distracted them, causing them to wander from their train of thought.

When they finally told them of all the events that took place on top of the mountain, everyone fell silent. They listened intensely to every word they spoke, and did not want to miss any of the details. The tale of the giants, and how the spirits of the land spoke to them, caused them to marvel. Magin, more than once wished that he had gone with them, and said so out loud. Finally, the boys described how the Yomiron grew excited with the war fever and began marching to war.

"Let's see, we left Neutria five days ago," Huck began to explain, counting the days on his fingers. "Ironbone carried Rullin and myself in his arms all the way from the gathering place. We didn't stop the whole time. Once in a while one of the giants brought us some nuts or some roots to eat, but this is the first meat that we've tasted in a week. They don't eat much, but they were always able to feed us, even though I would have preferred a little dear meat, or even rabbit."

"Well then, have as much meat as you like," Gordon said as he cut two slices from the roasting meat before them. "I think it's done?"

Everyone began to fill their bellies with the roasted meat, fresh with juices dripping hot and tasty. The boys continued their tale until finally, they came to the battle on the banks of the Angorium and Donnor Rivers.

No one spoke until they were finished telling the tale.

"There is more to the bone of the earth than I ever thought," Magin said. "You have given me much to think about. I think

I would someday like to go and visit this place you mentioned, Jothumland, and especially the gathering place, and speak with the Yomiron. I'm sure I could increase my knowledge of the earthways and the treasures buried within the ground?"

"And I would like to walk under the trees of the Wolf-Staak when the blackness within has been driven out," Milland said.

"Perhaps we might all journey together to these lands, if we come through this war alive?" Gordon said.

The boys finally completed their story with a description of the attack of the Yomiron on the Allomanian army. "And now you must tell us of the Battle of Ortangraal, and how King Amthrim and Caratium killed the Horzugal?" Huck and Rullin pleaded.

Milland began to recite their entire journey, from their departure from Neutria to the conclusion of the battle. When they came to the point in the story where they separated from Olaf and Pettin, he stopped. "I think our Tillenian comrades should tell us what happened to them, at this point," Milland said. "We were separated from the rest of the defending forces, when we sought protection within the western tower."

"Yes, but you must continue your tale and tell us what happened to you in the tower once we're finished," Pettin insisted.

"But first finish the story and tell us how the king and the centurion died," Huck demanded.

Pettin did not enjoy reliving the battle with the Horzugal, and had to fight back the tears when he told everyone of that fateful hour in the courtyard, before the inner walls. The others did not hide their grief. But their sorrow was lessened by the heroic way the king and the centurion killed the Horzugal. They had all come to admire King Amthrim in the short time they had spent with him and all his people. It was easy to admire men of honor.

"And what will become of Neutria?" asked Rullin.

"Prince Sagtrim is now the king, and I think he will make a good king," Milland said. Everyone nodded their heads in agreement. "I'm sorry for Princess Valenda. She does not yet know of her father's death, and I dread for the one who must tell her. There was a great love-bond between the king and his daughter. It was as great, or maybe greater than the bond between the king and the prince. But it often is easier for a father to love his daughter greater than he loved his son. A father's love for his son is mixed with pride, while his love for a daughter is purer, if you know what I mean? King Amthrim spoke to Sagtrim of Valenda before he died." Everyone fell silent.

Finally, when the silence became unbearable, Pettin spoke once more. "You must now tell us what happened to you within the western tower?"

"We locked ourselves within the tower," Gordon began. "The door was bolted behind us. Turahium is both brave and heroic, for the blood of Lothangia still runs both strong and pure in his veins. A fine leader off men he is. He cares greatly for their welfare. His love allows him to push them to the breaking point without them failing him. There is something more than flesh and blood within the golden armor of these knights, I'll wager."

Milland and Magin both nodded their heads in agreement, without speaking. Gordon continued with his story. "The undermen made an attempt to break into the tower, but we were able to keep them from breaking in when the door at the base of the tower was smashed in by the enemy. They began pouring in as the alarm was sent up through the tower. Before anyone else had time to react, Magin here, raced down the stairs shouting for others to follow him. 'For the Mark and the Light!' he shouted. We raced after him as fast as we could. I saw Magin swinging his axe as he jumped into a group of trogs, cutting and hacking."

Magin smiled as Gordon described his exploits. "I seem to remember you and Milland doing more than your share with your sword and knife," Magin said and then laughed.

"We all fought with abandonment," Gordon said. "Soon a troop of knights came charging to our assistance, leading a band of Neutrians right behind them. The trogs retreated through the door and regrouped, and gave us a moment to catch our breaths, but we were unable to close the door, which was broken.

"It was then that Turahium convinced us that it would only be a matter of time before the tower fell. We decided that it would be better if we made a last effort to break free from our soon-to-be tomb, and fight our way back to the inner walls. We knew that the chances of our making it was slim, but we thought that we had a better chance trying to fight our way back to the inner wall, and thus create enough havoc in the enemy's rear, as to get through. In this way we might even help those who were defending the walls.

"We then gathered together and rushed out of the tower, into the courtyard, right into the center of the enemy. We began fighting our way into their ranks, and paid dearly for every foot of ground we took. But we hadn't gone far when we heard a blare of trumpets from far off. From out of the inner walls, a band of knights rode in, followed by a large troop of Neutrians. We could see King Amthrim and Caratium leading the charge.

"Tarudium ordered us to fight our way to our comrades, as best as we could. But before we could reach where the king and Caratium were, we saw a black shadow descend from above. It was the Horzugal. What happened afterward has already been told, and I have no desire to retell it, so I will end my tale here."

Suddenly, Arlindor strolled up to them with Ironbone next to him. "I see you have all been busy reminiscing about the events of the last week," the druid said. His face was beaming with a smile. Everyone turned and stared at the giant standing over him.

Ironbone looked down on them with his flashing eyes and made a cracking sound, low and deep from within his throat. Arlindor introduced them to the Yomiron, one at a time.

"So you are all friends of these two pups," Ironbone said. "Huck and Rullin told me much about each and everyone of you. I'm glad to see that you have all come through the battle intact."

"Huck ad Rullin told us a great deal about you and your people," Magin said. "But I would like to learn more of the Yomiron."

"Would you? Craaaaak!" the stone giant said. "You are Magin, the earth digger, the stone mole, as I remember from the pups' description."

"At your service," Magin said, as he rose and bowed. "The people of my village are stone moles, as you say. We are interested in everything dealing with the earth's treasures. My friends and I have spoken among ourselves, of plans to travel to your homeland, if we survive this war. It would be an honor to visit with the giants of Jothunland."

"It would? Well, indeed," Ironbone said and thought about what Magin said for a moment. "Perhaps the time has come to put an end to the isolation of the Yomiron. Yes. You and your friends may come and visit with us, if you like, Magin of the Mark. We will speak together of the lore of the earth."

"Arlindor tells us that we are all going to the city of Lothar," Rullin said. "Will you be coming with us, Ironbone? I want my friends, Palifair and Tom, to meet you."

"And I would like to meet with them," Ironbone said. "Remarkable lads they must be, from what you and Huck have told me about them? But the path of the Yomiron lies to the west. We must go to close the Kil'org Pass, and prevent any of the slaves of Allomania from escaping to the north. But if you do come to Jothunland with your friends, you will all be welcomed."

"We'll try," Huck said. Rullin and Huck were disappointed at hearing that the Yomiron were not going south with them. Ironbone could see this, and it made him smile.

"I must now return to my people and finish the job we promised Arlindor we would complete," Ironbone said. "We still have a great deal of dead undermen to dispose of, and a great many of Truemans to bury."

Arlindor nodded his head in agreement. "And there is much we have to do before we leave in the morning," the druid said. "There is little time for us to waste. I suggest everyone try and get what sleep you can tonight. If all goes well, we should be in Lothar in three days. King Sagtrim is anxious to reach Lothar."

"King Sagtrim?" Huck asked.

"Yes, of course," Rullin said.

The sun was burning bright red when it made its appearance the next morning, rising over the tops of the mountains to the east. The king and his boatmen set out, down the Donnor River, like a flock of sailing swans. The Yomiron stood on the western bank watching silently, as the ships sailed by. Finally, they broke the silence by stomping their feet upon the hard ground like pile drivers, in a salute of farewell to the departing fleet. The sounds rolled through the valley like distant thunder. The men aboard the ships listened, with fixed eyes and stony faces, at the sound that bellowed across the waters. Far behind, to the west, rose an ever-rising pillar of black smoke from the fires set by the Yomiron. They were still burning the remains of the enemy. The men on the ships could see the black smoke in the distance, as they disappeared down the Donnor River.

A wind blew down from over the roof of the great forest to the north and filled their sails. Down the mirror-like surface of the Donnor River they sailed toward their appointment with Fate. The Neutrian boatmen strained their backs and arms to help their ships sail on their way. Ores pressed against the lapping waves to help the wind-filled sails propel the ships across the bobbing waves. The fleet sailed down the rushing currents that would eventually empty into the warmer waters of the Gulf of Aixia, under sunny skies.

"I wonder in what shape we will find our comrades, when, at last we are all reunited?" Milland said. He stood with Magin, Gordon and Arlindor on the deck of one of the ships.

"That I cannot say," Arlindor said. "But we might find that the currents that we ride on, through life, may at any time take us in whirls that double back on us? Do not be dismayed to discover more than one of our company has been changed in more ways than one, before this odyssey has come to an end."

"Changed?" Magin asked. "Have we not changed, or perhaps grown, since last we saw the comfort of our homes? But I wonder, on what paths these currents you speak of, could have led Blondor and the others?"

"Down roads better left untraveled, I would think," Arlindor said. "The road that Blondor was destined to travel down is dark." Arlindor shook his head as he spoke. "Truly that road is far blacker than the road we traveled. It's worst even than the blackest nightmare that you might have ever dreamed."

"What road could be that terrible?" Milland asked.

"The road that no one would pass through unless one had given up all hope of reaching its end," Arlindor said. "For no one passes through the Stygian Hole and comes out again unchanged."

"The Stygian Hole?" Gordon asked.

"Even my folk, in the East Mark, who love to travel underground, would dare not set foot in the Stygian Hole," Magin said. "What devilry could possibly have driven our friends into that foul pit?"

"Necessity, of course," Arlindor said. "It was the price that was needed to be paid to recover that which was lost. Nothing is ever achieved without a price, and payment for fulfilling the prophecies is often great. But now the Emperor Returned has set foot in Lothangia with proof of his rightful birthright."

"You're referring to Vesten, aren't you?" asked Milland.

"Yes," Arlindor said. "It was only through the Stygian Hole that Vesten could ever return to Lothangia, though he did not realize this truth. Only by passing through its darkness, could he be reborn anew into the realm of the Light."

"That would mean Vesten and the others have reached Palennoria?" Gordon asked.

"Correct," Arlindor said. "Before we left Wissenval, it was foreseen that Vesten needed to pass through the Stygian Hole. But our vision was clouded by the enemy, and we could not see exactly what would transpire. The Lord of Darkness kept the knowledge of what road to travel from us, but it's said that all roads lead to the Light, and all highways run to the city of Lothar. So we can expect to meet our friends in the capital when we reach that city."

"The legends and prophecies about the emperor returning, and all the stories surrounding Vesten, Palifair and the White Stone are about to come true?" asked Milland.

"That's why we are fighting this war," explained Arlindor. "But that will not happen unless we are able to reach Lothar in time to prevent the city from falling to the Dark Armies of Allomania. We must bring the Red Stone to Lothar. That's why we are in such a hurry. That's why both the Lord of Darkness and Wargana tried to stop us at Ortangraal."

"Will we reach the city in time?" asked Magin.

"We must reach the city by the 26th of this month," Arlindor said. "If we don't, it'll surely go down as the blackest day in the history of New Earth."

"Look!" Rullin shouted.

Everyone stopped talking and turned to see what caused Rullin's excited behavior. On the east bank of the Donnor River they saw a team of Maxthoium Riders. Behind them marched the Army of Tillenia.

"I think we should speak with our allies," Arlindor said.

King Sagtrim, General Junthumor, Bolthur and Huntulheim, as well as other Neutrians were already waiting for the Tillenian Army when Arlindor and the others joined them on shore. They stood and watched the great mountains of muscle, tusk and hair filed up to the banks of the river. About them were thousands of heavily clad Tillenians with battle axes, and armor covering their thickly built bodies. Their round faces were red from marching, and their laughing eyes shined and hid the fact that they were marching to war, and perhaps, to their deaths.

Then from the lead maxthoium, Tharokon jumped down to the snow-covered ground and approached those waiting to greet him. He held his helmet in his left hand and salute them with his right hand.

"Hail King Sagtrim! Hail Arlindor and all the friends and allies of Tillenia!" Tharokon said.

"Hail Tharokon, Commander of Tillenia!" King Sagtrim said and returned his salute. "Are the men of Tillenia ready to move south?"

"Yes, my Lord," Tharokon said. "We're anxious to move at your command. We are a proud people, like the men of northern folds. We lust for vengeance against the Dark Alliance, that has inflicted so much pain on our people. Perhaps, together, we'll find the strength to break the iron ring that is laying siege on Lothar, if we reach the city in time?"

"We must," Sagtrim said. "Too much blood has been spilled to date, for us to now let victory slip away without a fight. I don't want to miss our opportunity to spill some of the enemy's blood.

Some of the blood that has been spilled so far, flowed through my father's veins. Every last Neutrian will fight to the last to avenge our lost, and safeguard our freedom."

"The same holds true for Tillenia, my Lord," Tharokon said. "We've been fighting Wargana's armies for over a year now. But I think that Fennoria will not be able to send any more raiding parties against Tillenia now, not with her army destroyed at Ortangraal."

"Let us hope so," Arlindor said. "She has lost much more than you might know. The power of Fennoria will wane in time, and her witches will dwindle in power and numbers, but there is still the Lord of Darkness. Compared to his power, Wargana was a mere nuisance. But there is still something else that troubles me."

"And what is that, Arlindor?" Sagtrim asked.

"Nowhere among the dead have we discovered the remains of the Mount of Fennoria," Arlindor said. His face was dark and grim.

"The Mount of Fennoria? Still alive. Are you sure?" Tharokon asked.

"I can't be certain, his Life-Force is hidden from me. I can neither detect his life or death, but there is no indication to the contrary," the druid said solemnly. "I don't know what it means, and we can't delay here to investigate. We must move south with hast."

"You're right," Sagtrim said. "Tharokon, give the order to your men to move south along the road. Try to keep our ships within sight. We will do the same, as we sail down the river. It will do no good if our two armies reach Lothar at different times. If our assault against the Dark Armies is to have an effect, then we will have to attack together."

"Yes, my Lord," Tharokon said. "I'll give the orders now. We will push ourselves to our limits, to reach Lothar in time." Tharokon was about to turn and walk away, but spoke once more. "But before we depart, I would like to invite Gordon and the two Marklander lads to come with me for a moment."

Rullin's and Huck's ears perked up at Tharokon's request.

King Sagtrim smiled at the boys' reactions. "Go on, lads, but do not tarry long. We leave as soon as our ships are in formation."

Gordon and the boys followed Tharokon back to the Tillenian army. He led them to a troop of maxthoiums, fitted with battle armor. On the back of each mathoium was a large coach, in which Tillenian archers rode into battle. Mixed among their ranks were thousands of heavily armored Tillenian foot soldiers, waiting for the word to move out.

"Look!" Huck cried, as he pointed and ran toward two large maxthoiums. "It's Brimkonor, with Tonok and Kellock!"

Rullin ran right behind Huck. They ran right up to the Maxthoium Rider, who was standing in between the two giant beasts. His round, red face was beaming with the biggest smile, as he waved. Gordon followed behind the two boys, pleased at their reaction.

"Hi! Ho! There you are!" Brimkonor called as he greeted the two boys. The maxthoiums raised their trunks and trumpeted their pleasure at seeing their friends again.

"Brimkonor! What are you doing here?" Huck asked as he came to a halt before the stout man. The two maxthoiums greeted him by gently sniffing Huck with their trunks. "Tontok, Kellock, it's so good to see you both once more." Huck said as he patted their hairy trunks.

"They remember you," Brimkonor said. "We wanted to see our friends again, before we ride into battle. I'm only sorry Palifair and Tom are not here, but perchance we will run into them again?"

"I hope so," Huck said, as Gordon and Rullin smiled at the way the two wooly beasts showed their affection toward them.

"I hope that you all might come back to Jassinburg someday, after we have finished with this war," Brimkonor said. "Your stay in Tillenia was too short, and disturbed by war and the need to leave in a hurry."

"Perhaps we'll all have the opportunity to return to Jassinburg, someday?" Gordon said. "I want the opportunity to learn more of these great wanderers of the northern waste lands."

"Yes, of course," Brimkonor said, delighted at Gordon's interest in the maxthoiums. His eyes flashed with pride. "They are wondrous to behold, but you must see them in the wild. There they roam the tundra wilderness above the Great North Sea. They roam by the thousands in great herds, just below the great ice wall that covers the top of New Earth.

"I will hold you to your promise, my friend," Gordon said. "For such a trip, I'll single-handedly win this war, if I must."

"Then I make the offer a promise between comrades," Brimkonor said. "But now, we must go. We all have a date with the Lord of Battle, in the south. There we will all dine as friends reunited, I hope, when this war is at an end. I'll be expecting my two young friends to join us again in Lothar, when we all have a chance to break bread together."

"We're looking forward to it," Rullin said. Then they all said farewell to each other, and Gordon and the boys returned to the ships that would take them to Lothar.

As they walked back, Gordon spoke to the boys. "They are good men, these Tillenians," Gordon said. "Short and jovial, as they are, they ride into the jaws of death with a song in their hearts, and a laugh dancing in their throats, just as if they were back in one of their great bear halls, in Jassinburg. But if they had a choice, I'd wager they would rather chose their halls, with all their rich ale and mead to drink, over fighting."

After all the farewells were exchanged and signals of readiness were made, the ships set sail. Their sails were filled with the winds and ores pushed hard against the blue currents of the mighty river under the straining arms of the Neutrians. The golden rays of the morning sun danced across the armor and weapons of the Tillenian Army that marched along the banks of the Donnor River.

And so, Arlindor and all the others who set out with him from the Lost City, sailed down the Donnor River in the company of King Sagtrim, brother of Princess Valenda. With them the hardy men of the north sought to keep their appointment, with either the Goddess of Victory or the Hag of Doom, in the south.